FROM THE EDGE OF YESTERDAY SERIES

FIND ME IN THE TIME BEFORE

**When one moment shifts the
entire history of the world.**

ROBIN STEVENS PAYES

ALSO BY ROBIN STEVENS PAYES
THE EDGE OF YESTERDAY SERIES
A MULTIMEDIA TEEN TIME TRAVEL ADVENTURE

www.edgeofyesterday.com
www.edgeofyesterdaybook.com

TRANSFORMING LEARNING THROUGH STORY

Edge of Yesterday: Book I
Da Vinci's Way: Book II
Saving Time: Book III

FIND ME IN THE TIME BEFORE

EDGE OF YESTERDAY
BOOK IV

ROBIN STEVENS PAYES

Woodhall Press | Norwalk, CT

woodhall press

Woodhall Press, 81 Old Saugatuck Road, Norwalk, CT 06855
WoodhallPress.com

Cover design: Melissa Brandstatter
Layout artist: LJ Mucci

Library of Congress Cataloging-in-Publication Data available

ISBN 978-1-954907-32-4   (paper: alk paper)
ISBN 978-1-954907-33-1   (electronic)

First Edition
Distributed by Independent Publishers Group
(800) 888-4741

Printed in the United States of America

To a new generation of dreamers, doers and makers, time travelers of the imagination, who are inspired to connect history to the present and dream a new future into being.

Get inspired by their work at the www.edgeofyesterday.com/time-travelers

"To be yourself in a world that is constantly trying to make you something else is the greatest accomplishment."

—Ralph Waldo Emerson

"It sometimes happens that work and study force genius to declare itself, like the fruits that art produces in a soil where nature did not intend it. But these efforts of art are nearly as rare as natural genius itself."

—Émilie du Châtelet

Contents

A Time Traveler's Cheat Sheet Covering the Past 502 years and 48 hours

In which the future is an ever-present reminder of the past,
and today is but a point in time

You know how everyone's worried about time? You're going to be late to school! If you don't get good grades, you'll never get into college. Remember that time in seventh grade when . . .

And then, there's the familiar parental yawn: Back when I was your age . . .

And then there's the super-creepy #TimesUp!

Even when it's not . . . yet.

———

Welcome, dear reader, to my world.

My original time travel adventure starts out like a spy movie. I was visiting my dad's office for their totally lame Take Your Child to Work Day (they wanted us to take selfies with our parents and post with #TYCTW but, *eww!*), and I held back from the usual tour (been there, hated that). I told Dad I had a homework project to work on so he could go to his meeting with the Big Chiefs who paid his salary and our mortgage, and unexpectedly stumbled on what turned out to be a top-secret government program: Operation Firenze (OF).

For the record, Dad is not a spy, but there was something deeply suspicious about me, then a mere thirteen-year-old, gaining access, all while attempting to do some research using Dad's computer at his work, just because he never gave me his office Wi-Fi password to log in from my tablet.

A scrambled screen, screechy audio into my earbuds, and I accidentally crashed the thing. It took me a hot minute to reboot. But instead of the normal static desktop on Dad's computer, things started shifting. It was like someone—or something—had implemented a mad screen-share program to make things move around on their own with dizzying speed: Google Earth map images start showing up: a close-up of Takoma Park, er, that is, home, then Florence, Italy, and some old landmarks. And without my doing anything, it then maps a trajectory like the flight path of a supersonic jet—or the orbital plan for a SpaceX rocket. It keeps morphing, a sort of 5-D holographic projection of Earth, spinning wildly, but here, east to west instead of its normal rotation. A timeline at the bottom is counting back in decades, starting at this one.

What looked to be documentary video clips matching history's highlights for specific years paraded above the timeline, going all the way back to the 1500s, when there shouldn't *be* any video clips. Columbus not really "discovering" America. Pilgrims landing at Plymouth Rock. Their first Thanksgiving with the indigenous Wampanoag—nothing like what we think today. That sort of thing.

And then it gets faster. Colors in the projection slide in and out like a kaleidoscope. These images are literally jumping out at me. And I don't even have any VR goggles on.

Did this have something to do with Dad's work?

And then in walks this weird dude with an undefinable foreign accent who says his name is Kairos, which apparently means "just in time." I thought he was just a random IT guy they brought in on a high-tech visa, but then he tells me he's a "knowledge management specialist." And that he's looking for *me*. He left me with this weird horse statue and a golden compass *exactly like the one I found on the metro.*

Have I lost you yet? 'Cause even as I write it, it still sounds like a bunch of you-know-what.

But it gets better.

Because Kairos sent me a message (he didn't even have my phone number or Instagram) and a cyber code to hack the technology behind OF using something called the Qualia Rosetta to access— wait, are you sitting down?—*a temporal/spatial reference from fifth dimension; or reality from outside time and space.*

A four-dimensional illusion from some fifth-dimension reality. Yep. Time travel.

Meanwhile, for our science fair project, Billy and I were actually working on building a model of a time machine based on one of Leonardo da Vinci's drawings. Popsicle sticks, Lego bots, a make-shift solar battery—very primitive. Billy wasn't really buying all this Kairos/fifth-dimension mumbo jumbo, but even he couldn't resist tinkering with the mysterious formula and the golden compasses, which seemed like pieces to a puzzle we were on the verge of cracking.

No one thought it would work, least of all me. But these elements of mass, matter, motion, and velocity fused into a single structure. As awkward as our time machine was, it possessed undeniable power.

Still, there was a missing element.

It took a rogue kiss in the back of the garage from Lex, star jock and class hottie (and my best friend Beth's main crush—had she known, she'd probs have Instagram'd an embarrassing pic of me, hashtags #jealous #traitor #hatingoncharley)—that knocked us into the workbench holding the time machine to accidentally ignite the whirl-a-wind that sent me reeling back five hundred years, across six time zones, to land in an empty field at midnight, under a hail of cannon fire, and come face-to-face with the Renaissance genius himself.

Meeting Leonardo da Vinci: DREAAAAMMMM!

So, irl, no, not a dream. My messing with spacetime had real-world consequences.

Like having to teach Leonardo the science of Newton and Einstein to help me reverse-engineer the time machine from low-tech ancient Florence in order to blast me home ASAP when I found out Mamma, on tour in modern-day Florence with the National Symphony Orchestra (her day job: violinist), might be dying. And

I might just have gotten Dad fired for a major hack into the OF system he was in charge of.

Like creating paradoxes in the timeline, where I might no longer exist.

Or at a minimum, be grounded for life.

But I *did* make it back. Not to mention Billy, who came to so-called "rescue" me, along with sexy Lex, who never got home (that's a whole 'nother story!).

And so now how'm I supposed to *not* do it again?

Once a time traveler, always a time traveler. There's no turning back. Meeting Leonardo in his own time was an eye-opener. 'Cause if travel is enlightening, imagine time travel as enlightenment to the *nth* degree. Why not try to meet *all* of my personal heroes of history to find out their secrets?

And for that, I need Billy's help. And maybe Bethy's as well.

So hang on to your phones, everybody, because if what's past is prologue, as Shakespeare wrote, this is where my world is about to get really messy!

I.

In Which I Wake Up

Nightmares, school, zits, boys, and other things
that torture teens in the night

"I know the truth! You can't take that away from me!"

There are torches surrounding me; the flames glint off the pyramid of gold, silver, and ancient art treasures piled high before me even as flames lick my feet. A massive outcry comes in the shouts of men, the wail of babies, and a babble of women's voices in a language I can't understand.

"*È troppo tardi, Carlotta!*"

I wake up sweating.

"Charley! Carlotta! You're too late—you're going to miss the bus!"

It's Mamma. And I'm home, in my own bed. And about to be late for school.

"Coming, Mamma!"

The secret of my singular experience has haunted me ever since two years ago when I really was almost burned at the stake. True story . . . but I don't dare tell Mamma or Dad. I don't think they would ever believe me. No one would believe me.

Except for Billy, that is. Billy was right there with me.

I take a few deep breaths. I brush back the coiled curls from my eyes. I have to compose myself: I'm in 2019, not 1492. The dream—it wasn't real. Not this time, anyway. Was it ever?

One look at my nightstand confirms the truth: the golden compass. A tangible reminder of my adventure into a time both distant and ever-present. A reminder of Leonardo da Vinci and my wild ride through Renaissance Florence. The geometry that unlocked a power to travel back in time.

I journeyed there not knowing that a world of enlightenment can also contain a great deal of darkness and evil. That the history we learn in textbooks provides very little of the actual experience of the past. That interacting with the past can change the course of history—and one's very life.

And that the Renaissance genius Leonardo da Vinci, my Florentine idol, who I hoped would let me in on his secret superpower—inventing the future—would remain enigmatic, even after spending a night and a day, and another night and a day, in his presence.

No. I cannot speak of that experience. To anyone.

I shuffle into the comfort of my fuzzy purple slippers and make my way to the bathroom, trying to calm my mind: No one is out to burn me at the stake. I am home and safe. This time, the nightmare was merely a dream.

I glance in the mirror. Eyes hooded in half-sleep. Hair like Medusa. Face full of freckles and an annoying pimple beaming like a lighthouse above my lip.

Naturally.

I turn on the faucet and splash some water on my face before lathering up with the Cetaphil that will hopefully attack the bacteria that led to this facial formation of Mount Vesuvius. As to the hormones underlying the breakout, I have no control over them.

"Charley?"

This time, it's Dad's voice booming over the noise of the faucet.

I sigh, exasperated. "Can't you even let me wash up?"

I know I shouldn't be annoyed. After all, it's my fault I overslept. Billy and I were texting about our next project, working out the math until two o'clock in the morning when I finally fell asleep.

The parentals think I'm slaving away on the high school science fair. I've shared with them my ambition to explore the lives of the superheroes of history and make a podcast series about what I've learned—Leonardo, Einstein, Mozart, and lesser-known but equally ahead-of-their-times female polymaths like Marie Curie, Hildegard von Bingen, and the totally badass Marquise Émilie du Châtelet.

Mom and Dad are fully on board with this obsession because they think it means I'm on track—for school, for college, for career. Good stuff for a future college essay.

Maybe so, but in my humble opinion, that is their idea of a life, not mine.

My plans for the immediate future include interviewing these superheroes in their own times. Personally. Correspondent Charley Morton, reporting live from the scene.

It's bold, but I am living proof that this is possible.

"Hey, Charley? Just checking—did you fall in?"

Meanwhile, I actually have to wake up in the here-and-now.

I smear a dab of toothpaste on my electric toothbrush, feeling the whir while the bristles tickle my gums. Last night's dream—I am bound to a pole, hands tied behind my back. There's a hood covering my eyes, but I don't have to see anything to know that someone has put a torch to the pyramid of wood piled at my feet. The smoke burns my throat, even now.

Dad knocks loudly. And the twins begin babbling their weird wordless tune. Reality ready to pad in on footie-pajama'd feet.

Carrie and Daisy, those wild-and-crazy two-year-olds, are the main reasons for my staying home as long as I have—since, well, the bonfire of the vanities on that long-ago March day in Florence. My baby sisters are the most lovably exasperating creatures to have come into my life since then, and the only possible thing that could tamp down my ambitions to attempt another jump through time . . . for now. Time being relative, that is.

"Champ?" Dad says.

I spit into the sink and grimace into the mirror.

"C'mon." Dad sounds angry. "Open up, kiddo. Or I have one word: *Grounded.*"

"I'm brushing my hair!" I try pulling a wire brush through my waves and get caught in a rat's nest of curls. I usually wash my hair before bed; gives me an extra half-hour sleep in the a.m. and I can still usually make the bus. Downside? Knots. Lots and lots of knots.

"Youch!"

I can't wait for the day I'm allowed to get my hair straightened professionally. A present from the parentals for my sixteenth birthday, less than six months away.

"Charley!" This time it's Mamma, yelling up the stairs. "School bus is not waiting on your beauty routine."

I hear the bathroom doorknob being rattled and tugged on. When I open it, two little drool-meisters stare up at me with oatmeal and applesauce caked on their jammies and smeared all over their faces.

My heart lights up. "Somebodies love wearing their breakfast!"

I kneel down and stretch out my arms. Carrie climbs in. Then Daisy scrambles closer to edge out her sister, slobbering me with face-sucking kisses. I lock them in my arms and squeeze. They squirm to get out, but not before gluing my sweater with oatmeal hands.

"Babies! You've got me all messy." I sigh. "See? Now, I need to change."

"Jerry, what is the problem? Charley needs to get her butt down here. NOW!" Mamma shouts up the stairs. "Her oatmeal's getting cold."

As I pry my little sisters off me, the prospect of oatmeal is suddenly less than appetizing.

Dad frowns. "Looking at her now, Gwen. Twins have finger-painted her with breakfast."

"Thinking maybe a bagel to go, Mamma," I yell back. "If it's not too much trouble."

Dad sighs in resignation. "Guess I'm driving you to school again this morning."

"Thanks, Dad," I grin. "You're the best!"

II.

NEXT ASSIGNMENT

How a ban on collaboration can lead to creative solutions—
and drive your BFF crazy

"Hey, Charley," Billy hurries up to me on the way to the school cafeteria, striding on those long, gangly legs. My mom says he'll grow into his height, but at fifteen, he's still pretty much a stilts-walker.

"Hi, Billy," I say, peering around surreptitiously to make sure there's no one noticing I'm talking to the tenth-grade science-geek poster boy. "What's up?"

Texting late last night about how to refine the operating system for what's now morphing into a time travel app led us down a rabbit hole of cutting-edge research on quantum physics that might have some bearing on its refinement.

Seems like physicists and cosmologists are urgently collaborating to advance research into quantum principles like nonlocality and quantum transport to retrieve valuable information from the past to guide our present. And maybe the future.

Apart from the very interesting experiences time travel has augured for me personally, it would be impossible to speculate on the "why" of that urgent research. Maybe they are working to bring back cures from the future for some pandemic or plague that is new to humankind, a threat to the globe. Or to solve global warming.

Come to think of it, the health and environmental angle could open up new possibilities for applying IB—information biology. Which is taking unlocking our DNA code to a whole 'nother level.

Or it could be something that I completely haven't thought of . . . yet.

It's not like I could ask Dad what his office is up to. I've lost any rights to that 411 from Jerry Morton.

Like, whatever!

All's I know for sure is there's research being done at the top levels of secrecy, with enhanced cybersecurity.

And we broke the code.

For the record, though, since revealing the deets of our extraordinary excursion to the fifteenth century is strictly verboten, we had to scramble to come up with a new eighth-grade science fair project that wouldn't involve risks to our national security. So, on the fly, we came up with a question about prolonging human life span in the cloud—cloning our brains, so to speak—based on groundbreaking, Nobel Prize–winning research on telomerase, a sort of cellular clock that governs life span. Totally rad, and another form of time travel, as it were.

But our rule-breaking hack into the backup server bank in Dad's workshop in our garage remained a stain on the record, nonetheless. Ever since, our relationship, Billy's and mine, has to be on the down-low. We can be classmates, but putting our brains together to hatch the next science fair scheme or any other project is, per all parents involved and by explicit agreement with the high school administration, also verboten.

Nevertheless, geek or no, Billy is my best friend, and also the smartest guy I know—at least in this century—so it's only natural that we'd make a formidable team to enter the only science fair competition that really matters, the USA National Science, Engineering and Arts Fair. (That would be SEA-Fair, for anyone following the acronym soup of government-ese, a Washington lingua franca.) SEA-Fair, because it comes in the fall, is the one that gives students the edge on college admissions, and ultimately hands out college scholarships, giving students access to internships (like my own personal fave—the FBI Teen Leadership Program, because, well, forensic anthropology) and rock-star mentors. To life-changing opportunities.

Which we could totally win if we put our two minds together.

"Charley, I think my parents are finally over our little rule-break— you know, your dad's top-secret classified plans for Operation Firenze. I've now done approximately 137 and a half hours of community service, volunteering at the Kids' Museum and Science Center, plus my room is so spotless you could eat off my desk." Billy hesitates. "Er, not that you'd want to."

I grin. "I've been working on my folks, too—beaucoup de free babysitting hours. Taking out the trash without being asked. Playing violin on Sundays at the senior center, and not even for service-learning hours. Works wonders."

Things are a little weird with us since the kiss that brought us home from the past. But I've known him since, like, second grade, and he's almost like a brother to me. My head says we're just friends, but my heart—and hormones—are telling me a different story. Best not to go there. Plus, what would people think?

"Now, we just need to work on getting Mr. Nestor to let us team up."

"Exactly," Billy confirms. "So, Carlotta, here's what I propose . . ."

"So, Carlotta," comes a snarky voice behind us.

Beth. We are best friends, on and off. (And while we're on the subject, what would be the acronym for that: BFOO?)

"Hey, Bethy," I say, slowing my steps until she catches up.

"What are you two brainiacs plotting for the science fair this time: a drone mission to the asteroid belt?"

"Not, really. Just talking."

She lifts her eyebrows. "C'mon, *Carlotta*. I know you better than that."

I let out my best fake laugh. Billy snorts and stops short, causing a traffic snarl in the hallway. One guy, a senior from the looks of him, and nose-deep in texting despite the fact that cell phones are banned during school, smashes right into me, leaving me splat on the ground.

"Ooph!" I'm mostly embarrassed, though I'm pretty sure something's bruised. Did I mention I'm something of a klutz?

"Hey, watch it, man!" Billy shouts.

"Jerk," Beth mutters under her breath.

"*Mademoiselle*, I am warning you!" the kid shouts angrily as his phone slips out of his hand, texting interrupted. It skitters to a rest after caroming off the bank of lockers lining the hallway.

"You better pray *ze mobile is* not *craqué!*" He must be French, what with the accent and all. But that's normal in my school—we have students here from fifty-seven countries. The DC area is *very* diverse.

The guy stares first at me, then at Billy. "You break it man, you pay."

Aiming for dignity, I raise myself up on my elbows and give him the look; he totally ignores me.

"Hey, Charley, you okay?" Billy helps me up, moving us out of the mainstream of traffic. I, in turn, manage to reach out a hand just in time to yank Beth into single file as a pod of school resource officers, maybe expecting a stampede, pushes through the crowd, shouting for us to keep moving. One of the security guys strides past Monsieur Distracted, recovering the phone from being stomped on, then grabs him by the arm.

"No phones during class time," he says. "You know the rules, Mr. Emile-Tonnelier. You can pick this up in the office after school."

This Emile-I've-got-tunnel-vision kid glares at Billy and hurries after the school cop to negotiate for his life and the phone before it makes it to the principal's office, where steeper punishment might result.

"I'll deal with you later," he snarls at us.

"Phew! I'm okay," I say, watching the passing students adjust to the new flow of traffic as if I'm not part of the scene. Beth is impatiently tapping her Christian Louboutins—those *très* expensive French shoes with the red soles. She calls them her "love shoes." Still, why she'd wear stilts like these to school, of all places, is beyond me. Of course, Bethy, being herself, is focused on fashion, style, and social media. And apparently, everybody besides me sees her as hot stuff these days; her Instagram following is legend, from guys propositioning her in the comments to the girls who are dying to *be* her.

"That's a relief." Billy pulls on his seriously nerdy glasses and arranges his face into a frown. "Anyways," he continues, "if you know so much, Beth, then you know that Charley and I are doing separate science fairs this year. As requested by the powers that be."

"Yeah, so I've heard. That's what I want to talk to you guys about," she continues, clueless to the cut. "I've got an unbelievable idea. Top-secret, of course. But I'll need a geek to help me pull it off. What say you, Charley?"

Billy and I exchange looks. Not for the first time, I notice how even ugly coke-bottle glasses magnify the long, dark lashes framing Billy's baby blue eyes. But this is business, I remind myself, and we've both had the same thought at the same time: Beth might just be the secret weapon to our working together on this year's project.

I trace an imaginary arc across the industrial polished-concrete floor with one cowboy-booted foot. "Hmm. Gee, I dunno. I might be interested, Beth, if . . ."

"If what?"

"If you'll agree to take me and Billy both on your team." I smile slyly. "They can't ban you from choosing us together."

Bethy looks from me to Billy. "Seriously, Charley. Webhead's gonna hate this project," she begins.

But I can tell Billy's catching the telepathic waves I'm sending his way. "I'll work with whatever you've got, Bethy," he chimes in, obviously not without effort. "After all, three brains are better than one."

"Well . . ."

"C'mon, Beth, it'll be fun. Just like the Three Musketeers," I cajole, raising my fist. "All for one—"

"And one for all!" Billy finishes, putting up his fist.

"Hmmph." Beth raises a limp fist to complete our team fist bump and taps tepidly. "Maybe."

III.

WEARABLE SCIENCE

Practicing the fine art of persuasion born out of necessity

"Charley, Beth is downstairs, and I'm off to rehearsal." Mamma sounds out of breath. "I cannot be late today. And now I can't find my music—have you seen the 'Eleanor Rigby' score?" The National Symphony Orchestra is doing a pops concert featuring the Beatles. A sure crowd-pleaser.

"Music's on the piano bench where you left it." I push open my bedroom door with one foot while hurriedly picking up clothes off the floor. Ever since the twins were born, I've had to relinquish sleeping in the attic bedroom, because they're not allowed up there and they love trailing behind me. But it's still my private retreat when I need my girl-cave time.

Mamma peeks in and frowns at the mess, then resumes hopping toward the stairs, stooping between shuffling steps to tug on her sensible black slingbacks.

If that were me, Mamma'd be all over me to slow down lest I fall and break my neck. I open my mouth to say something snarky, when Beth pops up the stairway.

"Hiya, science fair partner!" Beth looks glam, with her sparkly mauve eye shadow and pouty red lips. Did I mention she's something of a fashionista?

"Oh, hi, Beth." Before I can invite her in, she's already plopped herself on my bed.

"Your father will be back from the toy store with the twins shortly," Mamma calls up from downstairs. "I expect you to help him out."

"Okay, Mamma," I yell down. "Have a good rehearsal!"

"Be good, you two," she calls back.

"Those twins are so spoiled!" Beth observes as we hear Mamma opening the creaky door to the driveway. "Always getting new toys and stuff!"

I give her the eye. "It's not easy raising toddlers when you're my parents' age, you know."

I admit, it came as something of a surprise that my mom was even pregnant two years ago. I found out about it the hard way when I was in the fifteenth century—except I was scared that Mamma was deathly ill, and I couldn't get home right then to be with her.

"Oh, I'm sure!" says Beth, with fake sympathy. "Anyways, before they all come home and interrupt everything, let's talk science fair."

"But Billy's not here," I point out.

Ignoring me, Beth barrels on. "I thought it'd be cool to do something with fashion and technology. You know, like an app that would take people's measurements, and then we could use three-D printing to make custom designs?"

Beth is so obsessed with designing clothes and wanting to break into fashion, she even has her own YouTube channel, "Beth's Fashion Forward." She's got about 10,000 subscribers—well on her way to becoming a legit YouTuber.

I groan. "No, umm . . . I mean, that sounds totally amazing, Beth. But I know Billy's got ideas too, and—"

"Does Billy *have* to be in it?" she whines. "I mean, it's totally obvious you've got a crush on that gearhead, but really, Charley . . ."

"Crush on Billy! Me?" I plop down on my cushy blue velvet chair, careful to snatch my laptop out from under me before I plop down. "Ha ha. Anyways, why're you suddenly acting all jealous about Billy?"

"Jealous? Ha!" she exclaims, looking away. It's a little bit of a sore subject, because she was totally head over heels over this guy Lex before he moved to a different, well, time zone, without even saying good-bye.

Naturally, it was a huge source of school gossip at the time. But since Lex had been living with his aunt and uncle (his parents died when he was young), who are rumored to have been devastated after a police investigation turned up with no leads, it all falls into the category of unsolved mysteries. Seems disappearing into the fifteenth century and falling in love with a local girl in another spacetime is not a traceable "Missing Child" crime.

But that's a whole 'nother story.

"I could care less about your so-called love life, Charley. It's just, well, Billy is about as far from fashion-forward as you can get. I mean, have you ever seen him wear a matching pair of socks?"

She does have a point. Billy might not even remember to put socks on both feet some days. And because of those long legs, most of what he puts on them are flood pants. It's a little embarrassing.

"We don't need him to do the coding for the app," Bethy continues, "because you and I have got that covered as Scratch masters, what with all ten badges from the Sheroes coding competition."

Which is true. Billy's talents lie in more sophisticated levels of game coding and virtual reality. But to build a fashion app, Bethy and I together have got all the skills we'd need.

"So, what's the hang-up, girlfriend?" she asks, curiosity overtaking insistence.

The hang-up is, for this next project, Billy has got to be involved. Because I'm pumped for another trip out of time. Whatever else we do, we'll need to update the time machine, and Billy and I have got experience together in that department. Billy's been building an app with remote navigational controls. And I've got the whole-Earth GPS geocache (aka, EarthCache) STEM thing mastered, as any future forensic anthropologist worth her salt must.

Which I totally cannot 'fess up to with disbelieving Beth.

"Yeah, well, the fashion app could be kind of cool, I guess, Beth. Hmm . . ." I tap my fingers against my laptop. "Hey, I've got an idea!"

Beth looks at me expectantly.

"I'm thinking climate change," I say, as if that explains everything.

"You are totally changing the subject!"

"No, really. I mean, think about it. We've got 'til 2030 to adapt. Climate scientists project the average U.S. temperature to increase by anywhere from three degrees to twelve degrees Fahrenheit. Which is bonkers when you think about it—like, we'll be living in the tropics here."

"Like that's news? I mean, have you lived through a DC swampy summer, Charley?!"

"Yeah, but they think it'll be uneven—like, I just read a story in the *Washington Post* that said the western slope of the Rockies is warming at twice the global rate!"

Beth rolls her eyes so hard I can practically hear them creak in their sockets.

"Anyways, the point is, there may be very hot days, and very cool days. And the seasons are shifting, so the growing seasons in the northern latitudes will be more like Florida now—"

"Charley, I know. We've been in the same science classes since, like, preschool. Remember?"

"—and sun, snow, and rain are totally unpredictable, not to mention floods, droughts, hurricanes, slow earthquakes, and fires. I mean, since the polar ice caps have started their precipitous melting."

"And your point is . . . ?"

"My point is that the fashion-forward girl in this century will have to be prepared for anything."

Beth shakes her head. "I am *so* not getting you, Charley. We're talking about a fashion tech project for this year's science fair, not preparing the world for climate change."

"Why not? I mean, we could, couldn't we? What if we could create 'transition clothes' that could cover any changes in weather from hot to cold, and everything in between—you know, sort of like transition lenses from sun to shade?"

Beth considers. "Could they be cute? I mean, no pug-ugly Mars space suits or anything."

I note that the ice between us may be melting here, figuratively speaking. If Beth totally buys into my vision to create clothes suitable for the trendy time traveler, for adventure anywhere, at any time—past, present or future . . . climate change is as good an excuse as any.

"Sure, cute. Why not? And practical, too. Think about it, Beth. Maybe we could make them out of some kind of smart fabric that cools down when it senses you're sweating. Then heats up when the temperature drops suddenly. And you can turn it into fashion-forward!"

I start madly searching on my phone to see if anyone's already invented this.

"Ooh, I bet we totally could do something like that," she says excitedly, jumping off the bed to grab the watercolor pencils on my desk. She pulls a sketch pad and charcoal out of her backpack and starts drawing, then wets the pencils to fill in the color. "Maybe like this?"

I reluctantly stop googling to peek over her shoulder at her doodles. I see the shape of a swingy coat in a dusty rose color taking place under her hand. No question, the girl's got an eye for style.

BETH'S PRACTICING DESIGN THINKING

"And then, maybe we could make it reversible. See the gray collar?" She's shading a big shawl collar with Leonardo-like hatch marks. "We could use this color on the other side."

"Mmm-hmm. Yeah, like that, but you could add in, say, lots of pockets." For all the stuff I'll have to bring with me, I think.

Beth eyes her design, holding it at arm's length for perspective. "Oh, true, a girl always can use more pockets, for sure. And maybe a hoodie."

"Definitely a hoodie." Sometimes a girl needs a quick duck inside a hood to avoid detection, *just in case.*

"And I see some engineers have been testing out a metal-coated fabric that responds to changes in temperature, to heat and cool. But we may want to add in a smart-system cooling and heating technology to control for climate. And that's where Billy could help us."

"Billy?" she sets the drawing down on my bed and looks up at me, like she's already forgotten him.

"Yes. You know how he designs virtual worlds, right?"

She nods.

"And he can adapt the settings to approximate different climate conditions, so . . ."

"So?"

"So, we can test climate models using your costumes—er, umm, fashion designs—like in a virtual lab!" I finish, trying to sound like this is a solution to a big problem we haven't even come up against yet. In truth, I'm just stalling for time.

"Test? What the heck, Charley!" Beth stares at me like I'm out of my mind.

"Really, Beth, with your fashion sense, Billy's engineering genius, and my investigative forensic mind and strong emotional intelligence, aka, EQ, we'll make the perfect team."

Oblivious to my previous adventure and a way-too-up-close experience of the Inquisition, Beth sits on the edge of my bed, eyeing her sketch again. Looking like *The Thinker*, a hand under her chin, she frowns. Then, picking up a piece of charcoal, she slowly and deliberately adds quick strokes to the page, to draw in pockets and a hoodie. "I'm gonna have to YouTube this story, you know."

**THE THINKER BY RODIN, OUTSIDE
PHILADELPHIA'S RODIN MUSEUM**

Credit: CC0 1.0

I watch the gears spinning in her mind. "I know, Beth. No one will want to miss it!"

"Hmmph. You know what, Charley? I think that if an idea isn't crazy, it's not worth trying. So, let's do it!"

I sit up, amazed. What came out of Beth's mouth is brilliant, and totally the rule I live by. In fact, I wish I'd said it myself.

"Billy too?"

She looks up, all innocent, and gives me one of her beatific smiles— as if this were not a point of debate even five minutes ago. "Sure, why not. Billy, too."

IV.
#SOS

Look who shows up—just in time

I'm about to WhatsApp Billy (who's an Android guy to my i-Everything) when who appears on the screen instead but Kairos—he, who has the uncanny ability to appear anywhere, at any time, in the nick of time. We've talked occasionally, since that first TYCTW Day sent me on a mad adventure, but lately, he's been MIA.

But Kairos is also an expert on "knowledge management" (aka, KM), which I've kind of guessed is a thing that comes from him being from some unknown past or future—and being able to tune into information from then and now. To have a virtual visit from this long, lanky dude with the wavy hair in a weird cut—like a cross between short, straight-across bangs and what my mom would have called a "flip," a style that girls wore back in the day—and luminous brown eyes, it seems almost like he's been spying on me.

Now, from the looks of the background scene showing on screen, he appears to be, loosely speaking, in the neighborhood—there's an image of the U.S. Capitol behind him. Then again, it may just be a virtual background. With Kairos, it's hard to keep track of where—or when—he is at any given time.

The self-proclaimed specialist who programmed our original time machine to tumble me back centuries to a menacing confrontation with a lynch mob and a too-exciting meetup with my Renaissance "I can do everything" hero, Leonardo da Vinci, is speed-talking. He sounds panicked.

"*Dio mio!* You must help me right now, Carlotta! *La bambina Carolina.* She is missing!"

"What are you talking about, Kairos?" I ask. Carolina is Kairos's very precocious eight-year-old sister. It was my suggestion to name my little sister Carrie after her. (Note to readers: Do not, under penalty of being grounded without your phone, tell Mamma or Dad! Carrie's namesake must remain secret due to aforementioned circumstances, i.e., broken timelines, parallel universes, quantum fluctuations . . . or some other reasonable explanation for the phenomenon of my having time-traveled to some version of the distant past.)

Last I saw Carolina, I was winding up my time (literally!) in Florence; we were together at the magnificent Piazza della Signoria. In 1492. And the whole place was going up in flames.

CAROLINA'S FLORENCE

Credit: iStockPhoto

"Isn't she with you, Kairos?"

"No." He holds up a postcard to show me on the screen, but his hand is shaking so badly, I can't quite read it. It's the loopy writing of a child learning cursive. (Or a modern teen who never did learn how to write that way. But that's another story). The place on the picture—not a photo, but a sepia-toned drawing—is the majestic Notre Dame Cathedral.

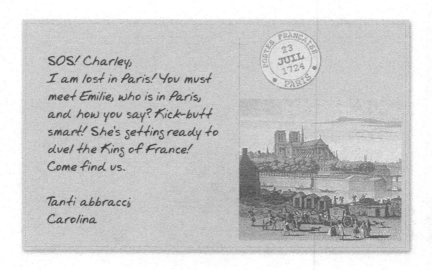

SOS! Charley,
I am lost in Paris! You must
meet Emilie, who is in Paris,
and how you say? Kick-butt
smart! She's getting ready to
duel the King of France!
Come find us.

Tanti abbracci,
Carolina

CAROLINA'S SOS

I squint to decipher the postmark. "Paris?" I observe with some nostalgia that the roof and flying buttresses here are intact. Pre- the devastating fire of 2019. "How did she get to Paris? In 1724 . . . what?"

"She hitched a ride on your time machine, Carlotta."

I raise a quizzical eyebrow. "How?"

"When you and Billy—and we—made the explosion to reverse the time, to bring you forward to your today, Carolina was also blown ahead. Just not so far as you."

"I saw she got blown forward—the little monkey!"

And now she's penned an SOS: a cry for help.

I scan my brain cells to think back to eighteenth-century Paris. What could have been happening back in the day that might get one small, mischievous girl in trouble: kings and duels, thieves and angry mobs, smallpox outbreaks, the Revolution and Madame la Guillotine . . . ?

"You mean . . . she's been by herself, in Paris, all this time?"

"Not quite *all*. As you know, Carlotta, time is relative . . ."

Before Kairos can launch into Einstein's equations, his substantial brainpower temporarily overriding his concern for his baby sister, I break in.

"Yes, yes, I know. It depends on the observer. So, get on with it . . ."

"Ah, so. She was not able to go as fast as you. Or as far."

"But Kairos," I remind him, "can't you go find her *alla Parigi*, as you'd say? After all, you're always—"

"Just in time. Yes. But look again, Carlotta. It is *you* she is asking for."

Yeah, I think to myself. Otherwise, why wouldn't Kairos just go get her himself? But maybe she just misses me like I miss her; why else the "wish you were here"? Is Kairos up to something he's not telling me?

"This Émilie she mentions, Kairos. She wouldn't happen to be the not-famous-enough-in-history STEM genius Émilie du Châtelet, would she?"

As it happens, the Marquise du Châtelet has been on my short list for possible time travel adventures for some time now. She was a brilliant mathematician, philosopher, and physicist—unusual enough for a woman living in the early 1700s, much less our own time. When she was young, her father recognized her brilliance and brought in tutors for her. By age twelve she was fluent in Latin, Italian, Greek, and German. Apparently, she was so good at math, from a very young age, that her father used to trot her out in front of guests to solve difficult equations—presumably without an abacus, or of course, a calculator. As a teenager, she dueled at the Court of Louis XV and, based on her aforementioned mad math talent, applied to counting cards, gambled to earn money to afford tutors and textbooks after her father lost his big-deal job at the Court of Versailles. I'm guessing, even today, she might be able to beat the house in Vegas.

My kind of girl.

Kairos laughs at my description.

"I have no idea what a stem has to do with genius, *cara* Carlotta," he replies. "But yes, the timing and the reference to a duel would indicate this Émilie is one and the same."

A mere three centuries ago. A quick calculation in my mind sets out the possibility for a visit with *la belle* Émilie. This changes the fashion statement for Beth's project: Carolina's rescue.

But first, I must talk to Billy.

V.

Ulterior Motives

Why secrets are sometimes necessary,
even under threat of detention

It's a good thing Billy and I have the same study hall. We got in trouble for laughing earlier in the quarter so, on top of everything else, we're not allowed to sit together. Luckily, Mr. Grigsby, the teacher who's monitoring study hall, is oblivious to texting in Google Docs, 'cause it's what we use for notes and collaboration and stuff, and schools block Snapchat and Instagram. Best part: Most teachers don't even know a chat app exists in it.

Just in case, I have my history book open to the time period we're studying this year, which is, conveniently, Europe during the Enlightenment, and I have opened up my spiral notebook covered in my notes and sketches, à la a da Vinci codex.

Timely, *non?*

I kind of expect Billy to respond immediately. When he doesn't, I stare at him across the room. He has his head down on his arms. Snoozing. After all, we were both up late comparing notes about the math involved in adjusting GPS to account for geopositioning relative to spacetime adjustments on a centuries-long scale. You know, leap seconds, Earth wobbles, and the like.

After all, navigating with greater accuracy to different time periods, more than Beth's fashion app, is what keeps me awake nights.

And what not to wear!

When I accidentally/on purpose time-traveled the first time, I was totally unprepared for the fact that the Peninsula that would someday be unified as Italy was going through a mini Ice Age, following the Medieval Warm Period. (Note to climate scientists: This level of climate change occurred when the major fossil fuel burn-off was from coal, wood, and peat, and certainly not at industrial levels. Which makes me wonder how much more CO_2 we're adding with all the detritus of modern, so-called civilization.)

Showing up during an Ice Age in a scoop-necked mini dress and leggings was, shall we say, awkward. And it certainly wasn't a useful way to blend in with the local Florentine population during the fifteenth century. Not to mention the fact that the only girls back in the day who showed that much leg didn't exactly earn the best reputation.

And I am *not* that kind of girl.

So wherever the future of time travel takes me, I'll need to be better prepared for whatever costume is more in line with the times. And local weather conditions.

That's where Beth's genius comes in. With her design sense, and integrating transition fabrics, understanding the body's biochemistry (let's call that "the sweat or chill factor"), and some IoT technology that I can help Billy rig up, our new fabric innovations will keep us climate-controlled and *appropriate* wherever we land.

For now, we'll need to keep Beth in the dark about the time travel thing, but as long as she's excited to YouTube for her fashion-forward followers, our plan should work.

Meanwhile, there's research to be done.

I search keywords: cooling, clothes, heating, technology, wearables, artificial intelligence. Looks like this is really a thing; there's even an e-zine for wearable technologies that goes far beyond your ordinary exercise tracker.

I feel my phone vibrating and, glancing over, see that Billy's awake.

> Billy: Wazzup?
> Charley: Did you see? You're in!

Billy:	Great. Just what I want. To be part of Beth's fashion show.
Charley:	You may think differently when I tell you another bit of news.
Billy:	??
Charley:	Talked to K last night.
Billy:	Kairos?
Charley:	What other K do you know!
Billy:	Well, there's OK, and IDK, for starters.
Charley:	Ha ha!
Billy:	So?
Charley:	It's Carolina. She's stuck in Paris.
Billy:	Carolina?! WTF?
Charley:	Tell you later. Gotta get to her. She needs us.
Billy:	*Us?* You're killin' me here, Charley.

I sneak him the hairy eyeball. But, of course, Billy's going to want to come with me!

Charley:	*Mais, oui.* But I need u. You'll need to look presentable. That's why Beth—
Billy:	Could care less about how I look.
Charley:	I know, but it's the only way we can work together. And you'll need to wear something that blends in.
Billy:	I'll get a pirate costume at the Halloween store. That's *if* I go.

Charley:	Anyways. If she can design us Parisian fashions for that time period—transition wear . . .
Billy:	Ha ha. How're you gonna get her to do that? Can't tell her the true purpose of your so-called "transition wear."
Charley:	YET! Patience, Iago, patience.
Billy:	First, that fez and vest combo is much too third century. These patches; what are we trying to say? Beggar? No. Work with me here.

This cracks me up. It's a scene from *Aladdin*. Billy and I used to watch it together all the time when we were kids.

"Oooh, I like it!" I type. It's Genie's next line.

A large, hairy hand suddenly appears under my nose. I slowly look up.

"Oooh, I don't," says Mr. Grigsby, in that fake, patient voice that teachers have. "Your phone, Miss Morton."

"Oh, I'm sorry, Mr. Grigsby. Did I say that out loud? I didn't mean . . . you know . . . it's just a thing . . . my dad . . . inside joke. Anyway, I didn't know we couldn't text during study hall," I say, making my eyes big in a way I hope conveys my innocence.

"I said, please hand me the phone, Miss Morton." Grigsby is nothing if not persistent.

"I'm so, so, so sorry. It'll never happen again," I say plaintively.

Mainly, I need to buy time to power my phone off completely, so he can't see the chat. Like, I'm pretty sure I have a right to privacy, but I just want to be on the safe side because we've all heard the horror stories.

I slowly hand it over. I mean, it's not like we've been sexting or anything. I don't dare make eye contact with Billy, either, although I'm sure he's laser-focused on what is happening.

"I could take this to the principal's office," he says officiously.

"Yes, Mr. Grigsby," I say humbly. I can feel my cheeks burning.

"But because I *know* you to be a good student, I'm going to be lenient."

I look up, hopeful. "Oh, thank you so much, Mr. Grigsby. That'd be amazingly wonderful, because I've got research for my Western philosophy essay on there," I explain ingratiatingly, without taking my hand off my device. "You know, don't put Descartes before the horse!" My bad pun fails to crack up the Grigsby.

Just then, the bell rings.

"Oops! Can't be late!" I grab back my phone and spring away as quickly as I can escape.

Billy and I meet up again a little way down the hall while kids are streaming by, slamming lockers and fist-bumping friends as they pass in a race to class.

I've got a quiz in philosophy next and Billy's on his way to AP calculus. He'd be taking advanced math classes in the physics department at the University of Maryland if he had his way, but his parents want him to learn to socialize normally with his peer group (he can be such a brainiac, it's true), so he's breezing through stuff he already knows. And tutoring kids having trouble in the class.

"Phew, close call!" I remark. "Almost lost my phone for the rest of the day, thanks to Grigsby the Grinch Who Stole Study Hall." Although I am not one of those people addicted to my device. At least I like to think I'm not.

"Oh, whatever am I going to do with you, Carlotta!" Billy says in a squeaky high voice, mimicking my mom.

"You should talk!" I retort with a smirk. Billy just graduated to a smartphone this year because his parents were worried he'd never speak to anyone face-to-face ever again. (Not true, by the way. He talks to me.) But now he's gotten into hacking into it, just to see how he can improve on the cybersecurity.

Billy continues walking at a sprint. I half-skip two steps to every one of Billy's.

"Anyway, let's not waste time on Grigsby," I say. "We've got bigger things to discuss. Like programming the time machine with the specific date, time, and place we want to travel back to. And then there's that whole thing about beta testing. 'Cause last time, we couldn't figure out how to verify whether our spacetime parameters would sync geopositioning of the Earth's orbit in space relative to the sun and other planets at the estimated landing date."

If we got this last calculation wrong, we might go back to the right date and year, but we might disastrously find ourselves on the opposite side of the sun from our planet in its 365-day orbit. Like I say, it gets complicated.

"Yeah, right. So, Carolina. You said Paris? What year are we talking? I'm guessing it's not 1492 anymore?"

"Of course not. We saw how Carolina got swept up in our time travel. After all, with that whole amazing Rube Goldberg contraption we built with Leonardo da Vinci's help back in Florence, to harness the sun's energy, with mirrors to amplify the fireworks and cannons during their Carnival celebrations, and the explosions that propelled our time travel home—"

"Oh, no, Charley! You don't think Leo's behind this, do you?"

That stops me cold. "Hmm. Didn't even think to ask K about Leonardo's current whereabouts."

"As improbable as it might seem," Billy reminds me, "we both saw where the famed Maestro da Vinci ended up."

It's true. When we got back from our first time travel mission, Billy was somehow able to capture and record an unusual livestream event on his tablet, one that serves as a kind of P.S. to our adventure. None other than Leonardo da Vinci sitting in Einstein's kitchen in Bern, Switzerland, debating Einstein's newly proven Special Theory of Relativity—and revealing to Einstein the future confirmation of the Higgs boson, a faster-than-light quantum particle. Mainly due to my having to reveal that future fact in order to get Leo to help us reverse-engineer our time machine to get back to the future. I mean today.

And they wonder where genius comes from!

"Nope. She mentioned a 'kick-butt' girl she wanted us to meet— someone out to duel with the King of France. So our specific destination is Versailles. Time period: the Enlightenment—1724, to be precise."

"So who is this girl who's about to raise swords against the King? That sounds positively treasonous, Charley! And why in God's name would Carolina think you ought to meet her?"

I can barely keep pace with Billy's sprint, and we've almost reached the spot where Billy will turn one corner and I will peel off on the other to get to class.

"Well," I pant, "you will recall that I've decided to survey all the polymaths of history to learn their secrets, no?" Theory: Big data could be a boon to my attempts to unveil the common personal attributes and historical origins of genius.

"But a girl?"

I stop abruptly and stomp my feet, forcing Billy to turn around. "Ahem! What do I look like?"

Billy looks at me. "You're taking it all wrong, Carlotta. I wasn't talking about you. I mean, girls, back in the day . . ."

"Actually, it turns out there have been many brilliant women throughout history. It's just that the men who write history books have inexplicably omitted them. Or shut them up. I mean, look at *Hidden Figures*, or *The Glass Universe*, and tell me those women 'computers' were not geniuses!"

"Okay, I catch your point, Charley. So, who are you planning to interview this time, Marie Antoinette? 'Off with her head!' and all that?"

"Don't be a dunce. Marie Antoinette was no genius. And her hairstyles were atrocious: three-foot-high wigs including birdcages, with actual birds inside. Imagine the chirping, twenty-four/seven. And the poop!" I scratch my head anxiously, just thinking about that avian interference.

MARIE ANTOINETTE, QUEEN OF FRANCE

Title: Queen Marie Antoinette of France
by Anonymous, 1775
Public Domain
The Queen is shown wearing a pouf created by her hairdresser,
Léonard Autié

"Right. So just who did you have in mind?"

"We're going back a little farther, to pre-revolutionary France. Look here at what Carolina wrote." I pull up a pic of the postcard I captured on my phone. "The year 1724. It's perfect!"

"What's perfect about that, Charley?"

"Well, you remember a couple of months ago in physics class, Ms. Jones told us about this totally cool physicist and mathematician from the time of the Enlightenment, Émilie—I mean the Marquise du Châtelet?"

He shakes his head.

"You remember—she translated Newton's writings into French for the first time, with a brilliant commentary explaining them. And they still use her translation in France today."

He still looks perplexed.

"And then she pulled a one-up on Newton's math by squaring the velocity of a moving object to calculate its force?"

I can see Billy's mind whirring to life. "I'm starting to remember something about an argument with Voltaire . . . ?"

"Exactly! *Force vive*, she called it: the living force. They totally disagreed about whether Newton's idea of a static universe showed the way things worked, requiring God—or some other magical intervention—to keep things in clockwork motion, or Leibniz's idea about a universe in motion. Émilie du Châtelet used calculus—an innovation at the time—to refine the math to prove Sir Isaac was wrong, and Voltaire, who idolized Newton, was furious!"

The bell's ringing.

"Yeah, well. The proof is always in the numbers," Billy confirms. "Speaking of which, I've got to finish my math homework and I've run out of excuses for not having it written down. Except that it's all in my head."

"Of course. You're going to love the Marquise, Billy. She's the real deal!"

I stash away a mental reminder to send him my notes about Émilie.

Then, I hesitate, tapping him playfully on the wrist. "And, yeah, can we also maybe talk about Homecoming plans?"

I'm not really crazy about things like school dances, but it's kind of a rite of passage. You've got to go at least once, just to say you've been. Last year, I went to the Homecoming game with a big group from our class, but I thought it was ridiculous to dress up and hang out with a gaggle of girls at the Big Dance, holding up the wall. This year, it's somehow different, though. I can't exactly put my finger on it, but I want to see what it feels like to go with Billy, and maybe even to dance with him.

When I first proposed the idea, Billy was adamant against it. But he finally came around when I said we could use it as a social experiment looking at modern teen rites of passage wherein we might observe the scene *in vivo*, as it were, and collect data points for a project examining cultural patterns and processes for AP Human Geography. I kind of like the idea of becoming a modern Margaret Mead of the species I'll call *homo adolescens*, aka, the American teenager.

"Homecoming? What's that got to do with anything?"

It's like he's already forgotten.

"Beth asked if she could come with us, since she doesn't have a date."

Billy frowns. "Please say you're kidding. It's like, Bethy this, Bethy that. It feels like we don't ever get to hang out together, Charley, just you and me," he points out, which is fair. "And I mean, what am I supposed to say? 'Oh, Beth, your hair looks so straight tonight!'"

"Whatever, Billy," I reply. "We need her to include you on the science fair project. So try and be nice, even if you have to fake it. You know Beth's really smart . . . even if she's decided to hide that fact."

"Okay. I'll try. But no guarantees. Meanwhile, oh-Brainiac-mine, think about whether we should go on the party bus to get to the dance. Might be less awkward than having one of our parents driving us."

"Ditch the parentals, stat!" I agree. "Speaking of parents: If I get in any more trouble today and the principal ends up confiscating my phone—my life!—and calling Gwen and Jerry, and if anyone were to ever read our texts . . . it'll be good-bye, time travel!"

VI.

ANOTHER HOMECOMING

Getting ready to rock-and-roll

Beth is getting ready for Homecoming at my house, mostly to avoid getting the third degree from her mom. ("You're not *really* going out in *that*, Beth, are you?")

She saunters into my room, noisily tweaks a few strings on my violin that I've left on my desk, and pages through the sheets on my music stand: Brahms's "Lullaby" is the twins' favorite to fall asleep to.

"Beth! Don't—it's fragile!"

"Ugh! It's so quiet. Just trying to liven things up. Could we at least play some tunes? Alexa, play party tunes!"

The noise is killing me. "Alexa, shut up!"

"You're no fun, Charley. And speaking of no fun, where are the twins?"

"Mamma took them for ice cream. She thought it might be too hard to get ready with them interfering."

In fact, this was not Mamma's idea, wanting to be here to see me off for my first big formal and everything. But she had promised the girls ice cream if they ate all their dinner. Since she's performing most nights, she hardly ever gets to spend quality time with them before bed. And babies' bedtimes, being what they are, it was the only time.

"But Dad's promised to take lots of pictures!" I reminded her, even though I do kind of think this should be more of a mother-daughter thing. If we didn't fight about my out-of-control hair. Which we totally would.

Beth has promised to sweep it into an updo, and plugs in her flat iron. I am skeptical, given the stubbornness of my curls.

A few minutes later, despite her repeated efforts, the flat iron isn't doing much to counter all that heavy boing-boing. I squirm at the heat against my head.

"Just sit still, Charley," she lisps, pulling bobby pins out from between clenched teeth, stabbing my head a million times as she tries to secure the twist.

"Ow! That hurts, Beth!"

"Sorry! I've almost got this . . ."

She puts the last pin in place before digging into the back of my head with pearl-encrusted hair comb to finish the look.

"There. What do you think?"

I stare at the stranger in the mirror with the sleek hair and red lips and wonder who in the hell she replaced me with.

"Well?" She pulls up Photo Booth on her phone to show me the back.

"I have to get used to it," I reply, squinting and turning my head from side to side.

Which is true. I mean, if I were looking at another girl who looked like the one staring from the mirror, I'd probably think she was *très chic*. But it is *so* not me.

I don't tell Beth that. But it seems not to matter, because she's already pulled her own dress off the hanger and is stepping into it. It's a strapless royal blue satin number, with just the right amount of sequins and lace on the bodice that hugs her body's curves and puddles on the floor, Morticia Addams style.

"Ta-da!"

"Wowee, girlfriend!" I exclaim, seeing her transformation as she slings on some gold strappy stiletto-heeled sandals. "You look *gaw-gi-o-so!*"

"My own dress design, of course!" Beth beams, and snakes over to look at herself in the full-length mirror hanging on the back of my bedroom door. "Not bad," she says, eyeing herself critically.

I pull my pink floaty dress up from my feet, to avoid messing up Bethy's coiffure. It's got a lot of tulle underneath the full skirt. It's kind of old-school, yet timeless. At least that's how Mamma describes it. I'm just happy that I don't have to wriggle around like Morticia every time I try to take a step. A problem Bethy's inviting with her own costume.

"Let me do your eyes, Charley." She pulls out some fake lashes, finishing them off with mascara to make it look more natural. "They say the Maryland cheerleaders use this mascara. It's supposed to last for a whole week without smearing."

I picture them sticking my eyelids shut. Or falling off. Beth DIY'd her own eyelash extensions, which you should definitely not try at home if you're like me, totally ham-handed.

"Ta-da!" Beth twirls me around, hugs me to her, and pulls out her phone to capture our glam. "Ready to pah-ty!"

Then she breaks into a grin, holding out an arm to link up with me and make our grand entrance, stepping gingerly down the stairs where Dad is waiting to capture the moment. Between Beth and the banister, I grip tight, even though my trademark cowboy boots substantially reduce the risk of my succumbing to gravity.

"Beautiful!" Dad exclaims.

"Take pictures, Dad!" I pass him my phone.

"Okay, stand over there, by the mantel. Your mother is going to be so sorry she missed this!"

"I know. 'Can't be helped!'" I mimic Mamma saying. "Let's text her."

"Okay—cheese!" Dad steadies the camera and takes several shots as we strike funny poses. "I don't know how you girls have gotten to be so grown-up. Seems like yesterday you guys were having no-sleep sleepovers and running around in footie pajamas."

"Dad!" I grimace. "That is such an old-fogey thing to say."

"Aww, gee, Mr. Morton," Beth says in her sweetest "impress the parents" voice, "we were just little kids then. It feels like a lifetime ago!"

Just then, the party bus pulls up to the curb blaring music and laughter.

"Right, then. Be careful in those heels, eh, Beth?" Dad warns, echoing my thoughts. "Don't want any sprained ankles on the dance floor!"

"I'll be fine, Mr. Morton."

My dad gallantly offers Beth his arm to help her step up and into the party bus without twisting an ankle—or ripping a seam.

Luckily, my pink dress is simpler, light and kind of floaty, falling just above the ankles. I prance right on board without assistance and squeeze in beside her.

The party bus is wired for sound. Literally. Speakers blasting "Two Tickets to Paradise." A huge neon banner says, *Your Ticket to Paradise*. I'm getting that's the theme. Laser light show. Everyone's standing as if it would be uncool to sit.

It's already giving me a headache.

Beth pulls out her phone for a selfie. A few guys crowd in close, like drone bees to the queen. George, one of the dorkier boys we know from way back in middle school, passes her a flask.

She takes a gulp from the flask and sputters, liquid extruding from her nose (think liquid boogers). George pushes her hand back toward her face, laughing.

"Lightweight!" George observes as I surreptitiously pass Beth a tissue. "What, never had a drink before? You chug, like this!" He holds his head back and pours the liquid down his throat, then offers it back to her.

"Chug . . . chug . . . chug!" the kids surrounding her chant.

"Beth!" I whisper in her ear, "you don't really want to—"

She frowns. "Don't be a prude princess. Nothing's going to happen," she says, caught up in the moment. "Besides, I can handle myself. I mean, I haven't been taking kickboxing for nothing."

I have to admit, spiking someone with those heels could be considered a martial art in and of itself.

"Okay, but don't say I didn't warn you!"

Before I realize that she's actually videoed me saying that, I hear the notification on my phone posted to her Instagram: #BratCharley #ExBFF #PartyBus #Homecoming. And there I am, looking like someone's mom, with my finger wagging at the camera. She instantly got 432 likes, and then I see #Charleypartypooper is trending.

I give her the eyeball, but she pushes me out of the way.

"Chug it! Chug it!" They've resumed their taunting.

Looking George in the eye, Beth takes a deep inhale and glugs from the flask. I see her hold her breath, willing herself not to spit it out. George snaps a picture and Instagrams it #BethFashionista #Chugit #PartyBus #Rockon!

I just stare out the window. Finally, the bus stops in front of Billy's house, and who doesn't step in looking all fine in a light blue seersucker suit and yellow tie!

Now George is trying to pass Billy the flask even before the bus doors close.

I squeeze past Beth, grabbing Billy by the arm.

"Hey, let's go sit in back, okay?"

"Sure. I was about to suggest the same thing," Billy yells over the beat, pushing away the flask.

We've only made our way through about half the crowd of kids, but I've already lost him. Something about the installation of the flashing LED light system seems to have distracted him.

I need to grab back his attention. "Ahem!" I start to model my new look.

"Oh, yeah." With an effort, he tears his eyes away to see me. "Wow. You look really pretty, Charley!" Billy steps one foot in front of the other, taking a courtly bow in front of me, and pulls out a wrist corsage—pink rosebuds with baby's breath.

I can feel my face flushing. Despite our long back-and-forth about whether we go together, or go as singles and just end up kind of hanging with each other, it seems Billy's been studying up on how to treat a date to Homecoming. There's probably even a YouTube for that!

He leans over to fasten it around my wrist. "Umm, you might want to smell them," he says, with a glint in his eye.

I bring the bouquet up to my nose and spy it—a fine gold chain hidden among the baby's breath.

"Ooh," I coo excitedly. "What's this?" I begin to pull the chain.

"Let me help you," Billy says as he sees me fumbling with it. Carefully, he unwinds the chain and, hanging on it, I see a small golden compass pendant, crafted in Au (the symbol for gold on the Periodic Table), and etched with its atomic number, 79. An essential tool for the time traveler.

"Wow! It's beautiful, Billy!"

Far more than flowers, that fade even when pressed, the golden compass is the perfect symbol for us, crafted with mathematical precision, and tracing the geometry of the spheres.

"Do you like it? It's multifunctional. It's not exactly like our original. But you can use it to draw circles, in drafting and design, to measure with . . ."

"And for time traveling!" I whisper in his ear, as he fastens it around my neck. "Oh, Billy, it's perfect." I pat the tiny charm now nestled against my neck. "Thank you!"

Whether it's the motion of the bus, which has just started moving again, or gravity, I feel myself swaying toward him. As he grabs my waist to steady me, I feel an unfamiliar spark.

We turn a sharp corner and I whirl into Beth, who's now dancing in the aisle. They're playing Drake, super loud. She drags me in to dance with her.

"Whoops. Sorry!" I stumble and grab onto the shoulder of some random girl as I try to right myself.

"Here, this hat will go good with your dress, Charley." George, apparently the life of this party, places a pointy, polka-dotted party hat on my head, pinching my chin with the elastic strap.

"Ouch!" I tug it off, feeling a second pinch, this one self-inflicted.

"Party time!" he blows one of those awful noisemakers in my face. His breath stinks and I feel his hand grabbing my butt.

I'm beginning to wish we'd taken a rideshare instead. Even the parentals might have been preferable to this.

"Hands off, man," Billy frowns, pointedly steering me out from under the long arms of George. "Idiot!"

"You're the idiot, idiot!" shouts George, but I can see he's already distracted as some other dude sticks his phone under George's nose, laughing at a Snapchat.

"Ignore that weirdo; I've got you, Charley," Billy assures me, wrapping me in a bear hug and crushing my dress. I feel myself blushing again.

"Billy, stop messing up her hair. After all that work I did on it!" Beth butts in and tucks my wayward curls back into the twist.

With that the bus jerks to a stop and the doors open.

"Welcome to Paradise!" the driver yells back. "Last stop!"

We get off the bus to a lineup of the Senior Welcoming Committee. And who's at the end of the line but the jerk who rammed into me in the hallway and dropped his phone. I notice he's sporting a fitted gray tux and a red cummerbund. Very Eurostyle. Very full of himself.

Worse yet, he's apparently recognized me.

"Now here's a surprise: the girl who fell down to Earth," he says, with a slight sneer. "What do you call yourself, anyway, space cadet?"

"Hey, you can't talk to my girlfriend like that!"

I turn in surprise. Billy has never publicly acknowledged that we're anything more than science partners.

"No one pushes *me* around," the dude smirks and pushes through, like he's ready to swat Billy out of the way.

I see Billy's face tensing up. I'm frozen to the ground, my mind snagged on that word: girlfriend.

"Billy, it's not worth . . ."

"Worth what, *girlfriend?* You scared I'll beat the crap out of him?"

To my surprise, Beth has stepped in. "Her name is Charley, and if I recall correctly, you ran into her!"

"Who smashed my phone and got me busted?" he shouts, waving his phone with now-cracked glass in my face.

"C'mon, Charley. Let's check out the punch table," Billy intervenes preemptively.

Beth seems intent on pushing the situation. "You can't bully my friends . . . you . . . you . . . wait, what's your name, anyway?"

"Guy Emile-Tonnelier," he says, pronouncing his first name like the French, "ghee," with a hard g.

I crack up, despite myself. A guy whose name is Guy.

"Guy—that's clever!" Beth replies, sticking out her hand. "*Heureuse de faire ta connaissance.* Are you from France?"

"French West Africa. Senegal, by way of Paris," Guy says, thrown off guard. "Originally. Now, here. My mother works at the Embassy."

"Wow. That's why the accent then." Beth leans in closer to Guy, none too steady on her feet. "I'm Elisabeth." She gives her name a French pronunciation too.

"Beth," I hiss under my breath. "Don't waste your time on this loser."

"I know what I'm doing, Charley," she hisses in reply, then turns back to the guy—who, I have to admit, is rather easy on the eyes. If you go for macho types, I mean. Which I know Beth does.

"Guy," she says, batting her eyelash weave flirtatiously, "why don't you ask me to dance?"

Turning on the charm, Guy replies, "*Un plaisir*, Elisabeth."

As he places one arm behind Beth's back to steer her toward the dance floor, I notice he's pulled out a flask from under his jacket.

"Beth?" I really don't trust this Guy person.

But Beth flashes me a confident smile, like, she's got this.

VII.

AFTER-PARTY

*In which school is still school, no matter how much the
AR looks like Paradise, and my date and I have more
important matters to discuss*

Billy and I ditch Paradise while the band is still blaring. Nothing worse than a bunch of teacher and parent chaperones breaking up fights in the school cafeteria as kids do what they will do in such circumstances: get all hot and bothered doing the bump-and-grind, make out under tables, surreptitiously vape in the courtyard, hang around looking awkward, or spew when they get stupid, stinking drunk.

I mean, what do they expect from a bunch of teens whose prefrontal cortexes are not yet developed enough to make healthy decisions?

Anyways, it was really not fun.

We decide to go to the Far-Tastier Diner, instead of the after-party. It's a favorite local place—advantage: It's open twenty-four hours. And since it's not too far from school, we can actually walk there.

The place is pretty empty at 12:30 a.m. We pick a booth and I flip the pages to the old-school-style jukebox, looking for some music to keep us awake.

"How about, 'Don't Stop Believin''?" I slip coins into the slot and punch A7. The music echoes off the walls.

"Never did," Billy quips.

"Homecoming over, hon?" queries the waitress, order pad at hand.

"Nah," Billy replies. "We left early."

"No kiddin'. Expect we'll be seein' a ton o' y'all streaming in soon. So, whatcha havin', kids?"

I order the French toast—sort of to get in the Paris mood—and Billy's going all out with the Triple Play: three eggs, bacon, sausage.

A few minutes later, I watch as he shovels it all in, including the hash browns, between two halves of a toasted English muffin. And downs it all with a large vanilla milkshake.

"You're going to make yourself sick inhaling your food like that," I observe. "Doesn't your stomach hurt?"

"Cast iron," he replies, patting his tummy.

Did I mention, he's still growing?

"So, it's decided," I declare. "We're going to France."

"Why do we always have to do what you want, Charley?" Billy gripes between bites.

"We don't always do what I want, Billy. Just last month, who went with you to Comic-Con as Black Widow to your Spidey?"

"Yeah, that was fun. But it's always your idea for the science fair."

"Billy Vincenzo, I do not understand how you cannot take Carolina's postcard as anything but an SOS call! I mean, she loves you as much as me."

"I guess . . ."

"One thousand percent true! And as you are the soon-to-be Eagle Scout here who knows how important our preparation will be to the success of this mission, let's make a list of what we'll need to bring with us."

You may not think there's much you can do in advance to prepare for time travel, but as a veteran of one such experience, I'd have to say that's provably false.

After I set my mind to meeting the great da Vinci in person to learn the secrets of his genius, Billy and I built the time machine from Leonardo da Vinci's own blueprints. We never expected it to actually work, but it did—so, like, be careful what you wish for.

I arrived in 1492 Florence with only my backpack, my phone, and a few sugary snacks to sustain me for what became a forty-eight-hour, five-hundred-year journey. Snacks, I might add, that went into a horse's mouth instead of my own.

So, this time, in my ambition to save Carolina and meet up with the great Émilie in 1724 Paris, preparation is key. Even with our updates to the Qualia Rosetta formula, we still need the golden compasses to trigger time travel. In our original time travels, somehow, the model of Leonardo's horse-and-rider sculpture worked together with the compass to get me to the right place and time. I do not know about this next trip, except, if that experience is any guide, it may need to be something personal to whoever I'm hoping to meet.

And although, as a scientista, I do not believe in magic, until our three-dimensional brains catch up with four-/five-dimensional physics, "magic" is sorta what it all feels like.

In the meantime, Billy's been improving the navigational controls and remote GPS capabilities, not to mention upgrading the renewables capacity for super-powering the solar batteries, for two years already.

That first roller-coaster ride was more than a bit of a hit-or-miss to the past. So my job has been to tweak the whole Earth-GPS thing, adding in new features to sync clock and navigation systems. After all, we don't want to leave to chance just where—and when—we leap in time.

Despite us having worked on refinements for the past two years, there's no sure way to know whether our controls, super-souped-up GPS, and other enhancements will actually work. I'd compare it to a SpaceX Mars launch, but without NASA's moon missions having paved the way, so to speak. Or maybe more like the Spanish sailing the Atlantic in search of cloves from India and trusting they wouldn't sail off the edge at the horizon.

But we can do a few mini tests while timebound in 2019, venturing no farther than Billy's and my houses: We can test out the time machine's new programmable remote-control features, and make sure that whatever I wear (suitable for the glam girl in any time zone!) can adjust itself to heat, cold, rain, or unforeseeable meteor strikes. I'm thinking a mix of the new experimental fabric and Kevlar for strength, but also IoT with an AI to automatically activate a heating or cooling element in case of dramatic climate change.

Plus, I've done tons of historical research, especially looking at existing energy resources back-in-whatever-day (you know, sun, wind, coal, wood, lightning, cannons, and the like) to know how to power our way back smoothly to the twenty-first century from just about any point in time.

I'm also determined to carry real food with me this time, to avoid the hunger pangs I suffered on our last trip, when we were in the land of pizza and pasta (*not!*—and for that, I've dished about common Italian food myths).

That's why our meeting later at Beth's house is critical.

"So, let's decide what goes on the packing list. We know what worked last time, and what didn't. The new supercharged solar battery is a can't-leave-home-without. And a portable power bank that uses the sun to power up the battery when there's no electricity to plug it into."

It's the only way to keep the electronics charged when you're, say, out in the woods camping. Or stuck in the deep, dark past.

"Hey, Billy, do you think this was before or after Ben Franklin's electricity experiments with the kite and the key?"

CAPTION: TIME TRAVEL PREPARATIONS

I take out my mini composition book to start taking notes. Like any determined design thinker, I always keep a pad with me, just in case.

But then it seems the dance must have just let out, because now a bunch of kids are staggering in, laughing, cursing, and yelling, making it harder to concentrate.

Billy puts his hand on my arm, stopping me writing. "Charley, I'd say electricity is the least of our worries."

"Shhh. Are you kidding?!" I hiss back, though it seems debatable whether anyone here has the wits about them to spy on our convo. "I know it didn't stop us last time, but we were really lucky, what with

Leonardo kicking in some of his substantial engineering genius to rig up powerful-enough fireworks that helped fuel our escape. And there's no guarantee we'll have anything like the fiery Tuscan sun to whip up the solar cells."

"You do know that solar battery power has advanced significantly since our first pioneering attempt, Brainiac?"

"Storage is still our problem, Brainiac. Not sure about activating the time machine for the return trip without carrying our own subatomic power supply. Which, given the instability of uranium isotopes and the turbulence of time travel, doesn't seem like much of a plan. Unless, that is, you want to rig up a stationary bike and keep pedaling?"

Billy, at that moment chugging his milkshake, starts laughing until he's choking. His face turns tomato red while the thick, milky liquid squirts out of his nose.

"Vincenzo, you're hopeless!" I quick grab a handful of napkins to staunch the flow. "Am I going to have to apply the Heimlich maneuver on you?"

Heads turn in our direction.

I scoot in next to him in our booth and squeeze my arms around his chest, but Billy spits out the liquid and manages to take a gasp of air without the Heimlich.

"Easy, now, you lovebirds!" The waitress who was taking the order of more Homecoming refuseniks at a large table nearby hurries over. "There are smoother moves to get your girl to make out with you." She takes a damp rag from the busing station nearby and starts to mop up the table.

"Umm, no, we're not really . . ." I feel my face flush, but luckily, everyone else is too hammered, tired, or themselves too busy making out to notice.

I turn back to Billy, who's now sipping from the water glass that the waitress set in front of him. He wipes off his mouth with his shirtsleeve before downing a big swill.

"You okay?" I ask, mopping his forehead and lips. "We can go home . . ."

But before I know it, Billy pulls me in tighter and I watch in what seems like slo-mo as he brings his face right up to mine and plants a kiss on my lips, gently at first, then again, more insistently.

And I find myself kissing him back.

It's only when the tables near us break into applause that I notice our waitress started it.

Billy's big arms wind around me, and I pray no one sees my flushed face. Despite the audience, this feels like a magic moment.

I don't ever want it to end.

VIII.

HANGOVER

Or time-traveler stylings that almost didn't come to pass

"It's after one o'clock already, and high time Beth got up, anyway, Charley. Just wait down here while I get her." Mrs. Cooper is clearly annoyed that her daughter's wasting the day away.

Feeling none too clear in the head myself, I am not going to be the one to tell her that her daughter was *literally* wasted last night.

On top of the Coopers' ancient oak dining room table sits Beth's sewing machine, beside which is a litter of material, patterns, drawings, and scraps that Bethy's been collecting from fabric shops and tailors' throwaways. Red carpet pix from her fashion inspiration, Tracy Reese—who designs very chic, very feminine clothes for Michelle Obama, among others—are tacked to a corkboard leaning against a mirrored breakfront to one side.

Naturally, our science project feeds right into Bethy's passions.

I have to touch everything. I finger one pastel-striped linen strip, holding the rose, white, and pale-blue swatch sideways like a mini French flag. Linen, of course, is one of the oldest-known fabrics on the planet, from the flax plant. The ancient Egyptians are known to have made most of their clothes by spinning flax threads into cloth—about the only clothing that wouldn't suffocate you during a Middle Eastern heat wave—and even used it in their mummification process. Good candidate for endurance.

A swatch of wool tweed catches my eye, all scarlet, black, and white. I press it against my cheek and feel its soft warmth. Last year, we took a school field trip to a local sheep farm in Maryland. The owner is an artist who used to teach at our school. She now raises goats for their wool and spins yarn on a giant wooden spinner to sell to clothing designers the world over. Her wools felt just like this.

"Charley! Why'd you have to come over so *early?!*" moans Beth, as she stumbles down the stairs squinting and holding her head.

"Science fair," I reply, trying to be cheerful at the prospect of working with a crabby girl with a hangover. "Did you forget?"

"Shhh! Why d'ya gotta yell, Charley?"

Mrs. Cooper scurries over with ibuprofen and a glass of water. "You'll have to forgive her today, Charley. Beth's got another migraine. Believe me, I know how it feels! Ever since she started on her period . . ."

"*Mom!*" Beth rolls her eyes and immediately shuts them again. "Ouch. Why is it so bright in here!"

"Now, then," Mrs. Cooper continues, "take two of these, Beth. And I'll make you both some hot chocolate. They say caffeine helps."

"Oh, gawd," Beth groans again, slumping into a chair at the dining room table. "Just leave us alone, Mom. I'll be fine."

Mrs. Cooper gets that "mom look" in her eyes. "Well, I'm not so sure about that! You and I are going to have a sit-down after Charley leaves."

Beth musters enough energy to give her mom a thumbs-up, but under her breath, I hear her mumbling, "Not if I can help it."

———————

"You look awful," I say, noting her uncharacteristically kinky hair and bloodshot eyes.

"Yeah, well you don't look so hot yourself." Beth tilts her head toward the door Mrs. Cooper just passed through. "You didn't say anything about last night, did you?"

"Nope, not a word," I assure her. "Wanna talk about it?"

"Nope," Beth responds brusquely. "Nothing to talk about."

"Really?" I give her the eye, aware that there are any number of ways a discussion about Beth and Guy and what happened last night might be revealing.

Beth isn't buying. "Yeah, well let's get on with it." She pulls a gauzy cotton scarf out of the pile and wraps it around her head like a turban, squeezing her fingers into her eye sockets. "Have you figured out what fabric you want to use yet?"

I sigh. I'm sure the Guy-talk will have to be had at some point. But we have more important matters at hand, since the science fair deadline is a mere two weeks away.

"I'm not sure it's here, to be honest, Beth." I start sorting the fabric into piles: good for cold weather, good for hot weather, nylon rain gear, fleece. I even think Mrs. C's stash of plastic grocery bags waiting to be returned for recycling might have possibilities.

"I mean, all of these could be good for one season or another. But all the seasons at once?"

"Well I can work with any of them to sew a prototype. You just have to decide."

Right.

"Hey, Beth, remember in eighth grade when your science fair project was observing how flowers reacted to incessant loud, screechy, acid rock music?"

"Yeah. Think it killed off some of the cochlear hairs in my eardrums, besides the plants. So?"

"So, plants also react to weather conditions, right? I mean, they bud in warm weather, and lose their foliage when it starts to get cold outside."

"Your point?"

"My point is, if we could understand how plants adjust to extreme weather conditions, maybe we can deduce how to adapt fabrics and other materials to help us do the same!"

This seems to wake her up. "Yeah, well my experiment showed that plants absorb sound through their leaves and roots but move away from harsher sounds. What does that have to do with—"

"The point is, they adapt to pollutants in the environment. And of course, to temperature and sunlight as well."

"Yeah, so . . ."

"Yeah, so we should see whether the same adjustments that plants make to temperature extremes could apply to how our bodies and clothes could interact to regulate heat and cold."

"No way, Charley. No plants this time."

I realize this may be a reaction to her science fair partner and major crush Lex's decision to move to Italy right afterwards. To another time zone. In the 1500s. Of necessity, Beth's only aware of the first half of that story.

I sigh. I guess we'll have to wing it.

"Anyways, we know about the materials research that they're playing around with. We're going to have to build in a temperature-control app, or adapt the Nest, or something responding to voice commands as well as changes in blood flow and body temperature. You know, like, 'Alexa, it's too hot?'"

I kind of wish Billy was here to weigh in on this.

"Alexa . . . ? I mean, I can't . . ." Beth makes a pillow of her arms and lays her head down on the table. "Just figure out what the hell you want, Charley, and wake me up when you're done thinking."

I'm losing her but I can't help myself. I have to think out loud.

"So, the question is, how can we construct something that can *predict* and *adapt* to fast-changing climate conditions? And also take the body's temperature into account . . . I mean, I've been thinking rain gear. But then, that stuff doesn't really breathe in hot weather, even if you put in zippers and vents."

I don't mention that the very idea of zippers in the eighteenth century . . . well, that would just raise the wrong eyebrows.

Mrs. Cooper walks in carrying two steamy mugs of hot chocolate topped with whipped cream, and what looks to be home-baked oatmeal cookies. "Here you go, girls. Thought this might help."

"Oh, yes, thanks, Mrs. Cooper." I take a polite sip. "Nothing like cocoa and cookies for inspiration!"

Mrs. Cooper glances over at our mess. "What's your science fair project this year?"

"Oh, Beth hasn't told you? We're planning to integrate temperature controls into clothing so, like, your running gear heats and cools based on your body temperature and the outside temp as well."

"Well, wouldn't that be practical!" Mrs. Cooper sits down next to the sewing machine. "You know," she continues, "I was just thinking when I was out for a run yesterday, wouldn't it be great to have some-thing warm for winter that lightens up as you build up a sweat, and—"

"Hey, Mom," Beth cuts in, cup to lips. "We're kinda busy. Talk about it later?"

An awkward silence as Beth looks expectantly at her mother, who looks down at her phone.

"Yes, well. Work. You know!" says Mrs. Cooper, getting up reluc-tantly. "It's just . . . Well, I know you girls are doing amazing things."

Beth waits until her mom is out of earshot. Bending down, she pulls a large plastic container overflowing with stuff out from under the table. I marvel at how gracefully she moves, hangover or no, and feel a little jealous—I would've no doubt crawled on my knees and bonked my head under the table.

"Depends on how it's designed," Beth muses, extracting a bright yellow rain poncho with Mickey Mouse on the back and pulling it over her head. "Like, if it's open on the sides . . ." She twists the poncho every which way around her, observing the movement of the plastic as she's thinking. To complete the effect, she pulls the hood over her turbaned head.

"Totes adorable," I say. "But really not that practical for very cold weather."

"Hmmph," she snorts. "What's your solution, then, Miss Know-It-All?"

"We'll figure it out," I say, not at all sure that's true. "Oh, and Beth? There's one more thing."

"What's that?"

"Well, whatever we design, once we figure this part out? It would have to be wearable in the eighteenth century."

"*What?*"

"Yeah, you know. Long, full skirts and petticoats for the girls. Pantaloons and waistcoats for the guys. And ruffles. That sort of thing."

"What the hell, Charley? Are you planning on wearing this to some costume party, or something?"

"A costume party. Yup, yup, that's it. After all, Halloween is coming right up, and I thought we could all go as historical characters."

"This isn't just another piece of your Leonardo da Vinci obsession, is it?"

"Leonardo? Been there, done that," I say, only half-joking. "No, I'm thinking about the Enlightenment this time. There was this brilliant woman scientist and mathematician: the Marquise Émilie du Châtelet. She was so cool, Beth! She was smarter than all the men in her life, even the brilliant Voltaire. I want to *be* her. I mean, for Halloween, that is."

"Oh, I see. Another one of your so-called geniuses," Beth bites back. Pulling a chair out with one foot and slumping into it, she drops her head to rest in her crossed arms on the table, apparently exhausted from the effort. "Your next fangirl project?" she mumbles.

"What do you suddenly have against smart people, Beth?" I bite my tongue before I let slip, *like you used to be.*

Beth squints up at me.

"Anyways, I've researched the styles back in Émilie's day," I continue, before she can snap a comeback. "See? I Instagram'd some of what I think might work." I push my phone under her nose.

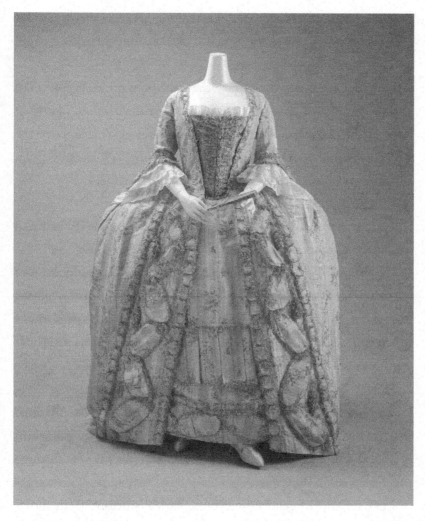

ROBE À LA FRANÇAISE: A DRESS FIT FOR A QUEEN

Beth pinches the picture to get a close-up look and frowns. It's a long, golden-toned dress with peach print flowers. Silk, brocaded within an inch of its life, with, like, twenty taffeta petticoats under it so that it poofs out and looks kind of like an upside-down tulip.

"You want to *wear* this thing?"

Want to wear is not the phrase that comes to mind. Frankly, I'm determined not to be caught out in modern-day clothes, like what happened in Leonardo's time. It was only Leo's cloak that saved me from becoming a victim of human trafficking. Which, back then, considering . . . well, slavery . . . was not even a crime.

This time, I need to be prepared.

"I admit, it's not all that, umm, comfy. But I thought it'd be fun. I mean, don't you have a costume for the Halloween Ball?"

"Costumes!" Beth gives a sinister little snort. "These look more like instruments of torture! So over-the-top!" She turns my phone horizontal, as if trying to understand the proportions. "And just how would you plan to get through the door of a room in a dress this wide?"

"Sideways."

"What?"

"A proper lady would enter a room sideways. Like this." I stretch my arms way out to the side like wings to approximate the width of a typical French Enlightenment dress and sidle my way through the dining room doorway.

"Ha ha. Don't forget, I know you, Charley Morton!" Beth snorts. "Wearing a balloon like this, I predict you'd end up bouncing off walls, like you're inside a pinball machine."

"Yes or no, Beth?" I'm getting frustrated. "'Cause if you can't make it, I'll find another way. I could probably persuade Ms. Jones in the design lab to let me three-D print it . . ."

"Go ahead, then, Charley! I dare you. An outfit like you're thinking about would only take, like, a month to print. And what about the technology that changes according to the weather and your own body temperature—are you going to print that, too?"

She's right. It *would* take forever. And it's already mid-October.

"And what's in it for me?"

"Winning the science fair. For once." I can't help being a little snide, as Beth is aware of her current second-place track record, next to me and Billy. As soon as I say this, I could kick myself, as this is not an argument to win Beth's heart.

"Hmmph. That is such old news—it's all 'Loser Lex's' fault. Who left school before we could even finish our experiment. And good riddance, I say!"

Deep down, I can tell she still cares.

"I mean, first off, the circumstances behind the death of Lex's parents are *très* mysterioso—like, were they *really* undercover? I bet they worked as spies. Or maybe Russian hackers."

I sympathize, this being in support of Bethy not being too hurt by his actually abandoning her for another girl . . . way, way back in the day.

"Hmmph. Lame. First off, we never even saw pictures of his parents, which is weird, right?"

If I'm not mistaken, Beth's eyes are red and welling up, and not just because of a hangover.

She bends down and pulls off the poncho, wiping her nose on her sleeve, presumably so I won't know she's upset. "Second off, his aunt and uncle—if that's who they even are—seemed genuinely mystified at not being able to find him," she sniffs.

"Which is totally why I'm saying the parents must've been working undercover somewhere out of the country," I say, "which would totally explain Lex's sudden disappearance." Which I hope is a convincing enough alibi, even if it's totally fake news.

Beth sets her mouth in a grim line as she straightens up in her chair. "Well, I'm not gonna let some dumb boy-crush stand in the way of winning this time, Charley. With you, or without you. So I repeat—if I make this ridiculous dress for you, what besides a thumbs-up on your Instagram profile pic do I get out of it?"

"You mean, besides getting to design and try out your custom-fit app in real life?"

She nods, folding her arms and throwing a "that's hardly gonna cut it" look.

"Well," I say, considering, "I'll help you with homework . . ."

"History papers?"

"History papers."

"For the whole rest of the year?"

"Whole year." It's not such a hardship, for all that it will take a ton of time. But then, time is, well, relative.

"Hmm . . ." Beth ponders a moment, as if dreaming up some other diabolical mode of extortion in return. She looks me up and down then glances back at the picture on my phone and grins.

"Well, okay then. Tick-tock! We're going trick-or-treating."

IX.

TEAMWORK—NOT!

Bicycle power: not such a lame idea

"Beth? Billy's at the door. Billy Vincenzo. And he's carrying . . . well, Billy, what is that contraption you have there?"

Mrs. Cooper pauses for Billy's response, but his words are lost as Beth yells back, "What now?"

"You may not bring that thing into this house, Billy!" I hear Mrs. Cooper saying as the two of us come running to the stairs.

"Was this your idea, Charley?" Beth asks, wiping her eyes abruptly, then leaning over the banister and spying Billy outside with what looks like a Ghostbuster pack on his back.

I have no idea what Billy's brought over but I need to head him off just in case he's about to spill the beans about our Plan A: time travel, to Beth's fashion Plan B: Halloween costumes. Even as I dash down the stairs to greet him at the door, I feel Beth's eyes boring into me.

"Oh, yes, Mrs. Cooper. Maybe Beth forgot to mention: Billy's doing the science fair with us!"

I'm just in time to see Billy backing outside again, grabbing the handlebars of a bike I don't recognize, with the aforementioned giant pack on his back.

"Umm, hi ya, Billy! Oh, yeah, glad to see you brought the, er, thing, for our science fair."

"Charley, I think I've solved the energy storage problem!" Billy blurts out excitedly. "You have to check this out . . ."

"Oh, you mean the AI for our transition-wear project, right, Billy?" I prompt.

"The wha—? No, it's for the time ma—"

Fortunately, Beth cuts in before Billy can finish blurting out the truth. "What, so you're training for the Tour de France now, Gearhead?"

"Beth, Billy's your friend," her mom warns.

"Sort of," I say. "It's one of his newest inventions." I pull Billy around—mainly to get a better view of the bike, which has no gears, no wheel as you'd know it, a small engine mounted behind the seat, and what looks to be a powerful magnet.

"No, really, we're . . . I mean, Charley and I are . . ."

"Oh, stop, Billy. We weren't going to tell yet . . . I mean about us being, umm, together." I grin in a way that I hope looks sincere.

"Together? I knew it!" Beth says. "So it's not fake news, after all. Not that I care . . ."

"Beth!" Mrs. Cooper interrupts. "Check your attitude, or you'll find yourself grounded for a month. Besides, Charley and Billy aren't going to want to work with you if—"

"It's okay, Mrs. Cooper," Billy says, beginning to back away from the door. "I agree, maybe doing this project together isn't such a good idea."

"Oh, but we have to!" Beth blurts out, immediately contradicting herself. "See, it's my idea! We were going to make an app to custom-fit clothes. And then Charley said, let's build in temperature controls, and Billy's made this kind of—awkward—Internet of Things control activation . . . and you know, Mom, this is really, *super* important if I'm gonna try to get on Fashion Fund, and all."

"I need to talk to you right now, Miss Fashion Forward—or no one's going to have a science fair project," Mrs. Cooper demands, pointing to the floor beside her. "Charley, Billy, you'll excuse us for a moment, won't you?"

"Thanks for almost ruining my life!" she mumbles under her breath as Billy and I march ourselves into the mudroom, where Billy's left the new wheels.

"Charley, I'm quitting if Beth keeps on being her drama-queen self," Billy starts in.

"Got that covered," I assure him. "I've promised to ghostwrite her history papers."

"You what?!"

"Shhh!" I touch my finger to my lips, knowing how Billy's voice carries. In fact, I can just make out Mrs. Cooper's lecturing voice in the kitchen, and a few of her words.

"I don't like how badly you're treating your friends . . . ," and, "I don't know where you get that . . . ," and, "I didn't bring you up to be rude . . . ," and ". . . or your father will go through the roof!"

I motion for Billy to follow me away from the door. When we're far enough out of earshot, I speak low, with some urgency. "We cannot let on about time travel, or the real reason for transition wear. Beth thinks it's for Halloween costumes."

"What the heck, Charley! You mean I almost let the cat out of the bag?"

"Forget about it. What's with the bicycle—and that ridiculous thing on your back?" I ask, knowing that getting Billy to geek out is the only way to really change the subject.

"Right. When you mentioned pedaling a bike to generate and store massive quantities of power last night, it came to me. The whole weather in Paris thing. That is, if you're still determined to go through with this Charley-to-the-rescue thing to find Carolina." He's got this dubious look on his face. "'Cause honestly, Charley, I'm pretty sure, knowing Kairos, he could just go fetch her if she was in serious trouble."

I'm thinking that finding Carolina is only one part of the equation. There's gotta be something more to it, because Kairos made such a big deal about it. Not to mention Carolina sending a postcard, 'cause I'm pretty sure the French *poste* "dead letter file" system back in the 1720s could not possibly last this long.

This could be once-in-a-lifetime—again. Continuing my interview series, up close and personal with my Superheroes of History so I can learn what makes genius is the real goal here. And on that score, *Determination* is, like, my middle name.

"Whatever, Billy. Here we have a chance to prove the new tweaks to the time program, and you're getting cold feet! Let's just get on with it: Paris can be cold and rainy this time of year. So?"

"So," he sighs, "we need a way to generate and store energy reliably and safely if we're going to get you there and back."

"You're not coming?" I notice the omission.

"To solve that problem," he continues, ignoring me, "I've been working on designing a portable minibike with a small engine that has wiring inside the frame. The wiring connects to digital controls on the handlebar, generating additional power through friction when you slam on the brakes, sort of like they're doing with electric cars now."

"You've got all that worked out already?" I marvel. "And you didn't tell me?"

"Well, kinda. At least on paper."

"We absolutely have to add in my GPS calculations—essential to improving on accuracy." I find myself getting caught up in the problem solving. "Remember how Kairos gave us the coordinates for a timeline five hundred years back and a thousand miles away? I've been working to refine the formula. You know, like the moon, global warming, and any weird meteor wobbles."

"Sure, Charley. Sure. We'll add in that formula. And Bluetooth. Don't you see? This is like a freakin' miracle bike!"

When Billy gets excited, his voice gets louder.

"Shhh, Billy! Do you want Beth and Mrs. Cooper to hear?"

He drops his voice down to a low growl, his version of a whisper. "Meantime, I'm working on installing voice-recognition controls on the tablet. 'Course, this one's just a prototype from my old bike, and some spare parts," he says, sliding the thing off his back.

"Your mind," I whisper admiringly. "Inventing is like your second language."

"Yeah, well." Billy tugs self-consciously at his newsboy-style cap. "Anyways, the bike folds into the backpack and the wheels compress—they have no spokes. Of course, we'll need to figure out a way to manufacture this thing using much lighter materials if it's going to time-travel with you."

"Hmm. That bike's gotta be pretty indestructible. Don't know if you'll recall the last time we went through the wormhole, but that is one rocky ride!" My body begins to quiver just thinking about it.

"I got the idea from you, Brainiac," he says admiringly, and pulls me close.

"Billy, focus!" I say, drawing in my breath. "We really don't have time to waste." The two arguing voices inside have abated and I'm expecting an angry Beth to stomp over at any moment.

I pick up the pack from the floor where Billy's sloughed it off. "Whoa, you're right. This thing weighs a ton!"

"Well, yeah, I'm still playing with materials," he admits. "I need stronger magnets, for one."

"Sick!"

"Anyways, I've integrated the bike with the tablet, and I'm creating new code for our app: On-Time Byclotronics™, I call it. Get it? Like a bicycle cyclotron."

In real life, a cyclotron is a powerful particle accelerator that physicists, mathematicians, and engineers have created to produce intense particle beams of protons and neutrons and stuff. It's kind of like the world's most powerful video game, but they use it for medicine and space travel, for starters.

"The kind of power you'd need to produce the beams just by pedaling? That's impossible."

"*Nothing* is impossible, Charley! Time travel? We are living proof of that," he reminds me.

I can see why Billy might think it could be useful for time travel because, honestly, no one really knows the consequences of manipulating those particles. They have them at CERN—the underground research center in Switzerland where scientists first detected the faster-than-light particles known as the Higgs boson, among other wonders of the quantum world. When CERN's accelerators were first turned on, people were afraid that the lab's powerful magnets might create a nuclear reaction and open up some kind of black hole that would suck in large portions of Switzerland, France, and Italy.

That was a while ago. So far, no black hole. But you never know.

Of course, Billy's copper-and-magnet byclotron couldn't have anywhere near the power of an actual cyclotron. But still . . . when you're talking bending spacetime, anything's possible.

"I'd be a little worried about the lithium battery. They don't even let those in airplanes, you know—exploding phones?"

"It has some bugs, okay, Charley? But I'm working on it."

"Obviously!" I can get ahead of myself when I'm excited. "Have you test-driven it yet?"

He nods. "The ride's good. And it's easy enough to set up. The geosynchronous settings are a little wonky at the moment."

"Yeah, like not crash-landing on rocky crags in Tuscany and cracking an ankle with cannonballs raining down," I reminisce with a shudder.

Billy gets a weird look on his face. "Well, what do you think, Charley?"

Before I can answer, a contrite Beth wanders back over, her mother looking on. In what sounds like a rehearsed speech, she says, "I'm sorry I lost my temper, Charley. And sorry I was so rude, Billy. I promise not to do it again."

She throws a glance at her mother, who's leaning against the doorframe, arms crossed, and frowning. "Satisfied?"

Mrs. Cooper nods and looks at me.

I consider. It is much harder dealing with Beth on this project than I would've imagined. Still, her fashion genius and experience at custom-tailoring her own clothing line is essential to our success. Not to mention, Billy and I literally cannot team up without her.

"Sure," I say, and elbow Billy in the ribs.

"Hunh?! Yeah, guess so, Beth," he says.

"Well, then, that's better," says Mrs. Cooper, smiling again. "Now you all let me know if you need anything. I, for one, am looking forward to seeing your project take some awards at the science fair."

I smile reassuringly, and, as Mrs. Cooper leaves, I walk over and twirl Beth around, so I can look her in the eye. "Beth, I'm sorry, too. Can we try a reboot here?"

She purses her lips and looks at me, then at Billy, then sighs. "I don't know what you two are cooking up in those big wonky brains of yours. But if we're gonna make this thing work, then you've gotta tell me what's really going on here."

I glance over again at Billy. She'll never believe it if we tell her. But if we don't, she's not likely to put her heart into it.

And I've learned over time that truth is always best. As far as it goes.

I glance over again at Billy, whose raised brows pretty much sum up how I believe Beth will take this.

"Okay, but I think you'd better sit down." I take a deep breath. "So, you remember two years ago, the eighth-grade science fair? Well, I was at my dad's office for Take Your Child to Work Day, minding my own business, when this weird dude Kairos shows up, and hacks me into a secret program there, Operation Firenze . . ."

As I unravel the complicated tale of Billy's and my first adventure—how Kairos was not only an IT guy in our time but was completely at home as Leonardo da Vinci's apprentice in Renaissance Florence—I decide to leave out the part about Elisabetta, Beth's fifteenth-century doppelgänger, and how she seduced Beth's then-boy crush Lex to stay there.

Beth can be very jealous.

" . . . and then, after I explained Newton's gravity, and Einstein's Theory of Relativity to him, Leonardo da Vinci himself helped us reverse-engineer the time machine with enough firepower to get us back. And the rest is history."

Beth is silent for a heartbeat, until she manages to put up her Sphinx face.

"Ha ha, Charley. Good story. Now, tell me what you guys are *really* up to."

I can see Billy holding up fingers behind his back, putting an evil hex sign on her.

I sigh. "Yeah, you're right, Beth. It is a good story." The truth is, I want a Halloween costume in the style of the French Enlightenment. And if we want to go to the Haunted Forest at Rock Creek Cemetery after the dance, it needs to be something I can wear comfortably in intense heat or bitter cold, rain, sleet, or black of night."

"You sound like an ad for the postal service," she quips.

"More like the Pony Express," Billy mumbles.

X.

FIELD TRIP

Hearing voices from the past—there be magick

It's happening again. I'm hearing voices. Now, unlike the first time—where I was somehow tuned into a long-ago scene out of the life of Leonardo da Vinci—this time, I'm hearing the voice of a long-ago woman.

And the explanation's a lot simpler, but nonetheless compelling. I'm watching an actress playing Émilie du Châtelet in a performance of *Émilie la Marquise du Châtelet Defends Her Life Tonight*:

> Émilie: What matters, what lasts? If lasting even matters. What's the point? Asking tricky questions is what I do best.

It's also what *I* do best. All the time. Much to the annoyance of my parents, teachers, friends . . . and just about everyone I know. But I really can't help myself. And besides, how are we expected to evolve our thought if we don't challenge what everyone assumes to be true? How would Leonardo have advanced our vision to include the possibility of manned flight? How would Galileo have changed our view of the heavens and Earth, or Newton the laws of gravity? How would Émilie have challenged Newton's Laws of Gravity, for that matter?

But I digress.

This Émilie is not wearing anything like the elaborate petticoated and hoop-skirted costume that Beth and I are rigging up for the science fair.

"Look, Charley," Bethy whispers to me in the darkness during intermission. Émilie remains onstage, so we can examine her as she continues to go about her business, advancing the equations for kinetic energy. "They don't have her dressed right."

In fact, she's zipped into a long-sleeved tunic with a peplum. (Zippers were not invented until 1893, but I will refrain from getting into a Twitter war with the costume designer to point out this anachronism. That would just be obnoxious.)

"That's because she's dead, Beth." For theatrical purposes, Émilie is doing a life-review after she's just died in childbirth, looking back on all she accomplished, or wished she had. "They want to just *suggest* the clothing. Because fashion really doesn't matter all that much to her at that point."

"Hmmph," she replies. "Fashion matters. Or you wouldn't care about this so-called costume for Halloween. But remember in our research about the farthingale? Why do the other women wear just those donut things around their waists that pop out their behinds?"

The farthingale in question is like a rounded pillow popping out horizontally above Émilie's butt, and tied around the waist. It's what gives eighteenth-century women such an unusually round tush (aka, they liked big butts).

"They're more traditional," I proclaim. But, in fact, one of the characters, Soubrette, is a youthful stand-in for "alive Émilie," and she's wearing a farthingale tied to her corset. So I guess Émilie, back in the day, had to play the fashion game. But liberated from life in that time . . .

"
Silly women follow *fashion*, pretentious ones exaggerate it; but **women of good taste** come to terms with it.

– Émilie du Châtelet

EMILIE DU CHÂTELET'S TRUTH!

Credit: Melissa Brandstatter

It's as if I can feel "dead Émilie" in the drama struggling against the stays, the lacings, the rules, and the social trappings that would befit a lady—a marquise—during the French Enlightenment.

In truth, by the definition of her day, the Marquise was anything but a lady. She was obsessive. And smart. And stubborn. She enraged her parents. And Voltaire, with whom she had a fifteen-year love affair, while married to the Marquis. Who loved her as passionately as she loved him. (Voltaire, that is.) And hated him. They fought about ideas that mattered.

In short, Émilie is my kind of kick-ass, take-no-prisoners girl.

But if I am to visit Émilie in her own time, I'll have to play by that society's rules. Which means the full *robe à la française* for me.

"Traditional, yes. But your Émilie seems to be anything but traditional. In fact, I'd say she'd be the kind of woman today to fit the meme, 'Nevertheless, She Persisted.'"

SENATOR ELIZABETH WARREN'S TRUTH!

Beth is referring to an exchange on the floor of the Senate years back that was supposed to be a put-down of a woman senator who, despite being interrupted by a male senator, dared to continue to read the words of Coretta Scott King, Martin Luther King's widow, about enforcing voting rights laws. Instead, the comment became a symbol of pride for many women—because women's public speech has been silenced for far too long.

"That's what's so cool about Émilie. She persisted in a man's world. Three hundred years ago."

"Cool. So why do the big dress, Charley? You could just throw on a long skirt and be done with it. Like they're doing here."

"It's a play, Beth. They can do whatever they want."

"It's *Halloween*, Charley. You can do whatever *you* want."

But I'm not dressing up for Halloween. I am dressing to go live in another time.

"C'mon, Beth, it's cool. You can put your awesome fashion talents to work. And we can add in the technology that will make our science fair project rock. You want to win, don't you?"

"Well . . ."

"College scholarship?"

"But . . ."

"Fame for your pioneering environmental fashion?"

She taps her foot.

"History papers . . . ?"

"Oh, well. Since you put it that way . . ."

I feel her resolve melting away. "Maybe even a runway fashion show?"

Halloween is only two weeks away. The Ancients thought of Halloween as the time when the veil that separates the living from the dead is thinnest. When the spirits of the world beyond life are best able to communicate with us, the living.

Cool thought, to be able to communicate with the dead.

Sort of perfect that, in the play, Émilie was reviewing her life from the afterlife.

Sort of a perfect time of year to connect with the past. Although, of course, as a girl of science, I am not in the least, ahem, superstitious.

Beth, with the weight of history off her own shoulders, has made progress on the fashion front.

"I found a pattern for a rustic shepherdess dress online. It's the simplest pattern I could find for that time period—and it still has twenty-three pieces, including linings and petticoats. So this is going to be a really big deal to sew. What do you think?"

I study the picture. It's sort of a "spring picnic" dress. Tight yellow bodice showing a wildflower print, with an overdress on it. They called that a *casaquin*. Three-quarter-length sleeves. Long blue skirt. Perfect for a shepherdess to go frolicking *en plein air*. The girl in the picture is wearing a wide-brimmed straw hat decked out with real flowers and fruit. Think Little Bo Beep who's lost her sheep.

It would be perfectly hideous for anything but a costume party. Or the actual eighteenth century. I can see now why the costume designer for this performance stuck with undergarments.

"They call for broadcloth for the skirt." Beth shoves a Prussian-blue swatch under my nose. "Well, what do you think, Charley?"

"Umm, maybe we can skip the overdress. And the hat."

"Good point. Especially if we've got to add in IoT technology to account for heat and cooling."

"Right," I reply. "I wish we had more time to try to come up with a fabric that does this automatically, though."

I sigh. For now, that's a pipe dream.

Anyways, the dashboard to combine all of our bells and whistles into one app is coming along. Billy's miniaturizing the controls, playing with stronger magnets for the batteries, and looking into whatever lighter materials—or ready-made new bike frames—he can scrounge up. Kairos is particularly useful at coming up with unusual "found objects." (And best not to ask questions where Kairos is concerned, I've learned).

Luckily, Billy's dad is handy, too, especially since asking my dad for help this time would just get us back in trouble. Billy and his dad tinker every weekend in his dad's basement workshop, complete with CAD-design program, and all kinds of weird gizmos. Kinda knew Mr. Vincenzo, who's a materials engineer for NASA, would be totally into this challenge!

I'm working on ways to automatically shift the temperature—sort of like built-in AC and heating, depending on how hot or cold it is, whether you're inside or out.

Billy's just texted me something on this topic—a battery-powered technology regulated through your phone that pipes water through tubes running inside whatever garment you're wearing that can go from heat to AC at the tap of a screen.

"Too complicated," I say aloud, as I tap a reply to Billy, looking at the photo. His solution is designed for marathon runners, not time-benders.

"Pretty straightforward, I should think. Although that whole farthingale thing. . . . Wait." Beth turns as if she's just heard me. "What's too complicated?"

"Something Billy sent me. A heat-to-cold system. Ugh! Looks like the plumbing for a water fountain, with water running through plastic pipes."

She glances over my shoulder at the photo on my phone.

"Are you kidding!? No way I'll run my masterpiece through with thick plastic tubes like that. It would absolutely ruin the lines . . ."

"How's a thin pipe any worse than stays?" I point out, thinking how they used to use whalebones in corsets, and how women couldn't breathe once they were laced into them.

"And you're supposed to be so smart," Beth hisses. "You know as well as I do there'd be condensation around the tubes . . . really, Charley. People would think you'd wet yourself!"

I'm thinking more that I couldn't support the weight of all those petticoats, a corset, and a hoopskirt, plus all that water running through it. I shiver just thinking of that cold plastic against my skin. And what if the thermostat breaks down when the battery dies? (Likely.) Or the tube springs a leak? (Also likely.)

I admit, this is not an easy problem to solve.

"Yeah, I get you. No worries. We'll work it out, Beth," I say, adding under my breath, "like my life depends on it."

XI.

NECESSITY IS STILL THE MOTHER OF INVENTION

Because running hot water through pipes is so old-school

I quick do a Google search: #wearables #technology #fabric #nano-bio #transitionwear. Using hashtags could find some trending innovations via social media. Because, if Beth's example as a YouTuber is any guide, there are other young makers/influencers out there coming up with out-of-the-box ideas.

"I need to capture your body from every angle, Charley, so we can see the steps we'll need to take to create my self-measurement app," Beth says, hovering above my head, standing on a chair and aiming her phone to take pix down my neck. "I know they have this down for men's shirts, but women's bodies can have so many more variations."

I see her sizing me up. Boy's body. Flattish chest. This is an old theme between us: Charley's arrested development. A sore spot.

"Beth! Let's. Not. Go. Through. This. Again."

But she seems unable to stop herself.

"I think we can confirm how much those curves matter from personal experience. I mean, real fashion designers would pin the fabric on mannequins to mimic your shape. But that technique is so old-school. Here, we can create a three-D model Photoshopping all your body parts in layers. We're gonna need to take pictures from all angles."

I go back to scrolling through Google. I'm getting some hits from the search that look promising, 'cause apparently there's a demand for this. And then, a weirdly on-the-nose match—very close by. Some research I've been following for a while now—materials science and all that. But now, they've got the actual fabric to show for it.

"Voila!" I feel like jumping up and down but instead, I just snap my fingers in the air.

Beth jumps down from the chair and is circling me, doing a body-360 to take my measurements. "Stand still, Charley. Raising your arms is not helpful."

"Yes. Nanobiotechnology. That's the future of fashion!"

"Charley, I have no idea what you're talking about. *I* am the future of fashion."

I groan. It's so Beth to make this all about her. But I can't waste time on that: I have to share my find with Billy right away. I text him.

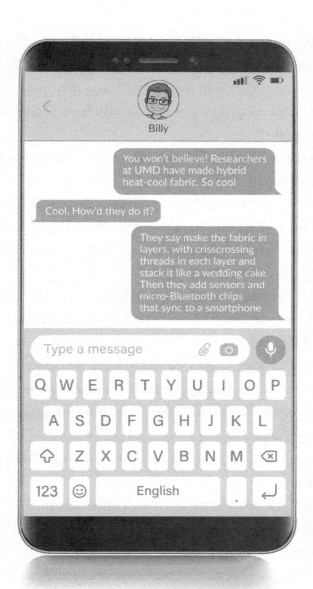

I follow a link to an article about it in the *Washington Post* and see there's another start-up that's in on a similar innovation.

I start texting Billy with the details. "It says they make the fabric in layers, with crisscrossing threads in each layer, and stack it like a wedding cake."

"What the hell are you talking about, Charley?" Beth asks, looking at me crossways.

"This cool hot-and-cold fabric invention," I explain. Might as well get Bethy in on this, since she's doing the tailoring. "Then they add sensors and micro-Bluetooth chips that sync to a smartphone. Seems doable," I conclude.

But I'm thinking we might need to integrate magnets, too, since we'll need to recharge all these devices in a pre-electrified time zone. I shoot Billy a link to another article for future reference.

"Earth to Charley . . . get your heads out of the clouds, girlfriend! Like just how're you planning on getting hold of experimental material that nobody's ever seen before, much less getting enough of it for your big dress?"

"We can totally do this!" I finish texting Billy. Now I can't help dancing.

When I look up from my text, I see Beth is squatting behind me, evidently taking pictures of my derriere.

"Charley, if you don't stand still . . ."

"Beth, there is no need for a butt shot. The farthingale will cover all the sins of my missing hips and tush."

"Charley, once and for all, this is not about you!"

I groan. She's always projecting. "Yeah, I know. It's about you."

I begin scanning a story about the University of Maryland product: strands coated in carbon nanotubes; fibers of two different synthetic materials—one attracts water, the other repels; and, according to the scientists, it can block infrared radiation. Which should be handy as a sunscreen if you land in a tropical zone, post some climate apocalypse. Or a shield against whatever weird waves we might endure while time-traveling.

Calls to mind a play we once did in school, *The Effect of Gamma Rays on Man-in-the-Moon Marigolds*. Which also calls to mind Bethy's marigolds-and-music science fair experiment with a certain no-longer-in-the-twenty-first-century Lex Campbell.

Which calls to mind my current interest in Émilie du Châtelet, whose once-famous experiments on the nature of fire revealed the infrared spectrum (though the discovery was credited to a dude, William Herschel, some sixty-plus years after her paper. So what else is new?!). But back in the day, she was awarded an honorable mention by the French Academy of Sciences for her discovery. A first for a woman. And if Émilie could do it, way back then, well, there's no excuse for a twenty-first-century STEMinista, aka, *moi*, not to follow her dream.

"Whoa, so cool!" I boot her away from my ankles. "We're not measuring for sweatpants, you know, Beth."

"Stop it, Charley—you're ruining the whole thing!"

"Huh?" I see my kick sent her butt on the floor. "Oh, sorry. But we are so done measuring here, girlfriend. Once we get our hands on this fabric . . . that's gonna be our ticket to ride!"

At this point, I have no idea how it will work, or whether their fabric is something we could just sew into a dress. But I do know it's legit: The research was published in a famous American scientific journal, *Science*.

So, not fake news.

"We're going for it!"

Beth is annoyed. "App for me, Science Fair Part One. Fabric for you, Part Two."

"You don't understand. None of this is gonna work if we don't get the fabric right." I tap on my phone screen to make the point. "Materials that heat or cool depending on the environment. And look . . . engineers at the University of Maryland have been working on it, right in our own backyard! We're gonna need Billy right away."

And we need to get our hands on whatever fabric they've already tested. I quick text him.

"Billy, again." Beth rolls her eyes and sighs. "Do we gotta?"

"Beth, you know Billy's engineering brain. I think he may need to make some modifications to his app—especially if we don't even need to pipe in hot or freezing water back in . . . umm, er . . . some hypothetical customer wearing it in some unknown climate future."

"I do not care about your stupid fabric. How's that gonna help me?"

"Oh, but it may. I mean, who knows, we could have a plague or something, where girls can no longer go to a store to have their prom dresses fitted in person. And this fabric's gonna keep them comfy, calm, and dry, no matter what. And that's where you, Miss Fashion Forward, will be so far ahead!"

"Yeah, well. Good hypothetical . . . not gonna happen."

While Bethy's letting off steam, I text Billy one last time: "Want to meet the inventors at UMD and see if they'll let us *borrow* some of their textiles for a test run? Like, we put it to the test *in vivo* under extreme environmental stress, and when we get back, our results could even be worth a write-up in a professional science journal."

Imagine! Me and Billy publishing our beta test results as tenth graders. Billy's gonna love it.

"Hullo! Earth to Charley. Have you heard anything I've just said? I just have, like, three more shots to get your whole body in digital images. So, like, *freeze*, girlfriend."

Beth's nagging hurts my ears. But it does remind me: Billy and I may need to give her a credit on our paper, too. I mean, the custom-fitting app idea is hers, even if it's not directly linked to time travel.

But we could integrate both into our dashboard: Transition Wear Fittings from Afar, or TWFFA, we could call it. I can already see it trending—in fashion magazines, sports blogs, whatever!

"Okay, I'm a statue." I freeze in place, stretching my arms out like Leonardo da Vinci's Vitruvian Man so she can continue taking pix of my elbows. Or whatever.

"Say, Beth, what would you think about having your name on a research paper in a big-deal science journal for your app and our transition-wear fashions? Could make you a social influencer for reals!"

"Okay. Got it." She's swiping through all her pictures and I see she's captured every possible angle. "Just checking to make sure—if you can turn around slowly one more time, Charley . . . oh, wait. What did you say?" she stops, mid-bossiness. "A published paper about my app?"

I nod. She begins tapping her forehead, her fidget for thinking.

"You know, that might be interesting. I bet it would look good on my college application. Fashion design school. I've been thinking New York. Or maybe Milan. I mean, *Vogue* has been really shining a spotlight on the design coming out of Italy."

"*Vogue.* Uh-huh," I agree with a slow blink. Not that I care.

"Or ESMOD, the best fashion school in Paris. Did you know they invented both the mannequin and the tape measure there? So I'm sure they'd love my app—to bring them into the twenty-first century."

"Yep." I can practically see the wheels turning in that shrewd little brain of hers.

"And Paris Fashion Week. That would be . . . *fantastique.* So, *ma chère amie* . . . just what did you have in mind?"

XII.

ONE BIG BREAKTHROUGH BEGETS
A BONUS

*Or how a bike, some bagels, and a shmear can lead to a
heist that baffles the experts*

When Billy finally chug-chugs up Beth's driveway on his red machine, I can hear that little motor humming from inside the house.

I rush outside to meet him, only to see he's upgraded the bike even more since the last time I saw it. And when he wheels around to the side, I see another secret he's been hiding: The bicycle's now built for two!

"Take you for a spin, Charley?" he asks, blinking behind his coke-bottle glasses. Billy never could manage to shut just one eye. "I've installed some enhancements. Really working out the bugs. I think I've finally got the magnet strength turned up to rocket-propel this baby."

Beth hurries between me and Billy, grabbing the handlebars to stop me from hopping on.

"Hey, lazy bones. What's the matter with your legs—can't pedal a two-wheeler?"

I just give her the hairy eyeball—on Billy's behalf. But he's not even paying attention.

"Making sure the solar battery is fully recharging the engine. For ti—I mean, for it to do what you need it to do, Charley."

I walk around admiringly. He's installed a tablet, Peloton-style, between the handlebars. And a basket, because, well, we need a place to stash junk.

"See you've improved on the prototype here. Can you show me how it works?"

"Better yet, I can show you how to do it yourself!"

He touches the screen and logs on with a password. The dashboard lights up and he's got icons for everything: charging, solar battery, speed, terrain. And he's integrated my asynchronous GPS program, based on a multilayered graphic overlay of the ancient maps that I've found on Wikimedia and in the Library of Congress on Capitol Hill—where I got my official LOC library card last year! And also topographical maps that are pretty eternal except for like, volcanoes, floods, melting glaciers, and Category 5 hurricanes that would have indelibly rearranged the landscape.

"Is the, you know, the formula uploaded?"

"Even a heart-rate monitor to track your health, and all that."

Integrating all this data, we can now tap into a wide variety of old location maps in real time and not only, like, Google maps now.

"Brilliant. Just brilliant."

This crowning achievement leaves me momentarily speechless.

But Beth isn't.

"Yeah. Great. Now Charley and I can ride it to UMD to meet the engineer dudes who invented this magic fabric Charley's going gaga over."

She slings a leg over the bar, both feet on the ground.

"Hold on, Beth. This is a very finely tuned robot, with its own AI. It's not just for tooling around." Billy has his own hand on the handlebar opposite Bethy's. "If you don't know all the controls . . ."

"Ridiculous. I know how to ride a bike, Webhead." With that, Beth climbs astride and puts her foot on the pedal. "Gimme your helmet, Billy."

But before he can even say "No way," the bike starts moving under her and picking up speed.

"How the hell do you turn this thing . . . oh, no!"

The bike veers off the driveway and into the yard, headed straight for the giant oak tree.

"No, no, no! Beth! Squeeze the right handbrake . . ." Billy shouts running after her, pulling back to slow down the bike and trying to pull on the left brake himself.

Too late. Bike's crashed. Beth's bashed, crumpled in the mud with the bike on top of her leg.

I run over to her, and pull the bike off, leaning close.

"You okay, Beth? Where are you hurting?"

She opens one eye, grips her leg, grimacing. "Ow, ow, ow. I think it's my knee. WTF, Charley?! Billy's trying to kill me."

Billy, who's been inspecting the wreckage to his wheels, looks up and manages a wry smile. "Same old Beth."

"Billy!"

Managing to fake his concern, he sets down the bike and comes around to look at her.

"Nothing broken. Looks like the patient will live."

"Can you stand up, Beth?" I help her sit up, then help her pull her leggings up to get a look at her knee. Scraped pretty bad. Definitely swollen. "Let's get you inside and put some ice on it."

She tries to get up and crumples back down. "Can't. Hurts."

"C'mon, Billy, we need to get her inside."

He squats down on one side of Beth with me on the other and we each put an arm around her waist.

"Okay, now," I pant. "Just put your arms around our shoulders, Beth, and we'll help you up. Ready? One—two—three ... and up!"

We manage to pull her upright without tumbling over one another, Beth groaning all the while.

"Guys, please don't tell my mom about this. She'll never let me out of the house again."

As she says this, Mrs. Cooper calls out from their back porch, "I bet you all are hungry. I've got some hot bagels waiting!"

"Okay, coming, Ma!"

"My mom's answer to everything is eating," Beth groans as an aside. "Like a bagel's gonna help anything."

"I don't know," I respond, tummy grumbling. "Couldn't hurt!"

We start slowly toward the house, arms intertwined for support and letting Bethy, panting, hop along. "Hurts, all right. Why'd you make me do that, Billy?"

Billy looks stunned at the accusation, since he'd tried to stop her. "Wait. What?"

"It was an accident, Beth, that's all. Don't you want to let your mom look at it and see if you need to see a doctor?"

"I'll be fine. I will be *fine*," she insists. "It's not like I need stitches. We'll just use an Icy-Hot and wrap it in an ace bandage."

"What if something's broken?" Billy asks, sounding sincerely concerned.

"If my mom finds out I was riding your stupid homemade, not-smart motorbike, I'll never be allowed to get my learner's permit. Probably be grounded for life. And I *cannot* miss the Halloween costume ball, now that Guy—"

"Guy!" Billy and I exchange a glance.

"Yes, Guy!" she repeats. "Hashtag: guy of my dreams!"

This little meme has cracked her up.

"Okay, Beth. Your call. But if you're okay, I've got to make it over to UMD to get my hands on those guys' magic material."

We awkwardly sit Beth down on the picnic bench on her porch to catch her breath.

"Oh, yeah. That. No, don't mind me, guys. And sorry to hurt your chances for a Nobel Prize, Charley," Beth says acidly.

"Sorry about the knee, Beth," Billy apologizes, a delayed reaction. "If you'd only let me give you a lesson in how the bike works . . ."

"Whatever. I'm so over this."

"No, Beth. Remember, we made a deal? We work together on the app. You help me with the dress, and I've got you covered on history papers for the rest of the year."

"Oh, yeah." She scowls.

"Anyways, don't know how you're gonna get to College Park. The battery-motor-tablet interface needs to be completely reconfigured," Billy chimes in. "Why don't we just call those guys?"

"I've got to get my hands on that fabric, Billy. We cannot dematerialize the fabric and just, like, *beam it up*; it's not like *Star Trek*."

Beth has a speculative look on her face. "Okay. So, look, Webheads, here's the plan: You guys go on without me. Bring me whatever magic fabric you want. I don't care how you get it and I don't really want to know. I'm going to tell my mom I'm staying here and working on our science fair project. That'll make me her 'little angel' again. And keep me off my feet for a hot second."

"Sure. As long as you're gonna be okay, Beth."

She rolls down her leggings to cover the puffy area, pushes herself up off the picnic bench, and tenderly puts her foot down. "Once I ice this thing—"

"Billy, you up for this?" I ask. "We'll take the Metro then I've got to get my hands on that fabric, Billy."

Of course, Billy's just the guy to manage something like this. What with his experience sneaking into Dad's office under high security last time, and all.

He looks skeptical. "I'm not sure this is such a good idea . . ."

I finger the necklace Billy gave me before Homecoming. It's the golden compass—the key to our time travel past. "That's where you're wrong. 'Cause I'm pretty sure it's destiny!"

XIII.

MISSION ACCOMPLISHED!

Found the lab, the fab, and grabbed a bag—now,
for proof of concept

"You would've been so proud of me, Billy," I conclude, as we meet back up at the UMD Metro to head for home. Billy peeled off before we made it to the Nanocenter, where they have the fabrics lab. Naturally, he was distracted by the budding engineers all busy designing cool stuff."

"Uh-huh, yeah, well, sorry I couldn't get there in time to help, Charley," Billy says, not seeming at all sorry. "It's just that I met these other guys who showed me their new hyperloop train they're constructing as part of their SpaceX competition."

I'm about to chew Billy out for getting distracted, again, but it doesn't matter—I have the prize fabric in my backpack.

"The research director there couldn't have been nicer. I told him this was our science fair project and—this is where Beth's being part of it is priceless—that we were prototyping a fashion line that would go anywhere, anytime, using his fabric. He immediately homed in on the commercial use of their discovery."

I pause for a reaction, but Billy's head seems elsewhere.

"You know, these guys are always looking for real-world applications. And he's such an engineering brain—like you, Brainiac—that he's thinking space suits and deep-sea exploration. But, of course, when I explained how climate change is about to radically change our idea of fashion design . . . Billy, are you listening to me?!"

"Huh? Oh, no. I was just thinking about a suggestion that guy made for our chatbot. Instead of just inputting data, I can program it to translate the program into actionable analytics. So, you can say, 'AI-Dude, text Billy location data.' And it'll automatically pin your location for me, and also give you live, on-the-ground information for that time zone. No need to reprogram—or to wait for a next move in TeenWords—to pinpoint your whereabouts. So obviously, I'll need to make a bot here that talks to your bot there. Like 'Hey, Siri, find Alexa.' There needs to be some additional AI integration."

These are fantasy technologies well beyond the scope of our current project. A big distraction, when time is of the essence. (Pun intended!)

"Earth to Billy—you are totally missing the point here. I have successfully snagged the first experimental output of transition-wear fabric direct from the laboratory where it was made! And we're set to create a dress that will keep me cool in hot water, or hot in cold water, or whatever . . . and Beth can weave her fashion magic so I totally don't look like a dork in old French society. And I didn't even have to steal it—the guy *offered it to me for nothing!*"

I don't mention that he probably took pity on me, since by the time I found the place—no one was there right away—when someone finally came in and asked me what I was doing there (as if I, a mere high school girl, were there to steal state secrets, or something), my heart was palpitating so hard that I was out of breath. I was so nervous and angsty (which I know, dear reader, is hard to believe, since I have found myself in much worse predicaments over time!) that I felt nauseous, until he brought me a bottle of water and had me sit on a metal folding chair and showed me a pressure point on my hand that supposedly relieves the feeling. Which worked, luckily, but also made him nervous enough to want to get me out of there as quick as possible. Hence, the gift of the fabric.

"Besides, we're going together, right, Billy?"

It seems unfathomable to me that Billy wouldn't come along for the adventure. I mean, I even found a ready-made court costume for him that we can order online.

But Billy's back in his own head, undoubtedly mapping out a new technique to automate data input to his AI on the fly in low-tech environments. Or some other radically awesome innovation that will set the French Enlightenment further into the future than Newton or Voltaire or Émilie or Montesquieu or Rousseau or any of those philosopher-scientists could ever imagine. Thanks to our upcoming adventures to a past that will soon come rushing to life!

I tap him twice on the shoulder to let him know we're coming to our stop.

"Oh, and for the record, it's gotta be Esmerelda. My chatbot's a girl, okay?"

Billy grimaces and jumps up before the "doors closing" announcement cuts us off.

"Okay, coming. I've got it: female chatbot. Esmerelda. For all we're about to dive into a lot of drama—past and present, I can't afford any drama with you, Charley."

I grin, satisfied. No drama on this end. Next up: climate-dress for success, and then the rest!

XIV.

TRICK-OR-TREAT?

Moonlit graveyard, scary clowns, and zombies—where's
the treat?

They search bags and backpacks at the arching black wrought-iron gates to Rock Creek Cemetery. That would make me feel nervous enough, what with all I've got stuffed inside. I mean, it's Halloween; they make you come in costume. Which is my excuse if anyone were to challenge my weird conglomeration of normal teen gear and always-with-me time travel preparations—especially, the all-important golden compass that launched our Renaissance adventure. Like the Girl Scout motto: Be prepared.

I've got on my Émilie costume, of course. Which, at the time, I thought would be a hoot. But now I'm rethinking it. First, the humiliation of the Halloween dance, to which I was unsuspectingly late, doing my awkward sideways entrance through the main hall doors right in the middle of the principal's "you all have fun and behave yourselves" speech, where I suffered slow claps and stares and hoots of "Char-ley! Char-ley!" under the observant eye of Principal Norton.

And the kids commenting:

"... Uh-mazing ..."

"Really ... incredible ..."

"That hair ... so, umm ... poofy!"

Beth was beaming the whole time because, of course, she designed it: wig, dress, and all. And Billy and I were able to weave in the new fabric that we got from the UMD Nanocenter. I added a skin sensor to the app that tracks with my digital assistant / fitness tracker / translator—I call her Esmerelda, or Esme for short—to monitor the temperature remotely, just in case.

For those not in the know, Esmerelda was a famous gypsy in Victor Hugo's *Hunchback of Notre Dame* way before the Disney version.

Anyways, I'm praying the technology works in real life; we couldn't really try it out without attempting actual time travel. This is our test run, so to speak.

I sneak a peek at the tracker for a baseline temperature reading: 55 degrees outside in the night air, but in the nested layers of my dress, a comfy 78.

So, not shivering. Mostly, I'm focused on not tripping over the train of this Cinderella gown and further humiliating myself. The potential for tripping seems far worse in a "haunted" cemetery, what with footstones, headstones, and tree roots, and rocks and freshly dug holes awaiting their post-human inhabitants.

"This is freakin' creepy!" I whisper, my skin crawling under the voluminous petticoats and stays.

Beth's response is the crunch and crackle from a bag of Cheetos she brought along. She's limping a little—the remnants of her recent mishap with the tandem. But she insisted on coming.

"What?!" she says when I turn to see what she's up to.

"Beth. Focus!"

"Hungry!"

I sigh. The stupid farthingale (and whose brilliant fashion invention was that, back in the day, I wonder irrelevantly) keeps snagging on bushes and gravestones. Which is super annoying. But it also contains a hidden pouch large enough to stash the solar power bank, my phone and earbuds, and any other essential time traveler must-haves that I need to keep close at hand, er . . . under my backside.

Although I am most definitely staying present for this Halloween night, I've been stocking up on essentials for the next journey, and never bothered to weed through this junk in my backpack before we set out tonight. So, besides my tablet, programmed like my phone with Esmerelda, I have two sets of earbuds, in case any accidental plus-ones get swept away with me; a portable solar charger; Carolina's postcard; some ancient coins (two silver French écus and a supposedly rare *half-Louis*, as in the Sun King, a coin minted in gold, which I purchased with babysitting money at the coin shop in Takoma Park); mini composition book and ballpoint pens in case all power-to-digital fails; Kleenex; matches; and water filter (because last time, I mean, the dead stuff floating in the River Arno!).

Ditto, my favorite corduroys, and an umbrella that Mamma must've slipped in there after I came home from school drenched one day.

My learner's permit I had in the front pocket of my backpack; I move the coins and ID to the pouch. Less likely to lose track of them there. Ya just never know when you'll need to show ID, and it's the only one I've brought tonight.

In running my fingers down the side of my backpack, I pull out this old-fashioned red ceramic box that the coin shopkeeper had thrown in with the coins. "A snuffbox," he said, "Antique. No charge." Then he added, "I thought you might appreciate this."

No idea what he was thinking. I know that, back in the 1700s, as soon as the tobacco trade with the Americas was up and running, snuff became the addiction of choice in the courts of Europe. I tuck it instead inside my dress's pouch, along with my phone.

Anyway that's mostly the low-tech stuff! Aforementioned portable charger goes in the pouch in case I need a power boost. Earbuds. Check. Phone containing Esme? Check. Because of Billy's latest obsession with AI, Esme is programmed with a virtual version of the time machine itself. I've packed a bigger solar battery in my backpack to power my homecoming. Getting stuck in the past can have dire consequences. Believe me, I know!

FRENCH COINS DEPICTING KING LOUIS XV, 1717

And, of course, I carry the golden compass, one of two. Billy is guard to the second. In inventing our original time machine, we discovered that these are the geometrical keys to making time travel possible. And now, with Billy's unexpected gift before Homecoming, a mini version. I wear it on a chain around my neck and close to my heart. Although I have no idea if it holds the power of the originals.

I ditched the hideous "Marie Antoinette" hairpiece earlier; who knows what kind of bird might have swooped in to nest in it out here. The weight of that wig on my head had at least one good side effect: flattening the boing-boing of my real hair.

We've come to the edge of what serves as a portal to the section of the cemetery that has been cordoned off for the All-Hallows Eve "experience" and brush off a fake spiderweb. The cemetery's become a

Halloween tradition for teens too old to trick-or-treat after somebody had the brilliant idea to set up a Halloween haunted forest.

Like a plain old graveyard could lack for spookiness.

"It's awfully quiet around here. Where is everybody, anyway?" I whisper.

A gust sweeps up a swirl of leaves around us, and we hear distant laughter and screams that could be from other kids doing the haunted forest.

"This place *is* pretty creepy, Charley," concedes Beth, now that she's done scarfing down her munchies.

Beth, aka, Wonder Woman, trails behind me. Why she's wearing high-heeled Wonder Woman boots to a haunted forest with mud-sinks is beyond me. Having to pull her feet out of that suck-swamp leaves her trailing several paces behind me.

"Whose dumb idea was it to be Wonder Woman anyway?" she asks self-mockingly, as she wraps her cape tighter around bare shoulders and arms against a rising wind.

"Told you to add in sleeves and use some of the leftover fabric from my costume. Or at least bring a fleece," I observe.

"Yeah. Well. Anyways." It's as close as Beth can come to acknowledging I'm right.

The full moon casts weird shadows among the trees, and I hear a hoot owl in the distance. The leaves crunch and crush under our footsteps, and my long skirt swooshes them around. Despite these sounds, the night is eerily silent.

I try to keep a conversation going, mainly to calm my nerves.

"It's not like Billy to be late, Beth. Halloween is, like, his favorite holiday."

Mine too. It was so fun taking my little sisters around the neighborhood earlier tonight for trick-or-treating. Mamma and I stuffed their little Tweedledum and Tweedledee costumes to make them so round they could bounce off each other like squishy balloons, which then became their favorite thing to do.

But then, I took off for the school trip here—I've been doing it since I was like, eleven, so it's tradition—despite the babies begging me to help them sort, count, and eat their candy.

And, despite the weirdness of this haunted Halloween experience, traipsing around cemeteries and the like is something I hope to do professionally as a forensic anthropologist one day.

Nearby church bells begin tolling the hour.

"I wonder if Billy got lost. I'm going back to the gate to look for him," I announce. "You comin'?" I can't just leave her 'cause we're on the buddy system, although I have my doubts about whether she'd stick around for me if the boot was on the other foot.

The sky's suddenly less bright as the wind picks off the last leaves from the trees, the moon ducking behind gathering clouds. A miasma of fog has settled in, making it harder to see.

"What the hell! Just text him, Charley."

"Right. Text him." I fish under the overdress of this costume to pull out my phone from the pouch, not looking where I'm going, and almost running smack into a tree. A tree root jumps up out of nowhere to trip me. I grab onto a bush and lose my balance, sending my phone flying.

"Oh no!" I drop to my hands and knees to see. If I've lost that phone, I'm, like, Dead Girl Walking. I'm praying I didn't leave the ring on silent.

"Hey Charley," yells Beth. Her voice sounds distant now. "Where'd you go? Did Billy text you back?"

"I dropped my phone. Can you ping it?"

A raucous raven crying out in the distance is the only reply.

"Beth?" I try again, trying to feel under the leaves. The ground is slippery. "Beth!"

I hoist myself up over a low tree limb to see if I can get a better view. "Hey, Beth. Come on. This isn't funny."

A whoosh of wings overhead. A shiver down my neck. "Nevermore," I whisper into the night, like feeling wings flutter by.

Nothing looks familiar anymore. Swaying branches above and around me dangle and dance in the moonlight like skeletons in the wind.

"Hey! Anyone there?"

I jump down and right myself on two feet, now totally alone. No Beth. No Billy. How could my best friends abandon me? Marching forward amid moving shadows, I skate over fallen acorns and almost slam my knee against an old grave marker.

"Holy hell!"

Suddenly, the moon totally disappears as more black birds wing overhead. I feel like any moment, the dead might rise (although, for the record, as a science girl, I don't believe in zombies). I feel my way past the gravestone and almost stumble into a freshly dug grave.

I've almost given up on the phone. But then, I spy a notification light flickering dimly in the grave hole. Is it ringing? Falling onto all fours, I thrust my body halfway over the edge, making sure to wedge my feet under a root so I don't fall in.

I listen, hoping for a sound. I can barely hear a ringtone—not mine, but Beth's!

"Beth are you down there?! 'Cause if you are, this is one freakin' dumbass trick."

"Oh Charley! Charley, where are you?"

I jerk to my feet.

"Billy? Billy!"

"Hey, Brainiac!"

"Yes, it's me! Over here, Billy!"

I hear his big voice ringing through the woods. "Charley, it's been over an hour and the bus is getting ready . . . and the kids are getting super-annoyed at waiting."

"Oh, Billy!" I yell as loud as I can. "C'mere, Billy. I need you!"

"Charley?" he calls again, but his voice is fading. "Char-ley!"

It's then that the phone in the hole rings again.

"Billy . . . it's Beth—I lost her!" I call out louder. "Hey, where are you, anyway? Can you hear me?"

At that moment, I hear the sweet ping of my own phone. I follow the sound, but it stops before I can get a read on it. "Billy, call me again!" I shout. "I've lost Beth, who's lost her phone, and I almost lost my phone but I heard you just now . . . anyways, just call me again."

I hear my own phone ringing, this time closer, and I am just in time to nab it as it flickers beneath the same tree I just climbed down from.

"Oh, thank God!" I quick check my screen—it's not cracked any worse than it was before, or I'd really be up a creek. "Now call Beth's, Billy." I scramble down to my knees again by the empty grave, waiting.

Nothing. I'm praying the battery didn't die.

"Billy? Can you hear me?"

But now I can actually call him. I look at my phone and a TikTok pops up, starring none other than Beth herself, or at least the back of Beth's head, with her red-hooded Wonder Woman cape.

"What the . . . ?!" As astonishing as it is to see Beth on my screen when I know her phone is, literally, six feet under, there's a butt-shot of some other girl wearing a big dress. They're in a big, formal garden. Fountains, statuary, and the like. Flares of gold, flickering candles glinting on metal maybe, show it's a breezy night.

It's impossible to imagine there's any other explanation. I mean, there are statues like that here in Rock Creek Cemetery. And maybe she's lost with another girl from school.

Or not. Girl trafficking and the like—these things have happened under less scary circumstances.

"Beth!" I holler again, cupping my hands around my mouth and yelling into the phone to amplify.

The Beth-on-screen stops and turns, staring hard into the camera as if she's heard me, but then I realize, it's not me she's listening to. Another face crowds into the screen frame, mouthing some words I can't quite lip-read. Somebody else in Halloween dress.

I've got to find her. Beth can't ever be parted for long from her device; she's got to be worried about the phone.

I drop down again and scootch my body over the grave's edge, seeing if I can somehow reach it. But my arms are too short, and if I inch my body any more over the edge, I'll fall in.

Two long, icy hands grab me. One covers my eyes. The other grips my arms.

I freeze. Through gritted teeth, I bite off, "Get. The hell. Off me!"

Then I yell as loud as I can, and begin kicking my feet. "Off me, freak!"

XV.

Time Stands Still for No Girl

It's a Slo-Mo-Past-No-Go

"B^{oo!"}

My heart's beating out of my chest. "Billy? *Billy!* I could kill you!"

"Here you are! You wandered off and I was so . . . Charley?"

"Oh my God, Billy. You scared me half to death!"

He pulls me up and I notice the anxious look in his eyes.

I sit, stunned. "Thank . . . thank God you're here," I say. "I need you . . . to grab Bethy's phone," I pant.

"Is that what you were doing, Charley? Looking for Beth's phone? Why doesn't she get it herself?"

"Beth's . . . missing. Phone . . ." I can hardly breathe the words out. "Look . . . down . . . there." I shine my own phone toward the grave's edge.

"Missing?" Billy squats down next to me. It's comforting to feel the warmth of his body. "Okay. I think I can . . ."

This is one time that gangly body comes in handy. He dives into a prone position at the edge of the hole. I grab him by the ankles and he torques down into the dank depths of a grave.

"Got it!" he shouts, pulling himself back from the abyss. He hands me Bethy's phone. "But what the hell?"

"Oh, thank God." I brush off the leaves and cobwebs, using my dress to pat it dry. "I need to let Beth know . . ." I close my eyes, fear finally washing over me.

Billy sits down next to me, drawing me close. He dabs my eyes with his T-shirt. "Don't cry."

"I'm not crying!" Still, it feels good to be cradled. It feels like he's kissing the top of my head.

"I just don't know what's happened to her, Billy. Look."

I pull up the TikTok. Still there with that other girl.

"What the hell, Charley? Looks like Wonder Woman Beth has pulled a disappearing act. But where is she—and who's that with her?"

But I can't answer him. A second TikTok shows Bethy with a ghastly makeup job, fingering this other girl's outfit and eyeing it with a seamstress's eye. Her ruffled blouse is covered by a vest that looks to be heavily embroidered and made out of much nicer fabric than mine. This new girl—I think it's a "she" even though her head's weirdly cut off in the screen, and her legs are covered with what look to be old-school riding breeches—Beth is gabbing with her, and suddenly begins jumping around—showing off some fancy footwork. I wish I could hear what they're gossiping about.

Again and again, Beth struts, turning on tiptoe to imitate high heels. Apparently showing off the art of the fashion influencer.

Glancing down at my own big dress, I wonder if maybe Bethy's been hit on the head, lost her mind, and weirdly mistaken that other girl for me!

"No. Umm, no . . . I have no idea where she is, or who she's with," I reply belatedly to Billy's question. "My phone. I dropped it and now it's showing me random TikToks with Bethy in them. It's like it's a fake account or something."

"Yeah, well that phone—there are some changes I'm making in the app . . ."

He starts explaining in Billy-like detail, but my head is elsewhere. It's rather inexplicable, given that I am mad at her, but I'm feeling a slight tug of jealousy about Beth not even seeming worried about being who-knows-where-that-is-not-here. And apparently with a new best friend.

FOMO.

"Charley, we should get back, y'know?"

I pull my eyes off the screen, pull away from his arms, and give him a peck on the cheek.

"Billy, you really are my hero!" I say this, even though it feels like we're more in the middle of a potentially precarious situation than at the end of one, and the one who needs rescuing is Beth. "You're right. Maybe we should let the chaperones know."

I hoist myself up using his shoulder for leverage. My long skirt is full of leaves, pebbles, and straw, and tangled awkwardly around my legs.

"Charley, knowing you, we'd better take it slow." Awkwardly, Billy tries to help brush stuff off and untangle me. "Looks like they're digging here, and what, with that dress . . . And who knows how long they might have been looking for us."

"Sure. Why don't you go ahead and let everyone know I'm coming. I've got to find her. Bethy's got to be missing this." I flash Beth's phone in his face. "And besides, you're faster than me with this big dress."

"Are you sure? I could carry you piggyback."

That could be a disaster waiting to happen, him hoisting me up, what with the wind flapping all this material in his face and imperiling both of us.

"Now don't you worry about me, Billy Vincenzo. I'll be fine."

"Well . . . if you say so." He stops, knowing that once I've made up my mind, arguing is futile. "But call me right away if something happens . . ."

"What could possibly happen?" I say, my voice dripping in sarcasm. We both know only too well all the things that could go wrong. "They've got to know about Beth, Billy. Hurry!"

With a quick backward glance, he sprints off on his long stilt legs.

I put my phone and Bethy's in the pouch for safekeeping and step carefully away from the grave. But wouldn't you know, almost immediately after Billy's out of sight, my dress snags on something sharp. I yank on it, walking forward at the same time, notwithstanding the graveyard's uneven ground and deep holes.

Just then, I feel a something snag me around the ankle. The one I hurt last time. I stomp the ground with my free foot and yank.

"Off me!" I begin crying, not knowing whether it's an inanimate object or something scarier, like a snake. I look down, but it's snared my dress, too, and as I pull harder, I hear a rip. It sends me pitching forward, headfirst.

In what seems like slow motion, I find myself flying into the abyss of another open grave—my own.

"HELP!"

I imagine the headstone reading: *Here lies Charlotte Morton, 15. Lost to this world before her time. She dreamt of inventing the future.*

"Charley? What's happening. Are you okay?!" Billy, hearing my cry, comes tearing back, on hyper alert.

Still suspended in time, his voice comes as a blur in my ears. "Charley? CHAARLEEEYYY!"

Too late.

Once again, I've fallen over the edge.

XVI.
There's No Defying Gravity

Breaking the bounds of time, or holy teacups,
here we go again!

I've fallen off the edge of the world. Gravity's tugging me apart at the limbs, tearing my head from my body. My skirt flies up around my head, much as I try to hold it down.

If I were a hawk, I'd be coasting across thermals, soaring one minute, sinking the next, spiraling through an endless void. It reminds me of the kites in motion I once watched outside the Maestro's atelier, then taking flight on the page as Leonardo da Vinci sketched them from life.

I am a spiral in motion with no spacetime orientation.

I know what this is but, once again, it's moving so fast! I didn't have time to prepare. For all that, I am traveling through wavelengths of heat—it's only Esme keeping me temperature-regulated in my costume—and light so blinding—split into its spectral colors: infrared through ultraviolet. A rainbow in a crystal universe.

And there is music in this color. A *whooshing*, low-pitched whale song sliding octaves up the scales, to what I imagine are frequencies higher than any dog's ears could detect.

Time travel. For the uninitiated, it's like riding Space Mountain in the Mad Hatter's Tea Cups; spiral motion in cosmic space spinning and tumbling inside a holographic reality. Once again, I am Alice down the rabbit hole. The pressure is squeezing my lungs out of my chest.

Although . . . this ride seems smoother somehow. Or at least less like the heavy-duty spin cycle on our clothes dryer. Maybe Billy's made some advances to Esme I don't know about. . . . Wasn't he just saying something about the app?

"Breathe, Charley!" I tell myself, fighting for breath—if I could only manage to open my mouth.

But there's no machine, or even a model here, and no remote control to trigger the reverse Earth's spin remotely.

If it's what I think it is, I don't know what will happen—will they be looking for me at the cemetery? Did Billy tell them about Beth? Did Billy even make it back safely? My head hurts too much to think about it.

It's then that I hear the crack and rumble of thunder. The sulphur scent of a match fills my nostrils. Another blast sends shivers down my spine.

The stench of death is in the air.

"I'm dying!" I scream, knowing there's no one to hear.

I wrestle with the reality as fear takes root in my mind.

"Dammit, Charley, you've just got to get through this nightmare ride," I remind myself, gritting my chattering teeth. "For the sake of Carolina, you've got to make it whole to the other side."

XVII.

Après Moi, le Déluge

In which it appears we are out of this world

Here's why it's important to know dates in history: When you're a time traveler, you can never be sure where you'll end up. Or whether your digital device will withstand the ride. I don't care how good your AI is at waking you up in the morning, there are historical forces at work that may not appreciate her cheery, "Good morning, Charley!"

Hence, when I put in my earbuds and check Esme on my phone, I am not that surprised to hear that she's, shall we say, jet-lagged. Back in the future.

"Today in Takoma Park, we'll see alternating clouds and sunshine. There will be a high of 50, and a low of 38."

"Shut up, Esme," I snap. "That's not helpful!"

Esme, disappointment showing, fails to respond. I have no use for a digital assistant stuck in the future.

I stash my earbuds in my pocket for safekeeping. I'll have to figure out how to reprogram her to work without any modern GPS. I wonder if Billy's thought about an app for that?

First, a body scan. No noticeable aches or pains, besides the usual crash landing. Arms and fingers attached—check. Feet and legs moving—check. Head on straight—check. Eyes open—check. Bruises to all of the above—check.

I make a mental note for Billy: Add parachute and popcorn packing like the Mars lander.

I squint and try to take in my surroundings in the bright of a moonlit night. There's a scent of decay—something like rotting pumpkins—in the air that I don't recall noticing earlier. Shadowy looming tombstones and ornate crypts make me wonder whether what I was thinking happened didn't. Except for the putrid smell, this could still be Rock Creek Cemetery and the wild ride nothing more than being caught up in tornado-like winds as a derecho roars through.

I wander guardedly down one row and squint to decipher the faded markings of the gravestones.

DAME FRANÇOISE GELLAIN, CROWNED BY THE FRENCH ACADEMY

Photo: Robin Stevens Payes

I suck in my breath.

"Paris!"

I walk over to get a closer look, the leaves crunching under my feet. I tense up, but hearing nothing but my own breath, I trace my fingers against the stone.

"Wow! Someone was crowned by the French Academy," I whisper, having mentally summoned the rudiments of my tenth-grade French. Whatever that means!

I read her name out loud, "Françoise Géllain. A woman? Wonder who . . . ?"

"Who!" echoes an owl.

A simultaneous tap on my right shoulder makes me practically jump out of my skin.

"Who's there?" I turn my head, but find no one. Maybe it's my imagination.

I take a few deep breaths. Another "who" from the left.

"Ha ha, Beth. I'm done playing hide-and-seek. Come out!"

"*Calmo!*" declares a familiar voice. "Or shall I say, *Calmes-toi?*"

I'm now standing in the long shadow of someone, advancing toward me. I turn around quickly and pounce.

"Kairos? I could kill you!"

I feel him brace for impact as I barrel into his arms.

The light of a rising harvest moon scatters light enough for me to reassure myself that this is truly his familiar face, with those dark, inscrutable eyes.

"Please, we are already too much among the dead. I prefer to live!"

He twirls his black cape, Zorro-like, across his long, lithe frame and I begin to breathe again.

"Are you ever a sight for sore eyes!"

"Your eyes, they are sore?" he asks, frowning.

"It's an expression," I explain impatiently. "It means I'm happy to see you."

"And I, you. Though your eyes are quite beautiful."

It's a joke between us. This is how Kairos introduced himself to me two years ago, before the original jump back in time.

But I'm too jittery to joke. The owl perched in a tree above my head has resumed his hooting. The tombs cast long shadows in the moon's glow. I shiver—whether from cold or fear, it's hard to say. "Why are you here?"

A church nearby slowly strikes the hour, the chimes echoing across the stones: one . . . two . . . three o'clock.

"Just in time, you have arrived," he replies, cryptic as ever.

"Looks like we're not in Kansas anymore!" I whisper.

"There may not even be a Kansas yet," Kairos points out, ever the rational one. "We appear to be in a time before."

Irritated, I pick up my voluminous skirts and stomp my booted foot on stone. "A time before. Very funny!"

Kairos fixes his smile into a scowl.

"From one cemetery to the next. Without even a prototype of the time machine that took us out of time last go-round. How'd you even know I was here, Kairos? And where's Bethy?"

"Sit down a minute, Carlotta," Kairos implores me. "You have suffered a great shock!"

I'll say. Because how I managed to get wherever I am is still an open question, "ancient cemetery theory of time travel" notwithstanding.

It occurs to me that Billy's apparent hacking of my phone might have something to do with it. Wonder if he installed a remote-control system to Esme that gives the wearer greater control? Bit of a genius, that boy.

I plop myself down next to old Françoise. "Should've beta tested her, though."

"Beta?" Kairos asks. "As in the second letter of the Greek alphabet?"

"As in whatever new dashboard Billy's installed on my device without telling me." It's exasperating. "Is Billy ever gonna get a piece of my mind!"

And then I wonder when "ever" might be.

"So really, how did you know to find me here, K?"

"Carolina," he says, as if that explains everything.

I glance around, but Kairos's little sister is nowhere in sight.

When I first met Carolina, in 1492 Florence, she was a precocious eight-year-old, curious about everything. She seemed to want to hang around me a lot, and honestly, I loved being with her, the little minx.

"I just assumed she was with you, no?"

Kairos gives me an odd look. "All will be revealed in time, Carlotta. But for now, we must collect your belongings and find her."

Carolina. Responding to her SOS was my mission. I rise and start down the stone-and-mud path. Heat sensor or no, the place has me goose-bumpy.

"Sit down, Carlotta!"

A wave of nausea hits. I sit back down, shock setting in.

"At least I didn't break any bones this time!"

Kairos laughs and takes off his velvet-lined cape to wrap over my shoulders.

"No broken bones. In a cemetery full of bones. You are very funny!"

I frown, failing to see any humor in the situation.

"At any rate, your *sac*, that you have filled with treasures from your own time," he points down at the ground, "may not be so fortunate. See?"

My eyes pick out evidence of a sadly deflated backpack lying a short distance down the path. I train my phone's flashlight on the ground, where I can make out some very twenty-first-century detritus among the stones: my old French *monnaies* from the coin shop at home. And, of course, my normal street clothes.

"Great. I'm dead here without this stuff!"

"Mademoiselle, all evidence to the contrary, you can acquire all that you need here. After all, France is a civilized country!"

Civilized, but not modern—at least by my definition. Despite Kairos's assurances, I am on my knees, crawling over the cold, hard ground, around graves, scraping the dirt and looking for all my other must-haves under the circumstances, including, of course, the all-important golden compass.

Which gives me momentary pause.

"Billy!" I yell, as if he were here. I have a feeling he'd have an answer to this new riddle.

Kairos has already chosen a nearby graveyard alley to investigate. "You see Billy?" he calls back to me.

"Hell's bells, no, Kairos. It's just . . . but then . . ." It hurts my head to think about it.

Anyways, first things first.

"Where's my compass? It's got to be here . . ."

I pause to flash my phone and look for a glint of gold. After all, if I have time-traveled, that compass is my life!

I stop in front of an open grave. It's almost as if we never left Rock Creek, with a big exception—this burial spot is piled with bones. A potter's field, apparently; not a coffin in sight.

"Oh, no"—I take an in-breath at the apparition of so many skulls staring up at me with empty eye sockets—"what if it's dropped into this bone pit?"

This must be a time before the Paris catacombs opened, the underground burial grounds they had to use when the cemeteries of Paris were overwhelmed with the mounds of decaying bodies and bones left from centuries of plagues. The number of corpses overwhelmed the living residents of an increasingly populous city, even though its size here must pale in comparison to the Paris of my time.

The annoying hoot owl is following me, perched on a crypt not three feet away, a specter amid the shadows. Eerie feeling, him letting me get this close. "Shoo, shoo, shoo!" I stomp my foot. He stretches his massive wings and takes to the sky overhead, crying out to the dead beneath us.

I feel like I'm about to throw up. I had read about the plague taking thousands and thousands of lives at once, so many that the grave diggers couldn't keep up, but still . . . this is too much.

"Stay strong, Charley!" I tell myself. "You're the one who wants to be a forensic anthropologist someday."

Truth be told, the whole idea of unraveling life in the past through the study of the dead fascinates me. But I never fancied myself a tomb raider—more of a crime scene investigator. So it's important to get comfortable being around the dead. You never know what secrets they will give up.

Forcing myself to carry on, I again train the flashlight on the path as I walk once more down this Death Alley. There are flowery inscriptions on the tombs and stones that surround us. Of those that are still legible, some appear to be quite ancient—Gabrielle Le Grange Bisset, AD 1607–1639; enfant Bisset, 1639. This poor woman must've died in childbirth.

Jules Charpentier, Anno Domini 1632–1690. Of those where the incised names and dates are barely legible, a few appear to date back as far as the twelfth century.

Have I overshot the year?

To collect myself, I plop down with my back against one small tombstone—it's hard to avoid them, they're so closely packed. There are stars above us and, as in Florence, I notice how bright even the darkest sky is without the light pollution that seems to rob the twenty-first century of the stars.

The small stone in front of me seems especially new. Judging by the dimensions of the fresh-turned earth, I judge it to be a child's grave. I rub my hand over the engraved number—1724. Is that the year we've landed in?

There's a name: Georgette de la Tour. And a poem:

Ainsi tout passe sur la terre

Esprit, Beauté, grâces, talent

Telle est une fleur éphémère

Que renverse le moindre vent.

"And so, all passes on earth," I translate, consulting the translator on my phone. "Spirit, beauty, grace, and talent. Such is the ephemeral flower that blows away in the slightest wind."

EPITAPH POEM

Photo: Robin Stevens Payes

If life and death weren't already so close here, the poet's words would drive that message home. I should make a stone rubbing, just to prove to everyone back home, and to myself . . .

The owl hoots again, breaking the silence.

"K?! Umm, Kairos?" I call out, mostly to make sure Kairos is still here.

I rub my hands together against the cold. Why didn't we think of gloves? Would this still even be Halloween—*la Toussaint*, the French call the holiday: a time to visit cemeteries and commune with the dead.

"Have you found my spiral notebook, Kairos? Could use a sheet of paper here, and a pencil."

"It is here, but I am still collecting," replies K. "There are clues here—symbols I haven't noticed before. Must add these ciphers to my collection."

I'm just a tad annoyed. Ciphers for his collection, is it? Here's Kairos talking algorithms and code when we should be memorializing lost human lives.

"Never mind! I'll come get the notebook myself."

I stomp back in the direction he originally set off, wanting to share my theory about the new grave and the year. Maybe that means we are close to where Carolina sent out the SOS.

"K? Can you talk so I can find you?" I'm still shaking.

"K, can you talk so I can find you?" he mimics in a high-Charley voice. Despite myself, I have to laugh.

"Oh, K!"

"'Oh, C!'" he chortles. "Don't you know? We are now in the Land of the Dead. Where life begins again."

"Cut it out with the riddles. Now you're just being annoying!"

Still, as long as I can follow his laugh to keep the sound of his voice in my ear, I'll be able to keep from weirding myself out, seeing the long shadows beam and flicker as I light the path with my phone's flashlight.

I am reaching the limits of the cemetery where its walls loom high and spooky.

"Up here!" he shouts.

I look up into the shadows of a series of vaults, chambers, and lofts at the cemetery walls, carved out of stone. I swing the beam in his direction. "There you are!" Looks like he's scaled the wall of what looks to be a particularly imposing vault.

"Carlotta," he whispers, waving me close. "*Viens ici.*"

"Oh, so it's to be French now." I adopt my bravest voice. "*Tu parles français aussi?*"

"I learned that *belle douce langue* in a different time and space," he says.

I can see he's about to launch into his mysterious provenance when I reach his side.

"Look, I know, you're from the way past, or maybe the future, and you're here just in time, but really, can we just stick to the facts. We're in a cemetery. It's dark. All these graves?"

He stretches out a hand to pull me up beside him. "You must see this!" He swings open a wooden door.

I ignore the hand. "Since you know so much, aside from the creep-out factor, what are we doing here? It's cold, it's dark, I've lost my home and everything that means anything to me, and besides, the stink is getting to me."

I can smell death through the bandana covering my nose and mouth.

"Look here," he insists, "it's a charnel house."

"Charnel—what's . . . ?"

Kairos reaches down his hand to help me scale up beside him on the second-story platform, and takes my phone to train the flashlight into the open loft, moving the beam around like a lighthouse.

"See—it is a work of art! The *Danse Macabre*."

He points the flashlight at a ghastly mural painted on the wall. Death, dancing. And above it, a massive stone crypt with a roof partially open to the stars, piled high with bodies in varying states of decomposition laid atop bony decapitated skeletons, their skulls tucked in beside them.

I gasp. He's opened the gate of a massive stone crypt with a roof partially open to the stars, piled high with skulls and skeletons.

CHARNEL HOUSE, ST. INNOCENTS CEMETERY

Credit: Creative Commons, Wikimedia

At the very top of the heap: layers of fresh corpses. Decomposing.

A crow settles above the open attic, then swoops down to peck at the eyeballs of one not-yet-disintegrated body.

"Shoo!" I shout, stomping my foot as he caws back at me. This only seems to attract all his cronies. I wave my hands to fend off his black-feathered friends, as crows circle and scatter noisily around us.

I stomp off in the other direction, hoping they'll scatter.

"I'm finding a gate out, Kairos. If this is Paris, and we're here for your sister . . ."

But the birds are following me. Their feathered black bodies whir into motion around me, scattering in the loft amid the new bodies. Their pecking jars yet another corpse until it belly-flops at my feet.

"Ahhh!" I freeze. After a moment, the crows seem to have lost interest. They take off into the night sky.

Unfreezing myself nerve by nerve, I squint to take a closer look. The female body still sports the tatters of a blue ruffled dress under a red silk shawl. And a red hood.

"Kairos?" I rasp. "C'mere! You need to see this."

I shove my boot under her hip. Too heavy to turn the body by myself. I stoop to scrutinize the fringes at the bottom of her shawl.

"Who are you? How did you die?" I whisper, almost imagining she might answer me. I briefly wonder whether she was a victim of disease, or murder and mayhem of another sort. The plague? Which plague. Without gloves or a mask, I'm afraid to touch.

It is moments like this that spur me to want to study forensics in college. Maybe join the FBI as a forensic anthropologist someday. They say it's a fast-dying field (ha ha).

I have to kick away dirt and stones to see if there are any identifying marks. These remains look fresh. Weird, I think.

And then I see it. Atop a tangle of hair she's wearing a red cap. One that looks suspiciously modern.

**A WASHINGTON NATIONALS CAP IN KING LOUIS
XV'S COURT**

Photo: Robin Stevens Payes

"Beth?" I shriek, in shock. "Kairos, c'mere. Quick!"

XVIII.

Arresting Developments

In which we find out that even back in the day, police aren't always looking out for us

S uddenly, a sharp whistle and the clip-clop of horses' hooves alert me to the fact that we are not alone. Torchlight blinds me. *"Qu'est-ce que vous faites ici, mademoiselle?"* An absurdly costumed man with a perfect red plume in his furry helmet draws his sword.

FROM THE UNIFORM OF THE KING'S GENDARMES

Exhibition: New York Metropolitan Museum of Art
Photo: Robin Stevens Payes

I feel my knees begin to quiver. Even without Esme, I get that he's asking me what the heck I'm doing here.

"Well, monsieur," I attempt. "I think this may be my friend—er, umm—*je pense que ce soit mon amie.*" I kneel down by her side in a protective stance. It occurs to me to check Esme to see if I've got the grammar right, but, no matter, this guy's not about minding his Ps and Qs.

"*Va-t'en! Vous êtes résurrectionniste?*" He grabs me by the arm. "*Comprends que vous serez sous peine d'exécution pour un tel crime?*"

"Execution?! But I'm just trying . . . Kairos!" I yell again, seeking reinforcements.

"I've got you, Carlotta!" Kairos huffs, jumping down. He drops to one knee beside me and clasps his strong hand around my shoulder. With the other, he slips me my backpack, and slyly helps me stick my arms through it, under the guise of rearranging his big cape, which has twisted around my body. I just about manage to pull my earbuds out of my pocket and pop them in, praying that Esme will not fail me here.

"Everything you need is here," he whispers, patting me on the back before standing to address the gendarme—French for police officer—if that's what he is.

"*Seigneur,*" Kairos explains in flawless, heavily accented French, "*cette jeune fille n'a aucune intention à voler un cadavre. Elle croit, par erreur, parait-il, que ce soit sa sœur.*"

This sounds like so much blah-blah-blah, except for his last word: sister. But Beth is not my sister. In fact, far from it, these days, although maybe we were like sisters, once upon a time.

"*Désolé, monsieur,*" the guard replies, in what sounds to be an accusation, not an apology. "*Mais je dois l'arrêter immédiatement.*" With that he whips out heavy iron manacles connected by a short chain and clamps them around my wrists.

"Wait, what about my Miranda rights?" I can hardly think straight, but I know from watching lots of *CSI* that the accused is always entitled to an attorney. "Why am I being arrested?" I shout. "What about justice!"

"*Tais-toi*, Carlotta," Kairos whispers. "We are some years before that revolution in thought."

And now, it seems Esme has automatically adjusted to translating from French to English, with added narration. "The slogan of French liberation—*liberté, égalité, fraternité*—does not yet exist."

Liberty. Equality. Fraternity. Them was fighting words. The French Revolution was (would be?) fought over those ideals. Inspired by the American Revolution.

"The charge," says the police officer angrily, "is body snatching. The punishment: six months locked up in the King's prison."

The King's prison. Would that be the infamous Bastille? What was the Bastille like at this time, and could one escape from it? My mind is churning.

"I am innocent!" I shout, stomping my foot on the officer's boot and preparing to run, if necessary, although I'm not sure how I could outrun the gendarme's stalwart horse.

The officer gestures at the church and then all around us. "*Mais oui, mademoiselle.* We are, indeed, in the midst of the church yard of St. Innocents. But *une jeune fille* like you—alone with a man in a place like this before dawn's breaking—here to steal the remains of the sacred dead? I declare you are no innocent!"

"How dare you!" I blurt at this insinuation, as Kairos, in turn, stomps me on the foot.

"Youch, Kairos. Did you hear what he said?"

"Hush. Go quietly, Carlotta, and do not make a fuss," hisses Kairos under his breath, grabbing my wrist and twisting it gently to show that, actually, the manacles are too large to keep my small hands from wriggling out. "And do not worry—I have a plan."

"A plan! But Kairos, if that's Beth . . . and if she's . . . ." My eyes tear up. "And I'm . . ."

But before I can even gather my jumbled thoughts into a coherent sentence, the guard grasps me by the manacles and drags me to his horse. I wince. He tugs at my arms and grabs me around the waist, coarsely throwing my supine body up and over his horse's back.

The beast seems immense and resolute. The elaborate sculpted and studded saddle, that undoubtedly represents something about the guard's social status or family wealth, is cutting into my rib cage, making it hard to breathe.

I flash back to my wild ride through Florence on Leonardo's horse, Macaroni, and the racing ostriches that blocked our passage, and pray that no such flightless birds populate Paris in this time. Said gendarme mounts behind my prostrate body and spurs the horse into motion.

"Do not fear, Charlotte," Kairos calls out as we clip-clop away over cobblestones on the guard's giant black horse. "I will find you. For you, as for Elisabeth, this is not the end. In fact, we are just beginning."

As I watch Kairos's shaky image fade to black under the jolt of the horse's trot, tears pour out for reals.

"Yeah," I murmur as we pick up the pace past the church that fronts this field of Death. "That's just what I'm afraid of."

XIX.

Bastille Day without the Parades

Being imprisoned in the Bastille is no day to celebrate

At least we are out of the graveyard. From the backside of the horse, I try repeatedly to object that I have done nothing wrong, that my intention had nothing to do with "resurrecting" anyone, dead or alive (as if such a thing would even be possible!), and that I had only been trying to identify my friend—or sister, as Kairos called her.

But then the guy on the horse behind us jumps down and puts a gag in my mouth, which, when combined with the manacles, makes for an extremely awkward situation and is not conducive to truth-telling in any way.

I pray that Kairos will somehow find a lawyer and make it to the Bastille in time to clear this mess up—before I am condemned to spend eternity behind the walls of a French prison. One that in the not-too-distant future will be the place that revolution starts.

The indignities the advanced time traveler must suffer!

Paris is waking up, it seems. It's kind of surreal to see how dirty and cramped the streets and alleys are. Ripe for the spread of disease—which explains, for example, plague. I can understand why the famous Baron Haussmann would want to tear the whole place down and start over—about 150 years from now, as Esme informs me.

At least Esme has rebooted with whatever non-satellite GPS system Billy's managed to program in this time.

I am surprised to note the twinkling candlelit glass-and-metal lanterns hanging on posts all along the route. And while not as bright as, say Times Square on New Year's Eve, it's enough to dim the stars. So this must be when they decided to make Paris the City of Light, I think.

We pass through Les Halles (for the record, the French say this like *ley-all*), the market that was an early prototype for the modern French *hypermarché*—the Costco of its day.

As its name would imply, it's a market made up of halls—long, low buildings—dedicated to dry goods like wheat and grain, and sugar, tea, and coffee. Or to fabrics and threads for weaving, like linen and hemp (yes, hemp is ancient for its use in clothing).

LES HALLES MARKET

Credit: Felix Benoist, Public Domain

But the outdoor market surrounding it is redolent with sounds, scents, and colors. And people waking up to trade gossip along with their goods. In this smaller-than-today city of tight-knit neighborhoods, there is no dearth of news to share.

Finally, we pass by stalls containing multitudes of fragrant spices, herbs, and tinctures that would go into the healing recipes of the apothecary. Naturopathic remedies. A sort of pre-CVS outdoor drugstore. I wish I could nose around.

Our progression stops abruptly before a massive stone archway. I lift my head to see crenellated towers and wide gates, with avenues guarded by some wearing the same regal-looking uniforms as my not-so-friendly escorts.

What's surprising is how much traffic there is—people milling about, teams of horses, and even expensive-looking carriages—going in and out.

SKETCH, COURTYARD OF THE BASTILLE
Credit: Jean Honore Fragonard, Public Domain

So this is Bastille Prison, I think, stunned to note the high, thick stone walls and towers with unsmiling sentinels, their lances thrust through the narrow window openings.

We are stopped on a bridge attached by heavy chains to the gate which opens to the avenue that crosses the moat for entry into the massive castle.

Maybe it won't be the terrifying place that history reports, I think, mainly to buck myself up. Looking down into the moat, I wonder what kind of reptilian creatures swim in the muddy waters below.

As we ride unceremoniously through the gates, now escorted by members of the royal guard, I feel a level of panic rising in me. After all, I didn't expect to come here, much less find myself a captive of royal forces for an alleged crime I didn't commit, and for which I have no defense.

Unlike the time before, when my journey to fifteenth-century Italy came from a deep desire to master time travel, learn the secrets of Renaissance master, Leonardo da Vinci, and get back in time to win the school science fair, my being here in the eighteenth century seems like a big, fat mistake.

Except . . . Beth. And Carolina. And the brilliant Marquise Émilie du Châtelet.

My captors are conferring in hushed tones with the guards.

"Mademoiselle!" barks one of the King's guards, his long spear aimed at my heart. "Dismount!"

This I find difficult, given the chains around my hands. With effort, I slide off the horse's back and promptly spill into a pile on the ground. So humiliating.

"Rise!" commands the guard, yanking me up by the arm. He uses a short dagger to cut my gag.

Now I'm mad. I spit out the filthy wad of cloth that kept me silent, the spit flying in my captor's face. "How dare you, you bully! Of what crime are you accusing me?"

"You are charged with despoiling the sacred resting place of our honored dead. Of robbing corpses, a crime against both Church and State. The King's guards will now usher you inside to face charges."

"But Your Majesty . . . I mean, *monsieur*. This is all a mistake." I fake-curtsy to show my fake-deference. "I can prove—"

"Hold the explanations. That is for the court to decide. As you are evidently not a subject of the King"—here the bewigged guard sneers at me down his nose—"until such time as the *Parlement* calls you to trial, you are to be locked up here at Bastille Saint-Antoine."

WOMEN ARRESTED FOR PROSTITUTION TAKEN TO PRISON

Credit: Étienne Jeurat, Public Domain

My heart drops. I look around to note that I am not the only girl accused without evidence. A wagonload of girls is pulled up right in front of us. And what were their crimes, I wonder? And it requires an act of Parliament just to have our cases heard! So now, I'm to be locked up without evidence of a crime. No trial, no proof, no assumption of innocence.

I pray Kairos will be true to his reputation for showing up "just in time"; hopefully he will have found a fair-minded advocate for my defense. Now would be good. Because I have done nothing wrong!

The guards start pushing me forward, and while my mind wants to protest, I am aware of the glinting swords clanking at their sides.

"Where are you taking me?" I ask.

Their grunts are their answer.

We are descending deep inside the Bastille now, where the walls are probably miles thick. Flares line the walls at intervals, and tears blur my eyes in the dim, smoky halls.

To say I'm scared is an understatement. I remember that during the French Revolution criminals were sentenced to hanging, or the guillotine. And I have watched way too many episodes of *Law and Order* not to fear that the worst injustices can be pursued with the flimsiest of evidence—even in this so-called time of the Enlightenment. I feel the shame of having been caught committing some grave crime, though I have not.

We walk past cells with metal grillwork covering high interior windows, and the hushed silence of prisoners as we walk by. We walk past bolted doors with heavy, seemingly unbreakable locks. Some doors require you to mount steps to enter.

We walk by one cell from which a light is emanating. As we pass, I notice a bewigged prisoner commenting loudly on the scene, his voice dripping with sarcasm. "Our wretched species is so made that those who walk on the well-trodden path always throw stones at those who are showing a new road."

"Who's that?" I ask my guard, Esme prompting me with the translation. I try to point, lifting both of my chained hands to indicate the eloquent speaker.

"Bah!" My escort is dismissive. "All high and mighty, that one. Always asking for favors. His manservant just brought him a load of books from Cardinal Mazarin. Snuck in some wine and coffee to accompany his five-course suppers."

The other guard behind us picks up on this trash talk.

"And they say he is writing a play to be mounted at the Comédie-Française. Gets too many favors, if you ask me. Critical of the King, they say! That sanctimonious toad, Monsieur Arouet."

Arouet—alias Voltaire! The playwright, poet, and philosopher who will team up with Émilie du Châtelet in science experiments and introduce her to the works of Sir Isaac Newton. Or has that happened already?

Either way, I'm a huge fan. Wish I could get my phone out for a selfie. I stop and try to give Monsieur Voltaire a celebrity shout-out, but another guard grabs me under the arm and hustles me forward.

Still, it seems that I've succeeded in at least gaining V's attention. He waves a white kerchief out from behind the grate in our direction, cautioning, "Judge a man by his questions rather than by his answers."

I nod back. Is it my imagination, or do I see him wink in reply?

Another five minutes pass in what seems like hours before the guard pulls a large skeleton key from the giant ring around his belt and opens a screeching wooden door. Behind that door, another one. And finally, a floor-to-ceiling grated gate. Each with its own separate key.

The two guards surround me, mumbling over my head. Something about waiting for questioning by the commissioner. "*Mais elle n'a rien à craindre,*" they conclude.

Nothing to fear but fear itself, as a future president of a future United States of America would say about a future state of the planet where a future Second World War would become inevitable not too far from this place.

I am shoved into a dimly lit octagonal-shaped room, landing humiliatingly on my butt. The first thing to assault me in this lockup are the heavy scents: smoke, straw, BO. It takes a second for my eyes to adjust to the dimness.

I try to get up, but it's awkward and painful trying to rise with my hands locked together and my backpack weighing me down. As one guard puts a boot on my leg to keep me from running, the other at last unlocks me from my shackles.

"Just you wait," I spit indignantly as he makes to depart. "Justice will be served!"

"*Au revoir, ma p'tite!*" he shouts back, wiping a dirty sleeve dramatically across his eyes. "You may be here for some time before Justice serves."

It's humiliating. I hear their laughter fade as one door after the other clanks shut, followed by the clicking twist of a key in the lock.

"Jerks."

The fight in me dissipates with his departure. Rubbing my wrists and brushing myself off, I struggle to regain my sense of dignity. As my eyes adjust, I quick glance around my new surroundings. The cell looks to be about ten or twelve feet wide, with stone floors. Small beds draped with green curtains—for privacy, I'm guessing—are arrayed around the room, heads against the walls and straw mattresses, with hay poking out of the coverings. Next to each bed is a small table covered by a dirty cloth on which are found brass candlesticks and a flint meant, I guess, for the tallow candle. Which might have to double as soap, 'cause it's next to a stone pitcher of water and a metal basin for washing. Chamber pots because, of course, no indoor plumbing. And who knows what kind of vermin live in the squalor underfoot or beneath the straw.

Next to a stove, the only source of heat for the cell, there is an open tinderbox with twigs and more straw for kindling. I wonder where they vent the smoke.

I have to say, next to this, Orphan Annie had it good.

I sit on the bed and shield myself behind the curtain while I slip off my backpack and quietly search for my phone that I'm praying Kairos stuck in. I tuck the backpack under the little table and arrange the cloth to cover it.

It's then that I realize I am not alone. The ringing in my ears subsides enough to notice the voices. In fact, my unceremonious entrance seems to be the source of fresh gossip among the women and girls here.

I wonder what their crimes might be.

My hand lands on the familiar case of my phone. I quick stash it in my pouch along with the solar battery—later, when I know it's safe, I'll see if Billy's been able to contact me.

Now that the adrenaline rush is gone, what with the arrest and all, I'm feeling quite alone.

"*Quelqu'un?*" I request tentatively. "What am I supposed to do now?"

"*Tu dois être fatiguée.*" An old woman with a kind face shows pity. She has lifted the curtain and is patting my hand, which feels gnarled, but warm.

"*Ne t'inquiète pas, chérie. Tu vas t'en habituée.*" She motions for me to lie down.

I have no intention of getting used to prison, but I'm overwhelmed with fatigue. I realize I haven't slept in ages. And I mean that quite literally. Even though the only bed here is made of scratchy straw, and who knows who has been here before me or what kinds of germs they may carry, I sink into it. And sleep.

XX.

A Day without Sunshine

Let them eat twigs

My eyes shoot open as a stream of daylight from a window on high hits my face.

"Too bright," I say aloud. I blink and rub my eyes. I was dreaming that some burly guards had cuffed me and sent me to prison.

Looking around, I realize maybe it wasn't a dream, after all.

I roll off the lumpy straw mattress and squint into the beam of light, trying to regain my bearings. *Charley, you're in the freaking Bastille!* my mind shouts. And I want to shout back, but what good would that do except bring those guards back? What with a bunch of women and girls in here with me, and no friends to vouch for me. I have a dimming hope that Kairos is fetching a lawyer, but why would he not have shown up right away?

I need a plan.

I think briefly about checking my phone—I swear I'm not addicted, but under the circumstances, it would be nice to have a little reminder that someone at home, aka, Billy, has noticed I'm gone.

"*Hé, ma fille!*"

I turn to find a girl about my own age poking me on the shoulder with a short stick, frayed at one end. Under the cover of my cape's hood I slip in my earbuds to make sure I'm understanding correctly.

"Hey, yourself! Stop poking me!"

"*D'où tu viens?*"

Where do I come from. This is the question I fear answering most. Because "the future" seems such a lame answer, and, in the past, can get you tortured or, you know, guillotine'd.

I settle for, "*Loins d'ici*"—far from here. Which is true, technically speaking.

"Here," she says, handing me the stick, as if that would be the self-evident response.

"*Non, merci.*" I wave it away. I'm wondering if she's a hardened criminal, or was also picked up on some bogus charge. Like being a "resurrectionist." *Like, me voilà.*

She taps the twig on my cheek now. "*Bâton à mâcher,*" she says. And opens her mouth and pantomimes chewing.

She wants me to chew the stick? Is she crazy? I wonder if Esme is malfunctioning.

She grimaces, opens her mouth and fans it.

"Ew." I cover my mouth with my hand. "Bad breath . . . ?"

She nods and hands the stick back.

Before I can decide if her germs are worth the trade-off, there's commotion in the chamber. An official-looking dude is approaching the cell, ornately dressed from foot to head in what must pass for eighteenth-century noble finery—black boots, knickers below the knee, a white linen blouse with lace trim around the neck, gold-trimmed blue coat, and, of course, the requisite powdered wig.

All the girls around me snap to attention.

My toothbrush-bearing friend whispers in my ear, "The commissioner. He will question you. Do not act too smart. You must not arouse suspicion, or we shall all be punished."

Telling me not to act smart is probably the wrong thing to say, as this just triggers my skeptic's instinct to question . . . everything.

I slip my backpack on surreptitiously under my cape in case this is some kind of search-and-seizure exercise.

"Which is the girl who has been plundering the sacred dead at St. Innocents?" he barks as he strides imperiously into the chamber, followed by the guards from last night.

One by one, all the other prisoners fall back behind their bed curtains, until there are only two of us still standing. Only my new friend is brave enough to stand with me.

"Er, umm . . . *moi?*" I reply timidly.

"Follow me," he commands. "You are to face questioning."

"Wait, *monsieur*, I think there's been a terrible mistake." I summon up my most humble demeanor, and pray that Esme is operating at peak efficiency.

"Shhh—did I not warn you to stay quiet?" hisses my friend. "He is the police commissioner and reports to the Comte de Maurepas, minister to the King. A very dangerous man."

"You, hush!" commands Monsieur le Commissioner. Looking me in the eye, he continues, "*Le resurrectionisme* is a serious crime."

"I think you have the wrong girl," I venture. "I was just . . ."

But before I can protest further, he grabs me under my left arm and commands the guards to open the door to the cell.

As they march me away, I glance back at my friend. The frown on her face shows that I can likely expect nothing good to come out of this.

XXI.

Expecting the Unexpected

Ghosts are not real, but there really are unseen forces at work in the universe

I am being fast-marched out of what seemed at the very least a safe space. As the commissioner marches me out from behind the many heavy doors, commanding his guards to lock each one in succession behind us, I feel my panic rising. The guard at the lead is carrying a torch to light the dark hallways, throwing flickering shadows against the walls.

At one turn in the thick maze of hallways, I catch sight of a prisoner leaning against stone blocks stacked on top of each other, with an iron ring chained around his neck. He seems to be almost hanging from the wall. He is mouthing obscenities and yelling at the shadows as we pass by, clearly delusional.

It is easy to see how one could go mad in the Bastille.

"I demand a lawyer—or, umm, *un avocat!*" I try to sound commanding, but the demand comes out more like a squeak.

"Quiet, girl. Did you not hear your friend warn you to keep your mouth shut? And hurry! Or do you want to end up like him?" He tilts his head toward the hanging man and I quicken my pace to escape the same fate.

At least they didn't clamp the manacles back over my wrists, settling for the fact, I guess, that there's no way I could escape by making a run for it with homeland security all around me. And what with the fact that *Monsieur* has an iron grip on my arm.

We seem to be marching back through the same hallways that I was escorted through earlier. I glance over to see if I can spy Monsieur Voltaire, but his window now has a curtain drawn over it. I guess the famous here get private rooms and are allowed to sleep in.

"Who are you and where are you taking me?!"

"Ysabeau." He grumbles under his breath. Esme translates this as, "He is handsome," but he so clearly is not.

"What? I don't understand."

The commissioner halts and turns, wherein I almost barrel into him through sheer force of momentum. "Ysabeau!" he repeats, thumping himself on the chest. "*Je suis Ysabeau!*"

Finally, I get it. "Oh, *bonjour, Monsieur Ysabeau*. I am Charlotte," I say, curtsying politely. (It's a skill I learned in Leonardo's time. Who knew it would come in so handy?)

I immediately bite my tongue. Even revealing my first name might be a mistake that would get me worse than the Bastille.

"Charlotte. I know," he says, and resumes our earlier chase.

"Wait, how do you know?"

"*Ton oncle, Monsieur Arouet.*"

My uncle? Arouet? That the great playwright and satirist soon to call himself Voltaire knows my name—how could that be?

No time to ponder this or any other cosmic coincidence. As we step lively past another prisoner "hanging" around the hallway here, I am reminded that the King doesn't really need a reason to arrest people.

IN THE GRIP OF THE BASTILLE

Credit: Tighe Hopkins, Public Domain

We are nearing the great door that emerges out into the courtyard we entered from yesterday. It is a noisy place; the sound of horses, carts, preachers, and supplicants fills the air.

"Monsieur Ysabeau, if I may be so bold—did my friend Kairos come looking for me?"

"Bah! Kairos." He spits on the ground. "No. You have a missive from a noble of very high rank who has taken an interest in your case."

"Oh? And who might that be, pray tell?"

He grunts, as if the question itself is an insult, and hands me a sheaf of handwritten papers with a very official-looking gold seal, tied together with a forest-green velvet ribbon.

My hands tremble—the tension of spending the night in this place, after falling through the Earth from one graveyard to another some three hundred years and an ocean away, and a chance arrest, where I encounter the legendary Monsieur Voltaire, who's a fellow prisoner ... I cannot describe what a toll that has taken on my mental state.

"Pull yourself together, Charley—you've survived worse!" I mumble to pick up my flagging spirits, and notice that my voice is trembling as well.

"*Tais-toi*, you ungrateful wench!" orders the guard, as another guard, bearing a very sharp pike—of the very sort an executioner might use to hoist the head of a convicted enemy of the King—appears out of the shadows.

I wonder at the charge under which they have arrested me: resurrectionist. That apparently makes me a very dangerous criminal in their eyes.

I shake as I untie the ribbon and break the official-looking wax seal; when it comes loose too easily, I lose my grip and send some of the bottom papers flying. I wonder how unseemly—or provocative—it would appear for me to bend down and collect them.

Out of the corner of my eye, I detect quite the commotion in the far end of the courtyard. The guards are pointing their swords at one of their celebrity inhabitants who seems to be defying established decorum here at the Bastille. The bewigged prisoner is wearing a fine pale-blue velvet coat and reading aloud from an open book.

"It is better to risk saving a guilty person than to condemn an innocent one."

Voltaire. The guards aren't taking too well to his recitation. As he marches toward me, he gallantly stoops to gather the packet together, examining the handwriting and nodding approvingly. He hands the gathered documents back to me with a gracious bow.

"I believe these are meant for you, mademoiselle."

"But . . . "

The guard with the pole draws up to attention, while Monsieur Ysabeau chuckles. "Heh, heh, heh. *Ton oncle, eh, mademoiselle?*"

Aware I am being judged for my every move, I curtsy in return: hand over heart, bent knees, head slightly tilted forward.

Voltaire strolls toward us, quill in hand. "The Baron de Breteuil," he says in his perfect Parisian accent. "*Père d'Émilie*, whose bounteous charms—and uncommon skill at picquet and the duel—are well-known at the Court of Versailles. He has pulled some royal strings to secure your release."

"Monsieur Arouet?"

"*Oncle*," he insists, taking my hand and bowing. "Man is free at the instant he wants to be."

I blush at his attentions. "But why do they keep you here, *mon, er, oncle?*"

"That Chevalier de Rohan was too, shall we say, cowardly to face me in a gentleman's duel. To save the family name, they went to the King to have me arrested, instead."

"So unjust!" I declare sympathetically.

"It is clear that the individual who persecutes a man, his brother, because he is not of the same opinion, is a monster."

I stand astonished. I can't believe he just said this out loud. After all, in the France where we are, there is no First Amendment right of free speech—not under the King of France.

The guards lift their swords again, and Ysabeau orders, "Silence, monsieur! You shall not mock the law!"

"You may want to be more careful with your words, monsieur," I urge in a loud whisper.

He appears to slough off the threat. "No opinion is worth burning your neighbor for. As for you"—he squeezes my hand between his two and leans close to whisper in my ear—"fear not. We have pulled some strings to forge papers with the signature of the King's minister, Monsieur de la Rennie, to gain your release."

The King's minister! A forgery of some magnitude indeed.

I am about to say something about how it's not right to fake someone's name—something Bethy used to do by forging her mom's signature on a note to get out of swimming—but the pressure of his hands covering mine tells me not to question the means to this end.

"We who?" I can't help but ask.

"Read the damned papers," he hisses in my ear.

I quick fumble through them. It's kind of hard to decipher the flourishing sweep of handwriting—and the weird French. I note the year—1724—a clue that puts things into perspective about *when* I am: fifty-plus years before the revolutions, either in America or France, under some King Louis or another. *Noblesse oblige* and all that sort of Divine Right of Kings nonsense.

I manage, haltingly, to read the opening aloud, "Monseigneur Nicholas le Tonnelier, Baron de Breteuil, the chief of diplomacy at Versailles under *le roy Louis XIV*, requests that the Countess Charlotte of Maryland, whose noble estates were established under the protection of the late Prince George of Denmark, be immediately released."

"Who?" Both Ysabeau and I query, in unison.

Rather than answer a question that might be damning for both of us, Voltaire's voice takes on an admiring tone.

"Ah, what fortune for you to join the company of the fair Mademoiselle Émilie," he tells me, ignoring the question. "Her conversation is agreeable and interesting. And her family well received at Court. As you shall see, *chère nièce*."

He winks and points to the page. "I believe you must sign here."

Despite my impulse to protest about not being his niece (remembering from my European history class, how the great man later takes up with his actual niece, about which, despite my admiration, I am so, like, ugh! #timesup), I try to focus my skittery brain on this parchment.

As I scrutinize the words, I notice there are some notable misspellings in this official decree: no accents in places one would normally see them; French orthography is apparently not yet standardized. I scan to the bottom of the last page and take a quick in-breath at the large, looping signature, written in a different hand altogether.

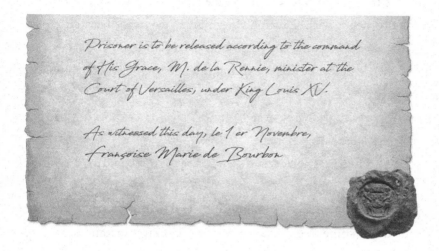

Prisoner is to be released according to the command of His Grace, M. de la Rennie, minister at the Court of Versailles, under King Louis XV.

As witnessed this day, le 1 er Novembre, Françoise Marie de Bourbon

ROYAL CITATION
Credit: Melissa Brandstatter

My eyes widen. Who is . . . ?"

Voltaire throws a sharp glance my way. "Silence: the book of fate is closed to us."

Then, to Ysabeau, who has been grumbling about people wasting his time with too much talk, Voltaire declaims loudly, with a nod in my direction, "Judge a man by his questions, not his answers."

"Judgment! Isn't that the whole misplaced point of this charade?" I begin my protest, only to be silenced again as Voltaire offers me his pen.

"You are free. This next chapter is yours to write. After all, what is history? The lie everyone agrees upon . . ."

It's then I realize that this whole situation is the result of a vast fake to begin with. I scribble my name (we never learned cursive growing up), Countess Charlotte of Maryland.

With a polite bow, I try to hand Monsieur Ysabeau the packet of papers.

Apparently, he's not over Voltaire's arrogance, flouting the playwright's status as prisoner.

"Monsieur Arouet, you will return to your cell, sir!" commands Ysabeau.

"*Eh, bien, monsieur le commissaire.*" And turning, to me, "We must one day resume free discourse under other circumstances. Perhaps over a glass of ice cream." There's a mischievous glint in his eye. "Ice cream is exquisite. What a pity it isn't illegal."

As the guard rushes forward to grab him, Voltaire, with a graceful bow and a glance back at me, saunters back inside.

Finally, after an "ahem" from me, the commissioner / prison warden—as that feels like his job here—looks over my papers. I have the feeling he doesn't know how to read. Ysabeau examines the broken wax, the seal, and the signature, grunting this Rennie dude's name aloud. I guess, whoever he is, he's a high-enough noble to get me sprung.

"Release this girl," commands the commissioner, and turns to walk away. The guard with the pointy spear roughly grabs my hands and officiously marches me outside the gates.

Still holding Voltaire's pen, I consider what the real gift of my encounter with my new fake uncle is—the notion that mine is the next chapter of history to write. Souvenir and inspiration, I quick sneak this plume into my pocket, wondering what story I am to write. Above all, I'm a girl of science, and the whole improbability of my journey to this time—or any other—is hardly a story I feel could be received in my lifetime as anything other than a fiction.

But I must put the skeptic's voice out of my mind. After all, I am undeniably here.

XXII.

EASE ON DOWN THE ROAD

Calm mind, better problem solving; think, Charley, think!

Just outside, I feel at once relieved and excited. I rub my wrists, aching from where Mr. Avant-Guard grabbed me.

Mindful of the precariousness of my position—after all, I now know of all the eyes upon me, from the highest ministers to the lowest of body snatchers—I take off briskly in what I think must be the direction of the Seine River. If nothing else, I know the Seine runs through Paris, and in the bustle of the big city, I can surely find someplace to hide until I figure things out.

I had forgotten how much more precarious life is in the past. Even among the noble classes, with war, disease, and the Unknown having the upper hand, every day is a battle for survival.

In my head, another battle is shaping up: Terror versus Reason. Since I've fallen from the future, I have encountered Death. Stealing. Capture. Prison. Voltaire. Royal edicts. Warnings by those who would do me harm. The events of this morning trigger the terror that I first felt on another early-morning ride—through Florence— long, long ago.

And also, Kairos, here; it's almost like he's been stalking me. And the awareness that, somehow, the Baron de Breteuil—father of the one, the only Émilie du Châtelet, mathematician-physicist-philosopher and, apparently, gambler and duelist—is aware of my existence. It seems an omen that I am meant to be here, to meet the amazing Émilie.

So far, though, Terror seems to have the upper hand. How do these improbable puzzle pieces fit together?

Once I feel a safe distance from that den of thieves and philosophers, I slow down to consider the evidence. Where am I supposed to go from here? The answer isn't obvious.

Because, first off, this time travel wasn't even supposed to happen—there being no explanation for me having jumped the veil, so to speak, without the time machine or any other technology.

And second off, while I am truly dying (well, maybe that's not the best word to use at the moment—let's say eager) to maneuver a meeting of the minds with the fair Émilie, my grand entrance to this spacetime has not made my encountering the Marquise du Châtelet a done deal. Like scoring an interview with Leonardo, it is my mission to plumb the secrets of her amazing scientific and philosophical and mathematical mind, woman to woman.

Third off, what could be the deal here with Carolina? She called out an SOS from this century to my own. Does she know I've arrived to save her? And why doesn't Kairos seem concerned about his baby sister? If it were my baby sisters who were lost, I would be frantic! And what about that Bourbon person who signed my release from prison . . . another clue?

And, last but not least, Beth. Because . . . the baseball cap and cape. Because Bethy seemed to have disappeared before I did from the haunted cemetery at home. Did *she* somehow time-travel? And could she have perished in the process? Even with my experience in the roller-coaster rides between times, and Billy's and Lex's subsequent time travels, we yet don't have enough evidence that this is actually not a life-threatening state. After all, even roller coasters can sometimes come off the tracks, to horrifying effect.

Or, horror of horrors—was that Nats cap on the cadaver at Les Innocents evidence of some earlier time traveler caught up in the considerable tailwinds (spoiler alert to readers unfamiliar with my Renaissance Florence adventures), where the heat literally got turned up over the course of Lorenzo de' Medici's Carnival carousals. Look at what the hell happened to me and Bethy II, aka, Elisabetta. Burning "witches"—aka, women who tell the truth—is probably still a thing in this century. After all, it's evidently still a practice in my own time—just that the "burning" is now in the fingers of social media stalkers.

Lost in my head, I'm so shocked when I hear a ping on my phone that I gulp in too much air and start coughing.

It's Billy.

"Where r u? Went all through Rock Creek searching. U and Beth: disappeared."

Was this here before? I stop cold. Does anyone at home besides Billy realize we're gone?

Panic tightens its grip. So many lives may be at stake.

Time waits for no one—trust me, I know. I need to respond to Billy, but what would I even say: "Time travel without warning. Might've killed Beth?"

But no. Not enough evidence to confirm. Best wait 'til I find out the facts.

XXIII.

Now You See Me, Now You Don't

Bicycle power: not such a lame idea

First things first.

I start following a well-trodden route toward what I hope is the (right) river, wondering how long it will take me by foot to reach some recognizable landmark—Notre Dame Cathedral comes to mind, as that was the image on Carolina's postcard.

Given where and when we are, a real carriage is probably reserved only for the aristocracy. So, I am half-hoping to see Kairos ride up on horseback to hurry us along.

Instead, he pedals up on a bicycle—or more accurately, a tandem—gallantly dressed in a ruffled shirt, a mini-skirt-length, embroidered green waistcoat, and tailor-made breeches, looking very . . . well, the word that comes to mind is ridiculous. Because the idea of him being perched atop Billy's bike with the bright red wheel hubs and now a straw basket replacing the wire one is such an anachronism.

But as Kairos, who left me in the Bastille without a "get out of jail free" card, rides 'round me in circles, I am boiling mad.

"How. Could. You. Abandon. Me. You—you traitor!"

He lifts one dark eyebrow and narrows his eyes to slits. "How is it that I am always finding you in trouble, Carlotta?"

"Huh! More like getting me *into* trouble, Kairos! Imprisoned and all alone . . ."

He brakes the bike in front of me so fast, I almost trip over him. "To have to petition . . . beg for permissions . . . craft the papers to get you, how do you say, *sprung*? Even in this day, France is a very bureaucratic country!"

Thoughts swirling, I try to seize on his words. "What do you mean, petition? Don't tell me you were behind that!"

He opens his mouth to respond, but I'm too fired-up.

"And what's with all that other crap—under King Louis . . . signed by some other person I've never heard of. And if it was you, why'd it take you so long? Answer me that!"

"*Silenzio, Carlotta*," he hisses. "There are spies all around us."

I turn my head left and right and spin around. There's literally no one in sight.

"We appear to be quite alone on this road."

He hops off the bike, which drops to the ground with a clatter, and lowers his voice to a whisper.

"While they don't have your twenty-first-century tools of surveillance, the King has ears everywhere." He nods his head toward the massive hedgerow that lines the road and I note something gold and glinting that flashes in the sun. Or did Kairos just plant that suspicion in my head?

"And what does any of this have to do with me? I am innocent of the crimes they've charged me with."

"But guilty of the far greater crime of *knowing too much*," he warns. "Your knowledge of future events, of revolution against King and country, could get you locked away forever, Carlotta."

This last warning rings true. I know for a fact that kings don't take lightly to assassination plots, real or imagined, even if this one only turns out to be real for another Louis in 1789.

Which brings up another subject.

"How'd you come by these wheels, anyway? And who else has seen you with them?"

Kairos picks up the bike off the gravel road and wheels it back around, apparently relieved I am done with cross-examining him.

"Billy notified me of this latest invention," Kairos informs me. "It is, as you would say, portable!"

I seize on this. "Billy—is here?"

"Not exactly."

He wouldn't come. But he sent the bike. Rude!

Grabbing a handlebar, I can tell Billy's updated it. Our last conversation about it—Billy's and mine—was all about boosting its electric power by installing a magnet free-energy generator, explaining it wouldn't require gasoline or battery power. Or even solar.

The idea makes sense: In a pre-electrical world, magnets would still be plentiful. Plus, they'd be better for the environment.

I see a message button, too. It's flashing. When I go to touch it Kairos grabs my hand.

"You may regret . . ."

It's too late. On the screen, Google Earth is spinning again. Round and round it goes, and where it stops, nobody knows. It shows a pin in the heart of Washington, DC, close to home. Which would not be the nation's capital from this time in history, as there was no nation yet.

I can see crowds gathered around the Washington Monument, where I seem to have a bird's-eye view. It looks like a protest, an ocean of people as far as the eye can see, spreading down the National Mall. It reminds me of the Women's March, a thing that happened in 2017. Has the Wheel of Time spun just short of my own DC in 2019?

But zooming in to a ground-level view, I notice that most everyone's wearing a mask. Not like trick-or-treat—which might have been fitting—but surgical masks. Many people are carrying signs. And they're chanting, "I can't breathe!"

"Charley!" I hear someone calling my name. "Carlotta!" I look around, but the sound is coming from the screen.

"Charley, I've lost you!"

"Billy!" There in the center of everything, is Billy, looking all mad.

But here, in this present, Kairos is getting all riled up.

"Carlotta! You do not know what you are doing!" he shrieks at me.

"Billy—I'm here. Can you hear me? I'm right here!" I tap on the screen, as if that might get through to him.

He cups his hands around his masked mouth as if to amplify his voice, but the noise of the crowd is drowning everything out now.

"Why are they all wearing masks? What kind of protest is this, anyway?" I demand. "And what the hell is Billy doing there?"

I look up at Kairos, who's usually got all the answers and some rational response that will calm me down. But he doesn't look calm. Instead, he's leapt in front of the handlebars to block my view of the screen. I have never seen Kairos look this animated. The dude who is simultaneously everywhere is pulling the bike away to regain control of the screen.

"Stop! Stop, I tell you. You are playing with fire, Carlotta. You must not toy with time . . ."

XXIV.

BIKING BACKROADS THROUGH FRANCE

Day-tripping: off roads like no tourists ever . . .

I think of the famous Butterfly Effect. You know, the idea that a butterfly flaps its wings in Africa and it creates a storm in Indonesia?

What if we have a different version of that here: My imprisonment in the Bastille leads to a revolution in the future—my twenty-first-century future, that is.

Although Billy and I certainly pondered time travel to the future,
the idea of having, like, some kind of crystal ball to see into that
future never crossed my mind. And if Billy is in it, where am I? And
does he still have a bead on our location?

As if reading my mind, Kairos says, "Billy is keenly aware of where
you are, *cara* Carlotta. And how you will need a way of navigating back."

Back from where? From Carolina . . . or a dead Beth? On a magnet-motorized tandem?

And then, another thought: What happens if we're caught riding it? I'm already under surveillance, it seems, having been caught grave robbing, or whatever that crime was that got me sent to the Bastille. And I know that gaining a high-tech profile in a low-tech time is a shaky proposition. More trouble in Seine City.

But there's no time to muse about all that with so much at stake.

Kairos is keen to get the show on the road.

"Focus on what is going on here, Carlotta. We do not want anyone to track us here. You have already seen what can happen when you attempt what history has not—cannot record."

He mounts the bike and walks toward me, beckoning me to hop on the back of this bicycle built for two. "*Allons-y*, Carlotta. To track down my roving little sister."

As I glance around the countryside and think back to my impressions of Paris earlier, looking so hodgepodge, so dirty, so different from the iconic Paris of today, and most recently having departed from twenty-first-century Maryland, I realize again the profound truth of our science experiment. Time-traveling once may be a fluke; but a second leap is scientific confirmation.

"Right. So where are we going?"

"To the Palace!" says Kairos. "Versailles."

"Versailles." I let that sink in a minute. From DC to *Paree*—from pumpkins to prison to palace—all within twenty-four hours.

Kairos starts to launch into his "all time is relative" speech. It's irritating.

"Carolina, though," I interrupt. "Notre Dame Cathedral—the picture on the postcard. Wouldn't we find her there?"

Kairos seems reluctant. "Perhaps when the time is right . . . "

"C'mon, K. She's *your sister*, for God's sake! I mean, aren't you even worried about her?"

"Worried indeed. My heart says yes. But that postcard was some time ago, and my mind says that those signatures on the papers releasing you from the Bastille—and their royal provenance—are warmer . . . clues, if you will. We must follow the trail. So, to Versailles?"

Of course, he's right. The postcard was ages ago—in any time frame. "Think, Charley!" I mutter to myself. "Think!"

"*Allez, venez*," I order my tandem captain.

At once, I feel my mind let go of the tension that had locked it. We're leaving this terrible place behind.

We glide down one of the narrow avenues that winds along the banks of the Seine, around behind the Louvre where, Esme informs me, King Louis XV lives currently—although he is too young to rule—onto the street that goes in front of the palace and across the bridge. I am glad that we're biking mostly magnet-powered, as pedaling in this infernal dress could only result in fabric getting caught up in the gears or twisted up in the wheels, which could only result in tandem malfunction. As in *kaboom!*

As it is, everywhere we pass, people stop and stare at our vehicle, attention which Kairos seems to relish, but which makes me feel exposed (note aforementioned burning-of-witches practice) until we cross the Seine again, this time to the southwest corner of Parisian civilization, where we eventually reach the walls of the old city of Paris proper.

I squeeze just a tiny bit on the brakes fitted into my rear handlebar, knowing this is probably my once-in-a-time-travel chance to study a place like this. 'Cause in just a little more than a hundred years from now, the blink of an eye in cosmic time, Paris will have been completely rebuilt to look more like the City of Lights in our day.

"Let us not delay, Charlotte!" Kairos says, kicking up the gears on the bike. "We have leagues to go before we rest."

We continue on, bouncing over a rutted country road. We skirt the edge of a forest. At this point, remembering the long, spooky shadows from the night before, I am happy the sun is now high and brightly shining.

It reminds me of a serious bit of unfinished business—the thing that got me into royally pardonable trouble in the first place, and that is driving us to escape Paris, thanks to Émilie's dad's considerable clout to get me sprung from prison.

"K, you need to tell me—that body, back in St. Innocents. Was it . . . ? I mean, could it have been, well, Beth? I mean, all those plague victims . . ."

"Uncanny resemblance, I agree." Kairos's voice assumes a serious tone. "But I told you, Carlotta: Your Elisabeth is in no danger here. As you well know, there are many strange coincidences across time—people look alike."

"You mean, like, there could be a Bethy III?"

I think back to my "uncanny" meet-up with Bethy II, aka, Elisabetta, in Florence during Leonardo's time.

Which leads me to wonder: Could Bethy I, aka, my once and former BFF, be somehow a descendant of Bethy II? And could the instant romance that grew up between Bethy II and Lex, who was Bethy I's boyfriend-wannabe in the twenty-first century, actually have been the liaison that would one day pass down a gazillion generations since then to become "my" Beth?

Reminds me of a goofy song that the twins love to listen to: "I'm My Own Grandpa," about a man who marries a widow whose daughter marries his father . . . but with a time-travel twist. The implications are too freaky to ponder. And certainly not covered in our ninth-grade biology class curriculum on genetics and heredity.

But I can't let myself go down that rabbit hole.

"Yeah, well. But you haven't really answered my question. How do you know Beth's okay? Is she here?"

"Where is . . . *here* . . . exactly?"

"Ugh! Stop it, Kairos!" I squeeze the brake for real this time, bringing the bike to a screeching halt. I stomp my foot down hard as we emerge onto a wide, gravel path, and almost flip us over in the process. "No more games. Is Beth here or not?"

He sighs, and turns around to look me dead in the eye.

"Your curiosity will be the death of you, Charlotte. Yes, your friend is here. You will soon see."

From his look, I gather that I may not like what I see when I do. "Hmmph."

"Now, shall we continue?" He turns on the motor so, feet on pedals, the magnet power kicks us into higher gear.

"But what about your sister—don't you know where she is?"

"One can never tell with that one," Kairos says with a hint of sarcasm.

"But what if she is still at the cathedral? Or has been picked up by child traffickers? Or is wasting away somewhere on the side of the road?"

"Your overactive imagination puts us all in peril, Charlotte," he says, not without reason. "You must trust me."

We ride in silence for a while, my mind fighting with itself over all the "what-ifs" in the decision to leave Paris. Sheep grazing. Geese honking overhead. I barely take in the changing countryside as we pedal past.

"We're almost there now. Look, Carlotta!"

I jerk my head up. It appears that we've stumbled onto the grounds of a humongous private estate, overlooking a series of vast, manicured gardens, graceful fountains, and a giant castle.

"Are we . . . is this—Versailles?"

"Oh, crap." Kairos is jimmying with the control panel. "Billy seems to have installed an additional feature that requires activation. I think I've almost got it . . ."

"Esme, what is this place?" I ask. In my ear, I hear Esme begin her travelogue: "The Château de Saint-Cloud was first established by a family of Florentine bankers, the Gondis, in the sixteenth century. Philippe, Duke of Orléans, the younger brother of Louis XIV, adopted the estate as his own." I climb off the tandem to stretch my legs.

But of course. The Gondi family must've been friends of the de' Medici, right? And would know my old pal Leonardo da Vinci. And this brother of the now-dead King Louis XIV built up the beautiful castle and grounds and made them his own.

Kairos grunts, apparently satisfied at whatever he's figured out.

I watch closely as the screen lights up with Billy's face. It's a picture I took of him at Homecoming, looking all dashing, and not at all the everyday Billy.

"A chatbot Billy!"

The bot emits a thought bubble. "Charley, it's me. Really."

A prompt asks me to type my reply

"No duh!" I type, not imagining that this chat will ever see the light of the twenty-first century.

"Where are you?" the chatbot's response pops up. I have no idea if this is preprogrammed or live, an artificial intelligence, or Billy's.

I again consult our surroundings. St. Cloud would mean nothing to him. "Near Versailles." I type. "France."

I wait.

No reply.

"So that was all preset. Not so intelligent, after all," I say with a sigh.

"Patience, Carlotta. It must learn as it goes," Kairos interjects. "Ask it a question."

I forgot that Kairos is the ultimate IT dude. A tiny spark of hope springs in me. After all, Billy could hardly test a prototype that would send signals across centuries before I jumped. So, in design-thinking terms, this is our test drive, so to speak.

"Do you know where Beth is?" I type.

After what seems like an interminable lag time, a response. "I don't get it. Can you elaborate on your question?"

So it's not a live Billy replying. NLP—Natural Language Processing. It's how computers interact with human language. Like spell check. Or Alexa eavesdropping on personal conversations to learn how people speak. Sometimes, it requires human fact-checking.

I started to create my own chatbot over the summer after I interviewed the CEO of an AI company as part of a summer coding camp. But life got in the way (aka, too much homework!).

"C'mon, Kairos. Billy thinks machine learning is the future, but, in fact, this machine still needs its human. Which could take an eon from here."

I sigh, and swat at a moth that's flitting around my face. "Go away!"

"Do not go so fast, Charlotte," Kairos interjects. "Look."

Seems a new chat bubble's popped up. "When?"

Maybe Billy *is* on the case in real time. "Seems like Louis XV just made King here," I type. "Searching for Beth—did she jump too? Saw Nats cap on a corpse. Can you get a live fix on me thru GPS?"

"When?" immediately pops up for a second time. Which makes me wonder about a bug in the system, even as I swat away the pesky moth; it seems to have dropped from a tree overhead.

Again, a lag time, but now, I am riveted. If Billy knows how to track me in real time—or past time—maybe we can synchronize and he can get a bead on what's happening in the outside world here.

"Stay. Where. You. Are. Things getting weird at home. New virus."

What's that even mean, weird at home? This is not what I expected to hear.

"Here's not safe!" I argue aloud with the Billy bot. "Do you even know what's going on here?!"

But then, of course he doesn't.

"Carlotta!" Kairos places a hand on my shoulder to calm me down. "This is no way to problem-solve. *Calmes-toi.*"

"Calm, calm, calm. I am being calm!" My frustration's boiling over. "I mean, how can I be calm when Billy's being so cryptic. Stay here, he says. New virus, he says. What does that even mean, new virus? Like, avian flu? Get a flu shot, people!"

"*Calmes-toi!*" None too calm himself, Kairos's voice rises. "The chatbot works only through digital prompts. And we have limited energy to communicate. Save power for our mission."

Our mission.

Collecting myself, I type in at the prompt: "What the #$@!%, Billy!"

A new bubble pops up: "But everything's fine for now. Don't worry."

For now, he says. Don't worry!

I start pacing. As if all the chaos happening here isn't enough, there may be a new plague afflicting the world. My real world.

"Kairos, what's he mean, fine? You're a man about time. Answer the question!!"

I start yelling and tapping on the screen to ask him myself, but as I tap, it dims. I pound on it to keep it alive. And now a second moth, flying after the first, has landed. "I want to go home . . ." But the light goes out before I can finish. "Reboot, Kairos. It's got to work!" I bang on it with both hands.

"I. Will. Make. It. Work!"

"Charlotte, your beating on this monitor will not bring it back to life," Kairos says, as he pushes me aside.

"With the technology of this day, we may not have the tools to fix it."

"No! That's not the answer. It's just in the code, right? We can make it work!"

Because if not, somewhere on the road to Versailles, some cold time in 1724, there is a modern girl who thinks—who knows—that her life is over in the past because of something that won't happen for another 275 years or so. And she, with all her advanced knowledge of technology, history (futurestory?), and science, is helpless to change it.

I sit my butt down on the bike seat and curl over the handlebars so Kairos can't see the tears burning in my eyes.

I've killed the Billy bot. And probably Bethy. I'm trapped in a time and place I do not get at all. And as Shakespeare wrote (and I saw inscribed on a statue when we took a class field trip in ninth grade to the Library of Congress in Washington, DC, where I got a coveted library card to do research with original materials), "What's past is prologue."

WHAT'S PAST IS PROLOGUE

Credit: Mike Peel, CC BY-SA

Or as we might say in my time, "What goes around comes around."

But time is catching up to me. I'm tired. I'm thirsty. And hangry. And determined not to die of starvation like I almost did in ancient Florence.

XXV.

Meet the Royals: A Boy and His, umm, Mule

Stow the bike, or sow a revolution?

"How many leagues to Versailles from here, Kairos?"

"Not too much farther by bike. On wheels, we should be there within the hour."

But I don't know if I can last a whole 'nother hour.

"Can we rest a minute? Maybe there's a market nearby where I can find some cheese. And a croissant. And clean water. And a pit stop—or whatever passes for modern plumbing."

"*À ton service, mademoiselle.*" Kairos bows graciously. He's always saying he's at my service. I have no idea why. But I'm not arguing!

"But we cannot linger on the duke's lands," he warns.

"Wait, can I grab a pic first?" I realize I should be posting all of this on my private Instagram account, @charley.private.journal, for the record.

"*Absolument pas!*" he exclaims, in his heavily accented French. "After all, one does not set foot on royal property without a formal invitation."

"Oh well, then, *allons-y*," I agree reluctantly. "But first, maybe we should hide our transport." Even though we have eluded suspicion parading the tandem around the countryside so far, there's no telling when the King's goon squad may descend again.

We pass a small wooden signpost announcing the village of Marnes-la-Coquette, and follow the road past rustic farmhouses, a watermill, people who one might call peasants working in the fields, and yellowing meadows where cows and sheep graze and lay placidly under the sun. It looks almost like a movie set.

We stow the bike in the woods at the edge of the village.

"Just how far would we be from there now, K? I mean, now that we're walking?"

"Two, perhaps three leagues by foot. A few hours, at most."

Even though I used that antique term of distance earlier, I really have no idea the length of a league but, in my present frame of mind, the idea of walking from here to the Court is basically a nonstarter.

At that moment, a daydreaming boy wearing a slouchy hat rides up atop a mule cart stuffed with straw, passing by without noticing us.

"Eh, *garçon!*" I shout, waking him from his stupor and distracting Esme from her travelogue to translate. "Can you give us a ride to Versailles? We'll treat your ass to some straw and water. And you, to a refreshment in the village."

He stares at me noncommittally, then glances over at Kairos who pulls out a coin and tosses it to him. *Garçon*, as I'll dub him, bites it and, apparently satisfied, jumps down. With a slight bow, he offers to relieve me of my backpack and stow it in the straw in the back of his cart.

I stuff away my fears that I may never see said backpack again and hop up on the rough board next to the driver's box—riding shotgun, as it were—and we progress joltingly over the pocked and rutted road into town. Kairos walks beside us.

Once we glimpse the steeple of a church, I note how quickly traffic, both on foot and by carriage, begins to pick up. I'm guessing it's what passes in these parts for rush hour.

From my vantage point atop the wagon, I see a scattering of country houses, a town hall, and a village square. I'm guessing it may be a pastoral retreat for the wealthy from the filth of Paris.

The scene revives me. "How charming!" I clasp my hands together in pleasure.

Though we are every bit the weary travelers we must appear, Kairos and I rumble into the heart of this quaint little French village—all stucco houses with straw roofs, a farmers' market, a butcher shop, a barber-surgeon with his striped pole to mark the spot, anchored by the town hall—for a short rest and refreshment at a raucous local tavern before setting off again.

GAITÉ TAVERN

Outdoor Tavern Sign, Versailles Exhibition,
Metropolitan Museum of Art
Photo: Robin Stevens Payes

Next stop: Versailles.

XXVI.

LIVING LIKE A KING?

*In which the Sun King's royal palace sure ain't
what it used to be*

Despite hitching a ride with Garçon as far as the royal village that bears the same name as the Palace of Versailles, we couldn't exactly enter its golden gates riding a hay cart.

Luckily, here they offer sedan chair rentals, a pre-motorized equivalent of a modern-day rideshare service. And no, there's no app for that.

After Kairos asks some skeptical locals, we proceed to the official rideshare offices on the *Rue des Coches* (how convenient that they've named it the Street of Coaches, assuming you should be otherwise oblivious or from out of time) where we hire a sedan chair, to be carried on poles by human porters. I always assumed that was a thing that only the Sultan of Turkey or the emperors of China rode, but it turns out they're quite common here. After a slight kerfuffle having to do with the cost of said chair—twelve sols, or *louis* (like the king), and my only having ten such coins, which cost me a fortune at home—we enter the deluxe carved and gilded cabin of said chair, hoisted smoothly into position by regally costumed porters, and quickly proceed on our way.

SEDAN CHAIR

Versailles Exhibition, Metropolitan Museum of Art
Photo: Robin Stevens Payes

We are transported up the long avenue toward Versailles Palace. I am expecting nothing but magnificence, as I have explored an interactive map and YouTubes of the modern-day palace.

In person, it is much more grand than I ever could've imagined. Gold gates glitter in the sunlight. I stare out the window as our coach bumps past mythic statues of grand proportion—the Sun King astride his majestic mount; Neptune, God of the Seas, lounging amid angels and cherubs, marble limned in gold and rimmed in the dew-washed backlit sunrise. And Apollo, god of practically everything.

Our man-powered buggy—hardly bigger than a public bathroom stall—proves to be a brain-rattling ride as we are jogged over the uneven cobblestoned streets.

As the sun rises higher in the blue sky of autumn, I begin to notice something else; these gardens are anything but manicured, and the majestic fountains, renowned back in the day across Europe for producing fantastical water shows, are spouting in fits and starts, dribbling into green, algae-covered founts.

In fact, the place looks a bit run-down. It makes me wonder again about the state of the Second Estate (aka, nobility). I vaguely remember that Louis XV was just about my age when he inherited the throne, and imagine that a too-fast learning curve from boy to king might mean that a few things are overlooked.

On the other hand, I have to imagine the King would have a whole retinue of workers to take care of the grounds, and knights to make them hop to—a staff to dwarf the number of civil servants working in the entire office of the Landscape Architect of the US Capitol, for example. (I know a tiny bit about this because said landscape architect used to be our neighbor.)

As we perambulate up toward the palace, there's barely a Swiss guard in sight to stop us. I'm nervous they'll ask for IDs to prove we are who we say we are. Not sure they'd know what to make of my learner's permit.

"While everyone was busy faking signatures to get me out of the Bastille, you should have forged some papers to show we belong here, Kairos," I whisper, leaning over to be heard above the increasing level of street noise: horses clip-clopping, traders and envoys from the corners of Europe, merchants arguing with one another—ostensibly over who has the right to sell linens, leather, and jewels to the courtiers—aristocrats, soldiers, and serfs all here to petition the Court for favor.

He gives me that inscrutable "keeper of secrets" look that makes me think his day job may be less knowledge management (as in IT, in my day) and more spy.

"I'm sorry to disappoint, Carlotta. Such a feat would require a royal declaration from young King Louis himself, which, after your recent imprisonment, would be unlikely. I would hardly expect him to offer you the title 'Duchess of Maryland' at this moment. The forger would be at great risk, as would you."

I sigh. It occurs to me that even in our own times, official documents—birth, marriage, voter registration—can lead to suspicion.

"I dunno. Could've at least brought some sealing wax."

We are drawing close enough to the palace that we begin to see courtiers and soldiers milling about. And boys and girls who look like mini courtiers, dressed in silks, their little skirts dragging in the dust; such fancy little duds that I can't imagine how they would ever play, run, dance, roll in the grass, or get holes in their stockings.

Or maybe playing's against the law here.

"These kids—what happens if they get dirty?" I half expect Esme to provide narration, but she has fallen silent.

I drape my arms on the sill of the open window and crank my head around to watch a bewigged boy of about nine or ten running past while twirling a hula-hoop-ish thing, while a girl shrieks and chases after him. I smile at the black-and-white spotted spaniel yapping at her heels.

CHILDREN'S GAMES

Credit: Pieter Bruegel the Elder, Public Domain

"I mean, it's not like somebody just throws their embroidered finery into the washing machine. Don't you think that's strange, Esme?"

When Esme still doesn't respond, I throw the question to my just-in-time pal.

"So, Kairos, what's the rule on childhood here?"

"Rule?"

"Yeah, you know. Like 'Children should be seen and not heard?'"

"Oh, no, Charlotte," Kairos corrects. "This is the age of 'natural' pedagogy, where children are given microscopes and gardening tools and instructed to explore the natural sciences. You may have heard the theory about children as blank slates, their heads waiting to be filled with reason? 'Instruction with delight,' they call it. Rousseau's theory being all the rage."

"Rousseau," I repeat, scanning my memory neurons for a reference from history class. "The Noble Savage? He was obsessed with Native Americans, wasn't he?"

Noble savages, uncorrupted by civilization—the idea is bizarre to my twenty-first-century brain. It makes me wonder how Beth, as a mixed-race, African American girl, would be received here.

But first things first.

Apparently, the reason Esme's silent is that she—or my phone, rather—is running out of juice. I need to somehow recharge it in case Billy's devised some sort of remote-viewing dashboard to spy on us from home.

"Oh, crap!" I look around the sedan chair in a panic. "Just what I was afraid of."

"What's wrong?" Kairos queries.

"First off, you'll recall that our bike tablet's navigation is far more than navigation. And, second off, said bike is stashed somewhere back in the woods outside nowheresville. And third off, young Garçon back there, who seemed so simple? He was shrewd enough to abscond with my backpack!"

"Oh, I would not worry yourself," Kairos says with assurance.

"Oh, you wouldn't, would you?! That tablet's only my life."

"You look very much alive without it," Kairos laughs.

I glare at him. Kairos knows the truth of this crime-in-any-other-century better than almost anyone besides Billy.

"What is that Simple Simon going to do with your tablet, Charlotte? Pawn it? No one in their right mind would touch your 'magic' box. If he tries to implicate you in some scheme, who's going to believe him? And he can't open that device without your eyes, no?"

"My eyes. Ha. Ha. That tablet's been souped up, and it syncs with my phone . . ."

"May I remind you, fair Dudette, that you were the original time-travel beta-tester using our original cloud programming? So now that you've downloaded an upgraded Operation Firenze from the cloud to your own tablet . . ."

"The Time Travel Express. Can't leave home without it!" I exclaim, trying halfheartedly to joke about it.

Except now I have.

"Well, I'll at least charge up my phone while I can." I pull my phone and the solar charging bank from my pouch and then sit my butt on the open window and, with my head out, affix the charger to the outside roof of the sedan chair where it can soak up the sun.

Luckily, I modified it to stick onto anything, grateful to Post-it note technology—so it can be removed without a trace. Nothing would be more disastrous than having a twenty-first-century device fall from the sky only to be smashed under the weight of a team of horses—or picked up by some nosy nobleman who might then start a witch hunt. I mean, no one would want to go through that trial-by-fire again.

"We are charging!" I cry, managing despite the bumpy ride to mount the charger on the roof of the sedan chair.

That taken care of, I slither back inside the cabin and see if I can get my bearings based on that map. The closer we get to the palace, the glitterier the place looks. Majestic statues, deep green gardens, landscapes and forests. The famed fountains. But topping it all, the gigantic palace shimmers. The roof, doors, gates, and windows gleam with gold leaf. I wonder whether King Louis might actually be in residence.

"*En garde!*" shouts a girl's voice off to our right. It is rejoined by a familiar charge. More karate than épée, "*Ki-yah. BANZAI! Hai!*"

I stare at Kairos, stupefied. It can't be.

Beth.

XXVII.

WHEN WEST MEETS EAST

What looked bad before suddenly gets weirder

"*A*llez!" A different female voice is carried by the breeze. I poke my head out the window to get a closer listen.

"So it's '*allez*' to get started?" Again, the familiar voice. In English, no less.

"Beth?!" I marvel, bringing my head inside the carriage again.

"To commence, *oui*," that other girl replies in accented English. "Follow me, now, as I lunge forward, then back, and parry with my sword."

"This is nuts. We've got to see if it's her, K."

"*Vite, messieurs, à droite*," Kairos calls to the porters, knocking twice against the ceiling.

Our porters trot right onto a cobbled path toward another splendiferous fountain, this one actually fully operational, where shiny bronze dragons and sea nymphs undulate out of the basin, gargling water and spouting sprays into the air. The center one shoots water high overhead, with the play of morning sunlight dancing off the droplets as they descend.

VERSAILLES BASIN OF APOLLO FOUNTAIN

"Wait. No. Stop right here!"

As two young women with swords come into view, Kairos knocks three times, and we stop short. I almost fly out of my seat.

Grabbing the hem of my copious skirts, I can hardly push open the sedan chair door fast enough to jump down, almost forgetting to grab my phone and charging pack off the top.

"I can't believe . . . Beth?" I shout, seeing the familiar figure of my BFOO hopping around holding a sword using both hands, and lunging at her sparring partner, a tall, gangly French girl, who looks to be a little older than us, dressed in men's trousers.

"I thought you were dead!"

"Ciao, Charley!" says Beth with a grin—a calmer reply than I would've expected after my drop-dead remark.

I note she is wearing a short red jacket with a hood and a full-petticoated skirt atop her Wonder Woman armor, her chest covered with a heavy leather vest, and it's the Beth in the TikTok. Weirdly, her face looks pale under heavy makeup, with rouged cheeks, in the style of the day.

"Hey, check this out. *En garde!*" Beth slashes the épée through the air right in front of me, barely missing my nose.

"Beth? Where the heck . . . cut it out! I'm serious, I thought you died! After I saw your Nats cap on the head of a dead girl back at the cemetery . . ."

"It flew off my head, what with that massive wind last night," she said. "And I almost threw up when that wind picked me up and dropped me down on my head. I must've passed out for a hot second, because I lost you and woke up at some other spot in the cemetery."

She looks at me, suddenly not sure of her story.

"Wait. Didn't you get blown up in that derecho back at the cemetery?"

"Yeah, well, no. Almost one hundred percent sure that's not what happened. Not in Rock Creek Cemetery anyway."

"Whatever. Anyways, Charley, I'm almost a hundred percent sure this is, like, the best dream ever. Except for that awful stink at the cemetery." She stops and ponders a minute. "Say, how'd you get into my dream, anyway?"

I struggle with how I'm going to break the news that that was back then. And we've both landed in a different now. After all, Beth's like the biggest time travel skeptic ever.

"It's like . . ." I start to explain, pointing with my left hand in the direction of where we came from. And then, with my right, wave my fingers like, hey, this sure is a future in the past we didn't plan for.

"And, so, now, we are here. Wonder Woman with baseball cap on and Fencer Girl with baseball cap gone. See?"

"Nope, don't get it."

Beth grips with both hands to heft the sword again. "*Allez!*" she cries, stepping forward into a lunge. I jump away to avoid an accidental stabbing.

Immediately, I bump into the other girl, who stops me in my tracks. She looks vaguely familiar—was she the girl in Beth's social media posts?

Disregarding the fact that I've almost knocked her down, TikTok girl takes her own starting position. The way she brandishes the sword, while Beth can barely heft it with two hands, I get that someone has been working out. Her blouse is ruffled and laced up the front, with a hint of a bosom underneath. I'm guessing the puffy sleeves, like a man's shirt in the style of the day, are what gives her the range of motion for dueling. (Mind you, the whole getup leaves her super exposed to injury compared to the gear serious fencers sport today, with their near impenetrable spacesuits and face masks.)

Her hair is piled on top of her head, her face is painted white, and her cheeks are rouged in red. To my eyes, she looks almost painted for the stage—but in this day and age, a girl masquerading as a boy.

PORTRAIT OF ÉMILIE

Credit: Marianne Loir, Public Domain

"Hey, Charley, meet my new bestie, Émilie. She's teaching me how to fence. But I keep mixing in karate terms. Right, *sensai?*"

"Bestie . . . umm . . . Em—Émilie?" I stare, dumbstruck.

At this, Émilie plants her épée in the soft grass next to the fountain and stares right back at me.

"You're Émilie?"

"*Comme tu veux.*" Émilie relents with a charming twinkle of laughter. She raises a hand.

Before I can figure out if I'm supposed to shake it or kiss it, she turns and slaps Beth's raised hand, clearly a modern move Bethy's taught her.

"*Tape m'en cinq*," she shouts, and they both let out a laugh.

High five.

"*But of course*." Beth manages to mimic the accent, a sort of pidgin Franglais.

I gasp. "Émilie. *No.* It's not . . ." I turn to Beth, then to her adversary, then back. "No. This is so wrong . . ."

"Gabrielle Émilie Le Tonnelier de Breteuil." She turns toward me and bows.

"Hey, Émilie, meet my best friend from home, Charley."

"Charlotte Morton," I curtsy, at a loss about what the expected Court greeting should be in this day and age.

"Charlotte," Émilie moves in and kisses me on each cheek, twice. "*Enchantée.*"

"Yeah, same here. I mean, *Oui, enchantée.* But wait: Beth, how did you . . . ?" I twist my head around to see Bethy beaming with satisfaction. "And Émilie, how did you . . . and Beth . . . er, meet?"

Beth jumps in. "Charley, you wouldn't believe. She lives in this beautiful place in Paris, and she was on her way here"—she gestures, to take in the whole royal landscape—"and when I explained I was a little lost, she said, Why not join me; I'm going to the palace. And so, here we are!"

I see Émilie nodding, confirming Beth's account.

"And this is, like, the most amazing cosplay. Émilie's father has this cool apartment here, and we rummaged through her closets—more like a designer boutique dressing room—to find me this costume for the duel. Like a female Musketeer." She does her model spin. "And the cosplay makeup—don't you love?!"

Kairos comes up behind me, startling me. "You look stunning, Elisabeth," he murmurs.

She stares. "Do I *know* you?"

"You have," he says, cryptically.

"Oh, where are my manners? Bethy, Kairos. Kairos, Beth and Émilie." He bows.

"Kairos is an old friend from home who . . ."

"You know, it's like I'm in a dream, or some AR game," Beth interrupts. "Hey, Charley—I lost my phone. Could you take a pic of me and Émilie here?"

Cosplay. Dream. Augmented reality. Delusional.

It's then I remember I have Beth's phone. "Here—I found it." I'm practically in shock about the whole thing.

"Uh-mazing! You're the best, Charley! Umm, next to Émilie, here." She grabs the phone from my hand to unlock it and opens Photos. "Okay, go!"

As Émilie and Beth strike various poses in front of Versailles Palace, I use her phone to start a video instead. If the phone survives the journey back to our world—that is, if *we* survive the journey ahead—no doubt Bethy's gonna want to YouTube it.

"Here ya go." With that, I slip Beth back her phone, double-checking phone cases to make sure I don't accidentally mix it up with mine.

"Um-hmm. Good. Your hand's a little shaky, though." Bethy flips through the video, and on to recent photos. "Wait, this is from before, right?" She's checking to be sure our earlier Halloween videos—in Rock Creek Park, no less—are also still there.

"Wow, some of these are really bad. We'll have to reshoot."

If she recognizes the vast spacetime chasm between her then and now, she's not showing it.

She starts to tell Émilie about her "Fashion Forward" channel, and that she should really check it out because she's going to be going to fashion design school in a couple of years.

"I must admire any girl who dares attempt what only men are encouraged to do," says the cross-dressing (eighteenth-century-style) girl standing in front of me.

"Yeah, Charley. What Émilie said," Beth echoes.

"Really, Beth?"

"After I lost you in Rock Creek Cemetery, this wind blew up and carried me along with it. Next thing I know, I'm in a whole different part of the cemetery."

I stand with my mouth agape. "Beth . . ."

"Anyways, Émilie was the first person I met who could understand a little English. She shares my fashion passion, and we got to practice—um, how do you say—martial arts?"

"*Mais oui, un des arts maréchaux,*" Émilie affirms.

"Yeah, and then there's the whole dueling thing. She says I'll be good enough to fight the duel master if I keep at it."

Challenging the master to a duel? Is that even a thing girls do here?

"It's like, so amazing!"

"Umm, Beth . . . ?"

"I'm not exactly sure how I got to dreaming in French," she continues, "except that after that whole Homecoming thing with Guy . . . you know, hanging out with him has really helped me improve my comprehension, even if my conversation skills pretty much suck."

"First we tried Latin . . ." Émilie throws up her hands. "*Impossible!*"

"I told her I'm fluent in Ig-pay Atin-lay." Bethy giggles.

Émilie gives Beth another *tape m'en cinq*.

"Her French must be perfected," Émilie confides, coming close, "if she is to meet my friends at Court. A beautiful girl with dark skin—she shall be *bien célébrée—la belle de Versailles!*"

"Famous. *Moi*. Imagine!" Beth's practically out of her mind at the flattery.

Beth's dark skin. Émilie's last comment—what it intimates is slightly horrifying. As a girl of color, Beth might either be considered exotic—something to go on display—or dangerous. For a Black girl at home, well, there's a whole debate going on about fairness and equity, but for an African- American girl at the Court of Versailles . . . ? Well, suffice it to say that, in 1724, that would be impossible, given that it's almost certain she would have to be here as someone's property.

I stop for a moment, torn between conversing with the future Marquise du Châtelet and getting Bethy to pay attention to what's really going on. Another impossible thing.

"Let us practice *encore une fois*, Elisabeth," Émilie says, pulling on her fencing gloves and picking up her sword.

"Watch and learn, Charley." Beth pulls on some old fencing gloves and assumes the fencer's stance again.

"*Allez!*"

Beth charges at Émilie, who parries and spins, confident as she is in the art. Even with a hard clash of metal, Beth's sword remains in her awkward, two-handed grip.

"*Brava, Elisabeth!*"

I am relieved when Émilie doesn't attempt another high five, but smiles in that polite, not quite sincere way that you see royals do in the movies.

Beth grins and turns to me. "Yep. That's how we do it. Right, Em?"

Seeing her opponent off guard, Émilie again parries, slicing through the air right at her student. Beth pivots away, but too late.

"You must not let your guard down, Elisabeth!" shouts Émilie.

A bead of blood forms on Beth's forearm. Almost immediately, it seems, a cloud of gnats and flies begins to swarm around her.

"Youch! It's so real here that I'd almost swear you cut me," she says, looking down at her arm almost as if it wasn't hers.

"Beth!" I fumble beneath my skirts to search for the tissues I swear I stuffed in my pouch. "You are not dreaming this!"

Before I can fish out the Kleenex, Émilie pulls out a monogrammed handkerchief (looks like the initials spell out **GET-B**) from beneath her ruffled sleeve.

"*Desolée, m'amie.* But proof. You are indeed flesh"—she applies pressure to Bethy's arm—"and blood." Swatting away the bugs, she wraps her *mouchoir* around Beth's wrist.

I get a flash of insight into how the French words *mouchoirs*, meaning handkerchiefs, and *mouches*, meaning flies, could be connected.

Émilie, it seems, suffers no illusions about our being in Dreamland.

"I have always been fascinated by the possibility of many worlds, many suns, and another girl like me who inhabits a different time," says Émilie.

"Many worlds, many . . . wait. What . . . what are you talking about?" Beth grabs the hankie, squeezing her arm, as a spidery capillary of blood from her wrist soaks its way into the linen.

"It's quantum physics, Beth. You know, the class we're in together?! The multiverse theory?"

"Shhh, Charley. Don't be rude! Let Émilie explain it." Beth seems to be developing a girl crush.

"Of course, I enjoy the material comforts here," Émilie continues undaunted by our interruption. "The balls, and games, the gossips at Court. And my jewels and clothes!"

Beth nods, not even noticing that the kerchief is now soaked in blood. She worships at the altar of the glamorous world Émilie describes.

But Beth's bleeding out, and I've got to keep her alive, if only to get us back to our own reality someday. I fumble again through my pouch. "Er, umm, Beth, I've got some Kleenex . . ."

Too late, I extract the tissues and try to pass them over to my BFOO. I'm a little annoyed at her getting Émilie's attention. And Émilie being more a Beth clone than the Enlightenment brainiac I was expecting.

"Surely, though, this is but one reality we inhabit," Émilie continues, looking over at me, like I'm supposed to edify her on a mathematical proof that supposedly links string theory, multiple dimensions beyond the three or four we know, and the idea that we are living in a universe of many universes—the multiverse.

"Many suns?" I repeat, wondering if she might have more of a mind than I was giving her credit for.

"*Oui*. Suns. *Soleils?*" repeats the French girl, looking me up and down now as if for the first time.

"I guess so. *Peut-être*, I mean."

I apply pressure with the clean tissues on Beth's arm. It would be too hard to untangle the math for her without using my calculator. And even if Esme could help, well, that level of calculus might raise an eyebrow or two.

She seems disappointed, like she was expecting a different answer.

"*Mais, à vrai dire*, your manners, Charlotte, are *barbarian*. Your dress is barely acceptable in civilized society. Nor your speech. I must imagine you are, like Elisabeth, *à l'étranger?*"

Strangers abroad. Understatement of the year! But we can't let on to being *that* strange—as in, *girls from three hundred years in the future* strange.

"*Oui, c'est vrai*," I respond slowly. "We're from *l'Amerique*."

Beth lifts the hankie. The bleeding has stopped. She eyes the wound in wonder, then taps her arm to see if it's real. "Sore!"

"*Oui*, so Elisabeth has informed me. I have read horrifying tales of the natives of your land," Émilie says. "That they are savages who kidnap white women and brutalize them. And your people, Elisabeth? Are they noble savages, or beasts?"

"Whoa! So. Not. Cool, Émilie." I feel compelled to protect her.

But Beth's already wandered off. (And she calls *me* ADD Girl!) I spy her some yards away, lifting the épée, examining her arm to make sure the bleeding's stopped, then lunging and stabbing at the air. "*Hai-ya!*" She runs back in a whirl, quite full of herself.

"Did you see that? I mean, it's wild! This feels like the real-est, most immersive virtual reality game ever. They're really getting good with the technology," she says, acting like she's suffering a manic episode. "Like, how you're even part of my experience, Charley! Amaze-balls."

I'll admit, it sounds like a fish tale, and if I hadn't lived it myself, I wouldn't believe it either.

But for someone who's a disbeliever, who's just been stabbed, with real blood, Beth seems remarkably blasé (it's cool that the French invented that word for "chill" long before we got hip to it).

Émilie, who, to be fair, has likely never seen a person of color before (and I can't blame her for being a girl of her time, when slavery is still legal and the French are off colonizing Louisiana), has been taking in Bethy's ranting.

"Charlotte, is something wrong with your friend here? I am concerned she is acting *complètement bête.*" She circles her finger around her ear and rolls her eyes.

I suddenly flash back to doing karaoke with Billy to a scene from *Aladdin.* "Sadly, yes. She is my sister. She's a little, how you say, crazy." I circle my finger empathetically.

Bethy is shocked. "I am so not crazy. And I am most definitely not your sister."

I grab Bethy by the hand and shake my head. "She thinks she's to marry the Sultan!"

I think to myself how Billy would immediately chime in, "She thinks the monkey *is* the Sultan!" We used to act out this scene as kids, just like this, so many times.

In the pause, Émilie rushes to Beth's defense. "A sultan! This is a marriage so many young girls have dreamt of! And of course, your skin! *Bien sûr*, she would be a *Mahométane*."

Muslim. Clearly, the cultural references have all landed wrong. This could not possibly be going any worse!

"Beth, I think we should go," I whisper in her ear, grabbing her by the hand.

Beth appears to be suffering a bit of delayed shock.

"Before your arm . . ." I take off the bloody handkerchief and daub it gently with my remaining tissue.

She pulls her arm away. "I'll be fine. It's a scratch. And it isn't even real."

"Well, if you're going to be so stubborn!" I stomp my foot. I really want to punch her, but she's the one with the sword.

Émilie grabs her handkerchief back, balls it up, and stuffs it into her bustier. Which frankly, kind of grosses me out. She looks at the ugly scab pussing over on Bethy's arm.

"Elisabeth, I must agree with Charlotte, here. You really must allow the Court doctor to look at your arm," Émilie says. "For now, perhaps a sniff of tobacco to ward off plague . . ."

She pulls out from her sleeve a beautiful red enamel snuffbox, looking much like the one I bought from the coin shop at home, and opens it gently lest the powder pour out accidentally. I get a waft of some perfumed scent.

"What a lovely little collectible box, Émilie," Beth says, forgetting the scabbing arm. "And that perfume—do I detect Chanel?"

"I do not know any Chanel, but I have a whole collection of snuff-boxes. If you'd like, you may take this one."

"But what do you do with it?" Now Beth's curious.

"Beth," I warn in a low voice, "this snuff tobacco is cancerous. They make it smell good to get you started and then deliver a wallop of nicotine to keep you taking it. You know, like flavored e-cigarettes?"

Émilie looks at me like I must have fallen from the sky. Which, all things considered, wouldn't be that far from the truth.

"I believe this *marque* is derived from your colonies. Maryland—do you know it?"

I turn red and squeeze Beth's arm so she can't blurt out our own provenance. "Youch, Charley! That hurts."

But Émilie is back at her demonstration. "You take a pinch of powder, like this," she demonstrates the amount, then shoves it up her nose and snorts. "It will ward off unhealthy miasmas until you can see the good doctor."

Beth leans over, just about to try it for herself, when I accidental-ly-on-purpose knock Émilie's arm hard enough to scatter the snuff, and keep just enough of my wits about me to grab her snuffbox for later inspection, to compare with the one I got from home.

"*Mon dieu!* What are you doing?" Émilie grabs my shoulder to keep from slipping, giving me just enough time to add the box to my pouch.

"Charley, how rude!" Beth scolds. "She's just trying to keep the infection from spreading before we can reach the doctor."

Now, I've watched *Versailles* on Netflix, and I know how all these King Louis kept the Court, with all its gossip, scandal, and intrigue around them. I even remember an episode where courtiers went around poisoning one another, including the doctor. No way I'm letting Bethy near that mad house of mirrors (literally).

I have a better idea.

"Em, would you happen to have, like, a first-aid kit? You know—arnica, bandages, clean water, and the like?"

"Arnica? My nursemaid has ointments in her medicine chest—yes, she will be brilliant at that. After all, it was she who raised me and my three brothers. Although, I must say, I have more often been the one who suffered from injury—jumping horses, playing *cligne-musette*"—which Esme informs me is what they called hide-and-seek—"climbing into trees, and the like."

Finally, here's the girl who sounds less like drama-queen Beth and more like me, levelheaded and sensible. And more tomboy than debutante, despite her status as the daughter of the Baron de Breteuil, former introducer of ambassadors, diplomats visiting at Court.

"*Suivez-moi*," she commands. And, as we proceed, I push Beth to follow.

XXVIII.

INFLUENCERS AND FASHION FAUX PAS

Hall of Mirrors fun-house ride and sipping on the King's
hot chocolate

Émilie's tastes are impeccable . . . What she sees, she wants and her
eyesight is remarkably keen.

—**Voltaire**

MUSIC ROOM, VERSAILLES

Photo: Robin Stevens Payes

We enter a grand salon inside this overwhelming castle, with its high ceilings and gilded mirrors. The white walls and doors are carved within an inch of their lives. I'm aching to get my fingers on the harpsichord. I've never played one before, but I've graduated from violin only to violin and piano, thanks to Mamma's ongoing prodding. I hate practicing, but I do love to play around.

And, of course, we're back to composing together, Mamma and me. After "Leo," there was "On the Witches' Express," which isn't at all like you'd expect. 'Cause in my experience, "witches" aren't evil, so much as misunderstood.

And now, I'm hearing music playing on that harpsichord that's just waiting for my fingers on its keyboard—maybe it's just a lullaby for the twins, that could go something like, "Leap-time, hearts a-fire / Dream time, magic-inspired." I definitely want them to experience the same passion for life, love of learning, and awe and wonder for the possible that has propelled me and keeps me going.

Bethy's in awe. Living in the gilded splendor at the Court of Versailles would undoubtedly feel like the most amazing dream ever for a girl with influencer ambitions.

I'm nervous. Walking into the palace, even escorted by our new friend, we encounter suspicious looks from courtiers, and women taking sidelong glances at us beneath their fluttering fans. And perfume to the high heavens and atrocious hairstyles powdered so thickly and shedding clouds of talc or something probably equally carcinogenic, that every time we pass someone, I sneeze.

And that's just the men!

I feel my heart beating out of my chest.

I can't help but recall that other time I was led into a palace where the leader of Florence found my tablet flashing all the accumulated knowledge of the twenty-first century, and immediately called for his armed guards to seize me for witchcraft.

I barely make it into hiding.

"Ooh, awesome. Is this your 'apartment,' Émilie?" Beth calls out, skipping along behind Émilie, evidently unawares of the very real threat of burning at the stake.

"Not ours. La Montespan."

Whoa. The Marquise de Montespan. This could be bad. I recognize her name from the Netflix series as the mistress of Louis XIV. I wonder if she is dead in this time zone.

Beth, distracted by the finery and stopping and staring as if she were at a museum, must run to keep up. "It's so posh. Em, do you think I could create a red carpet walk with Charley to video my YouTube here? I'm dying to show off her dress and explain the technology behind it. Think the Montespan would mind?"

This gives me the chills.

Émilie turns, her confusion showing. "What do you mean, *chère* Elisabeth?"

"Of course, if you have a couture dress, you could definitely be in my YouTube. I'd probably wanna redo your makeup, though. Who do you follow?"

Émilie raises an eyebrow. "*Whom* do I follow?"

"*Oui*. You know—Beauty Glam Paris? The Very French Girl? You know, the big fashion influencers."

They're all YouTubers. Hardly a household name here. Besides, I am definitely not up for being turned into a mannequin for Beth—in this time or any other.

"Oh, I'm pretty sure you'd have to get lots of permissions to shoot here, Beth," I chime in. "It being a historic place, and all."

An old schoolmarmy lady enters in a hurry. She is trim under her high-necked brown-tan-and-black-petticoated dress, a lace veil covering her graying hair. She looks salty, and harrumphs when she spies us. She must be Émilie's minder.

"Governess," says Émilie, grabbing Bethy by the arm to show her the wound, "would you be so good as to fetch some arnica for my new friends here? They are visiting from America."

Looking us over from head to toe, her servant turns up her nose in disdain, as if we're not worthy of her time. "We must first ask *Monseigneur le Baron* if he approves," says her servant, indicating that Émilie's father has VIP status and would judge us foreigners accordingly.

In other words, we should mind our Ps and Qs.

"First, *un chocolat chaud, grâce au roi.*"

A uniformed servant marches in, balancing a large, ornately decorated silver tray, three French porcelain cups and saucers, and tiny silver spoons that clatter until she sets the tray down on a side table.

Finally! I sigh—something to restore us.

From a steaming silver pot with a spout wafts the aroma of chocolate so strong, I can practically taste it. My tummy rumbles to remind me I haven't eaten in eons.

"I thought I might find you here, *mademoiselle*," says this Madame So-and-So. "I brought you all a *chocolat chaud*, the King's favorite, boiled up with the egg yolk of one of the royal hens." Looking down her nose at us, she sneers, "Let us see if it is to the taste of your new friends here, *mademoiselle*."

Behind my hand, I whisper to Beth, "Must be the hen that laid the golden egg."

"Not a goose?" Beth glances over at what's streaming out of the pot and stifles a giggle.

The governess adds, "Chocolate, of course, is known for its aphrodisiac properties—and this is the King's own recipe. The potion is perfect for a girl about to meet her future husband."

"Hmm, like, Love Potion Numero Uno?" Beth asks rhetorically. "Wonder if Chanel carries it. Or we could concoct something original—like 'A scent fit for royals, to win the boy—or girl—of your dreams,' or something—and talk about it on Fashion Forward. Just think, Charley; we'd slay it!"

Beth's imagination is clearly running away with her.

Émilie groans. "Another suitor whom *Maman* would have me marry for his money and title. It would seem as if girls are born only to deceive—this being the only intellectual exercise allowed them."

"Yes, yes! Exactly that! We are free in every way that men are. Free to learn; free to find a career; free to become mothers; free even to fly into outer space," I proclaim, then clap my hand over my mouth, recognizing my gaffe.

Too late, I detect the look in Émilie's eye, like *What do you know that I don't?*

I don't dare continue this conversation. Introducing our twenty-first-century ideas about gender equality would most definitely change the timeline.

I decide to take another tack. "Wait, are you to be matched up today, Émilie?"

"Let us choose for ourselves our path in life . . ." she muses.

But this girl seems to already have her own notions about the place of women: alongside, and not behind men. I think about my own choices, and wonder if I'm on the right path. And then I wonder what Billy's up to right now.

"But to have an equal partner in life . . ." Émilie wrinkles her nose into a frown and launches back into her diatribe. "If I were king, I would have women participate in all human rights—"

"*Mais oui, mademoiselle,*" interjects her governess, "but, alas, you are not. And your friends here seem to have odd notions about one's proper place in society."

She looks me up and down and walks around me, touching my dress. I can see her wheels spinning. She has no money or title. Apparently, no manners. She doesn't even bother with Beth, whom she's evidently taken to be my servant. Whether it's Beth's totes inappropriate costume, dark skin, or mannerisms, I'm not sure, but the governess's dismissive look is unmistakable.

"But of course, I have been remiss in introducing you. Elisabeth, Charlotte, meet Charlotte," Émilie responds by way of apology. "*Une autre Charlotte,* of course, Duchesse de Ventadour. She was young King Louis's governess, and now she is mine."

"That's a lewk," Bethy snarks in my ear, giving the duchess the once-over. I'm guessing she's insulted at being ghosted.

"Bethy, hush," I hiss.

Émilie bows in our direction. "Elisabeth and Charlotte are the daughters of a high-ranking trade envoy from the Colonies, whom Papa has previously introduced to the Old King."

The Old King. It was Louis XIV who built Versailles into a royal palace from a hunting lodge. I curtsy in a hurry and swat Beth on the back with a nod to do the same.

Reaching out a hand, I blurt out, "*Un plaisir, madame la duchesse.*"

"Alas, but I'm afraid my dear governess does not *tape m'en cinq*, Elisabeth," grins Émilie. "Such a greeting is a sign of highest honor and respect in America," she explains to her governess, who looks affronted.

"Yo, Émilie. I see you over there throwing shade," Beth exclaims, going in for a fist bump. It would seem this twenty-first-century gesture of congrats is about to join the high five as the Court's secret handshake.

I giggle despite myself. It is clear the governess thinks we are savages, and where Court etiquette is concerned, I'd have to agree. None of the bowing and scraping, or kissing of rings. I mean, freedom from the tyranny of kings was the purpose of the whole American experiment from the beginning!

But, for now, Duchess Charlotte (not me, dear reader, but the nanny) is here on another mission: to get Émilie in line for a husband. Whipping out a painted fan to hide her lips and in fast French, she begins scolding her charge, eyes afire with disapproval. And Émilie gives it right back. I catch a French, "Your *maman*," and, "Where have you been?" and Émilie's pissed-off "Mind your own business, you old fart." (I made that "old fart" insult up, but I got her tone.) "*Attends ton Papa, le Baron!*" Which sounds like, "Just wait 'til your father hears about this!"

The insults and upsets are flying so fast, even Esme can't keep up with their squabble, but I bet I can fill in the blanks.

Beth slides closer to the unfolding drama like she's thirsty for it. "What's all the yammering about?"

"Not sure of the deets, but it's not hard to get the gist. Sounds like her mom's mad and sent the royal babysitter to chew her out. You know, the usual."

After all, we've had the same mother–daughter fights.

"Or else . . . !" Her governess concludes, or something in that vein, apparently having won this round. She closes her fan in triumph, throwing Beth and me a harsh look before scurrying away.

"I am so sorry, *mes amies*, but, you see, I am off to the baths, or *Maman* will be scandalized," Émilie concedes. "She is forcing me to meet a new suitor and she has commanded me to look presentable. It's that, or off to a convent!"

Mothers! Every century's got them.

"Presentable? But where are you going?" Beth begs her new girl crush. "Can I do your makeup? It'd be so much better . . ."

Émilie lets out a peal of laughter. "Perhaps another time," she says, making a French exit.

First off, I look around the room to make sure there's no one listening in.

"Beth, we need to talk."

Beth's ignorance is turning into a hazard.

"You got that right," Beth replies. "I don't know who's behind this whole immersive tech, or whatever this is, but I have a feeling Miss Em is the brains behind this game. Like, it's one thing to do a virtual tour of Versailles online, but it's another entirely to actually walk into it."

We're in a touchy situation, and Beth is not making it any easier.

To give myself a moment to consider, I sip my hot chocolate, pushing a cup toward Beth.

"Sit down, and try this, Beth. I'm sure it's delectable, if the King drinks it." If it's not poisoned, that is. I shudder at the thought and take another sip to calm my nerves.

"Beth, first off, this is not a game, or a dream."

As I bring the steamy cup to my lips for a second sip, a flood of memory overwhelms me, remembering another hot chocolate Mrs. Cooper had made for us when we were first coming up with the design for this dress.

That was real life then. This is real life now. Where's the dream?

"Cool." Beth rises from her chair and moves over to see the harpsichord. She presses ham-fistedly down on the keys, striking a cacophonous chord. "Charley, you know how to play this thing?"

I want to say "Shut up, Bethy," but then I'm drawn to tickle the keys. To play music again!

But first, I must drum the truth into Bethy's thick skull.

"You gotta listen to me, Beth. Or it could be, like, death at Court!"

She sits on the bench in front of the instrument. "Hmm. Death at Court. I like it! Good name for a boy band. Anyways, Charley, spill the tea . . ."

"Tea is, like, where we are—when we are. It's kind of outside of our reality, but not in the way you think. It is *a* reality."

She scowls at me expectantly, like she's watching to see if my head explodes.

"We are actually in France. In the eighteenth century." I consult Esme, who is now narrating the fact that the French slave trade is very much alive and well. "As an *African American girl* you must know that you are in danger here. Because, well"—I look down again at my phone—"slavery."

"Yeah, ha ha. Slavery. *Seriously*, Charley?"

"Yes, seriously, Beth! Look around. First off, have you seen anyone else around here whose skin is anything but white?"

"Powder. And rouge. I confess the makeup is so overdone. But it's all part of the game—don't you get that?"

"How many times do I need to say it: This. Is. Not. A. Game!"

"Uh-huh. Well, let's pretend what you say is true. How come I can understand Émilie then? Even though Guy's been teaching me slang, and how to cuss, the only official French I remember from ninth-grade French class is how to ask to use the bathroom. Remember? I almost flunked."

I look at her to see if she's gone totally batty. "You get her because she's been speaking English to you, Beth."

Undeterred by this fact, she continues. "And she's wearing boy's clothes. As a fashionista, I know about these things—it would be totally unacceptable for high society girls to wear pants before, let's say, the 1920s, when Coco Chanel made women's trousers trendy. For the record, that was only a hundred years ago, Charley!"

I could tell her about Mademoiselle de Maupin, a famous French opera singer in the seventeenth century, who scandalized the world by wearing pantaloons. Or that Émilie herself wore (will wear?) pants again to disguise herself in order to be admitted into the famous Café Gradot, a men's-only salon in Paris, to join in debates over physics and philosophy with the most famous writers and thinkers of her day.

But I don't want to argue. There are decisions that must be made here, and I guess I'm the one who'll have to make them.

It's at this very moment that we hear a lot of commotion outside, and then something that sounds like metal crashing into a stone wall and a stream of French curse words, making me jump.

I yank on the golden handles of the French doors that open up to the outside. They're jammed. There's a narrow marble balcony, and I catch a glimpse of one of the fountains, but I can't see directly beneath us, which is where it sounded like the clatter came from.

I plant my hand against the glass and squish my face into it to peer out and down into the glare of what must, by now, be a noonday sun.

A small boy wearing a mask is jumping up off the ground from under the smashed-up remnants of a wheeled vehicle of some sort.

"You're kidding me! Looks like . . . that crook . . . *Garçon!*" That rube who snared my backpack dared to follow me to the palace. And the clatter below was him crashing Billy's bike into the wall. And now, he appears to be running in this direction.

"Stop, thief!" I shout aloud, attracting the attention of a passing member of the Swiss Guard—those guys in the fancy uniforms and funky high hats who guard the King and never crack a smile, catching me as I try again to yank open the doors.

He brandishes a sword. "*Mademoiselle, qu'est-ce qu'il y a?*"

As he approaches, I get a closer look. That face is strangely familiar.

Beth is trying to pick out "Frère Jacques" on the harpsichord and pays no mind.

But I bow and try, with Esme's help, to explain the situation and ask his help: the thief, the bike, the stuck window.

"*Silence, mademoiselle! Ici, nous sommes directement en-dessous des chambres du Roi. Ce brouhaha, c'est raison assez de vous arrêter!*"

Arrest us?! It's that boy thief he should be arresting, not us. Besides, I will not submit to another second inside that horrid French prison. It's positively inhumane.

"*C'est pas nous!*"

He reaches out to grab me by the wrist and pulls me over toward the harpsichord to grab Bethy, too.

But the commotion has stopped her playing. She gives the guard a sharp look. "Guy! The guy of my dreams!"

It's a joke with them. Or at least the Guy we know in the twenty-first century.

This Guy looks momentarily astonished, like he, too, has seen something in her. But almost immediately, he pulls his blank face back on. He nervously starts yammering back in official court French and I see Bethy get this confused look on her face, like she's so thirsty she'll say anything to get him to recognize her, like her boyfriend back home, and I kick her before she can get us into more trouble.

Then who should bound into the room but that bandito on the bike, a bandana tied around his nose and mouth, but acting nothing like the country bumpkin, and sporting far more upscale breeches and a waistcoat down to the knees. He's also weirdly wearing some carved metal casque atop his head.

Closing in, I'm about to command this Guy guard to arrest him for running off with my stuff, when our new visitor loses the casque, revealing cascading curls and simultaneously rips off the bandana, shouting, "*Tcharrli!*"

"Carolina!" I grab that Energizer bunny as she runs headlong toward me, almost knocking me over, and pull her in close for the biggest hug ever.

XXIX.

Jumping Bean to the Rescue

Fashion Forward styles royalty at the Edge of Yesterday

"How'd you know where I was? And did you bring my backpack?" Carolina looks down and swirls her booted toe on the polished wooden floor. Her swashbuckling boy clothes and low-cut leather boots with red heels are yet another sign of the Old King's enduring influence on French fashion. Another nod to Beth.

Beth looks from me to the Jumping Bean and back. "Wait . . . you know this girl, Charley?"

I ignore her.

"*Servizio,*" Carolina bows in Beth's direction. "At your service."

"Carolina, where have you been—and how did you find us?"

"Kairos told me you were on a quest. That we could do it together. Can we, Tcharrli?"

"A quest. Is Kairos the maker?" Beth interjects. "Carolina? And a quest—is she part of the AR game too? Unreal."

I take note of how Carolina's English has improved, or Beth wouldn't be understanding this.

"Kairos! He knew where you were this whole time?"

"Tcharrli, you would not expect me to be here in *la Francia* all alone, waiting for you to arrive, would you?!"

"And where did you sleep?"

"Eh, you know, the lands of Prince Philippe, the Old King's brother? You passed through them earlier."

"And my backpack!" I demand, although I do not see it with her.

"Kairos has it for safekeeping."

I stomp my foot and sputter, "How dare he think—he's gonna keep *my* backpack safe? He's been doing a piss-poor job so far! And the golden compass that he never found? That's the only thing that's gonna get me . . . er, us . . . back! What's he gonna do, disguise himself in my clothes from home? They'd never fit! And speaking of keeping things safe, what about me? I need my stuff!"

Amid my tirade, I notice Beth wandering off, obviously not tuned in to the urgency of this moment, no matter how much I've tried. Obviously, something glittery has caught her attention: A table is set nearby with the King's tableware, as if ready for a banquet. Perhaps this is where Émilie will dine with her intended.

Beth picks up a golden plate and turns it over—doubtless to see who's made it. She's always said no one should have to wait to get married to pick out her good china. I can just see her dropping it and it shattering in a million pieces. A priceless piece of the King's place settings. And Guy and the royal guard accusing her of some other crime against the King, for who knows what innocent infraction! And imprisonment for us both.

It's another disaster in the making, but I can't keep being Beth's keeper—and anyways, Guy the Guard's gone off who knows where to do who knows what.

Besides, I've got more pressing worries, like what is up with Carolina? And why are we here?

I turn back to the little Bean. "Anyways, you knew where we were all this time?"

"The Gondi family, they were Florentine bankers back in the day." She stops, as if that explains it.

"And . . ."

"They were enemies of the de' Medici."

"And so . . . ?"

"They owned it. Our cousins."

"Wait. So you're saying your cousins from the fifteenth century were the Gondis who bought the land that dead King Louis XIV's brother lived on, and that somehow their descendants knew who you were and took you in for two years?"

(Stick with me, dear reader; I know it's sounding convoluted, even to me.)

"No, not their descendants. It is them—they got caught up in your explosion during *Carnevale*, and . . ."

"What the . . . ?"

"*Si.* And they were blasted here, same as I. And live in this time. Same now as I."

I do the math in my head. "Wait, so they're also, what . . . some 230 years in the future—*your* future?"

"Got'eem!" she says triumphantly. Like she made that meme up.

This whole jumbled timeline—people jumping ahead, back, and everywhere into some future, past, present, whatever—is completely messing with my head. Einstein's relativity is no longer sufficient to describe what's going on here. Concurrent timelines . . . alternative futures . . .

I grip Carolina's hand and look her dead in the eye. "So, this whole thing isn't a mistake. But I don't understand—what did you bring me here for, Carolina?"

But before she can answer, Guy the Swiss Guard dude who earlier made a French exit, ceremoniously marches in, escorting his newly glamorous charge.

Reading the room, Beth looks like she's about to go into her Fashion Forward mode.

"Walking the red carpet, friends, is Gabrielle Émilie!"

Conveniently, Guy halts and turns to Émilie to get a clue as to what's going on. Apparently, English is not his forte.

Composing her face into the serious look of a celebrity interviewer, Beth grabs the butter knife from the fancy table, holds it to her lips, and starts in on her Fashion Forward banter.

"Here we see the gorgeous Émilie, looking all *Bridgerton* in an original French-royals retro look. Who are you wearing, Em?"

She puts the butter knife up to Émilie's red painted lips. Émilie whacks her hand away.

"*L'attrapez! Elle porte un couteau!*"

Beth does, indeed, have a knife—albeit an ornately carved silver butter knife from the tray that she's using as a makeshift mic. It's bizarre to me that Émilie would be making such a fuss. After all, she didn't care when Beth was slashing wildly at her with the sword.

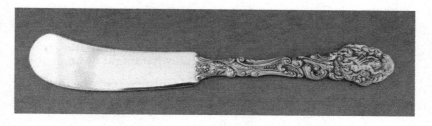

ANTIQUE BUTTER KNIFE

Credit: Antique Cupboard/Versailles by Gorham-Sterling

Apparently, this is different.

Guy grabs Beth's arms without a trace of hesitation. He unsheathes his own sword and holds it at her throat.

"*Mademoiselle*, I warned you," he growls in French, his meaning unmistakable in any language.

"Uh-oh," I say, letting go of Carolina's hand. "We've got to get out of here," I shout to Beth, who's locked between her two French crushes—a weird pre-Guy clone who's now got a sword drawn at her throat, and the very original Émilie who's suddenly turned against her.

I am not prepared for this sudden turn of events. I've got to think fast.

I know for a fact that all these ancient palaces have hidden panels and doors. For storage, or holding captives, playing hide-and-seek, whatever.

I put my ear to the wall and begin tapping, listening for a hollow place.

Carolina follows my lead, and when I hear her shriek "*Avanti!*" I come over to check for myself.

I look to see if there's a door, and find what might be an opening.

"This might be a good escape room," I whisper, realizing ironically that this would be a real experience in my own time. With that, I envision iron chains and lead balls, and other instruments of torture being stored there. Stop letting your imagination run wild, Charley, I tell myself.

Carolina's tapping on another wall adjacent to mine, but the room is so large, we might as well be on different sides of the planet.

"Come, Tcharrli," she hisses, her voice echoing through the wall to me. "Come!"

I follow her into a short hallway. "Wow—it's dark back here."

I shine my phone flashlight into the dark space, but it only lights a couple of feet ahead. I peer into what turns out to be a little room with a bed and a cradle in it—whether for a servant, or a servant's child, or, God forbid, the bastard child of the King's mistress, is anybody's guess.

"Tcharrli, look at this!" She pulls a china doll with a raggedy dress out from the cradle. It has one eye open and the other stuck in a permanent wink. It's a little creepy.

"Put that down, Bean. We're not here to play. We've got to find a back way out."

I advance a little farther into the space to see there's a panel with a handle on the other side of the room. "Found it!"

"Found you!" she calls back.

"Not playing, here! Beth is in danger. I'll see where this door goes. You go back and let Bethy know that everything's gonna be okay. We have an escape route."

"Si, of course." With that she scampers back into the main room.

"Just don't shut the panel all the way!" I call as she slips out.

I continue on.

The next door opens with a screeching sound that could wake the dead. I glance around to make sure no one's heard. All is silent.

This second room looks like it's for storage. As I ease my way around large dusty trunks piled high in my path, I can't help but wonder what inside. Costumes for the performers who come here to please the King? Musical instruments? Soldiers' uniforms for the French army? At any rate, it makes the going slow as I squeeze my way through the narrow passage and wipe a spider's sticky web off my face.

I feel a sneeze coming on, close my eyes, and hold my nose so I don't make too loud a noise. It's then that I stumble over it—an ancient trunk, out of which tumbles what look to be ancient books.

"Oh, crap!" I murmur, remembering the time I had to hide from Lorenzo de' Medici in just such a hidden closet containing ancient treasures, behind a palace wall. That time, in my clumsiness, I almost destroyed a world-famous and priceless painting by Botticelli and barely made it out alive!

Is history about to repeat itself?

XXX.

TIME LOOPS AND ECHOES

Magic spells and incantations—I am not a witch!

This time, my foot lands on what looks to be something of a literary treatise, unbound. I stoop down and pick up the pages, blowing off the dust carefully and then wiping everything gingerly with my sleeve.

"Oh my God, Carolina!" I shout, forgetting in my excitement that she'd returned to the main room. "Look what I just found!"

DE VIRIBUS QUANTITATIS

Suddenly my little apprentice is by my side, this time dragging a petrified Beth behind her.

"Why would Guy pull a sword for a stupid butter knife!" Beth is sputtering. "I would never threaten my new bestie . . ." She makes an attempt to pull herself together. "But then, it's impossible to really be scratched in a dream. Isn't it?" she looks to me for confirmation.

But I'm too excited about my discovery to address Beth's delusions. So long as she's safe.

I shine my phone flashlight on the pages of the book and motion to Carolina to look.

Scrutinizing the pages, she looks less interested.

"O, *si*," she says. "I recognize this. This is Fra Luca Pacioli's magic and mathematics work. Written with Leonardo, of course."

"Leonardo da Vinci?" The Maestro shadows me, even here. Or at least some of his writing does.

At once, we hear knocking on the walls from the outside and a rush of voices. I smell something smoldering, as if someone with a torch is trying to smoke us out of this room.

It's only a matter of time before they charge in—and I cannot bear to think what would happen if we—a deluded Wonder Woman, a Jumping Bean from who knows when, and me, so recently released from prison under the preposterous allegation that I was trying to raise the dead—what if they were to arrest us all together this time?

I look down again.

Leonardo's magic book. I could use a little magic right now.

I scan the pages, trying to decipher the Italian, when Esme (who has been long silent) kicks in with an explanation: "The treatise known as *De viribus quantitatis*. Written between 1496 and 1508, it contains the first reference to card tricks as well as guidance on how to juggle, eat fire, and make coins dance. It is also the first work to note that Leonardo was left-handed."

Like me.

"Juggling—that's funny," I say. "And making coins dance." I stare over at Carolina like she's got the answer to this riddle.

They're knocking on the walls of our escape room now, a chorus of voices shouting. It is all too familiar a feeling.

"We've must leave!" Carolina cautions. "I will assist. My title: magician's apprentice."

Who's the magician, I wonder.

"But what about Guy . . . and Émilie? Why's she suddenly so mad at me?" Beth chimes in.

I continue staring at the book. "What if Leonardo is leaving a puzzle for us to solve. Juggling. Making coins dance."

"Don't forget eating fire," Carolina adds.

Eating fire. Like this is the answer to our current conundrum.

"Think!" she challenges me. "Where would you find such an array of magic tricks?"

"A circus? The Medici Palace?"

"Where we are."

"Versailles!" I exclaim. "This palace holds the key!"

"And so do you," she reminds me. "The golden compass is your key to unlocking future worlds. And the secrets of fire."

"Future worlds. Secrets of fire." I'm so confused.

"Do not forget your secret superpower: time travel."

"My superpower. How'm I supposed to do this anyway? I only have Billy's compass"—I finger the tiny pendant around my neck—"since we never found the one I lost at the cemetery . . . and we always need two!"

Carolina takes off the bright blue scarf tied around her neck, turning it inside out to show the brilliant pattern of a peacock's tail. She twists it again, and it is now a red-white-and-blue American flag. (Note to self: From where we are, Betsy Ross won't be sewing the Stars and Stripes for another fifty years or so.)

"And now, *signorinas* watch closely! I will ask a friend to come up and help me with this trick," she continues. "Tcharrli?"

Although this whole exercise seems like a ridiculous waste of precious time, I go up and stand next to her. There is a pedestal on which she has placed the scarf.

"Anything there?" she asks.

I feel across the silk with my hand. The only thing underneath is the pedestal.

"*E cosi*," she continues, in what I think must be her native Italian (although I'm having doubts about where she—like Kairos—actually comes from). "*Alakazam uno, alakazam due, alakazam tre, e puf!*" She pulls away the scarf.

"Now give me your left hand," she continues, ever the clever young magician. She outlines my fingers and palm, then covers it with the scarf. I can feel only the silkiness against my skin.

"Please place your left hand over your heart." When I do, I touch Billy's mini compass charm on my necklace. At the same time, I hear the clang of metal against metal as something slips from the scarf down my bosom. "What the . . . ?"

"Please do one of your bows," she commands. As I curtsy, a cold metal thing slides down my bodice and hits the marble floor.

She bends down and picks up a second compass. She twirls it between her fingers and flips it into the air. "Ta-da!"

I gasp. "How'd you do that?"

"Shhh, do you not know? It's magic!"

I take it from her, that familiar golden compass, with all the pock-marks and scratches, well-worn from use over centuries.

I look at her, looking at me all wide-eyed and innocent.

"So you had it all the time! Did Kairos find it in the cemetery, Carolina?"

She shrugs, and walks back toward the panel where we first came in. "Shhh . . . !"

It makes me wonder what other magic tricks Kairos's baby sister has up her sleeve. And who taught them to her.

I keep two fingers on my necklace, just for security.

I see Carolina's mouth moving as she draws closer, maybe uttering some secret magic spell. Her finger stabs excitedly in Beth's direction.

"Fai la tua magia!"

I hear the rumble of voices, louder now, and choke from the smoke that's beginning to fill the room. Am I having flashbacks, or is this actually happening?

Nothing makes sense, and Esme has run out of juice, for now.

No matter. I stuff the phone in my dress pocket.

The magic had better be about to get bigger. Much bigger.

Beth has started coughing.

Suddenly the room feels like it's revolving. Maybe it's the smoke, or maybe it's PTSD, but this is more and more reminiscent of the bonfire of the vanities in Florence, where flames licked up around us, burning our feet and enveloping the air around us in smoke.

"Get down, Tcharrli!" Carolina cries as tendrils of smoke waft in to fill the room, until she is but a dim silhouette.

I squat low and cover my mouth with Kairos's cape to keep from inhaling the smoke. But I've lost Beth.

"Charley!"

"I've got you, Beth. Don't worry," I assure her, mostly for myself. "Quick, grab my hand!"

"This has turned into a nightmare," Beth whispers shakily, twining her fingers with mine.

I've never heard her so scared, even in the cemetery.

"I'm not having fun anymore. I'd do anything to wake up in my own bed."

"We're going!" I pull her close to me and we both lie down, cheeks resting on the cool tile where there is a reservoir of breathable air.

"Breathe, Bethy. Carolina, can you grab my hand?"

"Here," she calls out. I barely see a small lump a few feet from us—she must have thrown her own cape over herself for protection.

"Tcharrli, you must go. They are after Beth . . . and you!"

"Okay, checking out! But you—it's not safe here for you—you must come."

In all the hubbub, it occurs to me we haven't even planned out the when, the where, or the how. Even though Esme is right in my pocket, I don't know whether she's awake enough to program, or whether I could reset the dashboard with the right GPS calculations even if she was.

In the meantime, the spin of the room seems to be accelerating, along with the heat, and there's nary a breath of fresh air.

"Please, please, tell me we're not going to die here, God!" Beth implores. "Let me wake up and find out this is all just a hideous hallucination."

I pull Kairos's cape over Beth and me and pray we will not melt into the floor.

I dimly hear Carolina's excited echo, "K, we're out! Send me a postcard, Tcharrli!"

XXXI.
LEAP-TIME

An American exit: right portal; wrong off-ramp

I t's weird how, if you do a thing often enough, it becomes kind of second nature. For me, a fourth cycle through the clothes dryer of spacetime is not much worse than being struck by lightning while spiraling through Space Mountain with your eyes closed, no hands and no seat bars.

But time travel, even for the initiated, is still exhausting.

It's taken me a bit by surprise, of course. *Magia* flashes again in my mind. But magic is not a reasonable deduction for a science-adhering, evidence-seeking STEMinista, in any time zone. And our being in this time of the French Enlightenment and all, the sudden creation of a rare Earth–spacetime fart through which we may have popped would be a smelly explanation. But there it was . . . and here I am.

Like, wherever.

Until . . . *Bam!* Crash landing. I'll never get used to it.

Nevertheless, I have a massive headache, and Esme wakes up enough to inform me that we have switched time zones once again.

I can barely budge my brain, much less figure out where her voice is coming from.

I open my eyes a slit and detect that I'm tucked in a modern bed, under the covers, in a temperature-controlled environment. I follow a slice of moonlight streaming through lacy curtains and, squinting, see it fall on Bethy's sleeping face.

At a glance, I can tell we're no longer at Versailles, and judging from the fact there's no armed guard, no sword stands, and no Duchess So-and-So giving us the once-over, we must be safe. At least for now.

Feels like I should be doing a deeper scan to get my bearings, but my eyelids are so heavy, I can barely keep them open.

It's almost like I'm still hearing voices. I cradle the pillow around my ears to muffle the sound, and my hand closes on something small and round.

"Not now, Carolina," I mumble. "I'll do it later."

XXXII.

A Pandemic by Any Other Name

Whoopsie-daisy . . . looks like our GPS needs tweaking!

Someone gently rapping on the door rouses me enough to half-wake up. Squinting into a too-bright light streaming in through the curtained window, I hear a familiar voice. Somehow, I can't quite remember who it belongs to.

"Good morning, sleepyheads!"

"What time is it, Esme?" I mumble. I reach for my phone, which is plugged in to a modern wall socket, fully charged. In the process, I drop whatever it is I grabbed from under the pillow. It falls to the floor with a clunk.

I glance around. We're home. Or at Beth's house. And the thing I dropped—Émilie's snuffbox. I reach down to nab it before Beth notices and gets too curious. In the process, I almost fall out of bed.

"Morning!" The way-too-cheery voice is much closer now, practically screaming in my ears.

Quickly, I palm the snuffbox and somehow trigger a secret compartment. Two tiny portraits pop out. I glance down into my hand.

It's Émilie.

"Mom," Beth grumbles. "Too early."

And Voltaire.

"Rise and shine. The day is waiting!"

This is their familiar routine: Beth oversleeps; her mom tries to cajole her to come down and eat; Beth says it's too early; her mom sticks some waffles in the toaster and puts them out on the table with syrup; Beth complains she isn't hungry and definitely not for waffles; they end up in a fight to get Beth out the door in time for the school bus.

Typical teenager stuff.

I just about manage to squirrel away the box and the dollhouse-sized ceramic portraits just as Mrs. Cooper pushes open Beth's bedroom door.

"I brought you girls some yummy hot chocolate!"

"Nice!" I manage to squeak out, hoping I sound sufficiently grateful, even if I'm hardly feeling it.

"You are most welcome, my dear." She's wearing a white hospital mask that muffles her voice. Weird.

So now, trying to get a bead on *when we are*.

Riddle number one: How would a snuffbox from Émilie's teenage collection have a Voltaire pic inside when, as far as I know, they might not have even met by then? Riddle number two: How did it/I/we get here intact?

"Did you girls sleep well?"

Riddle number three: As she sets down the steamy mug, Mrs. C picks up a yellow-flowered cloth from next to me on the nightstand. I recognize the fabric from my Émilie dress. Then I notice it has elastic sewn into the ends to turn it into a mask like hers.

"I'm afraid I'm going to have to ask you to put this back on, Charlotte," she says, handing it to me. "I know you young people are much less susceptible to the virus than we older folks, but it's for everybody's protection, you know. And I promised your mother that having this sleepover would not turn into a mini-super-spreader event. It's only because we're all in a pod together that we even agreed to it."

What's she talking about—a pod? Super-spreader—what? Flu virus—how?

Better play along until I can get my bearings.

"Thank you so much!" I slide the elastic behind my ears, all the while wondering how the hell I'm supposed to drink through a mask.

Mrs. Cooper looks at me puzzlingly. "Oh, I didn't mean just yet, sweetheart. Of course, finish your chocolate first!"

"Right. I knew that." (Not!)

"Mom!" Beth groans exasperatedly.

"You're the best, Mrs. C!"

"We've got this," Beth's on autoresponder. "Oh, and yum! Thanks for the hot chocolate!"

"Okay. I don't want you girls to forget, you've got that big history project due on Monday. I heard you both working together late into the night, which is the only reason I said it was okay for Charley to sleep here, pandemic pod protocol, and all."

Beth gives a giant fake yawn. "Oh, yeah, so tired. Anyways, no worries, Mom. We got this!"

"And I'll remind you only this one time, Beth: You have to organize your portfolio for your college application. Your teachers may understand your needing more time since we're in virtual school right now, but Rhode Island School of Design will not."

Mrs. Cooper leaves the door ajar as she goes.

Beth gets out of bed and tiptoes to the door, looking down the hall to make sure it's clear. Then she yanks the door shut.

I blurt out. "Pandemic? Virtual school? College application? When the hell are we?"

I pick up the mug and throw the mask back on the reading table. Can't help wondering what's with all the hot chocolate—here, there, and everywhere.

"Thank God she's gone. My mom is crazy. I have no idea what she's talking about, but the best way to get her to leave us alone is basically to pretend to go along with her."

"Beth, your Mom's so nice—why d'ya gotta be so mean to her?" I ask, not for the first time. While this isn't a time for the hashtag-gratitude lecture, I need to figure out if Bethy went through what I went through. And then see whether she knows what a pandemic pod might be, and why she assumes we know we should wear masks, at home, on a sleepover, with our BFFs.

She falls back on her bed, squeezes her boyfriend pillow, and turns toward me.

"Gotta talk, Charley. I mean, you would not believe the super-real dream I had last night! There's princess girl, Émilie, then there's a duel where I got nicked after I nicked her"—here, Bethy pulls up her PJ top and, to my astonishment, I see a Harry Potter scar developing.

Beth hesitates a hot moment and stares hard at her scabbing skin—like, *What the f, did something really happen*—before apparently deciding to ignore the evidence and plowing on.

"Anyways, you showed up, and then we're in her castle . . . and she was going to walk the red carpet, but then something changed, and it was almost like the first time when the world started falling in on me and I was spinning and could barely catch a breath, there was so much pressure. Wait. Can you pass out in a dream?"

It's a question I really can't answer, just like how we got here from there, and what's with the pods and stuff.

I stare at her, just to make sure I'm registering this accurately.

"Ooph—you've still got that white schmutz on your face, Beth. It's probably got lead in it. Lemme just . . ."

I lick a finger and rub away the white makeup that would, in another century, have made her a French fashion plate and wipe it on the bedspread, and I launch into my "It's Not a Dream" speech before reminding myself it's hopeless. Besides, probably better that she not know the truth—she might start blabbing and ruin my and Billy's lives in the process. Again.

"Is it hot in here already, or is it just me?" I mumble.

I look down to note I'm wearing flannel jammies. Weird. I review the floor: my cowboy boots—check; a crumpled-up big petticoat, mud on its hem, and a tangle of yellow-flowered flowy fabric that, on closer inspection, still has tiny chips woven in.

Proof that I was there and now I'm back here.

Back before we left? That's what happened in our first adventure out of time, Billy's and mine.

But the clues don't add up. First off, when we left, it wasn't that cold—more like Indian summer but without the sunshine. The fact that we've got on flannels would point to the fact that it's not that hot out. And I suspect, the sunshine means this is not when we left for the haunted cemetery experience.

I've gotta check in with Billy. He's the only one who might be able to tell me what went wrong—or right—with the program.

But first, I want to get dressed. I'll have to borrow some of Beth's clothes; need to save the big dress for a costume ball, or something.

I attempt to kick off the covers, but there's a rolled-up quilt at the end of the twin bed.

"Aiii, no!" cries a voice from inside the roll-up. "Tcharrli!"

"Carolina!" I scurry to unpack her from the bed roll.

Beth starts cursing, all the alarm bells going off about "an invader" in her room.

Carolina, startled, curls up into a little ball and puts her hands over her ears.

What with my head splitting, and Beth panicking, I'm at the end of my rope.

"Shut up, Beth. Can't you see you're scaring her?"

"You shut up, Charley!"

She can't act this way to the Bean. "Okay. That's it." I put a protective arm around Carolina. "Time to go."

"No, wait. Just tell me who the hell you are, and how you got into my room!"

Slowly, Carolina unwinds herself. "*Servizio*," she squeaks.

"Wait, don't I know you?" Beth demands. "You were in my dream!"

Carolina ignores her and, freed from the cocoon of covers, begins her jumping bean routine. "Tcharrli, something terrible has happened. We are not supposed to be in this time!"

My inkling that we overshot our landing is now looking like more than a theory. "Esme! When are we?"

XXXIII.

BILLY!

One glimpse into the future is more than enough

"Today's weather in Takoma Park will be clear, with temperatures in the low forties, rising only to fifty," says Esme. "That gives way to cooler temperatures and clouds this evening, with the chance of a derecho. Trick-or-treat, Charley!"

Beth's still in a knot about finding a strange girl sleeping in her bedroom. I hear her plying Carolina with questions. Little Bean has put on her game face and is trying to answer her in the same convoluted way Kairos does—in riddles. Beth's got herself totally in a knot over all of it. Then, as if that isn't enough, this breaking news about the weather sets off a new storm of anxiety in my BFOO.

"Derecho!" Beth looks at me. After all, we've been through that, and it's no fun. "So, like, Carolina, whoever you are, did you just blow in with the wind?"

Carolina, upset that none of her explanations is sticking, throws her arms up in the air.

"Not funny, Esme." I frown, looking at the weather app. There is no storm of any kind in range. Besides, that's not what I was asking.

Giving up on Beth, Carolina hangs over my shoulder to check on the weather report.

"What's your magic slate say, Tcharrli?"

I ignore her. "Esme, what *year* are we?"

But before I can hear her response, my phone rings, and Carolina, curious, scrambles up next to me to look over my shoulder, as if she'd never heard a cell phone ring before. (Note to readers: She hasn't.)

My ringtone—from my old composition, "Leo"—takes me by surprise. 'Cause it's literally been centuries since I got an actual phone call.

Billy. It's like he read my mind.

I put him on speaker.

"Charley!" It's a relief to hear his voice. "Where've you been?"

"Oh, not you, Webhead. Whatever happened to your great invention for the science fair, Billy-boy?!" Beth snaps.

"Charley, take me off speaker, 'kay?"

Beth goes on ranting.

"'Kay. Shhh, Beth, we'll talk after, all right?"

Beth huffs, flashes me an angry look, picks up her phone, and starts texting.

Billy's voice sounds urgent. "Something's gone very wrong. Where've you been, Charley? You and Beth?"

"I was gonna ask you that. Where've we been—and 'specially, *when* are we?"

"Can't you two lovebirds keep it down!" Beth barks. "I'm 'bout to start an Instagram Live."

I cup my hand from mouth to phone so she can do her thing—and keep whatever news Billy's about to share hush-hush.

"That's just it. The thing misfired. It's 2020."

I let that settle in a minute. Is that why, still using my French connection, I could see people gathering in masks, protesting?

"Wait, so we've lost a year?"

"Not just any year, Charley. There's a worldwide pandemic here now. A worldwide coronavirus, COVID-19. For the year it first emerged—2019."

"What the frig?!" I can't help screaming.

"Shut. Up. Charley." Beth hisses, giving me the side-eye without ever losing contact with her followers on the screen.

"So, Fashion Forward Fans, now that I've had this France dream, I guess that makes ESMOD my dream school." Beth pauses and looks at me—"Get it? Dream. School?"—to see if I get the joke.

"Funny, Beth," I reply dismissively. Trying hard to wrap my head around this revelation of Billy's. "What's that even mean, Billy?" I whisper back into the phone.

It's like Beth heard me, but not the context. "Meaning, I'll need to start getting my French good enough to do some Insta Lives in

French. Might have to consider translating the name too, like, Bethy à la Mode."

"*À la Mode. À la Mode. À la Mode*!!" chants Carolina.

I push her over into the pillow with a "Shush!"

"Sorry to break the news all of a sudden, Charley. But you need to know that nothing's normal anymore."

"Nothing's normal." This confirms my worst fear. "Beth's mom said something about being in a 'pandemic pod.' What the hell's she talking about, Billy?"

"Can't explain everything. Just know you're at extremely high risk of catching a deadly disease. One-point-three million people dead worldwide. Eleven million cases in the US as of last week."

"One-point-three million dead!"

Beth glares. "What's the Webhead talking about now—the zombie apocalypse?"

"Zombie?" Carolina asks. It's the only word that seems to have registered.

"You may have upset the timeline, Charley," Billy's telling me, but I can't focus. What keeps popping up in my brain is that I saw a glimpse of this, this time of masks, in the time before.

"What timeline? I need to know! The one I left? Or is there some other time I've upset?"

Beth chimes in, as if she's the one I asked.

"Upset my Live. Because look how, since yesterday, I've lost, like, a thousand followers."

"Billy, can't talk now. Meet me at the diner, okay?"

"That's just it, Charley. Diner's closed. Coronavirus."

"Closed? From a flu?" I can't take any of this in. "Okay, Billy Vin-cenzo, just tell me where we can meet. *Pronto!*"

"Outside's the only place. 'Cause you've apparently traveled from a hot spot. France, right? Surging right now. They've closed Disneyland Paris and the Eiffel Tower."

"There's no Eiffel Tower when we were, much less Disneyland!" I insert, wondering how a flu might "jump" a timeline. "Plus, it's an old Paris that's dirty and decrepit . . ."

"Charley!" he yells. "Shut up and listen. We can go to the school track—walk and talk at the same time."

"Okay, okay. As soon as I brush my teeth and figure out what normal-ish clothes I can put on and walk over." I hesitate, thinking. "Hey, I lost my backpack somewhere—or some-when. Could you throw together a few things for me? Like maybe some snacks? And Tylenol. My poor brain can't take many more of these crash landings. Think I might be suffering a traumatic brain injury this time."

"TBI? That might explain things." Beth stares at me like I've lost my mind. Which I probably have.

"Sure, Charley," Billy says. "You'll be fine in—whatever. Everyone's either in sweats or leggings for the duration anyway. I'll drive over and pick you up on the corner down the street from Beth's okay?"

"Drive!" Times have changed. When we left, Billy didn't even have his learner's permit.

"Yeah. We'll need to put our two heads together to fix this mess."

I'm wondering if he means the virus, or the mess-up of the timelines.

"Oh, and Charley? You'll need to wear a mask."

I glance over at the mask on the nightstand. Is this what Mrs. Cooper was talking about?

"Right. Peace out."

XXXIV.

HIGH SCHOOL REUNION

When you've been gone so long,
you never know who's gonna show up to meet you
when you get back—or too far forward

I had to wheedle Beth into loaning me a pair of her ripped jeans, an ugly sweater, and a zippered tie-dye fleece hoodie to look even halfway 2020. I marvel at the speed of dress conferred by the zipper. Such a little thing but, considering the elaborate process of corseting and bodice buttoning that made getting dressed such a process back in the day, quite the innovation.

Of course, Beth, momentarily squashing her impulse to ghost me, wanted to straighten my mop of a head and do my makeup so she could record it as a Fashion-Forward moment. As I sit squirming under the burning tyranny of her flat iron, it occurs to me that I don't even know who this Beth is: from the past (she walked the red carpet at Versailles) or the future (not so much, and upset about me, Carolina, and why I'm not with the pod program here).

The paradox possibilities are almost too much to ponder.

"Let me do your eyes, too, Charley. Some green eye shadow to bring out your eyes. And black mascara to outline. Oh, and fake lashes. Yours are so—short. You'll look totally rad."

Influencers!

"Thanks, but no. I'm outta here." I double-check that I took everything out of the dress pouch and shove it all in my pockets. I grab a pair of skinny shades from her dresser top to hide the rings around my eyes and grab the mask off the bed table. "I'll bring these back, maybe. Billy's waiting!"

"Wait, what about me, Tcharrli? Let me come, too!"

Carolina. On the one hand, could get complicated if she comes and someone from school sees us together. Or Mamma and the twins—and how does that even work if we're in the year after? On the other hand, Billy knows her from Leo's time, and he'll be glad to see her. And on the third hand, I can't trust her with Beth. For all I know, she'll be dressing her up and turning her into a mini-me. And to blast images of Carolina out to all Beth's followers could invite trouble. After all, she's barely eleven.

Luckily, Beth's leggings fit her, along with an oversize T-shirt and a couple of sweaters from Bethy's closet. And she wears the same size sneakers as we do already.

"She looks redonkulous, Charley," Beth observes, peeking out from under the swaddle of her bed covers.

Looking her up and down, I have to admit she looks quite the ragamuffin. "It'll have to do." I grab Beth's mask before she can protest and pull it over Carolina's nose and mouth. "I can't tell you why," I warn her, "but don't take this off unless I say it's okay."

Beth yells after us, as we reach her back stairs.

"Shut up, Beth. Your mom!"

We'll have to tiptoe down so as not to upset Mrs. Cooper more than she likely already is. And that's just for the normal stuff.

But Beth can't turn it down. "And I still don't get what she's doing here!"

"Babysitter in training for the twins," I hiss back at her before taking to the stairs. "For when I'm not around."

I don't dare elaborate on this, as it's just occurred to me that this is one of the consequences my time traveling could've caused.

"Wait. Is this where you live, Tcharrli? Can I meet your family? Is Carrie named after me?"

I had to tell her about the twins since, in a weird way, they were part of the reason for my hasty departure from the fifteenth century, like, two years ago.

"Will they like me?" She does her little half-skip, weaving in front of me, now behind, from side to side and in front again, spinning around to walk backwards. "I bet I'll like them!"

"You know, you're exhausting sometimes, Carolina. Too many questions."

"Wait, what's the world like here? Does everyone have an Esme? What about earbuds? Can I have something to eat?"

"Things are weird. Billy said the diner's closed. And it *never* closes." For all I know, the whole world as we knew it BTT2 (Before Time Travel Two) is shut down, and we're all either doomed, dying, or in some kind of bardo.

"Is there a tavern where we can get something to eat?"

She did scarf down my hot chocolate, melted marshmallows and all, so she shouldn't die of starvation. But as for street smarts—that's a whole 'nother story.

"We'll get you something soon. But look where you're going!" Now, she's stepping one foot on the curb and the other in the street.

"Are these automatons?" she asks. "Leonardo made an automaton!"

I knew about Leo's automaton, but thought he only invented that much later in his life. Meanwhile, the only other "horseless" vehicle she's ever seen is the tandem, and that's foot-powered and not likely to kill someone.

Luckily, Beth's street is not too busy, especially on Saturdays, when families are usually out doing errands, taking their kids to soccer matches, football games, or the like.

Still, I'm not taking any chances.

We get to a corner bus stop under a glass shelter with a bench. "Sit down and don't move, Carolina," I command. "It's better I meet Billy before he finds out the news that you've also leaped time. Promise?"

She nods slowly, then reaches up for a fist bump. But at least she's staying put.

Meanwhile, I have my eye out for Billy. I have no idea what he might be driving, but assume it's one of his parents' cars.

So imagine my surprise when I see him chug-chug up on a little orange electric scooter, complete with sidecar. But it's not the same Billy as when I left a year ago. This guy's filled out, his hair's longer and wavy, and he's got on *Back to the Future* oversize aviators. He's sporting a black mask, so I can't see his expression, but his eyes are crinkled around the edges in a smile.

"Like it, Charley?" he asks, proudly hopping off. "It's from a kit I got for . . ."

I stomp my foot, a little angry that he's acting like nothing's happened. "What the hell, Billy!"

He glances surreptitiously around us. "Not here. C'mon. We'll go for a spin."

He motions for me to get into the sidecar, but before I can explain that we've got an extra rider, Carolina, human cannonball, dive-bombs Billy, knocking him into someone's front yard.

"Carolina!"

"*Bee-ly!*"

"Umm, surprise?" I offer up meekly.

XXXV.

A Plague o' Both Your Houses

Or how even a Shakespeare couldn't foresee the
consequences of this tragedy

The ride in the sidecar, with Carolina squished in beside me, is only slightly less bumpy than our head-spinning rocket rides through time. And although I am dying to get to the heart of what's going on, I insist Billy keep both eyes on the road and focus on driving, even though there's hardly anyone out today.

Pretty eerie, if you ask me.

Carolina, on the other hand, seems to be enjoying the ride. She's looking out the back, her face upturned and staring at the exotic (for her) landscape. Every once in a while, she chirps in wonder about a colorful playground and the tall funky standing flowers on poles in Sligo Mill Park, and all the bike sculptures from the ReCycle: Art of the Bike project. She seems particularly captivated by the clock on Carroll Avenue, with its Roman numeral–faced clock, including the year of my hometown's founding, 1883.

"Just like the Duomo clock!"

It's not at all similar, but it would take too much energy to explain the differences. Besides, I've got other things on my mind.

After what seems like an eternity of putt-putting across Old Town Takoma Park (time being relative), we stop at the school. Billy takes off his aviators, then his mask, which tells me I can pull mine off, too.

With a little bit of a shock, I can see a few beard hairs sprouting on his chin. What a difference a year makes!

Billy starts around to the field behind the school, walking the bike so as not to make noise that might raise suspicions about my being here now. (Unless there's another, older me here now, which, given the events of the last few hours, I can't even think about.)

I follow in his wake, Carolina keeping pace just behind me.

"So what's up with this flu thing, Billy?" I demand. "How'd we skip a year, where's the brainiac Billy I left behind, and why are we here?"

"Boy, are you a sight for sore eyes!" he exclaims.

"Yeah, you too. I think."

"Wait, did you bring that stuff I asked you about?"

"It's all here." He taps on a trunk in the sidecar I hadn't seen earlier but doesn't make a move to spring it open.

"Umm, first—a slight problem. I think I may have miscalculated, Charley," he says, as if that explains everything.

"C'mon, Billy. Spill!"

With that, he launches into an improbable tale about bat-to-human novel virus transmission that spread across the planet from something called a wet market in China, which is nothing like the local Takoma farmers' market. Whole countries have gone on lockdown; schools are suddenly all online; and everyone's gotta do this thing called social distancing. To demonstrate, he moves to a spot six feet away.

I think back to my release from the Bastille, meeting back up with Kairos, and the bike—when I accidentally triggered the GPS on the video monitor and caught a glimpse of a massive protest in front of the Washington Monument. I didn't understand at the time why Kairos didn't want me to see it; everyone was wearing masks there, too. The whole pandemic thing might explain the masking. But is that why people were protesting?

I'm kind of afraid to ask. Seeing into the future may not be all it's cracked up to be.

"Worst of all, Charley," he opines, "you aren't supposed to be here now. You're a year later than you should be, and I have no idea if there's some kind of granddaughter paradox or timeline fluctuation that could rip open the fabric of this universe just by your showing up in the wrong time and place. Not to mention her." He nods at Carolina, who's dashing up and down the track like a sprinter in training.

I have a million questions. Like, was he able to see where we were, me and Beth; and how can this be a different year; and could I be a carrier? But before I can even put them in words, Billy's giving me an anguished look.

"No, seriously, Charley. As much as I love you and missed you, you can't be here now. You've got to go back."

"But I need to know what's happening, Billy. Are my parents okay? The twins? Mamma was going on tour with the NSO—could she have been infected? I need to see them!"

Carolina, out of breath, inserts herself between me and Billy.

"*Bee-ly!* Can we go to the *casa* of Tcharrli, *per favore?*"

"Yes, I've got to go home, Billy. Don't you see?!"

Billy plops on the seat of his scooter, apparently frustrated that I am not taking his warning seriously enough.

"How do I get this through your thick skull, Charley? If you interact with your parents in the future, it may change the trajectory of your life when you do get back to where you started from."

"Wait. Is there something you're not telling me, Billy? Like, what do my parents make of the fact that I've been missing a whole year? Unless I haven't. Unless there's a future Charley here now. In which case . . ."

But Billy skips answering that. "There's another pandemic now: virus misinformation. Your mom and dad and the twins are definitely safer than they would be if you went into your house. And you're safer, too, because you haven't been here this whole time. We can't know if your being exposed to a fatal disease from this time will interrupt a whole and healthy girl from returning to that time—er, that is—if we were to let time take its true course."

None of this is making sense. This Billy's here talking to me now, and Mrs. Cooper saw me and Beth, and it didn't feel like we had disrupted time, except that we're now in a worldwide pandemic that wasn't here before.

"I've got to go home, right now!"

Billy shows no sign of turning on the ignition. "Slow down, Charley. You're a scientist. You know we have to think this through logically, right?"

I stand on one foot, then the other.

"First off, as a scientist, I'm like, whoa, everyone's getting bat-sick. There's gotta be a cure. Let's find it. Second off, I'm like, I want my mother! So I'm going home—with you or without you, William Vincenzo! And if you're not with me, step aside."

At that moment, Carolina comes up from behind and tumbles into the sidecar. "Going home with Tcharrli," she chants in a singsong manner. "Gonna meet her family!"

"No you're not," Billy insists. He turns around to try to shove her out of the sidecar. But Carolina's nothing if not tenacious. She braces her arms and legs and resists.

Seeing my chance, I hop on the scooter, push Billy aside, and putt-putt off as fast as this machine can take us, leaving him to lope after us. "Wait up, Charley!"

I push the pedal to the metal but we're already at full speed. Which cannot be more than 15 mph. I'm guessing it would go faster without the sidecar and Carolina in it.

I see Billy catching up, but he's definitely huffing and puffing. "We can outrun him, for sure!"

"Charley—it's about the golden compass on your necklace. It's not calibrated with the originals . . . hey, will you at least listen?"

Whoa, this gets to the heart of at least one question. Although I'm not really ready to stop, I power off the scooter and put a foot on the pavement. "I'm listening."

Billy stops, hands on his thighs and hunched over to catch his breath. "Gotta start working out," I hear him mumble.

"Your point . . . ?"

"Okay. Well. Yeah. I don't know how you got back here exactly, but . . . a year ago, when I could see you guys were in trouble . . ."

"You knew what was happening? How?"

"*La magia!*" exclaims Carolina.

Billy frowns. "Your magic didn't really do this, Carolina."

Her face turns into a pout. "You were not there, Bee-ly. You cannot know how it felt!"

"Stop, Carolina. Billy, what do you mean, you could see us?"

"It was more an energetic pull," he says, pulling a long face. "Almost like a pre-materializing ghost of a hologram. Very *Star Trek.*"

Since our first trip back in time, *Star Trek* has been, like, his technological North Star.

"But that was a year ago. You tried to get us back then?"

"It would have been a safer bet," he mumbles.

"And you waited a whole year?"

He looks almost defeated. "Charley, I don't need to tell you, of all people: Time doesn't wait. But this pandemic—and the panic that came with it—well, it has upset everything."

I feel bad for doubting him.

"Anyway, it took me awhile to figure out a bug in the programming: the charm. It was never meant to be combined with the heirloom compasses from Kairos."

I touch my necklace. "We needed two. And it's all I had to go with—hey, Carolina, show him the one you did the magic trick with back at Versailles."

"This?" She holds up one of the original compasses that powered our first journey, and the first leg of this one.

To get a better look, I get off the scooter, careful to keep it upright with the kickstand.

Billy nods. "The two ancient compasses are calibrated. They're tuned, in a way, to the same bio-earth fields."

"You're saying this wasn't calibrated the same way?" I ask.

"It's just a little charm, Charley. For us."

He touches the little golden charm lying close to my heart and I can feel a tiny electric spark. Whether it's kinetic energy, or an emotion connected to my heart, it's hard to know.

I blush, remembering how he gave it to me for our first dance, and declared that we were, like, together.

"Not for time. Or meant for anybody else. And definitely not tuned to the same magnetic and gravitational resonance frequencies as the others."

A love charm.

Like Émilie's little porcelain snuffbox, there is definitely a connection between physics and desire. Or, considering Émilie's way of thinking, love and philosophy. There's got to be a human connection to it all.

"That's it!" I shout.

"Wait. What?"

"You know how the original formula Kairos downloaded from the cloud into Dad's iPad, the Qualia Rosetta, sent us back to Renaissance times?"

I'd noticed that Carolina had drifted off—bored with our debate, Billy's and mine. Out of the corner of my eye, I could see she was busy collecting rocks and stones, balancing them carefully, one on top of another, beginning to take shape as a rock stack. At the mention of her brother's name, however, Carolina runs back, dumping a bunch more stones from her oversized sweatshirt onto the ground at our feet.

"*Si, si, si!*" she interrupts. "Kairos and I both have access to the cloud. The Qualia Rosetta is the key to unlock even more secrets . . ."

"Secrets? You also have access, little Bean?" I ask.

Billy scoffs. "We don't have time for your secrets right now, Carolina. We're getting away from the point—this may be life or death for Charley. She cannot be here."

"Hmmph," snorts Carolina. She stomps away again, back to her small but growing cairn, apparently hurt that we aren't paying attention to her.

"Right, Billy!" I jump back into the scientific argument. Realizing how I'd missed our convos, Billy's and mine. "Here's my point: how science and philosophy, as they called the science back then, radically advanced in the Enlightenment, thanks to Newton, Leibniz, and our own dear Émilie?"

"Right. So?"

"So the new compass wasn't calibrated to the correct spacetime. Just like you said, Billy. Brilliant!"

He blushes, even though I'm pretty sure he's not grasping exactly what he said that could have triggered that idea. And modesty being what it is (a quality Mamma keeps railing to me about), I can't lay sole claim to the breakthrough here.

"Uh-huh."

I continue. "And here we are, in an exponentially different time—some people say it's the Information Age, others, the Quantum Age—another major leap from Enlightenment times."

"Ancient news, Charley. The cutting edge is more like a Quantum Information Age, what with the powers of quantum computing, and all."

So?"

"As I was trying to tell you . . ." Carolina, coming back with more stones, has apparently been listening this whole time.

I ignore her interruption. "Yeah, so you know, the first leap-time here took me and Beth to 1724 Paris. When the teenage Émilie was hanging out at Versailles. Who was not at all the Émilie I've been obsessed with—her secrets being mostly about fashion and fencing."

"Totally Bethy's jam."

"Right. Which may be why she went back before me, even. I mean, we all know that the most minute Earth wobble, or a geosynchronous delay of a fraction of one degree, can throw off your GPS and can mean the difference between getting to Timbuktu or Takoma Park."

"Of course." I can see he's getting impatient. "So what's your point, Charley?"

"We've advanced leap-times since Émilie figured out that *force vive* required squaring the product of mass and velocity to measure the force of an object in motion."

"Old news, Brainiac," Billy concludes.

"Yes, but that one little *square* in the formula changed our perspective of reality, allowing Einstein to discover Special Relativity. It completely revolutionized our understanding of energy as mass times the speed of light squared. Thus, cracking open a four-dimensional spacetime."

Mentally, I flash back to the interview I did (will do?) with Einstein, back in the day—part of my personal project to learn from my "heroes of history"—and when he told me about his regret in not finding the Unified Theory tying together our proof that the physical and subatomic worlds can be proven using one unified equation. And that he practically dared me to be the one who pulls it all together.

I drag myself out of my daydream.

"Now, it's our turn. Our mission: to crack time by viewing four dimensions from a fifth dimension—not the square, but the cube."

"Yes." Billy gets that lost-in-space look, like he's gone deep inside his mind to unravel a mental mystery—or, in this case, a new dimension.

"Since the first leap took us back twelve years earlier than I was aiming for, it seems reasonable to assume that the little compass that triggered our second leap maybe transported us 'home' too far into the future. It's just a wonder that we got as close as we did to our departure date."

"I hate when you figure all this stuff out without me, Charley," Billy grumbles, scratching the red beard hairs barely sprouting on his chin. "I get what you're saying. But it's just a hypothesis. And any good scientist is going to look at your hypothesis and say, bull-doody, because it's untested. And frankly, even our time travel looks like bull-doody—because it's been tried out and worked only on a few people."

"So far," I remind him. "And the number of our experimental group is not one. There's me, you, Lex, and now Beth . . ."

"And don't forget me, Tcharrli," says the Bean. "And Kairos!"

"Which brings the number to six. Not to mention, apparently Leonardo da Vinci, who, at last report, was seen in the vicinity of Bern, Switzerland, in the twentieth century."

"Still, I don't get what you want to do about it, Charley. Reset our geo-spatial-temporal settings with the compass?"

"You don't think it's as easy as that, do you?" I demand. "Because now that we're here in 2020, I think this COVID-19 might have something to do with it."

"COVID-19! What the heck, Charley? Was there a plague back then, too?"

"Maybe. Not the disease, I don't think—but maybe its genetic markers. You know, all of life has a DNA signature, and we're nothing if not part of the life-chain."

"Yes, well they are working on a vaccine using a new technology, mRNA. It modifies a protein on this coronavirus so it's not so sticky to human immune systems."

"Yeah, it's gotta be something like that. Something about what sticks to us humans—or modifies what we have the capacity to grasp. I think that's what's novel here, Billy. What if it's our capacity to power-boost our DNA and change our reality?"

"Still not getting your point, Charley. It's like you're into the realm of science fiction."

"No—science. It's gotta be tested! And, Vincenzo, I'm gonna need your help majorly, this time. 'Cause I'm goin' back to meet the real Émilie. The one who out-Newtons Newton. She of the *force vive*: motion-mass squared. The woman who made the magic squaring her legacy, aka, doing the math to discover the formula for kinetic energy, who passed that square to Einstein two centuries later for Relativity. And who never got any credit."

"Like you're gonna change that!" Billy says snidely.

I stomp my foot. "Billy, you are not gonna stop me! If I can't go home, I'm going back." I feel a pang of homesickness, and wipe my sleeve across my eyes. "And I'm gonna get there with you or without you. After all, I traveled back once on my own . . ."

"And we all know how well that might've ended for you in Florence, if Lex and I hadn't come along!"

"Whatever. Are you with me? Because I've got to get to Émilie in 1736. Just after she moves back to her husband's estate, after Voltaire takes up residence. When she begins her Newton translation. And their experiments together at Cirey."

"And you're planning on leaving from here?" He looks around. "I mean, 2020, Charley. And what if we can't ultimately get you back to the time before you left—2019? That could totally mess up the spacetime continuum. And leave your folks super worried."

First, I note the "we." I take heart that Billy's as excited about this as I am.

"And your knowledge of a future pandemic? And a future me, even? What does that do to our timeline, Brainiac . . . yours and mine?"

This gets my head spinning in a loop. Like, is he insinuating that there really is a 2020 Charley I've displaced? What if she and Billy are still together in this timeline? And who—and where—is she?

But there can't be two of me here. Or what if I've entered some parallel universe? After all, that is theoretically the explanation for our having leapt back in time in the first place without causing a paradox . . . at least, not at that point.

After all, if experience offers any lessons, it's essential to get back before you've even left, unless you want to mess up the future—yours and everyone else's. Which I may've already done, accidentally.

"Okay. Means we've got to make some refinements to the energy synchronization between the antique compasses and my new charm," I say, touching the golden compass at my throat. "Like, maybe this'll require a three-compass turn. I'm guessing, given the advances and refinements in standards and measurement in today's technology, it might start with cubing the Rosetta formula."

Before I can even ask him if he's brought his copy, Carolina taps me on the shoulder and points to her rock stack, which is now almost up to her waist. I walk over to inspect.

"Beautiful, Bean. How'd you get them all to balance so precariously?"

"Ancient rocks balance to bring new harmonies from the Earth. Just as you will find a magnetic frequency to harmonize all three golden compasses."

"The Earth's magnetism . . . hmm!" I caress the top rock, taking care not to tumble her rock tower.

I think back to seventh grade and Earth Sciences, and it begins to dawn on me what she's driving at. The Earth carries a consistent frequency over time. I replace the stone on top of the stack, then lean lightly against it to see if it can bear my weight without tumbling over. It forms an amazingly stable structure. I marvel at Carolina's abilities—but then, like Kairos, there's a lot I apparently don't understand about her.

"Hey, Billy, look! Carolina's cairn is amazing . . ."

"Hmm?" Billy asks absently. I can tell he's been deep inside his head.

"Earth to Billy—strong magnetic field? Resonance?"

"Three compasses can form a quantum energy interaction—past to present to future," she explains further.

"Spooky action at a distance," I add, echoing Einstein's skepticism about the mystery of simultaneous interaction of quantum particles that are far distant in space. "But what if particles are interacting not just in space, but in time, since spacetime is the fourth dimension, after all?"

This seems to jar something in Billy's brain. "That phrase of Leonardo's: 'In rivers, that which you touch is the last of what has passed and the first of that which comes. So it is with present time.' It's all about perspective, right? We live in the present, we've been to the past—and somehow, Charley, you time-traveled to the future. If we could map out that whole landscape at once, model a five-D holographic roadmap that factors in spacetime together by controlling for and manipulating quantum uncertainty, including, like, electromagnetism, and beyond the limits of the senses and the human mind—that's gotta be the perspective to help us get to the next stage. Math's complicated. But maybe it's gonna show how to get to a Theory of Everything integrating human mind equals quantum electromagnetism-matter-cubed."

I pick up a stick with a pointy end and begin tracing in the dirt. I don't know whether it's the ghost of Leonardo that's taken hold of me—what, with his penchant for puzzles and all—or time travel's just catching up with me, but what started as a sketch of Vitruvian Man has morphed into a mysterious code that might depict "hearts and the cubing of hearts." A vision inspired by the math in our evolution of time travel: $Hm=[QE]M^3$. And about which, more, I have a sneaking suspicion, will be revealed..

FORMULA FOR TIME TRAVEL FROM THE FIVE-D

"Sick, Charley!" He pauses, and I can tell all the mental cylinders are firing. "It's so next level," he says, stroking that nonexistent beard. "Speculative five-D radicality. Where's the proof?"

"What if the proof is in the past?" Carolina asks, stepping behind her cairn.

I consider this. "Right. 'Cause you can't change the past without a fifth dimension to step into."

Even as I realize the next leap-time is inevitable, I feel a pit in my stomach.

I won't be seeing Mamma and Dad and the twins. Or wolfing down a plate of Mamma's yummy spaghetti pomodoro.

Not yet, anyway.

But science, history, and the future can't wait.

I nod. "Okay, then. I say we make like the Borg and synthesize before the pandemic locks me into an inescapable future!"

XXXVI.

EARTH TO CHARLEY: GET OUT!

Math, shmath—there's a vortex underfoot

"Hey, look who's here. It's Billy the brainiac! Hey, Webhead . . . I'll race you!"

It's a familiar voice. I glance over to see Guy—Beth's homecoming date—apparently out for a run along the track and now sprinting our way. I note that he's all sweaty, as if he's been working out awhile, and he's not wearing a mask, although he does have a gator around his neck.

I quick put my mask back over my nose and mouth and cover my head with my hoodie. Billy gives me his shades to complete the effect.

I turn in the opposite direction and lower my voice. "I've gotta go, Billy. I can't let Guy see me here now."

At some point, I'll fill Billy in on the Guy clone we met at Versailles and how he's become the enemy in two time zones, but now's not the time.

"Who's your new girlfriend, Bill?" Guy asks, pointing at me. "Bet you're going to make Charley jealous!"

"Guy, why don't you go spread your droplets somewhere else?!" Billy taunts him, pulling up his mask and pushing me away.

I have no idea what that means, but it doesn't matter—I have to go, immediately. The me who was here before I was may get wind of this me, thanks to Monsieur Charmant, here.

Without hesitation, I motion for Carolina to push her mask up and follow me. We fast-walk off in the opposite direction.

"What're you, scared I'll beat the crap out of you, Webhead?" I hear Guy parry back in the distance.

I want to yell at Billy to take off, too, but he's standing resolute—no doubt to buy us some time.

Carolina turns around to see, fast-walking backwards now. "Tcharr-li," she says. "Billy will be okay."

It looks like Billy is luring Guy back toward his "wheels" in the front of the school. I'm a little worried, 'cause even though Billy's grown into his lanky frame, I'm not sure he's ready for a face-off with Beth's boyfriend in this spacetime zone.

"We must return to those rocks," Carolina says. "They are positioned over an Earth vortex and they align with tonight's Halloween full moon in conjunction with the planet you call Uranus. While that is the sign of disruption and chaos, it will help you on your way to the destination you seek."

This is all feeling a little too woo-woo for me.

"What are you saying—to Émilie's Cirey? In the time of her major scientific achievements?" I ask. "But we only have one compass and the charm around my neck. And Billy says he hasn't sync'd up the necklace. We need the other compass from the backpack Billy brought me."

"Yet you have a talisman to magnetize your quantum entanglement with that time."

I glimpse back and note that indeed, Billy has disappeared around front, taking Guy out of sight. "But I feel naked leaving without my transition clothes, or anything I've prepared . . ."

"*Vene con me,*" she says, grabbing my shoulders and pushing me back.

The little cairn tower barely shows from this distance.

"Okay, okay, Carolina. Stop pushing! I'm going."

Although I'm still doubting Carolina's plan, I don't have anything better in mind. She takes off in a sprint toward the cairn and I huff and puff to keep up. It's not like me to be so winded—after all, I regularly play soccer on these same fields, or at least I did, up until I jumped the timeline. The vagaries of time travel must be getting to me. "Time to up the workout routine, Charley," I say through my teeth.

It's then that I feel my phone vibrating. I'd forgotten that I'd turned the ringer off.

I pull it out of the pocket—and thank God for pockets—in Beth's sweats. Checking as I jog, I see that Billy's sent me a video. He's now in his sidecar . . . and Guy is driving the scooter!

"Oh no, Bean," I yell. "Looks like Guy's hijacked Billy. He's zooming away with my boyfriend. I've got to help him!"

"Oh no, you cannot, Tcharrli," she rejoins, pointing around the side of the school. "Here they come. Look!"

I stop in my tracks. There's Billy in the sidecar, hefting his backpack in one hand. Guy's still at the wheel, but Billy must have installed some kind of remote control, because Guy is yelling and wrestling with the steering wheel that Billy's now in control of, and he's taking Guy somewhere, evidently, that he doesn't really want to go. It really does look like some kind of clown show.

Billy keeps yelling "Wait!" in our direction, without giving away who we are.

"Holy guac, I have to get away."

My phone's pinging again, and now it's Beth, saying she's meeting Guy at the school and telling me to call my mom, who's looking for me. (But which me? I wonder, irrelevantly.) I look a little closer and it looks like she sent the message just over half an hour ago.

"Tcharrli!" shouts Carolina, louder now. She's grabbed my arm and is pulling me. We're only about five yards from the cairn now, and Billy's driven up to the soccer goalpost, where he drops the backpack, shouting and waving those long arms.

"You forgot this, Cousin Émilie. You'll need it for your trip!"

For a moment, I'm wondering who he's talking to, as I don't think he has a cousin by that name, until Carolina punches me on the arm. "It's *your* Émilie, *cretino! Andiamo!!*"

"Don't curse, Carolina," I say reflexively.

Then, "Guy!" I hear from another direction. It's Beth. She's coming around the other side of the school now. I'm guessing Guy told her to meet him here.

"Émilie, don't you have a flight to catch?!" Billy's apparently trying to decide how close he can come before Guy sees me and the gig is up.

Beth's turned the corner now—I can hear she's all chatty with whoever might be her new best friend—and, suddenly, it's a horror show . . . she's with me! Not me, me, but a 2020 me—the me who's really supposed to be here.

"Holy shit! This cannot be happening."

I quick throw myself to the ground behind the rock stack. "The backpack!" I hiss.

Carolina dashes the ten feet to grab it and then throws herself on top of me behind the rocks, letting loose a string of curses in Italian, invoking the gods, fate, and Kairos to do whatever he has to do to get us out of there alive.

I quick sling the backpack over my shoulders.

"Hey, wait. Billy!" I cry, popping my eyes just enough above the cairn to get his attention. "Did you upgrade the dash . . ."

But the sky above me and the ground beneath have already given way and, in what's now becoming a sickeningly familiar feeling, I am spinning, twisting, falling, whirling, as my rib cage is crushing my lungs, in an ever-accelerating spiral through spacetime.

XXXVII.

ANOTHER HARD LESSON IN GRAVITY

How insurance is critical in any time zone

You know the old question about whether a tree falling in a forest makes a sound if no one's there? Well, ditto for a sudden crash landing from the future.

"Oh, V! I believe the new instruments from London have arrived."
Je crois que les instruments envoyés de Londres sont arrivés!

Delivered by the eighteenth-century home delivery service, no doubt.

"Linant! Linant, *vas t'en, cherches le paquet de poste, mademoiselle.*"

The voice is familiar—a little deeper, more anxious-sounding. But there's no mistaking the divine Ms. Émilie du Châtelet.

I rub my achy head and take a quick look around.

I've landed by a stream, in a grassy field. It's a sunny day in a Goldilocks zone—not too hot; not too cold. Thankful for that, at least, given my extremely inappropriate clothing.

There's a high hedge directly in front of me and, beyond, what looks to be a multistory brick building. From online pics, I recognize the redbrick and pale stone facade, its mansard roofline framing the upper floors of Émilie's château in Cirey, France.

ÉMILIE'S CHÂTEAU AT CIREY

Credit: François-Edmée Ricois and Isidore Laurent Deroy, Public Domain

Before I can collect my thoughts, the anxious voice breaks through again.

J'espère seulement que rien n'en sera brisé—nos expériences doivent commencer toute de suite, avant la compétition de l'Académie Royale des Sciences—l'épreuve de la nature de feu.

Émilie must be passing nearby, perhaps just beyond this wall, I think, excited to be so close to my actual goal of meeting *the* Émilie who is on the verge of some amazing scientific accomplishments—discovering the infrared, translating Newton, doing the calculus that Newton did not, and making improvements through her commentaries.

I feel a chill going down my spine.

Things being what they are, I set out to find the remnants of Billy's backpack which, as usual, has exploded at landing. Picking up the nylon sack for inspection, I once again marvel at how the strains of temporal dislocation seem to have added substantially to the wear and tear, stressing its normal life span. The backpack is frayed and battered, but still holding together. When I get back, I'm going to have to invent an indestructible backpack—one that might survive a Mars landing, or a Stone Age one.

I survey the contents that Billy packed, now scattered on the ground. Luckily, they don't seem to be as affected.

First, a box of sterile face masks. I wonder at how they have somehow become the 2020 version of condoms: Don't leave home without 'em. Even so, I'm wondering how it would ever be cool to show up at the front door of Émilie's house with what looks like a disposable diaper over my face. And since I never had time to ask what symptoms to look out for . . . Well, I'm hoping against hope Billy's somehow added a "2020 Breaking News" feature to Esme's app dashboard.

On the more practical level, though, I pick up his old tablet, still in one piece after the crash-burn landing. It looks like he's even thrown in a big gray skirt with built-in petticoats, one of Beth's preliminary designs, and a cloak. He's also packed the Marie Antoinette wig I'd ditched at Halloween the original year of my departure—something he's kept safe for me for over a year, I now know.

There's also a little book of essays, *Discourse on Happiness,* by none other than Émilie herself.

I flip through the frontispiece to find the publication date: 1748. This isn't encouraging, as it would be twelve years past my hoped-for destination. But it looks like Billy's inserted a postcard, again showing Émilie's portrait, in front of a different château—one that resembles a mini Versailles.

I flip the card over and decipher Billy's messy scribble: *"Space. And Time. Again? Heart and the cubing of hearts." Remember me always. xo, Billy*

I sit down cross-legged on the lawn a moment, to breathe and reflect.

I recognize these as lines from the Émilie play. But Billy wasn't even with me and Beth that night. Cubing of hearts. Clearly a reference to our last conversation before leap-time.

Remember me always. What does he even mean by that?

I pull the skirt over my head to cover Beth's sweatpants, and shove the wig over my boing-boing curls and stick the earbuds in my ears just in time. Looks like my well-traveled shit-kicking cowboy boots are well hidden underneath all that fabric.

"Well, Bethy, looks like we're not in Versailles anymore," I remark, shaking the skirts to see if I can straighten out the myriad wrinkles.

I hear Beth's voice in my head lecturing me about how I'll never make the red carpet looking like this.

"*Mademoiselle? Mademoiselle! À qui vous parlez?*"

"Who am I speaking to?" I repeat in English, completely flummoxed.

"Mademoiselle, this is private property!"

Thank God Esme's still doing her thing.

Looks like Billy's also upgraded the instruments in my pack: his compass. Check. Which reminds me—Carolina must still have the other one. I'm wondering just where/when would that little Bean have gotten herself to?

I scan more stuff around me. An hourglass—what can the sands of time reveal to me to inform the Age of Esme? Metal funnel. What? Silver pipettes. Dollhouse-sized glass test tubes in a tiny wooden rack, vintage-looking mini medicine jars with cork stoppers.

Hunh? Does the Billy I just left in 2020 know something I don't? No time left to ponder.

I struggle to tuck in the rest of the modern and vintage detritus emanating from my backpack without bothering to look at what else is inside.

Someone who looks like a lady's maid, sporting long brown skirts, an apron, and a little white cap, hurries over and, in a flurry of French exclamations, asks if I am okay—relates how she saw a flash of light and heard a boom like thunder outside the wall, even though there has been no sign of rain, even though Madame de Graffigny complains incessantly about the poor weather at Cirey and thunderstorms.

Cirey. An answer to my earlier hypothetical.

"Oh, but I was invited. *Invitée?*" I explain, switching to Franglais until Esme can kick in fully, which I hope impresses her. "Madame la Marquise would certainly require hand-delivery of the scientific equipment for her *laboratoire* contained in *mon sac*." I unzip it to show her a glimpse of the modern wonders inside.

"*Eh bien, excusez-moi*," she apologizes, helping me to my feet.

I realize this must be Mademoiselle Linant, the person Émilie called for earlier. She tries to pull my backpack away from me, but I pull back with equal and opposite force (with a nod to Newton, for sure!) to finagle it out of her grasp.

"But you see, I have been instructed by the insurers not to let the contents out of my hands until they are safely unpacked in the laboratory of Madame the Marquise. *Er, eh, les assurances?*" I repeat as Esme prompts me.

When this fails to impress this dimwitted chick, I change tack. After all, insurance might not have been a thing, back in the day.

"By the personal guarantee of his Majesty the King," I say, trying to sound official.

She gives me the side eye but relents. "The Marquise is receiving visitors, but you are welcome to drop your sack inside. *Suivez-moi*."

"Oh," I explain to her retreating back, still trying to keep myself together. "But I must actually unpack these instruments and sort them," I assert, aiming to make myself indispensable to the process. I do intend to stay awhile, to absorb some of Émilie's amazing genius. The fact that the equipment I have inside is quite a bit more advanced than, say, the weights and measures, test tubes, beakers, and thermometers that would have equipped even most the advanced labs in Paris and London, could only make what I know that much more central to the scientific method.

We swing around the wall to the front of the castle. I gape in awe as I see the beautiful arched doorway, above which Émilie and Voltaire attended to the creation of intricate carvings and sculptures, decorated with a two-faced Neptune (coming and going), seashells, and a phrase in Latin credited to Virgil. Not able to pull a translation from my rusty brain's Latin 1, Esme translates, "A god has granted us this leisure."

CIREY ORNATE STONE CARVINGS AROUND CHÂTEAU DOORS

Photo: Robin Stevens Payes

I wish my AI could give me context here, but I have to be satisfied with the amazing sculptures that cascade around and down one side of the stone archway—a world map for astronomy; a ruler, T-square, and, yes, a compass to represent mathematics; a plume for writing. On the other side, a palette for painting; a mallet for sculpture; and a bagpipe for music. I wonder briefly about adding a violin, which I know for sure was invented before now!

Truly, this is a place that mashes up nature, the arts, and sciences to show the interconnections between them in the way of Leonardo da Vinci, and so many others before him. A way of thinking we've somehow lost in my lifetime. And that I hope to revive.

Mademoiselle Linant pushes open the heavy "door to art and science" and bids me enter before her. The entrance hall is grand and filled with light. The walls, from what I can see, must have been recently painted, as they bear no scuff marks from any of the Marquise's children (by this point, I imagine they must all be kept somewhere to be seen and not heard).

I think for a hot second about putting on my mask to protect these poor people from whatever pox I may have carried back from 2020—but I'm at once distracted by the sight of servants running in and out, carrying buckets full of steaming water.

The grand room is bathed in light, with giant French doors framed by gold damask curtains pinned back to show off the pastoral landscape outside. The walls are painted a pale green, and I tiptoe over the white marble floor so as not to scuff it up.

Out of the corner of my eye, I spy a fireplace—this must be where the water is heated. There are a lot of people gathered around, but no one familiar-looking. I can't see if Émilie or Voltaire is here, for there's a crowd gathered. This must be their "salon"—a gathering of the Enlightenment glitterati who come together to share news and gossip that would be familiar in that time.

Then I hear the voice of Émilie, holding court before this gathering of well-outfitted guests, men and women, recounting some long story that even Esme is having trouble making sense of. Her more attentive guests laugh gaily at every *bon mot*; others gossip in whispers behind beautifully hand-painted Chinese fans. When I see one on the table by the entrance door, I grab it for myself—never know when it might come in handy.

A large gangly woman remains toward the back of the crowd, black eyes casting about as if looking for somewhere else to be—or someone better to talk to.

As if she can feel this defection from her salon, Émilie calls out, "Françoise, honored guest at Cirey—perhaps you will recite with me? I am thinking of that epic poem by our own dear V—'La pucelle.'"

I hear the crowd murmur. The woman in the back who'd been looking to escape is blushing to her beauty mark. Françoise, whoever she is, has no choice but to come forward and join in the recitation. Totally disarmed.

I admire the master stroke. Have to use that on Bethy sometime, I think to myself. When I get back to my own time. Or if . . .

My minder, Linant, still standing with me by the entryway, taps her toe impatiently. "Monsieur Voltaire was almost sent back to the Bastille for this poem," she says. "It is a scandal against Church and King. We cannot wait until *mesdames* have worked up the crowd with his treasonous satire, or we may have another arrest on our hands."

Scandalous. I think back to the first time I met "V," as Émilie refers to him. Another sojourn in the Bastille. The last place on Earth I want to revisit.

"Oh, uh, I'm kind of liking the vibe," I breathe, vying for time here.

But she does not hear. Linant puts her head down and inches forward through the throng.

"*Madame? Pardonnez-moi,*" I hear her interrupt.

"What is it, Linant?" asks Émilie, a note of exasperation in her voice.

"*Vos instruments scientifiques,*" she announces. "*Le messager du Roi . . .*" she begins tentatively, pointing back in my direction. "*Ne parlante que de l'anglais!*"

I rankle at this fake news. My French, with Esme's assistance, is *pas mal!*

A sudden hush falls over the room. Seems like this ill-timed interruption might be badly received by their hostess.

"Send him to me," commands a clearly excited Émilie, now using English. "I must inspect the delivery. Immediately."

At this point, I have at least the presence of mind to fish one of the masks out of my backpack and put it on. No use infecting all the Marquise's peeps here with a new virus—especially while they're still dealing with smallpox and the plague.

The crowd parts to let me through, craning their heads at this unexpected intrusion by a stranger, who is evidently not a "he," nor what anyone might describe in this day and age as the King's messenger.

But then it is my turn to stare.

Madame la Marquise is soaking in a bathtub. Naked.

XXXVIII.

PROOF THAT LOVE'S THE LIVING FORCE

When E + V = immodest to a fault

A LADY AT HER TOILET

Credit: Antoine Watteau, Public Domain

As I approach, Émilie rises. A male servant who had been carrying a water bucket almost drops it at her feet—and Linant rushes to grab a white chemise with which to cover madame.

Not quite in the altogether now, though her damp white chemise clings scandalously to reveal every curve—and nipple. Marvelously daring!

If I were to take out my phone with everyone watching, I could Instagram her pic as a companion to the famous Watteau painting on the wall behind her, right down to the puppy nestled in a yellow-and-blue basket by her tub. But I restrain myself.

The imperial Émilie steps out of the tub and gathers up to her full height—towering almost a full foot over me—and stands dripping, arms outstretched, while Linant enrobes her in a dressing gown.

"I thought, at first, this château is no palace," I overhear one nobly dressed male guest observe loudly as the woman standing next to him titters into her painted fan. "But now I see: It is a Temple."

Émilie doesn't seem in the least bit embarrassed.

"Well . . . ?" she says expectantly as I come near.

Even though I'm masked, and she is completely forthright and open, when she meets my eyes, there is a flash of recognition.

And here, dear reader, is where even the most careful time traveler, aka, *moi*, may have screwed up. Because, while Émilie is all grown up and transformed, I am still the same girl I was twelve years ago when we met at Versailles. Which would seem impossible to anyone who is not living the life of a time traveler. And, alas, there are so few of us.

She offers me her hand. Not sure what I'm supposed to do with it, as I don't think she counts as royalty, officially, or anything. And she's not giving me any clues.

Still, someone needs to break the ice here. "Charlotte Morton," I curtsy.

"Have we not met before?" asks Émilie, now clearly confounded.

Think quick, I admonish myself.

"I have important information for you on the, er, uh, laboratory instruments you ordered. I represent the English manufacturer." I rely on Émilie's excellent English to hush Esme for an instant.

The crowd seems to be drifting off now—perhaps because we're speaking a language they don't, or because the entertainment portion of the program has ended abruptly. Others are sampling the goodies now being carried around on trays: lemons, oranges, candies, and coffee. And an array of wines, champagne, and liqueurs that I would love to sample.

Émilie lowers her voice, which now takes on an urgent tone. Tying a sash around her robe, she grabs me by the arm. "We must go to my rooms, Miss Morton. To speak privately."

And to the dispersing *saloniers*, she waves her hands. "*Merci, mes amis. On doit retourner aux travailles! Pourtant, amusez-vous bien—ce soir, je vous invite de nous joindre en haut, au Petit Théâtre, où on monte une des petites comédies, par Monsieur le Voltaire, bien sûr, L'Enfant Prodigale. Une comédie écrite exclusivement pour nous.*"

At this invitation to the guests to join her this evening for the debut of a new play by Voltaire, in the château's own little theater, there's a polite smattering of applause all around.

"Alors, à toute à l'heure!"

Her guests seem more than content to schmooze among themselves, and cruise the counter, as it were, to enjoy an afternoon feast.

Émilie pulls me away.

"But what . . . where are we . . . ?" I blurt. In a flash of déjà vu, it feels like someone's always pulling or pushing me to get somewhere other than where we are.

She lifts a finger to her lips. "Not here. There are ears." She points to a bushy ficus tree in a blue-and-white Chinese vase, and though I'm not one to believe in conspiracy theories, I swear I spot movement in the shadows.

I hurry in her footsteps as we go down a long hallway to enter a bright bedroom paneled in a powder blue and pale yellow—evidently following the decor in evidence with the dog basket (if not the dog itself!) in the painting. A ladies' desk (because it's so small and delicate, I think) is strewn with pages and pages of French prose. There are equations, calculations, and cross-outs quickly jotted. They must be formulas! I'm dying to inspect her papers close up. I can't help but wonder if this isn't her not-yet-in-print translation and commentary on Newton's *Principia*.

A compass lies on top of it, along with a protractor and the requisite plume and ink.

Émilie's own girl cave, it seems.

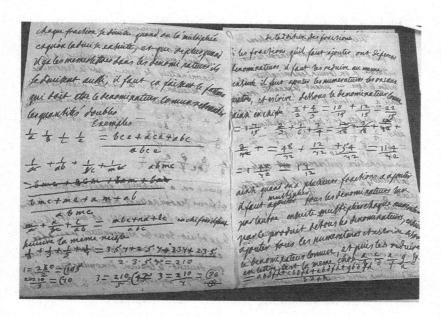

DRAFTS ON THE FOUNDATIONS OF PHYSICS

Credit: Émilie du Châtelet
Photo: Robin Stevens Payes

Catching my glance, Émilie says, "Oh, those papers. Nothing but the scribblings of a frustrated mathematician." She waves offhandedly. (Too bad I cannot convey how French is her accented English. But then, my American rendition probably sounds equally exotic to her.)

"Sit," she commands me, using her foot to pull out the small boudoir chair just beside her dressing table. I can see both of us reflected in the double mirrors—and realize that I look a wreck! I have the wig on backwards, with my own curls peeking out from under; the skirt Billy packed is humongous on me, and the hoodie over it looks redonkulous. No wonder the crowd fell silent when they saw me.

"*Eh bien!*" Émilie stands over me. "You are no messenger, correct?"

"Er, umm . . . well . . ." If she's going to interrogate me, first, I will need a cover story before I can decide how not to blow it. I shift uncomfortably in my seat.

"Well, yes. I am a messenger, of sorts," I say. "Just not for the King of France. Or any king." I glance up from under my wig to see how this is going over.

"*Évidemment.*"

"But I *can* share some information with you, to help in your, er, science experiments."

As I learned with Leonardo, "science" was not really a distinct subject back in the day, so I'm not sure whether she would consider her work to be advancing science. "Metaphysics" or "philosophy" seemed to have also encompassed what we now call science. "Your masterwork on Newton and Leibniz—*vis viva?*"

"My masterwork?" This perks her up. "Leibniz. *L'épreuve de force vive.* I am not sure how you are aware of my writings on this subject, unless you have been reading my correspondence." She looks me up and down suspiciously. "But it makes no difference right now; you have instruments that will help me in proving this?"

Again, I hesitate. The instruments I could show her are so much more advanced than anything available from London or Paris in this time. And the knowledge I have—about how her equations will lay down the predicate for an even more famous equation, $E=mc^2$ . . . Telling her about Einstein, as I did with Leonardo, could be even more dangerous under the circumstances.

"I find it hard to understand your words . . . why do you wear that covering over your mouth? Is there something malformed about it?"

Why indeed. I could try to make the case about viruses. The spread of germs through the air. But germs would not compute, thanks to the aforementioned discovery by Pasteur over a century from now. And I don't know enough about how this virus is transmitted to even attempt an explanation.

"You know of the smallpox inoculations that cure that deadly disease?"

"Well, yes, of course. The English noblewoman who must have endured exposure to this distemper when her husband was in service in Constantinople, in Istanbul—Lady Mary Wortley Montagu. V has written of her as 'a woman of as fine a genius, and endued with as great a strength of mind, as any of her sex in the British kingdoms.' A sister in science. There has been much resistance here in France to the variolation she promotes as a cure for *la variole*. Do you bring word from her?"

I am relieved to hear she is familiar with variolation, the earliest known process of vaccination, here against smallpox, where the scabs from patients with a mild form of the disease were blown up the nose of a healthy person as a way build up their immunity against more serious illness. A radical advancement in treatment against a deadly disease.

"Well, not exactly, but . . . there are a multitude of other easily spread 'distempers,' as you call them, that may not yet have a cure, or even a satisfactory treatment . . ." I wrack my brain to think back to what Billy was saying (will say?) about how new vaccines are being developed against COVID-19 that change the virus's DNA structure to make it less infectious.

"You have such a malady?"

"Umm . . ." There's really no way of knowing. But I cannot tell her that.

"Your words are getting lost inside your face covering. Will you not remove it, the better to hear you?"

In the end, there's nothing to do but comply.

As I peel away my mask. Émilie frowns. I can see the wheels spinning inside her head.

"*Et maintenant, ton perruque?*" she asks, wherein I pull off the wig.

"Oh! That feels so much better!" I scratch my head and let the air in. Although my hair has been partly smooshed, there's still a nest of curls around my face.

"We have met before, I believe. Was it at Versailles?"

Here's the crux of the matter: If I deny meeting her at Versailles, does that erase the history? Or would that be considered gaslighting? There is trouble enough in my own time with people trying to deny the truth of the past. And I don't want to get caught in a lie. On the other hand . . . how could I begin to explain?

"*Je m'appelle Charlotte,*" I say. I bow, just as I did that day so long ago.

"Charlotte," Émilie moves in and kisses me on each cheek, twice. "*Enchantée.*"

"Yeah. I mean, *Oui, enchantée,* I am sure."

"But you have not aged, Charlotte. *Comment expliquer . . . ?*"

I switch to French, aided by Esme. "*Eh bien, chère marquise, c'est une histoire incroyable—même à moi.*"

She looks at me hard, then at herself in the mirror. "*T'as trouvé la fontaine de jouvence, peut-être? On en a parler, bien sûr, en Floride, à l'Amérique.*"

"The fountain of youth? No, it's much more bizarre even than that."

"Oh, how interesting," she says with a little frisson of excitement. "How I love a good tale. You must dine with me this evening. Join me and Monsieur de Voltaire, and regale us with your marvelous story!"

It is not an invitation, but a command. Still, if it is dangerous for Émilie to notice my "eternal youth"—just think of what Voltaire's reaction would be to my presence here, when it was "*mon oncle Voltaire*" who saw to it that I would be released from the Bastille!

"*Merci beaucoup, madame,*" I whisper.

"Though first, we must make you look more presentable," Émilie observes, throwing open her armoire to show an amplitude of *robes à la française*, far finer than the one Bethy whipped up for me.

First, she dons one of her own beautiful gowns—an off-the-shoulder blue-and-yellow number. Given the match to her decor, I'm guessing these are her colors. Then she begins rifling through the rest of her dresses. "You look to be *un peu plus petite que moi.*"

Slightly smaller than her—an understatement. This might be a time to pull out Bethy's outfit-fitting app. But that would only raise further questions for which I have no good answer.

"Of course, this is only one part of my wardrobe, and *la Linant* can cinch you in to fit and pin up the hem," she is saying, looking me up and down. "Let us see the dress best suited for your petite frame."

She busily turns back to her wardrobe, pulling out one exquisite dress after another to find something closer to my size.

I have stopped paying attention, thinking this may be a once-in-a-lifetime chance to record history in the making.

First, the manuscript. I pull my phone from my backpack, surreptitiously snapping a pic for the record books. Scanning the room, I note that, positioned atop the mantle over the fireplace, is a framed parchment neatly scribed in a different hand. I walk over to decipher it.

Mais hélas, A + D - B / N'est pas = je vous aime." Signé, V.

VOLTAIRE'S POEM TO ÉMILIE DU CHÂTELET

Credit: Voltaire (François Marie Arouet)
Design: Melissa Brandstatter

Loosely translated: "Too bad no algebraic calculus can measure up to I love you."

I can relate to Voltaire's frustration.

There are more loose papers scattered on the mantelpiece, and a faint scent of perfume wafts from the pages. Scientific love letters (or love-of-science letters)—from correspondents as far away as Lapland, it would seem, from the postmark.

I marvel that here's the same pretty little snuffbox I have, with E and V's portraits painted on it, being used to weight down the edge of the page.

I pick it up to inspect; it looks so much like mine that I can't help but wonder if somehow, I haven't been here before. In fact, lined up against the wall is a whole collection of such boxes, each more lovely than the next. I can't imagine anyone would miss this one if I added the ceramic portrait-painted box to my collection a second time.

But the papers . . . that's the real proof.

I hold my finger down on my camera app and hear the whir: snap, snap, snap, snap, snap.

The camera click turns Émilie's head back in my direction.

"I recall now. You and *cette belle nègre, ton amie*—was it Elisabeth? *La mahométane?* You had this instrument at Versailles. It captured our portraits, no?"

La nègre. My friend. Beth. Her words sting.

Scanning my memory: What's the first Law of Holes? A comeback is in order, but I don't know what to say.

But Émilie's already moving on. She bustles out a gown of many colors—silk, with fine vertical stripes in gold, green, and scarlet, and white lace accenting the cap sleeves and square-cut neckline down to . . . who knows where—and brings it over to measure up against me.

"This ought to do, no?"

I cross my hands over my chest. While I've filled out a little in the boob department since middle school, I'm no Beth.

"*Ah, non, Charlotte, ma pauvre!*" Émilie sympathizes. "First, we will cinch you into a corset and stays to, *dis-on*—lift you. And the farthingale will draw attention to your hips"—I see her give my lower body a professional once-over—"and away from any, shall we say, deficiencies."

Before I can say, "Hey, no body-shaming here, Em," she's already begun tugging the corset down my body, under my chest, and around my waist, to tie me in. There are real whale stays sewn into the bodice of the dress, which should be made illegal here—first, to save the whales, and next, to save me. This being the real thing, and not something from a costume shop, it feels far more instrument-of-torture than fashion.

"Let us see if this will suit you. *Jupons* first," she says pulling one of the flouncy petticoats that go under these massive dresses up and tying it around my waist. Standing on a chair—no mean feat, given the dress and petticoats she has just put on—she lifts that no-doubt-expensive dress above my head.

She spins me to fasten the buttons up the back. There must be a million, or else time has stopped, for this dressing up leaves me feeling breathless and tired, unlike when Beth was taking a billion measurements for the first *robe à la française*.

"And finally, *une pièce d'estomac*."

A stomacher. I gather this is like a curtain they use over the top of the dress. It falls from shoulder to hem.

"This one accessory hides a multitude of sins, *chère* Charlotte."

It does indeed, being like a drape over my chest. Embroidered all over. Weird, but beautiful at the same time. The long silks swish as I tiptoe over to gaze at this new girl in the mirror.

"I give you Charlotte," Émilie says.

I wish Beth could see me now.

Inspecting me closer, she says, "We will find for you a more fashionable wig. And jewels. I see you have a lovely little necklace already. A gift from a lover?"

I feel myself blushing up to my ears.

"But of course. Perhaps we can add a gold ring and bracelets from my collection. Do you prefer rubies or emeralds?"

"No, jewels, *merci*. No, your generosity—"

"It's hardly generosity, *ma chère*. We must make you presentable."

Then, in a more ingratiating tone, she places her long fingers around my phone.

"And now. How can I know you are not reporting news for the *Mercure Galant* or, worse, that reprobate Abbé Desfontaines, capturing images of my private letters?"

Ouch.

It would make sense that she would be suspicious of me: a girl who popped in as a teen when Émilie was also a young woman, and twelve years later, popped in again, still a teen. I had studied enough history to know about the newspaper she referenced. It reported on fashion, Court gossip (of which there was plenty), the travels and travails of the nobility—always dedicated to the King. Meaning: Whether I'm reporting for the broadsheet or spying for the King, it's the same thing. Someone else could report on me, as easily as I might report on them. Meaning: Conviction for spying leads to a new visit to the Bastille, or worse, exile to a convent in the Louisiana territories.

I have little time to ponder such horrors, though. More immediately, how do I prove my innocence in the here and now? Especially since it is true that I have presumably captured some of her most consequential ideas and personal notes from her lover on my phone.

"Oh, this dress. The jewels. So beautiful . . . Truly, I couldn't, Émilie!" I exclaim, trying to change the subject. "It is more than I could ever repay you for . . ."

"Undoubtedly," she says wryly.

She eyes my phone again, like she can't let it go.

Maybe I can show her some of our girl pics from Versailles; would that be so horrible?

It's at that moment I realize it was Beth's phone, not mine, that captured our earlier meeting.

"Dammit, Beth!"

"Elisabeth is here?" she asks, genuinely interested. "I would like to see her again. Is she, like you, frozen in time?"

"No. Not here. Back in Maryland. *A l'Amérique.*"

As if that settles it.

I scroll quickly through my pics to see if I have anything even remotely presentable. Luckily, it doesn't seem to matter anymore, as Émilie seems to have dropped it.

"*Allons-y, dépêches-toi,*" she says, turning on her red-soled heels. "We do not have all the time in the world, *mademoiselle.*"

I stifle a retort. Because, in my experience, we kind of do have all the time in the world.

She crooks an arm for me to take it.

"*Je vous en prie, madame.*" I need to stop digging.

I secret my phone, the compass, and a face mask under the stomacher for temporary safekeeping.

"Now, earrings—tiny emeralds, to bring out your beautiful eyes. Pearls around your neck, perhaps? This delightful little necklace you wear—*le médaillon* . . . he is a compass?"

"*Mon petit ami . . . un cadeau,*" I begin to explain, faltering as she fusses over me.

"And for the crowning touch, your wig." She pulls a powdered model—something that would add at least four inches to my height—from a wig stand in the little dressing room. She adds a little more powder, which then flies through the air.

"Achoo!"

"*Santé!*" Émilie responds.

My health. I briefly recall that no one uses talc anymore in my time, if that's what they use to powder the wigs—something about it causing cancer—but I am in no position to argue.

She positions the wig atop my own curls, tucking them in.

"And more flour to complete the effect." She picks up a silver bottle, about the size of a flask, with a hose and a rubber end—sort of like Mamma's turkey baster, but smelling of roses.

A puff of powder escapes. And flour: It's like she read my mind. Good to know.

"Oh, no, you are too kind, Émilie, really! Now, if we're about done here, I wonder if I might ask you a few questions. Not spying or anything," I hasten to add.

But she's not done. I see her taking a velvet ribbon; it feels like she's weaving it through the curls, and then I can feel her poking pins strategically throughout.

I can't let this moment escape without getting in a few questions. After all, I came here to learn how this woman, back in the day, was able to so daringly challenge the conventional wisdom of her time. After all, most educated French people still believed in Descartes' scientific method—that everything in the universe could be described as matter, and not mathematics, as Newton's work revealed.

"So, Émilie," I turn to face her. "Woman to woman here: I think you're brave to challenge traditional women's roles. How do you stick to it, what with all your critics?"

"Stay still!" She pokes me in the head. I screech and turn back. "It is my passion to learn about the world," she says. "I want to know *everything!*"

We share this passion. "But you're the pioneer here. So cool that you're grokking Newton and all that." I stop a minute to reflect. Is she already working on her magnum opus French translation of Newton's Laws from the Latin he wrote in? "I mean, do most girls get to learn so many languages, and science. And AP Calculus AB?"

Oops, no Advanced Placement courses now. No public school. And probably no calculus as we'd take it in high school or college.

But she seems to catch the drift. "I was fortunate: Papa recognized early on that I was smarter than my older brother. He brought home books and hired tutors for me. *Maman* wanted to marry me off to someone of high rank when I was sixteen or seventeen. When I protested, she tried to send me away to a convent school—the only socially acceptable option at the time for a girl of high birth."

She's now pulling out a box overflowing with brooches and buttons, pearls and gold filigree bracelets. I am such an anti-frou-frou that, to me, they all look ridiculous.

"Okay, so what happened next?"

She curses, pulling out a tangle of gold chains. I'm hoping she's not going to cuff those around my wrists.

"To me, to be sent away to school with the nuns would have been a fate worse than death. I believed, along with Leibniz, that God was the Prime Mover of the Universe—a sort of force that set all things in motion. That is the only rational understanding for God. So, you see, I knew too much of the new science to go along with strict Church teachings." She clicks her teeth, deciding. "Now, then, do you prefer rubies or emeralds, Charlotte?"

I can't really picture all the bling she's added, but my neck bows under the weight.

Slapping dust vigorously from my neck and shoulders, she stands back to observe.

"Your face—we must whiten it." She uses a brush to paint on a white substance, to match her own white face. "It is the habit at Court, although I cannot for the life of me understand why Her Majesty the Queen refuses this fashion. And Monsieur de Montesquieu, he has criticized women for living under a mask, for fear of a tan."

Again, it's a product-ingredient thing that only we moderns might be wary of. I'm not sure what's in the white face paint, but I pray it isn't lead. I want also to affirm the link between sun and skin cancer—protection from the sun is not dumb.

I open my mouth, only to be accosted further with the brush.

"*Un peu de rouge à lèvres.* Your lips are so pale."

She's being kind—they're chapped and peeling from my biting them so much. I purse my lips as she paints them with a dusty rouge, adding a dab of it to my cheeks as well.

"*Et maintenant, la mouche.*" She affixes a star-shaped fake beauty mark she calls "the fly" next to my dimple, then turns to straighten the dress with its long train behind me.

"But . . . if you had been able to go to a *real* school?" I ask.

"If I were King, I would redress an abuse which cuts back, as it were, one-half of humankind. I would have women participate in all human rights, especially those of the mind."

My admiration knows no bounds. Career. Family. Social status. Studying. Writing. Even acting with the great philosopher and playwright Voltaire.

"Participating in society as an equal to men. Is that what drove you?"

"*Franchement*, life is too short. I am determined to get everything done."

"You got that right." Even a life lived in multiple time periods, I think to myself.

"*Eh, voilà!*" says Émilie, smiling in satisfaction. "A little tuck here and a big hem there," she says, spinning me around, "and we will make your lover blush. *Regards!*"

I turn once more to see myself in the mirror. I don't even look like me. Not even Beth's dress and expert makeup artistry could ever make me look so much like Cinderella.

For posterity, and for a future Fashion Forward Live, I film a selfie in facing mirrors, Émilie's face captured behind mine in ever smaller view, like the Quaker on the oatmeal box.

I try to imagine Billy blushing at seeing me this way. He likely wouldn't even notice. But it might be good if he were ever able to come here, in this time. He could see how super smart people can not only think, but also be fashion-forward, and engage in charming conversation as well.

Besides, I miss him.

An irritated male voice rings out, startling me out of whatever rabbit hole I might be diving into.

"Émilie! Have you seen the latest attacks on me by that ingrate, the so-called pillar of the Church, Desfontaines?"

"Ah," she whispers, "it is Monsieur de Voltaire. He is in a rare fit of mania over the latest accusations of l'Abbé. You would be better served to hide in here"—she points to the dressing room—"until I can calm him."

She pushes me toward the little room.

I have just enough presence of mind to grab my backpack. Whatever the scandal, hiding out will buy me a little time to get my cover story straight for V, aka, *mon oncle*, aka, Voltaire.

I duck my head and drag the dress behind me, squishing myself sideways through the low, narrow doorway just in time, for I hear him enter, cursing.

"*Espèce de salaud. Après tout ce que j'ai fait à garder son peau des feux de l'Inquisition!*"

Fires of the Inquisition. Still! I shudder. 'Cause I've had more than a bit of personal experience in that department!

Émilie kicks the door firmly shut behind me, almost catching the hem of my dress.

"I am so glad you have returned, and I want to hear all about your voyage. But first, will you please button me up, V? I have no idea of the whereabouts of that incompetent, Mademoiselle Linant—she has absolutely left me undone."

"*Comment tu m'as manquée!*"

"*Pas plus que moi!*"

My mind is too befuddled to think in French right now—thankfully, my phone is holding its charge. I look around for a plug—forgetting for a moment that we are in a pre-electrified world. Did Billy pack a solar charger? Not that there's any sunlight in here now. Digging at the bottom of the backpack, my fingers grasp a couple of Tylenol and crumbs from what must have been Billy's last sandwich.

"Hopeless," I exclaim.

In a side pocket, where I'm hoping to find more than crumbs, I see Billy's left me a spare battery—just in case. And last, but perhaps most, I drop the compass between my boobs, held in place by the tight-cut bodice underneath the stomacher.

I plop myself, dress, wig, and all, on top of the little dressing chair, with one ear pressed against the door.

"*T'as passé une bonne journée, mon cher?*" I hear Émilie asking.

There is a short little exchange in French—too low for me to hear. Émilie giggles; Voltaire recites what must be a short poem, followed by a peal of laughter from them both. I imagine there's a little make-out session to celebrate V's return.

"I bring you some small, but very dear gifts," he says, loudly, after a too-long moment, "to reach the heart of Madame Pompon-Newton."

"*Tu n'auras pas dû!*" she exclaims excitedly.

She must be unwrapping a package because the next sound is a little gasp of delight.

"Oh, V, you shouldn't have! More diamonds and rubies! I feel like the Queen herself."

"*Voilà.* Allow me, *ma chère!*"

Another gasp, and then dear reader, I can feel a blush starting at my toes. It's like, get a room—but then again, they're in it.

At that moment, I'm startled by an unexpected ping.

"No, not now!" I insist and clap my mouth for shouting that out loud.

"*Qu'est-ce que c'est, Madame* . . . ? Have you been hiding secrets from me, again?" It's Voltaire's voice.

I fiddle with my phone, which pings a second time. Esme! Before I can turn her to silent, I see a voice recording. "Charley, I have reset the apps on your phone. I think I can now track where and when you have landed. It's like GPS-plus."

"Billy!" It's like he was reading my mind. But, then, who is this Billy: the 2019 original? Or the 2020 version I hardly know?

Putting the phone up to my ear, I try to tune in. His voice continues: "You will not necessarily understand this, but COVID is highly transmissible, and . . ." The recording becomes garbled.

So it's the 2020 him.

"Billy? Billy!" I stab repeatedly at the play button.

Voltaire has started to rage. "Billy? Billy?! Who is this Billy?!"

Billy's voice pops back. "So, obviously you understand the dangers . . ."

"No, obviously I don't! What dangers . . . ?"

"*Arrêtes! Qui c'est, là-dedans?*" Voltaire interrupts.

With that, Émilie kicks lightly at the door.

"I believe it is *La Linant*. I have asked her to powder my wigs."

I clap my hand over my mouth.

"Linant. I do not believe you. *Laisses-moi voir.*"

"See? Linant?" she bellows. "Why do you doubt me?"

At that, another muffled round of, "*Je t'aime autant . . .*" "*Non, je t'aime le plus . . .*"

Ugh!

"There is no need for jealousy, my love. I speak of the King of Prussia, Frederick William, of course. For he is a dear Billy, to me. Whom you have presumably just returned from visiting, my dear—and I am dying to hear news of your travels."

Voltaire's voice has dropped to a grumble.

Despite being distracted by Billy's super unclear message, I turn my mind to a more proximal problem. Dining with Voltaire might turn into rather an existential event.

I finger my face mask. While putting it back on might not stop me from blurting out random stuff in sticky situations, it would certainly smear my lipstick and knock off the beauty mark. I'm beginning to understand how the face masks Billy gave me are not mere 2020 style accessories.

Meanwhile, I don't dare try sending back a voice memo, 'cause they can clearly hear me talking. But if I can record E and V . . . and send their voices across the ages . . .

I hunch over to type beneath the cloth-covered vanity.

NOT SURE HOW YOU'RE TRACKING. I'M IN ÉMILIE'S DRESSING ROOM AT CIREY CHÂTEAU (FOR REALS!) LISTENING TO AN EPIC CONVO BETWEEN HER AND VOLTAIRE. WILL TRY SENDING.

I must raise up the phone to see if I can activate Billy's enhanced magnification that presumably will work using quantum principles of nonlocality or, in Einstein's famous words, "spooky action at a distance."

But my hand is tangled in a lace cloth covering the table and, in trying to extricate it, I pull down one wig stand and another and another, all in a row. And these aren't Styrofoam forms, dear reader—they are heavy, carved wooden heads. They fall like dominoes. I try to keep them from hitting the ground, but it's too late—they clatter against the tiles.

As the flour flies, it sets me off again. "Achoo!"

XXXIX.

A Little Theater

Dying under the footlights in the room where it happens

With that, Voltaire busts in. The very guy who sprang me from the Bastille.

"You, *mademoiselle?!*" he cries out. "You are the one who has made all this clatter?"

It's clear he expected someone else on the other side.

Émilie rushes over, her neck and wrists now aglitter in diamonds and rubies, and gathers me to her bosom. "*Charlotte, je te présente Monsieur de Voltaire.*"

Her elaborate new diamond choker chafes against my neck. I pull away.

"Monsieur de Voltaire!" I exclaim, doing my elaborate curtsy, but it's clear Voltaire's brain has already begun working away.

He bows deeply and takes my hand. "Charlotte. We have met before."

It's not a question.

"Umm, er, eh . . ." I stammer.

Émilie lifts an eyebrow. "You have met? What? How?"

Voltaire turns to her. "The Bastille, was it not?"

My tongue is twisted. "Umm, well, as unbelievable as this may sound, I . . . or you . . ."

"Faith consists in believing when it is beyond the power of reason to believe."

"So, is she the girl?!" Émilie looks from V to me and back. "I heard a rumor—a report years ago while you were in that wretched prison, as it were, about a girl who was arrested for raising the dead. Is this she?" She fixes a stare at Voltaire.

"Well, I—if you will only allow me . . ." I stammer, thinking this deserves an explanation, only I have no idea what it will be.

Voltaire nods. "It is she."

Émilie turns toward me. "But how could that be! V told me you were taken for a spy and would be hanged."

"It seemed that was a case of mistaken identity," V replies. "Charlotte, here, was taken on trumped-up charges. Your dear departed father, *ma chère Émilie*, championed her release, thanks to his clout at Court."

"Appearances," I am finally able to pipe up, on my own behalf, "are what we make of them."

"*Le resurrectionisme*. Forces of unreason. Perhaps your appearance here, *mademoiselle*, goes beyond reason," Émilie suggests.

I wish I could dive into what we know in my time about quantum physics, entanglement, and Einstein's aforementioned "spooky action" to justify the possibility of my being here.

Instead, I must settle for a riddle. "Beyond reason, but not beyond possibility."

"It is said that the present is pregnant with the future," Voltaire replies, staring now at me.

"Yes, yes! *Exactement,*" I reply excitedly. "Er, not pregnant exactly, but . . ."

Voltaire throws Émilie a smug smile.

Emilie considers. "One might even argue that the state of an element being given to determine the past state, the present, and the future of all the universe—they all must coexist, as they each have a relation, each to the other. Gottfried Leibniz's system—where each object is pre-synchronized at the moment of its creation to unfold in *le meilleur des mondes possibles,* which contains its own inevitable past, present and future—would predict this," she smiles back.

In the mirror, I see Voltaire grimace as Émilie expounds on Leibniz's famous theory that we live in "the best of all possible worlds," but decide to ignore the playwright's distaste for the man and his philosophy (V being a confirmed Newtonian!). 'Cause speaking of an inevitable future, I know his future hit play, *Candide,* is a satire on Leibniz. As in, gotcha Gottfried!

I butt in to see if I'm grokking. "So if I'm getting you, here, Em, you're saying someone . . . or something . . . programmed us from the get-go to become all that we will be. *C'est ça?*"

"*Pas moi, ma chère, mais le bon Dieu.* These are the metaphysics of Monsieur Leibniz."

God as computer programmer. Not everyone would buy this in my time. I scan my memory banks to recall what Einstein theorized about time's unfolding.

"Weird, but the world's most famous physicist, Albert Einstein, wrote almost the same thing to one of his best friends, also a physicist. "People like us, who believe in physics, know that the distinction between past, present, and future is only a stubbornly persistent illusion."

"Ah, but then I must one day meet this Monsieur Einstein!" Émilie winks at me, raising her palm for a *tapes m'en cinq.*

Feels like we're all on the same wavelength. But I may be getting way out in front of my skis.

"For I have observed that the attraction of celestial bodies is proportional to mass, both in the attracting bodies and in the bodies attracted," Émilie says.

Which would definitely seem to apply in the *force of attraction* between E and V. Love and love's fire spark together in the Age of Reason.

"Yet this does little to explain who you really are, and why you are here," Émilie says, releasing her arm from around my shoulders.

Here's the kicker: Reason only goes so far—for when we dive into the quantum universe, not to mention the multiverse, of which this may be but one reality, things get wonky and reason no longer applies.

Voltaire, seeing me hesitate, responds, "But, of course, you have reason, my muse, my Minerva. But it is Monsieur Locke, the English philosopher, who has the last word on this subject: 'Not everything can be measured. Is not experience the source of human knowledge?' As for Charlotte, here, we experience her presence, and therefore, she is. Is this not true, Madame Pompon-Newton, in this best of all possible worlds?"

This discourse takes place in a dizzying Franglais, melding the philosophies of Newton, Locke, and Descartes, so that not even Esme can decipher it with any accuracy. Though my ears do pick up on his last words—I recognize them from Voltaire's *Candide*, and the musical version I got to see with Dad when I was a kid, with Mamma playing in the orchestra.

Under my breath, I try to hum a few notable bars from the musical: "There is a reason for everything under the sun . . . in the best of all possible worlds."

"Aha!" Voltaire exclaims. "She sings! Therefore, she must perform in this evening's spectacle, my dear Émilie, *The Prodigal Child!* It is a comedy, *chère Charlotte*. Oh, it is perfect, is it not?"

How amazing—and also terrifying—is this: Voltaire is inviting me to act in one of his comedies!

"Oh, really, V! I was so hoping Pauline could take on the role. My daughter," she explains to me, "is due to arrive later this evening from the convent in Joinville, where the nuns take care of her education."

"The convent?" I ask, a bit acerbically. Too good for the mother, but not the daughter.

"Yes, too bad. But I think Charlotte is made for this role. *Oui?*" Voltaire takes me by the hand, "Illusion is the first of all pleasures."

Émilie looks me up and down. "Can you make believe you are lying ill in bed while I, your mother, pray that you will be restored to me?"

I cough as if to audition, though, in fact, the cough is real. "While I'm not sure how my dying would be done to comic effect, Madame, and while I am completely unrehearsed, I am quite sure I can lie still onstage, if that is all that is required."

"That will do!" Voltaire shouts, giving Madame his own *tapes m'en cinq*.

XL.

THIS CASTLE'S TOO HOT

I hope this is not what I think it is

Almost as soon as this is decided, E and V disappear to their respective desks.

It appears by his quick escape that Voltaire's room, in another wing of the house, can be accessed by a secret staircase. I am dying to explore, but that might seem rude.

As night's shadows lengthen, a young maidservant who looks a little younger than me bustles in to light the twenty or so candles around the room. The flames dance, and Émilie's diamonds glitter, brightening the room even more. After the girl stirs the embers in the fireplace, the room blazes with heat. She makes a little bow and backs out.

Fuss all around her, and the goddess of science sits in her Temple, a model of focus, her brow furrowed. I'm curious to get a glimpse of whatever work commands her attention now. Imagine seeing this science mind at work!

With swishing dress, I tiptoe to spy over her shoulder, expecting to see notes for her translation of Newton, or calculations from her recent experiments on *force vive*. Instead, I see she's inked her plume to scribe, *Mon Cher V, Coeur de mon Coeur,* in big sweeping letters. Heart of my heart. It's almost like she's paper-texting her lover, even though he's just left her room.

I'd love to show her how much easier it is to send text messages, but there's that paradox thing again. Plus, it might erase her legacy. After all, who would ever preserve cryptic texts as a part of the historical record, like they do Émilie's and Voltaire's letters?

Noticing me hanging around, she shields the page with her hand, to wave me off.

"You must be famished, dear Charlotte. Go, find yourself something in the kitchen. Cook has been preparing for a big supper—and you may even find his thick, crusty, country bread, warm out of the oven!"

Okay, now she's speaking my language! As someone whose previous experience of time travel to the home of pasta and pizza (btw, let's just blow open that myth!) left me with nary a crumb to eat, I can't wait to sample authentic French cuisine.

Heading out, I have no idea where to find the kitchen, except by smell; I hope my nose will guide me true. I notice that I actually can't smell anything at the moment, which is weird.

I get detoured by the library, filled with books that might be the envy of anyone who loves reading and knowledge. I read somewhere that she and Voltaire collected something like 21,000 books. I imagine this would more than rival the much later collection Thomas Jefferson gave to the newly created United States to form the Library of Congress.

I am waylaid once again by Voltaire, who introduces me to the Cirey cast of players (and regulars, I gather, to the castle): Madame de Graffigny; the loud and very large Marquis du Châtelet in his naval uniform (yes, really, this is Émilie's actual husband!); the Venetian, Algarotti, whose writings about Newton's theories are aimed specifically at Italian women; and their Cirey neighbor, Madame de Champbonin—all staying here.

Voltaire, it seems, must regale his audience with the story of our original meeting in the Bastille, which is greeted with oohs and aahs—and which I, for one, wish he wouldn't brag about.

Thankfully, being himself, the conversation immediately turns to the regrettable power of the King to detain innocent men (and women) without evidence. And the high price of setting them free. The women seem more interested in details about the evening's entertainment later on, and Algarotti seems more than happy to conduct a brief focus group with the gathered ladies to add to his Newton dialogues.

I am getting that #newtonmania is sweeping the world, or at least this part of Europe. So much chatter and misinformation; it's all getting a little unnerving.

When I feel my phone vibrate under Émilie's dress once again, I am more than happy to tune out the whole discussion and try to catch a glimpse of any new message, in any form, that might save me from the plague of boredom.

I first touch the elastic from the face mask tucked inside my stomacher, reminding me of other plagues.

Finally, we hear a louder bell announcing dinner. Entering the dining room, with candlelit chandeliers, I see no servants, but two hatches—one for food, and the other, apparently, to clear dirty plates. Clean dishes and silver appear between courses. This novel form of dumbwaiter looks to be an innovation!

The feast looks sumptuous—that fresh-baked bread Émilie mentioned earlier, greens from the garden, a big steaming rack of lamb, little roasted capons (like mini chickens), an array of cheeses including brie, camembert, Roquefort, and others I've never seen before, a cornucopia of apples and pears, and an ample supply of wine and champagne—but I smell nothing.

For once, I am not hungry. Tired. Too much time travel.

But I know I should eat anyway. I cut into the skin of a little capon, careful to mimic the table manners of my hosts (knife in left hand, fork in right, without switching—and even though I'm a leftie, I follow suit), and steam pours out. Normally, I'd be salivating. I put a bite in my mouth but without smell, the taste buds seem to be shut off as well. It kind of reminds me of one of my favorite books as a kid, *A Wrinkle in Time*, when Meg and Charles Wallace are searching for their dad, off on the planet Camazotz, where, to Charles, the turkey dinner served up to them tastes like sand.

Ditto! I can hardly muster the will not to spit it out.

As the evening progresses, it seems playing ill should not be a problem. My throat feels scratchy. I feel headachy. I hope it's nothing but a bit of a sore throat coming on.

The talk at the table turns to gossip from Paris, though Madame de Graffigny seems intent on talking more about her friend Pan-Pan, whoever that is. Seems he lives in a place called Lunéville, part of Prussia (and also part of France, apparently—I find this part extremely confusing and wish I could search the Internet for it), where aforementioned Frederick William, aka, Billy, is the king. I gather they are all friends, or maybe frenemies.

Madame asks me which of the American colonies I come from, and where my people hailed from before landing on the Maryland shores. I manage to rasp out a few polite words (although saying my ancestors are British doesn't exactly inspire enthusiasm), but my throat is tightening.

Thankfully, Voltaire launches into his time in exile in jolly old England, arriving just in time for Newton's lying in state at Westminster Abbey, when he was first introduced to the work of the brilliant physicist, and yammering on about Newton's influence, and how he had written letters for Jonathan Swift of *Gulliver's Travels* fame, to come to France. And how that visit never materialized, despite their mutual admiration.

Either way, my head is spinning. It must be all the excitement, and the wig and dress are so hot. Indeed, there are furnaces ablaze in every room, although everyone at dinner besides Émilie complains about the chill.

Dizziness not resolving, I excuse myself from the table—after putting my dishes in the dirty dish hatch, as I've noticed the other guests doing—to go outside after dinner and before the play for some fresh air and to study my part. Luckily, it seems I don't have many lines; anyways, it's too dark out to read, and the flickering candles in the windows cast more shadow than light.

The hoot of an owl, the dark of the night, and the sound of footsteps approaching cause me to turn around (perhaps a little PTSD from my earlier experience in cemeteries!). But it is only Mademoiselle Linant, following me at a discreet distance. Makes me wonder if they still think me a spy.

I can't think about it now. I try to take deep breaths, but the corset keeps me from it, and the stays cut into my ribs. I wish I could ditch the whole thing and run around in my shift. I think about Émilie's bath earlier—bathing in bubbles sounds so lovely.

La Linant stays close to the house—perhaps she knows something I don't about what is out here—but I need to be away from all that to clear my head and give me time to think. I see a large shadow of a structure—it looks like a low outbuilding—and walk in that direction. It is very slow going, as now I'm getting chills. It's more than the hot hearth, the hot dress, the stays, and the wig; I'm feverish.

I feel myself falling. The sensation reminds me of how my time travels always start out—slow, then with dizzying and accelerating force. I pray that this isn't what's happening here. I don't know if I could stand the physical strain in my present condition, and besides, I remind myself, I have a starring role in one of Voltaire's plays, a once-in-a-lifetime performance with the maestro himself directing, and Émilie du Châtelet playing my mother.

Still, I feel the world spinning, spinning . . .

"When am I?" Always my first question. I come to slowly, sitting myself up on my elbows. Mademoiselle Linant, fanning me, has me laid out on a workbench next to a fireplace, with enough stacks of firewood to heat a factory, and a hood for ventilation. A bellows stands beside it. The chimney contains rows of jars and ceramic vessels, neatly arranged.

As I glance around, it seems we are in a dank workshop beneath the house amid all the chemical tools of another century: furnaces—presumably for melting lead into gold in pursuit of that age-old, get-rich-quick myth of practicing alchemy, scales to weigh it, prisms, thermometers, clay vessels, beakers for measuring, glass test tubes, metal buckets, a pair of small "state of the art" telescopes, a microscope, compasses, and other weights and measures neatly aligned on shelves or strewn on workbenches—works in progress—or tables pushed against the walls.

There are two globes on one of the tables—and a portrait hung above of a dude dressed in exotic (for France, at that time) winter clothes, is portrayed with one hand pushing down on the top of a globe as though to flatten it at the poles.

**PORTRAIT OF PIERRE-LOUIS MOREAU
DE MAUPERTUIS**

Credit: Robert Tournières, Public Domain

It's labeled Maupertuis, who I know to have been one of Émilie's calculus teachers, and also a lover. Beneath, a little poem (by V, no less!):

> *Ce globe mal connu, qu'il a su mesurer,*
> *Devient un monument où sa gloire se fonde,*
> *Son sort est de fixer la figure du monde,*
> *De lui plaire et de l'éclairer.*

> This little-known world which he knew how to measure,
> Becomes a monument where he bases his glory,
> His destiny is to describe the world,
> To please and to enlighten it.

And here I stand in the famous Cirey laboratory, where V and E seek to base their glory and to enlighten the world.

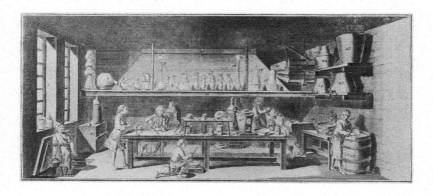

18TH CENTURY FRENCH LABORATORY
Credit: Engraving (CC BY 4.0)

Coming to my senses, I can still feel the room rotating. Or my head. It appears I must have fainted.

"Your fever . . . we must send *pour le médicin*," insists Linant. She then proceeds to tell me that the nearest reputable doctor is ten miles away, in Joinville. It is the middle of the night. Arriving by carriage will take hours.

No phones. No highways. No cars. No telemedicine visits. I think about the Tylenol I found earlier in the backpack and wonder if I can retrieve it . . .

I sit up, with difficulty. "*No, merci. Pas de docteur. C'est rien.*"

Even the sight of leeches makes me throw up, much less having them suck "bad blood" out of my body. And other cures available in this century—enemas, smallpox inoculation, amputation—seem less than equal to whatever I may be afflicted with. A country bumpkin of a doctor is the last thing I need.

"Allow me to at least send for my brother to get help. It will do no good to alarm *la Marquise et le Monsieur* needlessly," she insists. She is clearly more worried about the state of my health than I am.

"I am *fine*," I insist, pushing up from the bench a little breathlessly. "Besides, the show must go on!"

XLI.

LIFE MEETS ART

Or is it the other way around?

T he little theater is so charming.

While I'm offstage, I peek out from behind the folds of the blue curtain with its gold accents and fringe, into the audience.

"*Merde!*" I say to Émilie, hoping that even now it means good luck in the theater, and not, you know, something a little saltier.

The divine Madame Em raises her hand for the more traditional (by now) *tapes m'en cinq*. I meet her hand in more of a grasp.

"*Les mains, si froid*," she whispers, rubbing two hands over mine together to create friction, transforming kinetic energy into heat.

She ushers me in to take my place on the divan, center stage.

As the curtain rises, I squint to survey the little crowd from earlier that has reassembled. Anyone from earlier who's not in the play is in the audience. It looks like someone, perhaps V himself, stands in the box overlooking us—but upon further scrutiny, I can see that's a trompe l'oeil; the scene's painted on the wall.

With difficulty, I turn my head in the other direction—my aching neck notwithstanding—and see a frescoed set behind us using the same trompe l'oeil technique, and made to look like a country kitchen: a big fireplace, shelves on which are plates and cups, and a hook from which someone has hung actual pots and pans.

To the audience, I imagine, the kitchen looks quite real.

"*Ma pauvre Marthe!*" Émilie exclaims over her very sick daughter, aka, *moi.*

So my character's name is Martha. I can't remember if I have a line.

She speaks her lines in a loud stage voice. The French sounds foreign to my ears and Esme, it seems, has failed me. Or maybe it's more that my earbuds have fallen out.

I feel like an elephant is sitting on my lungs as I try, in vain, to cough. It's harder and harder to breathe. Maybe I really am dying.

I finally admit to myself that what started out feeling like a bad cold or the flu may be something much worse. It's weird that, for the first time in my life, I actually got a flu shot this year. (A random, and probably worthless, rabbit hole: Which strain of flu would've been around in 1736?)

With difficulty, I turn on my hip to face the audience, hoping to loosen the phlegm.

"*Maman* . . . Émilie, I think I really need a doctor," I wheeze.

"*Ma pauvre,*" begins Émilie again, dropping her stage voice, putting a hand over my forehead and scooting closer to the divan to support my back so I can rest more comfortably on my hip. "Thank *le bon Dieu* you have returned. But to see you in such a weakened condition!"

As if on cue, a too-familiar male voice starts lecturing. The worst possible timing for a butt dial; it seems I've accidentally hit play on Billy's message.

"The thing about this virus—you can lose your sense of smell and taste. And it comes from bats. Chinese bats."

"Bats!" I exclaim, my lungs squeezing inside my chest. From the audience, a peal of laughter. Why they should find this funny, I have no idea. It is well-known, at least in my century, that birds can transmit viruses to humans.

"I was raised by bats!" Voltaire exclaims, as he jumps out of his box, audience right, and onto the proscenium, seeming unable to restrain himself, "and no one here can fill your head with lies."

I can't help but look startled. There's a modern-ish band, Lair of Voltaire, that recorded a song by that title. I only know, because Beth made me listen to it with her over and over in her vampire stage. (She was *obsessed*.)

Automatically, I croak out the next line: "Why you gotta be like that?"

"Dare to think for yourself," he says, "for you, *Marthe*, are the prodigal child."

"My dearest girl, you must live at all costs," Émilie improvises, caressing my hair, er, wig; then looking at V, she adds, "We must send for the doctor. She will have care for her health!"

I swear, no one could make this stuff up! In what's turning into a parody of a *Saturday Night Live* parody, Voltaire replies, "The art of medicine consists in amusing the patient while nature cures the disease."

"But I don't have time to wait," I cough out.

On cue, a Dr. So-and-So, face covered with a plague mask and carrying a doctor's bag, jumps onto the edge of the little stage and shouts "*Medicus est in domo! Patientes estote ad examine mihi.*"

Kairos—thank God!

"You are a sight for sore eyes," I mumble, an echo from a time before.

"Worry not, fair Marthe," he says facing the audience. "I have my instruments."

But first he must push past an increasingly excited Monsieur de Voltaire.

"Is it the smallpox?" Kairos asks.

"I have already had la variole and so am immune. . . . Doctor, have you the requisite scabs from the pox to treat poor Marthe?"

V's apparently talking about variolation—the cure milady Mary brought back from Turkey. Which is crazy. No one in the world today . . . er, my world today . . . gets smallpox. It's been eradicated by vaccine.

But I can't exactly tell him that.

Kairos, thank God, has beaten me to the punch. "It is not the variole she suffers from, Monsieur, but another disease related to *le rheum.*"

As he explains the outlines of what may be the new coronavirus Billy warned me about, he adeptly places a modern hospital mask over my nose and mouth and loops it around my ears.

"Where did you get . . . ?" I try to puff out, but it is useless trying to speak—or to figure out the mysterious ways of K, man from the deep past, or perhaps the future.

"It may be transmitted through animal contact. Bats. There is as yet no treatment."

I hear everyone in the theater inhale—then, all hell breaks loose.

The stable boy interrupts. "The sheep in the meadow, cows at pasture—they have been showing signs of strange behavior."

La Linant covers her mouth with one hand and points at me with the other. "She—Charlotte—was headed to the stables before she fainted. I fetched her in from the freezing night air. I knew there was something strange about this girl . . ."

Madame de Graffigny, ever the busybody, starts buzzing even before rising from her seat. "I knew we should not admit her to the château. I must go to my rooms at once. I will write Pan-Pan about this."

Meanwhile, Émilie and Voltaire, still onstage, seem immune to the panic, acting as if this is all part of Voltaire's play.

XLII.

About Time!

Quacks, vaxx, and quantum time crystals—wait, what?

Voltaire squeezes in between me and Kairos and takes hold of my wrist as if checking my blood pressure. "She has weakened. *Docteur,* your diagnosis?"

Madame la Marquise is pacing downstage. "My beloved child! If only you had come home sooner, you might not be at death's door," she emotes. "You must live!"

At which moment, who should run up onstage but her daughter IRL, Pauline. "Fear not, *maman, j'arrive!*"

I try to push up on my elbows to catch a glimpse of the nine-year-old future duchess and lady-in-waiting to the Queen of Naples. She is tall and gangly, like her mother, and, it seems, just as impulsive.

But my head is foggy under the heavy wig, and I can feel that my glands are swollen to the size of golf balls.

"Ooh, I want my mamma."

"And just who is this imposter?!" Pauline says, indignantly. "I hurried here at your request, *Maman*, and learned my lines in the *post-chaise* on the way home, only to find you have replaced me—with her!"

"*Oh, ma fille!*" Émilie says, momentarily stepping out of character. She pulls her real daughter into an embrace without leaving my side.

Quite the tableau.

"*Desolée, mon chou*, but I didn't know when you might arrive. And Charlotte, here—"

"Charlotte!" shrieks Pauline. "*C'est qui, ça?*"

V jumps in, improvising again, as if this is all part of the action. "She is the Countess Charlotte of Maryland, of course. A visitor from the Colonies."

Amid all the hubbub, K leans over me and wipes my face with a cool cloth. "Carlotta . . . Charlotte," he whispers, "you can stay no longer in this place."

"How am I to leave, pray tell, Dr. K?"

He opens his doctor's kit and begins to sort through it. To my astonishment, I see he has three vials of liquid of the kind that go into shots in the arm.

"It is only due to this very cold winter that these vaccines do not spoil in transit," he says. "Lucky for you all."

What in hell's name . . . ?

I feel defeated. I swallow hard.

"Ah, but *monsieur le Docteur*, first, I must let my stage mother here in on a secret." I reach for Émilie's hand. "*Maman, Madame la Marquise*, Émilie—your *force vive* is just the beginning."

She looks at me in astonishment—I can see assumptions shifting in her head as she takes in what is surely an unanticipated twist.

But then, seemingly aware that there is an audience, and that we now have a prodigal child plus-one: "It is you, my child, whose *patrimoine* we must protect. Though you are young, I see in you such potential! The uncertainty of this world must not deter you from pursuing your dreams."

Now it's my turn to be astonished. It feels like she's talking directly to me, Charley, not *Marthe*. Or Pauline.

In a stage whisper, I respond, "The infrared. Your theory about light waves. The idea that different colors of light carry different amounts of heat. You must continue to pursue this—the doctor's instruments to measure temperature and a prism to refract the light—it is the way to prove your theory." I cough, trying to unblock the frog in my throat. "In my backpack . . . *sac à dos* . . ."

If only she could time-travel, just once, I think, she would actually feel the wave output of the rainbow for herself.

Voltaire seems delighted by our improv on stage. Rather dramatically, and pulling a tragic face, he turns to the audience to recite his ode to Émilie, a testament to the fact that she loves her experiments more than him.

Sans doute vous serez célèbre

Pour ces grands calculs de l'algèbre

Où votre esprit est absorbé.

J'oserais m'y livrer moi-même.

And here is where the whole play goes completely off the rails. Émilie seems to have digested my words. What she says next in a soliloquy makes no sense in the play, but then, why should it?!

"Judge me for my own merits, or lack of them, but do not look upon me as a mere appendage to this great general or that great scholar, this star that shines at the court of France or that famed author. I am in my own right a whole person, responsible to myself alone for all that I am, all that I say, all that I do. It may be that there are metaphysics and philosophers whose learning is greater than mine, although I have not met them. Yet, they are but frail humans, too, and have their faults; so, when I add the sum total of my graces, I confess I am inferior to no one."

She squints to gauge V's reaction before putting her hand up, expecting to meet mine in a high five.

She turns to take her bow and, following her lead, I slip off the divan and try to stand for a bow as well.

There's scattered applause by the smattering of audience members who have not yet fled.

Pauline cries out *"Non, non, non, non, non. Tout ceci, c'est pas possible!"* as she runs backstage to bring the heavy blue curtain, with its golden image of Triton, down.

Behind the curtain, V has begun pacing and complaining. "You have turned my comedy into a tragedy. The lines, you have twisted and tangled them."

I turn my head to Kairos. "K," I whisper, "how can we get out of here? I have so few of the tools we need. After all, it's not like anyone's going to airlift us . . ."

"What tools you do not have here, I have carried with me. Or we can find or fabricate them here."

This reminds me of the lab equipment Billy packed for me. "Backpack!" I croak, pointing offstage left, where I stowed it.

"Your necklace?" he asks, reminding me of the little supercharged charm. I feel for the little compass over my heart, which is pumping super hard. But Billy's necklace is safe.

He pulls a second compass, one of the originals from his bag, and tucks it into my dress. "Carolina's," he says, as if that explains everything.

"She knows . . . where?" I begin, but it hurts too much to talk now.

Kairos rushes to grab the backpack from the wings. "First, we must take care of you and our other latent patients," he whispers in my ear.

"Ready?" He pulls a syringe from his bag and carefully draws the plunger to fill it from the vial. "I will administer a vaccine designed to modify your RNA to boost your immunity . . ."

"Is this why Billy packed me so much medical stuff . . . youch!" I say, feeling a pinch.

Not a moment too soon.

K whispers something in Émilie's ear to distract her while giving her her own shot in the arm. I want to ask him what he said, but he's already on to the next.

Approaching her delicately, young Pauline is next to receive the jab. The girl bursts into tears.

K prepares one last dose and stands before Voltaire, insisting that this will not hurt, and V should just take off his shirt. When he refuses, K pushes V's white ruffled sleeve as high as it will go.

Voltaire objects because, of course he would. "Doctors put drugs of which they know little into bodies of which they know less for diseases of which they know nothing at all."

Kairos is much too intent on getting this over with to offer a riposte. He prepares the last vial.

"The more a man knows, the less he talks," broods Voltaire.

After much protest, he manages to get the shot in V's arm. With a dramatic flourish and a set speech that sounds straight out of *Julius Caesar*, Voltaire grabs his arm in pain. "I have been stabbed! *Et tu, docteur?*"

For your own good, Monsieur de Voltaire, I reflect. And not a moment too soon.

"As great as I'm sure your advanced medicine is, Kairos, I need to get home—in the right time," I breathe.

The chaos upstairs enables K and me to covertly scramble down the back stairs to get outside. He's grabbed his medicine kit and slings the backpack over his shoulder. I cling to his arm for support and then pull on his cape to cover me too.

"First, what's with the jab?" I pant as we go. "You know, why subject all the players to that?"

"Prevention measures," he says, as if everyone should know what the hell he's talking about. He slows down, and finally stops.

"Breathe, Carlotta. For now, you must save your energy."

"So, yeah, that's another thing," I pant. "Energy."

"I bring news on that front. But first, come outside," he insists, taking off the plague mask and replacing it with a hospital mask of his own.

Outside, the night is freezing. There's a sliver of moon, and Venus is bright in the winter sky. Orion's Belt is just visible above the horizon. I can't resist peeking into the eyepiece of another in the château's seemingly endless collection of telescopes set up on the terrace. The sky glistens with stars.

Since the little theater was so warm and toasty at the top of the castle, the temperature contrast is striking. I shiver, as much from cold as fever. When I try to speak, a weak stream of steam comes out of my mouth.

"Anyways. Back to the present. I've ruined V's play. Pauline hates me. I feel sick as a dog, with potentially some virus from the future, which potentially I have just spread into the eighteenth century. I need to get home. How do we activate Billy's app? Esme's charge is low. It's night. No fireworks, no solar battery . . ."

"You are in luck, my friend. The foundry, where your Émilie and Voltaire have been conducting their experiments on force. They are using primitive equipment—weights made of iron, and pulleys. The heat output required to melt all that metal is prodigious."

As he talks, my head begins to clear. I am starting to feel better. Whether it's the vaccine, the cold air, or the distraction of having to figure out a hard problem, who cares.

I start to get the picture. "The proof of *force vive*, kinetic energy, when combined with experiments Émilie will soon undertake about what we know of as infrared waves, could unleash just enough energy . . ."

"For starters, yes. But here's the breaking news: time crystals. Sort of a perpetual-motion machine that changes states—but without consuming any energy. Handy discovery, *n'est-ce pas?*"

"Time crystals?" It rings a bell somehow. Like I read about how Google was experimenting with this a while ago (ahead?). "But, no energy dissipation? C'mon, K. That would violate the law of thermodynamics and entropy. Surely you don't expect me to believe—"

And then I hear what sounds like the *ding-ding-ding* of a bike bell, punctuated by a familiar woot and a holler.

"Tcharrli!"

Carolina. Wearing a fashionable straw hat, ribbons flying, she wheels up shakily on the byclotron built for two that Kairos and I ditched back in Marnes-la-Coquette.

In 1724.

Just sayin'.

The bike has a new headlamp flickering on the handlebars with the spin of its wheels, its light shining a "V" that brightens everything in her path as she approaches.

I blink into the brightness. "Wait. What? Bean! Have you been here the whole time?!" I give her a squeeze.

"What time is that?" she asks, innocently enough, putting her feet on the ground for balance and squeezes back.

I see Kairos winding up to give me the "time is relative" speech. Not like we haven't all heard that before!

"You know what I mean."

"*Tout près*. After you left Elisabeth in the wrong time for you, I was blown back in your wake. To that earlier time. I had to free my cousin from the Bastille. She was bound for the Louisiana Territories. Her father . . . well, let's just say, I talked him out of deporting her."

Louisiana. Where wealthy fathers sent their young girls so they wouldn't inherit the family fortune. Where hurricanes toss up winds and waves with vast forces of destruction.

"Oh, yeah. *Laissez les bons temps rouler*," I note with sarcasm.

"Not such good times," Carolina replies with a frown, taking me literally.

"Wait, after we left in the future-future," I shake my head trying to figure out if 2020 even means anything to her, "you went back to when we were with Beth, and the Bastille . . . and Voltaire?"

She tosses an annoyed look at Kairos, as if this is something he should try to explain to me, but Kairos is busy trying to hurry us along.

"Anyways, look what I found in the way-back times!" she says, showing off the bike. "Quicker than those sedan chairs they rent to take visitors to Versailles, but not nearly as *cool* as Bee-ly's motorbike."

Before I can make any more un-PC comments, I hear a door slam behind us.

"*Fous-le-camp, rénard! T'es salaud!*" Émilie says as she storms out. Something about this feels familiar.

"Do you know what V told that fat biddy, de Graffigny? 'Madame du Châtelet is a great man whose only fault is being a woman.' *Imaginez ca!* After all I have done to support him!"

"Umm . . . er . . . Émilie, Madame, *je te présente ma copine Carolina.*"

"*Ta copine?*"

She looks from me to Carolina, then seems to remember her manners.

"*Carolina? Enchantée, ma petite,*" Émilie replies, ignoring the rest of us.

"*Bonsoir, madame.*" Carolina drops a formal curtsy, Renaissance style, before eagerly slapping Émilie a high five.

"I must introduce you to my daughter, Pauline," Émilie says. "As soon as we are on speaking terms again." She hesitates. "I know you two will become fast friends!"

Émilie kneels down so she's eye to eye with Carolina, and puts a finger under her chin to look the little Bean in the eye. "*D'où viens-tu?*"

Carolina drops the bike on the graveled terrace, pleased to be recognized. "*Firenze! Anno Domini quattordici . . .*" The rest comes out muffled, as I quick clap my hand over Carolina's mouth. No need to divulge her Renaissance provenance, nor her present-day royal connections. Although I'm thinking it might be good to get Pauline and Carolina together at some point, if only to help Pauline learn Italian, for her future royal job in Naples. And right now, Carolina could stand to take some lessons in patience from the nuns at Pauline's school.

Holding onto her hat, Carolina commences to circle around us, happy to connect us as part of her BFF crew.

"I am happy to see you are feeling better, Charlotte," Émilie says kindly, rubbing her arm where Kairos gave her the shot. "Though I, myself, am beginning to feel a little unwell."

Unwell. Uh-oh.

Kairos walks over. He pulls a super modern thermometer from a bag and holds it up to Émilie's forehead. "Thirty-seven Celsius. Perfectly normal," he mumbles.

"Celsius," she repeats. "The Swedish astronomer accompanied Maupertuis to Lapland to prove Newton's equations about the flattening of the Earth at the poles, you know. Maupertuis has written to me of Monsieur Celsius's findings from the expedition . . ."

Brow furrowed in thought, she turns back to Kairos.

"But who in the world are you, *monsieur le docteur?*" She grabs the instrument out of his hand and stares at the digits. "And what in the hell is this?"

"No, Émilie!" I warn, but the note of caution sticks in my throat.

"Kairos," he bows. "I thought the thermometer might be of interest to you. In measuring the wavelengths of color."

"Kairos!" I gasp, which turns into a coughing spasm.

Carolina, giggling, puts on a little robot routine. "*Regardez-moi. J'arrive de l'avenir.* Vaccines have wiped out illness."

"*L'avenir, tu dis!*" interjects Émilie, unfortunately only picking up on the part about Carolina coming from the future. "Such an imagination!"

Kairos goes over, putting an arm around his sister's shoulders, and whispers in her ear. "Right, Carolina?" he asks aloud. "Not the convenient moment to discuss what has not been foreseen."

"*Pas convenable à prévoir?!*" exclaims Émilie, still in a rage over whatever conflagration she and V might have been engaged in. "I have just had this stranger, posing as a doctor, stab me in the arm without my permission, then put a thermometer made by—*eh, eh . . . une civilisation,* no doubt extraterrestrial—up to my head, but it's not convenient to discuss it?!"

As she passes in front of our byclotron, its blinking light projects onto her dress, though it's weaker now than it was when Carolina was pedaling and generating full energy. She ends her harangue and stoops down, and now the light shines on her face, like a full moon in the darkness.

She stands up, drawing gracefully to her full height, towering even above Kairos.

"Or, there is Monsieur Newton's optics," she continues in English. She bends down once more to observe, and now the light is on her face. "What if . . ." She hesitates, as if whatever thought has just struck her mind is still baking. "I mean if I could just prove . . ."

She turns to face me. "Do you believe this thermometer can be calibrated to measure the heat of different rays of light coming through a prism?"

"Umm . . . er . . . ahhh . . ."

Fact is, I don't know. But I can see the situation is getting out of control. Temporal paradoxes can seriously mess things up. And we've got a bunch of 'em overlapping.

First, my clue to Émilie to find proof of infrared waves (many years before they were actually proven by some English astronomer). Second off, digital thermometer. And third, there could be nothing worse than the spread of a disease no one's ever heard of 285 years too soon, and twenty-first-century instruments that make these people think we're spies.

Or ETs.

A light from above captures my attention. I lift my eyes, half-expecting to see the aurora borealis dancing across the sky, a display of photons from the sun reflecting in the night sky, striking and exciting atoms in our atmosphere.

But no, it's a meteor shower, shooting across the dome of night and leaving a trail brighter than the moon and dimming its light.

It seems like a sign.

"Light without heat," Émilie murmurs, as if she's about to float some brand-new hypothesis. "What then would one make of heat without light?"

"Gotta get home, Kairos."

And Carolina . . . she's banging me on the arm. The one where I got the shot.

"Stop. That hurts, Bean!"

"Look, Tcharrli!" She points to the pasture where the cone of light from the bike extends. A megalith, a group of giant rock outcroppings, reminds me of the cairn Carolina created when we left the time after for this time before.

I'm tired, hangry, and very short-tempered. "What?!"

She pulls me by the hand.

"Okay, they have giant stones here. So?"

She lays out our original hypothesis, "You remember—Earth's magnetism? Three-compass turn?"

Émilie seems prompted to chime in. "In regard to the perceivable attractions of some bodies on Earth, such as those of the magnet and of electricity, they follow other laws, and probably have other causes than the universal attraction of matter . . ."

It's like a masterclass on her commentaries, with improvements on Newton's laws, IRL, and normally, I'd have a million questions. I wish I felt up to it. Before my mind can even formulate a question, I feel an amplifying vibration under my stomacher. I don't even remember stuffing it there. It's like, "ET, text me!"

Looks like Esme's still on the case. As I fish under the dress, my fingers graze over the old compass Kairos gave me before I manage to pull out the phone.

The text: $Hm=[QE]M^3$.

Seems Billy's a mind reader - he's updated the Qualia Rosetta code for a remote install, and not a moment too soon.

I steel myself for the next step: Leap-time!

XLIII.

LIKE DÉJÀ VU ALL OVER AGAIN

Forges and foundries and falling, Oh, my!

"As much as I'd love to hear all your views on gravity, Émilie, er, Madame," I say, "I wonder if I might visit your laboratory to conduct my own experiment on magnetism and *force vive*. It is of the utmost importance."

Her face lights up. "It is rare to find another woman who expresses interest in testing out these theories. I would be delighted, Charlotte—under one condition."

"What's that?"

"That I accompany you. That we do the work together."

"Me, me, me! Bring me, too!" Carolina jumps in.

I can't argue, although I wonder how I can ever hope to restore the natural order of the Universe when I have set off such a firestorm.

Kairos taps me on the shoulder. "I believe, *chère Charlotte*, that the *laboratoire* will be insufficient to your needs. There are furnaces, but one may need a place that supplies not only heat but a way to modify the molecular structure of . . . shall we say, other materials."

"You have a better idea then?"

He nods. "Madame," he bows, addressing Émilie in the most solicitous of tones. "I believe there are foundries nearby?"

"But of course. This is where Monsieur de Voltaire has been working on his own experiments to prove Monsieur Newton's hypotheses. In fact, it is why I have so few thermometers left at the château . . . and all of those measuring only in Fahrenheit. Whereas it would seem that Monsieur Celsius's innovations have not yet reached Paris—or Cirey. I must write Maupertuis to correct this deficiency."

Oy vey. Not only have we messed up with the digital thermometers, but they haven't yet even adopted the scientific standard for measuring heat scientifically.

"Can we go to the foundry, Émilie?"

No sooner have I asked the question than I hear the jingle of a bike bell in back of me. Carolina has already picked up the byclotron.

Although I worry that Émilie will want a ride, or at least to inspect the workings of our bike, it seems that the excitement of engaging in experimentation is stronger than her curiosity in the here and now.

"Fetch Hirondelle!" Émilie commands Kairos. "In the *écurie. Vite!*" She points to the stables I spied earlier.

Kairos obediently saunters off and returns a few minutes later astride a large, beautiful mare. He dismounts and Émilie lets him give her a leg up. He then helps me up in front of her. Drained of energy, it's all I can do to hang on.

"Are you coming, K?" I ask, for this all-hands-on-deck moment.

He jumps on the back of the bike and tips his hand in a salute. "Let us see who arrives fastest," he says with a wink. With a tap on Carolina's shoulder in front of him, she ding-ding-dings the bell and they push off, lighting a path into the night.

As they reach the edge of the woods, I hear our electric engine click on—making me wonder if somehow, someone, somewhere had upgraded the solar storage as, surely, moonlight, even supercharged by the meteor showers, would not be strong enough to power it.

Or Kairos brought back and installed that woo-woo quantum perpetual-motion discovery: time crystals.

"You cannot arrive before us!" It seems all Émilie needs is a challenge. "My mare is not just beautiful, but smart. And quick!"

With a swift kick and a *Ki-yah! BANZAI! Hai!* (clearly, her earlier association with Beth left its mark), Hirondelle—her name means "swallow," like the bird—flies off in a gallop.

———————

I am worn out by the time we arrive. In my present condition, I am not looking forward to the energy it will take to travel home.

The foundry is sort of like a primitive factory. Made of brick, with massive chimneys to vent raging hot fires burning inside, it is set for those who know their craft to smelt metal to pour into casts, to make church bells, or new gates for Versailles, or weapons of war.

It looks like workers here are pouring molds to make cannonballs. A pyramid of the lead balls stands beside one of the cannons that they must also forge here.

Weapons of war notwithstanding, here are casts for statues. I imagine that Leonardo da Vinci—he of my Renaissance time travels, when he was commissioned by his patron, the Duke di Sforza, to forge the world's then-largest mega-horse to stand in the main square of Milan—would have had to make a mold of such tremendous size for the project that it would have needed its own giant foundry for the manufacture.

But then, di Sforza went to war against the French and the project was called off. All the metal in the dukedom was repurposed for cannons.

Tragic.

The fires are kept burning day and night to fuel the massive furnaces. I kind of get where Kairos was coming from when he suggested this place. Last time, when I had to escape Florence in haste, we needed the bonfires of the vanities and a spectacular fireworks display to celebrate Carnival just to fuel my time travel escape.

Here, we have to improvise yet again to create enough firepower to activate a portal through time.

With metal castings and ashes flying through the air, I set off again in a fit of coughs.

I'm not sure how the new "time crystal" technology—however that may have turned out—figures into this, but I guess I'm about to find out.

Émilie is already talking to one of the foundrymen who apparently works the midnight shift. I see her pointing from me to the piles of wood and straw that stoke the fires, to the walls lined with iron ore, lead, and other metals, as she's screaming to make herself heard over the noise of the furnace.

INTERIOR OF A FOUNDRY

Credit: Léonard Defrance, Public Domain

The man is shaking his head.

While Émilie is trying to persuade him, Kairos arrives, carrying something that looks like an oversized pitchfork. I'm nervous he might launch it at the keeper of the fires—his chivalry toward those he knows and cares about is well known. It would do me no good to try to call him off; blasting furnace or no, I have no voice.

The man points to Kairos, who goes over to speak with both Émilie and the forgeman, who shakes his head again.

Carolina trails a little after him. She carries a big wooden bowl filled with water from the stream outside. The water lets out a hiss of steam.

"*Salot!*" Émilie swears, walking back toward me and the Bean. "If I were king!" she sounds off in frustration. I'm not sure if she's angry at the fire-tender, or Kairos, even though we beat him and Bean here.

Carolina runs over to greet me. On her wrist is looped the fan I pinched from Émilie's château earlier. I rip off the ribbon and flip open the fan in a panicky attempt to beat back the intense heat and smoke from the foundry.

"Look!" she exclaims. I peer into the bowl where I see something big, shiny, and gold. In the dim light, it looks like a goldfish.

"It's a new compass!" Carolina points.

"What? Why?" Still fanning madly, I'm barely able to cough out the words.

"Go ahead. Pick it up."

Still, I don't dare touch the sizzling thing.

Carolina fishes it out of the now-warm water and passes it over to me.

I barely hold on to it, it's so heavy, almost twice the size of the original antique one.

"Remember, the three-key turn."

I try to speak again. "Not calibrated, Bean. Need to get to right time—can't overshoot."

"It is all taken care of, Carlotta!" says Kairos, coming in at the last bit. It's so loud in here, he has to shout. "The original formula has been advanced to compensate for practical aspects such as polar shifts, geo-solar positioning, radio wave interference, disturbances in the photon belt, and other spacetime markers. Calibration is, shall we say, *baked in* to the fabrication process now. And as you may have noted, a much larger compass is required for activation of the time crystals from the primitive energetic state of this époque, however 'enlightened.' You will just need to activate the settings in the larger compass once you're ready."

"Baked in? Ready?" I glom onto the only words that register.

He drapes his arm around my shoulder and squeezes me close to speak directly into my ear. "You must trust, Carlotta. Not everything can be proven by your science."

Trust over proof. Considering the stakes here, that's a tall order.

Émilie has wandered back toward the blaze, staring into the furnace, captivated. Her face is alight, her mind on fire with new ideas, no doubt. How the heat and smoke aren't choking her, I can't guess.

The forgeman walks over to her, carrying a lump of melted iron.

Émilie nods her head, showing him ten fingers, then twenty. She then points back to the fire. It seems they are negotiating something. I wish I could listen in; I know she will use iron in her experiments to prove *force vive*. A scientific form of alchemy.

It reminds me of something I read about Newton himself believing in alchemy enough to spend his older years, after his writings on gravity, trying to accomplish the impossible—turning lead into gold.

But this alchemy is different—human experiments to set mass into motion, motion into force, force to yield symmetry, symmetry as beauty, and beauty metamorphosing into love, "and the square of love."

The forgeman uses a big shovel to thrust the lump into the blaze.

Kairos points to tracks along the floor going into the furnace itself. I imagine the tracks help convey carts or sleds of some sort that carry the heavy metals to the furnace for smelting or molding, or whatever it is these tradesmen do.

He then points to the opposite end of the tracks, where a ladder is built into the high wall, leading to a loft piled high with sand. No doubt to cool heavy molten objects. A bed of straw is beneath.

I give him a thumbs-up, like, "Cool," but Kairos keeps pointing from me to the loft, walking with his fingers to show I should climb up. I try to ask why, but there's no way I can make my voice heard.

Kairos and Carolina must have some kind of weird telepathy between them, 'cause she immediately laces her fingers through mine and pulls me toward the wall. It kind of reminds me of the time Billy and I made our mad escape from the piazza in Florence, under the rockets' red glare. Our first real kiss.

"What, Bean?" I ask. "Why?"

"Time to go home," is all she replies. She loops the straps of the backpack over my shoulders. It feels so heavy.

I turn to face her. "Where?"

Without explanation, she starts pushing my tush to get me to climb up the ladder. I drop the compass. Too heavy.

As I slowly pull myself up a cautious few steps, she follows, keeping up the pressure so I can't turn back.

Time to go home.

Yes. I think about the twins, Mamma and Dad, and Billy. My own bed. And some modern-medicine way to fight this bug that's burning up my body. Or even some of Mamma's famous spaghetti pomodoro.

And, this time, it seems like Carolina intends to accompany me.

She stoops to pick up the new compass. But I can't risk having her blow up the timeline again by coming back with me.

With Carolina pushing me, I rise, step by painful step. I brace myself for the pull of gravity, and a way to navigate through the ceiling of smoke that's hovering overhead without having another coughing fit.

Somewhere, I've lost the fan. Maybe I should put on the mask again.

The loft must be thirty feet up. From here, the sound from the blast of the furnace is diminished. But I am getting dizzier and dizzier. Whatever flu or virus I am fighting, dehydration from fever and fire, and whatever side effects the vaccine might have left me with, have done a mean trick.

With effort, I scramble off the ladder and into the opening at the back of the loft, where I throw myself on the pile of sand. Even as I lay down, I feel a familiar whirl of hot air encompass me.

"Help me, Tcharrli! Behind you."

Carolina lifts up her hand for me to grab on. She's too short to reach the loft; after all, these ladders were built for full-grown men, not small girls.

"You shouldn't be up here, Bean," I croak. But there's that determined set of her jaw. It's like nothing I say will talk her out of it.

I get down on my belly to grab her by the hand. This beautiful silk dress, on loan from the Émilie collection, is officially a wreck, I think irrelevantly. How will I ever repay her?

But Carolina. She keeps shouting. I try to pull her up. My hand is sweaty. She almost slips, dangling off the ladder until she gains a foothold on the step again.

This is nuts.

But she keeps at it. I try again. That dizzy feeling is getting stronger. I creep back from the edge for fear of falling, or failing.

"The time crystals!" Carolina cries, grabbing back onto the highest rung of the ladder. "Need to activate them. Ready?"

"Go back down!" I implore her, making sure she has a good handhold. "You cannot come this time." I pick up a nearby rake, on top of a hay pile. I start jabbing it in her direction to show I mean business.

"Tcharrli, no!" It's then I see what she's talking about—it's the new compass. She has somehow kept it cinched close to her body underneath her dress and still managed to climb the ladder. She manages somehow to extract it and shove it up for me.

Kairos has now reached the bottom rung of the ladder. He hurriedly waves Carolina down, then yells up at me. "Put the rake down, please, Carlotta. There is no need."

He sounds concerned—like I've come unhinged, even though he was the one who told me to come here.

"Carlotta, there is only one chance for you to find your wormhole: We must make sure that the spiral pulls you to your own time. A turn in the wrong direction could send you even farther into the future—or deep into the past. To activate the time crystals, you need all three compasses."

All three. I'm just exhausted. The newly forged compass is flopped onto the straw beside me. I touch my heart. Billy's charm still here. I start to panic—where's the third—in the backpack? And my phone?

"I need Esme!" My voice is lost to the roar below. It's then that I realize I've had them both with me the whole time, fastened beneath the stomacher.

"Good to go."

I look once more at my surroundings and commit to memory this improbable scenario—Émilie and her latest experiment. The foundry. The midnight ride of Carolina and Kairos. The jabs. The Prodigal Child. The very public bath. And a novel virus from a time after.

"Hurry, Carlotta," Carolina cries out. "Don't worry about the fire!"

I don't know what she's talking about. If anything, it is Madame who is too close to the fire.

For good measure, Kairos adds, "That furnace is like a volcano—it could erupt at any time."

"The taper is lit," Émilie screams from the forge. From this vantage point, it looks as if she's got Kairos's thermometer pointed into the forge. "Now, to determine whether fire always throws off light *and* heat."

It's like they're giving me a lecture on the nature of fire. Which makes no sense. At least not to my addled brain.

"Wait, Tcharrli!" And Carolina, something flashing in her hand from the glare of the raging forge, and again scurrying toward the ladder. "You're going to need . . ."

Too late. As if on cue, several sparks from the forge have jumped the apron of the furnace and sparked the woodpile.

"Fire!" I croak, as if anyone could hear. "Fire!" I try again, now waving and pointing from my loft.

Having sparked the wood, the fire is running through the straw below, coming dangerously close to the fuse attached to the cannon. I note the cannonballs and pray there aren't any loaded. From here, it looks like the newly minted cannon is pointing right up at me.

At that moment, a blast sounding like cannon fire blasts me to the back of the loft. A ball ricochets against the wall just beneath me, and the loft crumbles. I am falling . . .

XLIV.

ANOTHER TURN ON THE WHEEL OF FORTUNE

Round and round she goes / and where she stops,
nobody knows

Straightaway, I am in motion; forces of gravity squeeze my heart and lungs inside my chest in cosmic winds. An ethereal white light engulfs me.

Think though I might that I've mastered this, I'll never get used to these gale-strength energies.

I feel the wig blow off. I pry open one eyelid against the centrifugal force. As hay and straw and fabric fly up in my face, these derecho-level wind forces are shredding the dress. Time crystals notwithstanding, it feels like entropy is alive and well in the universe.

I try to pry my eyes open—if only to commit this scene to memory. No selfie can capture the reality of this experience.

But gravity, gravity, gravity. From falling to swirling, I am swept into a whirling vortex.

"*Au revoir à l'Âge des Lumières. Au revoir, Gabrielle Émilie Le Tonnelier de Breteuil, Marquise du Châtelet.*"

It seems a fitting finale to this light of the Enlightenment.

Even though I know this must all be moving in a flash of an instant, it's like everything is happening in slo-mo.

Before the wind, light, and explosions entirely engulf me, I see Émilie taking long strides into the same field of energy that encompasses me.

Émilie is about to be blown out of time.

This is so wrong. I wish I could scream. Her quest isn't yet over. She's about to change the world forever with her discoveries and translations and writings. A woman at the forefront of discovery. She can't go.

As I feel the dizzying whirl around me, I notice out of the corner of my eye that something else has gone wrong. Who is running beside the Marquise, in full silhouette: none other than the Bean, Carolina herself. It's like she still sees me in the loft—I see her mouth moving, but I can't hear anything.

Waving her arms with all her might, she opens her palm and flashes again whatever it is she said I'd need.

I squint, but the rockets' red glare all about me make it hard to discern such a small item from so far away.

I barely see Bean hurling whatever it is in my direction (the direction I was?) with all her might. Judging by the arc of the trajectory, I'm astounded at the strength of her arm.

Equally astonishing, the object is entering the energy field that has embraced me, but the headwinds are too strong, it seems, to withstand a collision between matter and whatever gravitational forces animate my experiences in between times. It shatters midair, but not before I perceive what she was trying to send me.

It was a snuffbox. And remembering how Carolina had alerted me to the talisman, I'm guessing it's the one with the miniature portraits of E and V.

With that glimpse, it's like atoms are reshaping around me. That world is slipping away.

To keep my brain from flying away with it, I attempt to mentally apply Émilie's *force vive* formula to figure out how much kinetic energy my twirling body could make on impact.

But before I even remember how to integrate the variables—*BOOM!*

Too late; I've crashed. Again.

Struggling to focus, I do a quick body scan to see what might be broken this time. Hard to tell—everything hurts. I lift my head and open one eye.

When am I? Did it work?

At first all I hear is my own heart beating and my breath in my ears, but rising underneath it is a dull, "Mwah, mwah-mwah, mwah-mwah."

It's the Grigsby.

XLV.

WAIT. DID THAT REALLY HAPPEN?

Life is like study hall: You gotta make the best of it

I open my eyes to my history book, once again (still?) open to the Enlightenment. I raise my head. Study hall. Grigsby's glaring at someone across the room for yet some other rules infraction.

In front of me, my spiral notebook, covered in my notes and sketches. The date on the whiteboard in the front of the auditorium: October 29, 2019.

Thank God and Kairos—2019.

That means it's two days before the Halloween Ball. Two days before the Haunted Forest. Two days before another out-of-this-world adventure that rocked my world.

C'est un miracle. Literally.

I go for a deep breath, and—start laughing. At the absurdity of it all. Here I am, poring over a history book's recounting of the Enlightenment (*sans* la belle Émilie, it must be noted), when I was literally in it. Living history.

Or changing it.

Grigsby gives me the look, and I smother a giggle and settle into my seat, scanning in case there's something I'm missing.

Like, am I still sick? Was I ever? Was that reality? Or is this?

I glance down at my phone. Esme still seems to be working.

It's then that I notice Billy's been texting me. Over and over and over.

Billy: What's so funny, Charley?

Charley:

Billy:

Billy: So what're we going to do about the science project? I am not doing the Beth fashion thing.

Billy: I don't care what you say

Billy: Excuse me? C, are you looking at me?

Billy: Did you rub my lamp?

Billy: Did you wake me up? And all of a sudden you walk out on me?

It's from *Aladdin* again. But not the original part we were texting in the time before . . . before . . . well, just before.

So history's already changed. I don't know what he knows. Or doesn't know.

I glance up, and there is gangly, nerdy, lovable old Billy, sitting in the same seat as before, as far away from me as before. Staring at me with laser eyes.

I better play along. At least for starters.

> Charley: I don't think so. You are getting your wishes, so sit down.

I give a little snort-laugh thing. I can't help it. I take out a tissue and pretend to blow my nose. But now, my outburst sets Grigsby moving up the aisle.

Sometimes I wonder if life isn't just one big cosmic joke on a repeating loop.

I hastily put my eyes into my book and pray that Billy doesn't text me.

"Anything interesting there, Miss Morton?" the Grigsby asks, tapping his pencil on the back of my chair.

"Oh yes, very!" I reply, a little surprised to hear my voice coming out too loud, considering I was only just recovering from barely having one. "For instance, did you know that during the French Enlightenment, there were women *philosophes*? And this one woman, Émilie du Châtelet, actually proved the formula for kinetic energy? And improved on Newton with her very own original commentaries. I mean, literally. And she was really good at dueling!"

Heads turn around me as kids who were previously sleeping or playing games look up, annoyed at my, shall we say, erudition?

Although I have to say, I'm used to it.

Seeing that I could go on and on about this topic, the Grigsby shuts me down with a simple, "Very interesting, Miss Morton. Keep up the good work."

As he moves on, I pull papers into my lap to better hide my phone.

I note quickly that I'm somehow in normal clothes: purple, over-sized, long-sleeved T-shirt and black leggings with pockets. Cowboy boots. Hair in a tangle of curls, except flat on top. Phew—no wig, no farthingale.

Charley:	Hey, ever heard of a coronavirus?
Billy:	Uh, duh. Common cold. Going around.
Billy:	Why—sick?

Was I ever!

Charley:	Like, every winter. But I mean a novel coronavirus?
Billy:	Umm . . . no. Unless you mean the 1918 Spanish flu?
Billy:	Funny you should mention: happened right at the end of WWI.
Billy:	When Wright Brothers' military flyer first used in battle.
Billy:	As you may recall from our visit to Air and Space 2 years ago.

Billy:	When we did your idea for science fair project.
Billy:	Now I get to choose topic.

Phew. No COVID-19. Which might explain my seemingly miraculous cure.

And Billy's off on his personal obsession about the technologies of war. Big yawn.

Think I'll wait until we have a moment in person before I share this latest news with him—if ever. 'Cause really, what would be the point. Except for that old saying about an ounce of prevention being worth a pound of cure.

Charley:	News about the science project. Meet me in main hall after class.

The rest of the day proceeds like most any other. Genetics in Biology. Pop vocab quiz in French. New paper for History: fifteen pages on the Scientific Revolution. Which I could write in my sleep. Although I have a vague recollection of, at some point, promising Beth I'd write hers as well. A little fuzzy on the timing of that promise.

I'm by my locker shoving books in my backpack—it's so ridiculous they weigh us down with paper when everything is online—when who should show up, but Beth herself. With a mask in her hand.

"What's up, Charley?"

"Hey, Beth. What's with the mask?" Makes me a little nervous; have to find out what she remembers. Or not.

"Homecoming dance. Heard you were coming down with something." She hands it over. "Maybe you should put this thing on. Can't risk you getting me sick."

So weird that one little sneeze in study hall and the whole school's worried about a pandemic. Which, now that I think about it, someday soon may not be all that weird.

I bat it away. "Allergies is all. No need to go all hypochondriac on me."

She gives me that "Gotcha" smirk. "Anyways. Want to come over today and work on the fashion app?"

Billy sneaks up behind her, putting his hands over Beth's eyes. "Want to come over today and work on the fashion app, Charley?" he mimics, grinning at me.

"Who asked you, Webhead?" she asks, squirming out from under those big hands. Besides, don't you have some new battle drone to build?"

"Aren't you supposed to do a Fashion Forward Live soon?" he counters.

"You guys!" I zip my mouth shut.

Beth's not having any of it. "No doubt I can't Fashion Forward you, Billy Vincenzo. Besides, not that it's any of your business, but I have an actual date . . . with Guy. He's guesting on the Live—and he actually is fashion-forward. So, à la prochaine, you guys."

"Breaking news." I murmur as she struts off on her familiar fashionable red heels. But the real breaking news to my mind is that the memory of Versailles seems to have been erased. Or maybe just a not-yet.

"Guy and Beth. Actually, they kind of deserve each other." Billy turns and waits until she's out of earshot. "Guy's got a thick bozone layer," he says without irony.

I bite my tongue before I reveal that there was a Guy lookalike at Versailles wearing this flashy military paraphernalia—ribbons and medals and the like—and that clueless-in-any-time-zone Beth actually seemed to fall for the uniform as much as for the guy.

"So, speaking of breaking news, Charley, anything special you want to tell me about?"

I really want to wrap my arms around him in a bear hug, but I don't know if I was exposed to the virus, or whether Kairos's jab was a cure. And I certainly don't want to be the first one to spread it.

Instead, I busy myself reorganizing my locker so he can't see the expression on my face.

"Umm, no. Usual. Classes boring. Twins annoying. Mamma on tour. Why?"

He pulls out his tablet and pulls up the Esme app that he's been upgrading. Or was.

"See, it's a livestream. Notification is cryptic.":

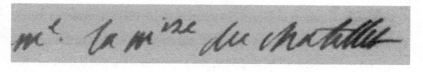

SIGNATURE OF EMILIE DU CHATELET
Photo : Robin Stevens Payes

"I don't know who or how . . . or why. But thought you might."

Émilie. Unlike the ping for Billy's audio memo, the one I butt-played at an inopportune moment during my unexpected debut stage performance—in 1736—this one is live, in HD, with augmented reality.

"Think you'll need these glasses to see this." He hands me a pair of AR glasses, puts on his own, and pushes play.

I have a sick feeling that I should confess all to Billy. Right now. He deserves to know the truth of my multi-leap experience; after all, he's my partner in all of it. And also, I don't want to keep secrets from someone I really do care about.

Plus, my beta-test showed there are some major glitches with our spacetime GPS calibrations, where our two heads might solve the problem better than just my own. And that whole future thing! Not to mention the disturbances of my heart.

Besides, he's the only one I can trust to tell any of it.

"Umm, Billy, there's something we should talk about first. . . . Like *force vive*—the living force. And love!"

He looks at me funny. "This is live, Charley. I don't think you want to miss this. I know I don't."

As the livestream starts, I have a hunch what we're gonna see. Because we first viewed another episode of this show when Billy and I got back from the Florence adventure: Leonardo da Vinci trespassing in Einstein's kitchen in Bern, Switzerland. In 1905. Einstein's *annus mirabilis*. His miraculous year. The real miracle in this timeline was that Leonardo, who died in 1519, time-traveled forward to meet his hero—because I introduced the Theory of Relativity to Leo back in 1492. Major time paradox!

It's a long story, and you can read all about it if you're curious.

It appears that, in episode two, as Billy's Esme app catches us up on the story, they have a new trespasser, who may just now blow my cover.

And for that, despite all evidence to the contrary, I will be eternally grateful.

XLVI.

PAST TENSE, PRESENT TENSE . . .

. . . Future even tenser

L ike before, I catch a glimpse of Leonardo and Einstein conferring, still in Bern. And who is with them, sharing her
mathematical proofs?

You guessed it.

"Wait—turn up the volume, Billy."

He checks around. The last-period bell has just rung, and kids
are streaming out of school—off to soccer practice or band, or ballet,
the convenience store, or wherever.

"There may be ears," he says, not without reason. He hands me a pair
of earbuds and puts in his own. Apparently, we can listen in tandem.

Leonardo and Einstein are sitting at Einstein's table—there is a blackboard at the head. And Émilie is scribbling out formulas in chalk while explaining her task at hand.

Unlike me after that horrific blowback, the Marquise looks perfectly put together, and game to challenge two of the world's most revered geniuses with her own foundational work.

The lone woman in the room. And not one of them seems surprised.

> Émilie du Châtelet: I visited an iron forge to do an experiment [she calls it an *exprès*] on whether fire is matter. It is for a paper—there is a contest by the French Academy of Sciences. While I was there, I had all the scales replaced.

I can't help but blurt out. "Wait. I wonder how, after I left . . . ?"

"What the hell, Charley?" Billy stares at me.

To tell the truth, if anyone but Billy was showing me what was unfolding on this artificial reality livestream on his tablet, I might have second-guessed myself on this whole tortuous experience. After all, it could've been some new Netflix show. Or an immersive 3-D hologram, like I heard about at Clos Lucé, the castle in the Loire Valley where Leonardo worked for the King of France until his death in 1519. You know, a pseudoscientific historical reenactment.

"The forge," I say excitedly, "where we went to engineer enough force to take the last leap. And the giant compass . . ."

I fish in the backpack—the product of Billy's packing job—and pull out the newly forged golden compass.

Somehow thinking the snuffbox should be here—but then, I remember.

Billy grabs it and stares. "Wait. So you leaped time without telling me?"

"Shut up, Billy," I interrupt. "They're like, about to take Émilie's *force vive* to a whole new level!"

> Émilie: The new iron scales were fitted with iron chains instead of ropes. After that I had both the heated and the cooled metal within the range of one pound to two thousand pounds weighed. As I never found the smallest difference in their weights, I reasoned: The surface of these enormous masses of heated iron had been enlarged due to their dilation, therefore they must have had less specific gravity.

> Leonardo: Do not despise my opinion, when I remind you that it should not be hard for you to stop sometimes and look into the stains of walls, or the ashes of a fire, or clouds, or mud or like places, in which, if you consider them well, you may find really marvelous ideas.

With that, the Maestro, using a charcoal pencil, begins one of his sketches.

Émilie: (moves to look over his shoulder to watch as the drawing takes shape) . . . but claiming that fire has weight is to destroy its nature.

Einstein: Concerning matter, we have been all wrong. What we have called matter is energy, whose vibration has been so lowered as to be perceptible to the senses. There is no matter.

It is here that I have to wonder: did Einstein give Émilie the idea for the squaring of F=mv to define what we now know as the formula for kinetic energy? Or was it she who inspired him before this moment to square his famous formula to define relativity?

Leonardo: (detailing his sketch) Fire destroys falsehood and restores truth, driving out darkness.

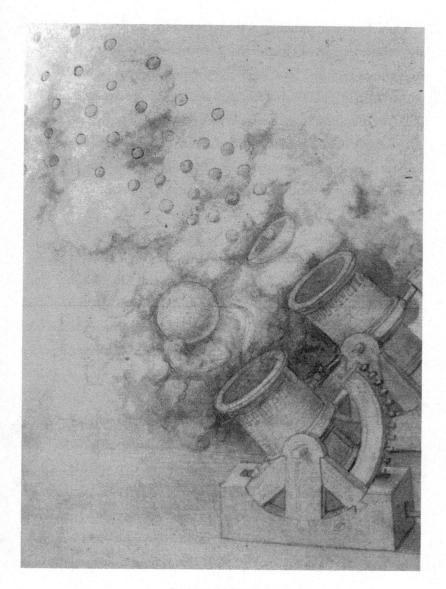

CANNON FIRE

Credit: Notebooks of Leonardo di Vinci, Public Domain
Photo: Robin Stevens Payes

"Ooh," I exclaim, squinting at the screen to see the drawing emerging from those long artist's fingers that I remember so well. "He's showing how the cannon fire that literally blew me away can be beautiful," I muse. "But, in real life, that force carries terrible, destructive powers."

"Move, Charley. I can't see!" Billy pushes me out of the way to rest his googly VR eyes practically against the screen for an up-close look at how these mad scientists are making eureka-like connections on the fly. "And stop blabbing. This is like watching the Marvel Universe of Science!"

> Émilie: As Monsieur Leonardo shows, it was by dint of fire that I find myself here. In this experience, I encountered light so blinding—split into its spectral colors. A rainbow in a crystal universe. It seemed to open a doorway to other worlds. I merely stepped inside.
>
> And what a joy to find myself in the company of Monsieur Einstein, whose reputation I know only from hearsay, but whose mind can take in worlds in an instant. How can this be?
>
> Einstein: Everything is energy, and that is all there is to it. It can be no other way. This is not philosophy. This is physics!

"Billy, this isn't right. They seem to be *obsessed* with each other, like they could keep talking about all this forever. But Émilie cannot remain in 1905—the following year, 1906, would've marked the bicentennial of her birth. She has yet to begin her greatest work—her commentary on Newton. She will have yet others who pull upon her heart. I'm afraid she won't want to go back. And how would she, even if she wanted to?"

Something's got Billy distracted. He seems focused on some commotion taking place IRL.

"Billy? Don't you care?"

He looks at me like I've just dropped in from *Micromégas*. (For those who haven't met Voltaire or follow him, this is his science-fiction tale about when giant extraterrestrials find earthlings as tiny little ants. And no, I am not making that up.)

But I need to pay attention to the livestream, as Émilie begins speaking again.

> Émilie: It is much easier for you to change the shape
> of the Earth. I implore you, leave, in the changes that
> you will make . . .

"Right. That—the changes you will make," I interrupt her. "Keep that in mind, Em. You gotta go back."

> Leonardo: (showing his ostrich egg globe) If you find
> from your own experience that something is a fact
> and it contradicts what some authority has written

down, then you must abandon the authority and base your reasoning on your own findings.

Émilie: The study of physics seems made for man; it turns upon the things that constantly surround us, and on which our pleasures and our needs depend. [She produces her own golden compass and pinches it to show that it is material.] I will not regret the trouble it will cost me and I will believe it well spent if it can instill in you the love of the sciences and the desire to cultivate your reason.

Einstein: Is it true that your old collaborator Voltaire wrote in one of his correspondences to a friend, 'Minerva [the goddess of wisdom] dictated, and I wrote'?"

Émilie: The companion of my solitude has written an introduction to the philosophy of Monsieur Newton, which he has dedicated to me and the frontispiece of which I show you.

FRONTISPIECE TO VOLTAIRE'S ELEMENTS OF THE PHILOSOPHY OF NEWTON

Written in collaboration with and dedicated to Émilie du Châtelet
Credit: Louis Fabricius Dubourg and Jacob Folkema, Public Domain

Einstein blinks and bows slightly to this "Minerva."

Is this recognition of the generosity of Voltaire toward her brilliance? So unlike Einstein himself, who ignored his first wife Mitza's substantial contributions to his world-changing research, and never acknowledged her contribution? Or simply a nod to Émilie's unique genius?

We may never know how this meeting could change that equation.

Émilie writes something in tiny script on the blackboard; I can't quite make it out.

Leonardo and Albert come up close to scrutinize it. Leo picks up the chalk and starts sketching whirls of wind. Albert writes out his famous equation. Émilie erases the lower part of the "E" to turn it into an "F," scratches out the "c" to replace it with a "v," and puts a heart around her formula: *force vive*.

Then, quite hilariously, this newly formed triumvirate breaks into a riot of whoops, dancing and slapping each other with jubilant high fives.

A burst of static disrupts this weird scene. "Wait. What?"

Billy stares at the interference, as though there's some message in it. "Umm, Charley?"

"Shhh." I hush him. "I think it's clearing up. As I watch, the static dissolves.

Kairos enters with the same doctor's kit he carried at Cirey. He pulls out needles, and a vial. Seems he's determined to give the men the jab, too. For what reason, I cannot fathom. Unless Émilie could now be a carrier—and how horrible would that be?!

"Kairos? No way. And he's giving them shots?" Billy asks. "Like there was a major flu outbreak or something in this in-between space where they've all gathered?"

Émilie hastily explains to her new besties that this is the new medical science. That it will not hurt, but confer immunity. Just in case.

Mission accomplished, Kairos hands Émilie a beautifully embroidered handkerchief, in which he's wrapped a new snuffbox for her massive collection. She opens it to find a tiny golden compass charm inside. "Like that of Charlotte," she acknowledges, "from her own true love."

She remembers me! I turn to Billy, who's blushing at this moment.

"See, Billy, the little compass charm. Like the one you gave me." I put my hand over my heart, where the charm lays. "So you're famous now, too."

But he's dived back into the Esme app, which he seems to be updating with new code.

Émilie turns and, hand over heart, bows graciously to each of them, bidding them adieu, expressing hope that they may meet again.

Now Kairos holds up one of the original compasses, matching it to Émilie's. How many compasses are now lost in spacetime, and who can follow the trail? The ubiquity of this energy to initiate time travel irks me no end.

Kairos scribbles something on the blackboard—I cannot quite make out the formula, but I bet I could guess.

"*Jusqu'à la prochaine, mes amis,*" Émilie calls out. And with that, *poof*—the Marquise has disappeared.

Billy turns, tapping his foot impatiently.

"First, Brainiac, you're gonna tell me how all this happened—your most recent leap. But second, and more to the point *right now*, what's this?"

He points to the Esme dashboard, where he's pulled up a second "livestream" as it were. I see a girl with a straw hat with ribbons trailing down her back.

"Carolina?"

She's walking down a familiar-looking street, with old Victorian houses, and some that are Sears houses—like mine—from the early 1900s.

It all feels too complicated for me to explain right now. Like, as if the statistically improbable meets the totally implausible.

Carolina glances around behind her, as if she's being followed. Suspicion confirmed.

"What the hell, Billy?!"

"That's what I was going to ask you."

And then I realize: It's my street. She's at my house, and the twins are playing on the front porch.

"Carolina—Bean! No!"

But she can't hear me.

"She said she wanted to meet her namesake," I murmur. "I've got to get home—right away! If she meets them, all bets are off."

"Carolina? Wanted to meet . . . I don't know what you're talking about, Charley, or what she's doing here . . ."

"She's playing with fire, that one. It could lead to major *timeline-us interruptus*. And we're ten minutes away, walking. How am I gonna get home in time to stop her?"

"Secrets . . ." I hear him mutter under his breath. Seizing Esme back from my hands, Billy takes off in a long-legged, loping run. "Meet me outside."

I shout after him. "Wait, where are you going, Billy? Don't you even care . . . ?"

Abandoned.

I sink down at the base of my locker, feeling deflated.

"After all this, and now, Billy . . . I never would have thought . . ." I sink deeper into my despair.

With that, I hear a little *ding-ding-ding*—a video message.

It's Billy. And the byclotron. It looks spotless. Like on its maiden voyage. But maybe *this* is its maiden voyage.

"This can't be happening . . ." I get a second wind and sprint out to the street.

"Hop on!"

I reach out for his hand to help me get on the front seat, but he's such a germophobe, he gives me a hand wipe first.

"Don't worry, Charley. We got this." He starts pedaling, picking up speed until the battery kicks in. "I've enhanced it—we'll be there in a nanosecond."

We're moving so fast, it's all I can do to hang on. We round the corner and chug up the hill. Daisy's busy digging up weeds in the front yard with a spoon. And here's Carrie, using one of the Popsicle sticks in my old collection to stir her famous stone-and-dandelion soup in a plastic bowl, offering it to Carolina, who's sitting on our front stoop.

Acting like this is all perfectly normal.

"*No!*" The future of the world, or at least my world, hangs in the balance. "Go back, Carolina. You can't . . ."

"Tcharrli!"

"Chahley!" yells Daisy, piling weeds into the bowl, adding water from the watering can by the front stoop.

I climb off the bike and run up to give the twins a big squeeze. Even though this situation is fraught, it's been eons since I hugged them. Just to know they are safe . . .

Carrie says, "Pwetend. Soup. Yummy . . . !"

They've played "Chef" many times before. Pretending. That could spell trouble when the Bean is around.

"Cawowina teaching," Daisy explains, as if this is all perfectly normal. "Where have you been, Sissie?"

"There's only one way to solve this."

I look at Billy, who's come up behind me. He nods solemnly.

"Carrie, where's Mamma. And Dad? Who's here with you?"

"Bethy! Boyfwend!" Carrie exclaims.

Bethy! So this is where she was going to do her Fashion Forward. Like she wasn't expecting me home. Where would I have been supposed to be, I puzzle, knowing that the whole timeline has been disrupted. And, anyway, where is she while all this is happening! The twins could be kidnapped—trust me, I know.

"Don't worry, Tcharrli. I am watching them too!"

"That's what has me worried, Carolina. You've got to get out of here—you know better!"

I pull out the giant compass—the new one Carolina gave me at the forge—and look around at Billy.

"Send her back?" Billy asks. "But . . . we're not optimized for . . . You're aware, Charley, this could crash the system . . ."

"Carolina, you have a compass, too, right?"

She nods.

"Crash, smash, Billy. All's I know is that we have got to get Carolina out of here, *pronto.*"

"I'm aware of the danger." It seems Billy has already begun modifying the code on the dashboard.

"Got it, Carolina?"

"But Tcharrli!" she complains. "I just got here."

"You're not messing things up for my sisters," I tell her. "They're just babies. You've got to go."

"But I can go anywhere, anytime . . . you don't need to . . ."

But I've stopped listening. "You in?" I ask Billy.

He pulls out his ancient compass. "Operation Firenze 2.0, here we come!"

I turn to give Billy a high five, and almost trip on the steps.

He grabs me and pulls me tight to keep me upright.

I turn toward him and right then, right there, he plants a kiss on my lips to seal the deal.

Looking down, I see something gold, glinting on the walkway.

And the world is spinning . . . again.

Acknowledgments

I am deeply indebted to my children, Ben, Dana and Ari, without whose inspiration The Edge of Yesterday adventures would not exist in any spacetime zone.

I couldn't time travel (and keep track of space-time) without a truly talented team: designer-in-chief Melissa Brandstatter and series editor Allison Gillis, who have stuck with me through multiple time leaps. Webmaster Andres Cuervo is our real-life "Kairos" – the IT specialist who showed up "just in time" to update and upgrade our "learning through story" platform at edgeofyesterday.com

I am grateful for the support of my travel partner, Sally Craig, who gamely ventured with me to stalk Émilie du Châtelet through Paris, Versailles and Cirey, France. We were thrilled to join in with a band of Émilie superfans representing the Madame du Châtelet Circle, which organizes an annual parade on 10 September through the streets of Lunéville, France, where the Marquise died in 1749, in childbirth, at the age of 42, and where she is interred at the Église St. Jacques in an unmarked grave.

The Circle's goal: to honor the legacy of this brilliant mathematician, philosopher and physicist. Our goal at the Edge of Yesterday: to bring the inspiration of a woman of genius to a new generation of creative STEMinistas.

And, finally, my thanks to Steve Eisner, founder of the When Words Count Retreat in Vermont, for seeing the potential in the Edge of Yesterday series, and for offering this author the extraordinary gift of space and time to chronicle these time travel tales.

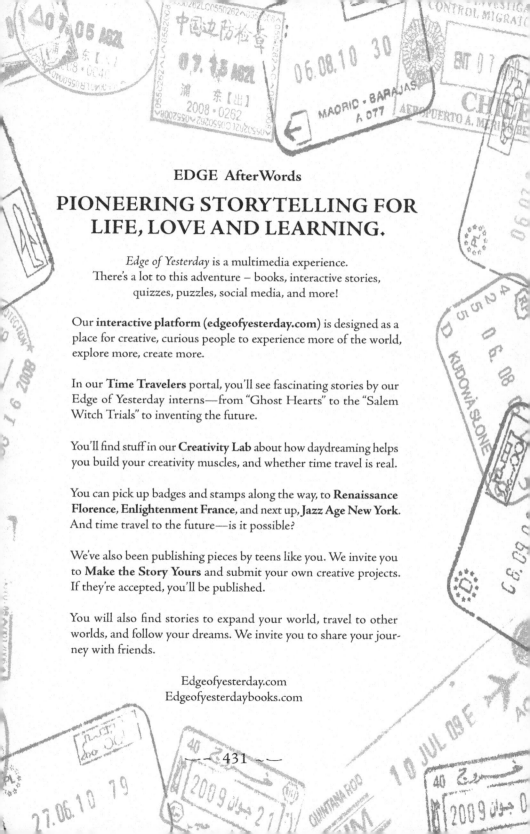

EDGE AfterWords

PIONEERING STORYTELLING FOR LIFE, LOVE AND LEARNING.

Edge of Yesterday is a multimedia experience.
There's a lot to this adventure – books, interactive stories,
quizzes, puzzles, social media, and more!

Our **interactive platform (edgeofyesterday.com)** is designed as a place for creative, curious people to experience more of the world, explore more, create more.

In our **Time Travelers** portal, you'll see fascinating stories by our Edge of Yesterday interns—from "Ghost Hearts" to the "Salem Witch Trials" to inventing the future.

You'll find stuff in our **Creativity Lab** about how daydreaming helps you build your creativity muscles, and whether time travel is real.

You can pick up badges and stamps along the way, to **Renaissance Florence, Enlightenment France**, and next up, **Jazz Age New York**. And time travel to the future—is it possible?

We've also been publishing pieces by teens like you. We invite you to **Make the Story Yours** and submit your own creative projects. If they're accepted, you'll be published.

You will also find stories to expand your world, travel to other worlds, and follow your dreams. We invite you to share your journey with friends.

Edgeofyesterday.com
Edgeofyesterdaybooks.com

About the Author

Robin Stevens Payes is author of the young adult science fiction book series, Edge of Yesterday. She is a mom of three, a science and education writer, a novelist, and a coach. She is especially interested in the complex dynamics in mother/daughter relationships. Her innovative system of "storytelling for change" has programs designed to help these women—from Boomers to Zoomers—use the art and science of story as a tool to take them on a journey of self-discovery that can transform their relationships.

Robin offers writing and creativity workshops and programs, and a six-week summer internship program for teens. Her mission is to allow moms and daughters the space and time to cultivate their creativity, curiosity, and connection while storytelling together.

Join us!
— edgeofyesterday.com
— edgeofyesterday.com/creativity-lab
— edgeofyesterdaybooks.com

Contact: info@edgeofyesterday.com